GUARDIANS OF HORSA

Legend of the Yearling

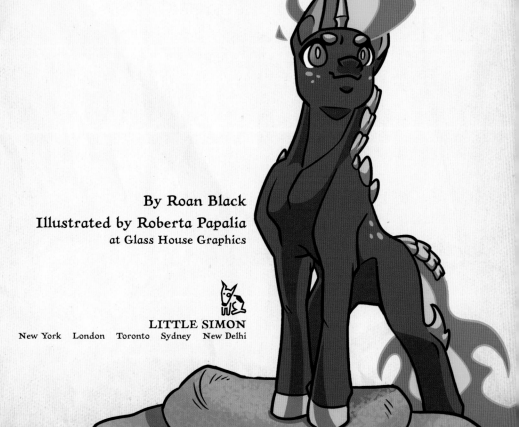

By Roan Black

Illustrated by Roberta Papalia
at Glass House Graphics

LITTLE SIMON

New York   London   Toronto   Sydney   New Delhi

LITTLE SIMON
An imprint of Simon & Schuster Children's Publishing Division
1230 Avenue of the Americas, New York, New York 10020
First Little Simon edition January 2023
Copyright © 2023 by Simon & Schuster, Inc.
All rights reserved, including the right of reproduction in whole or in part in any form. LITTLE SIMON is a registered trademark of Simon & Schuster, Inc., and associated colophon is a trademark of Simon & Schuster, Inc. For information about special discounts for bulk purchases, please contact Simon & Schuster Special Sales at 1-866-506-1949 or business@simonandschuster.com. The Simon & Schuster Speakers Bureau can bring authors to your live event. For more information or to book an event, contact the Simon & Schuster Speakers Bureau at 1-866-248-3049 or visit our website at www.simonspeakers.com. Designed by Nicholas Sciacca • Illustrated by Roberta Papalia at Glass House Graphics. Colors by Giorgio Antonio Pluchino and Antonino Ulizzi. Lettering by Giovanni Spadaro/Grafimated Cartoon. Supervision by Salvatore Di Marco/Grafimated Cartoon. • Manufactured in China 0922 SCP
10 9 8 7 6 5 4 3 2 1
Cataloging-in-Publication Data for this title is available from the Library of Congress.
ISBN 978-1-6659-3157-1 (hc)
ISBN 978-1-6659-3156-4 (pbk)
ISBN 978-1-6659-3158-8 (ebook)

CONTENTS

Chapter 1

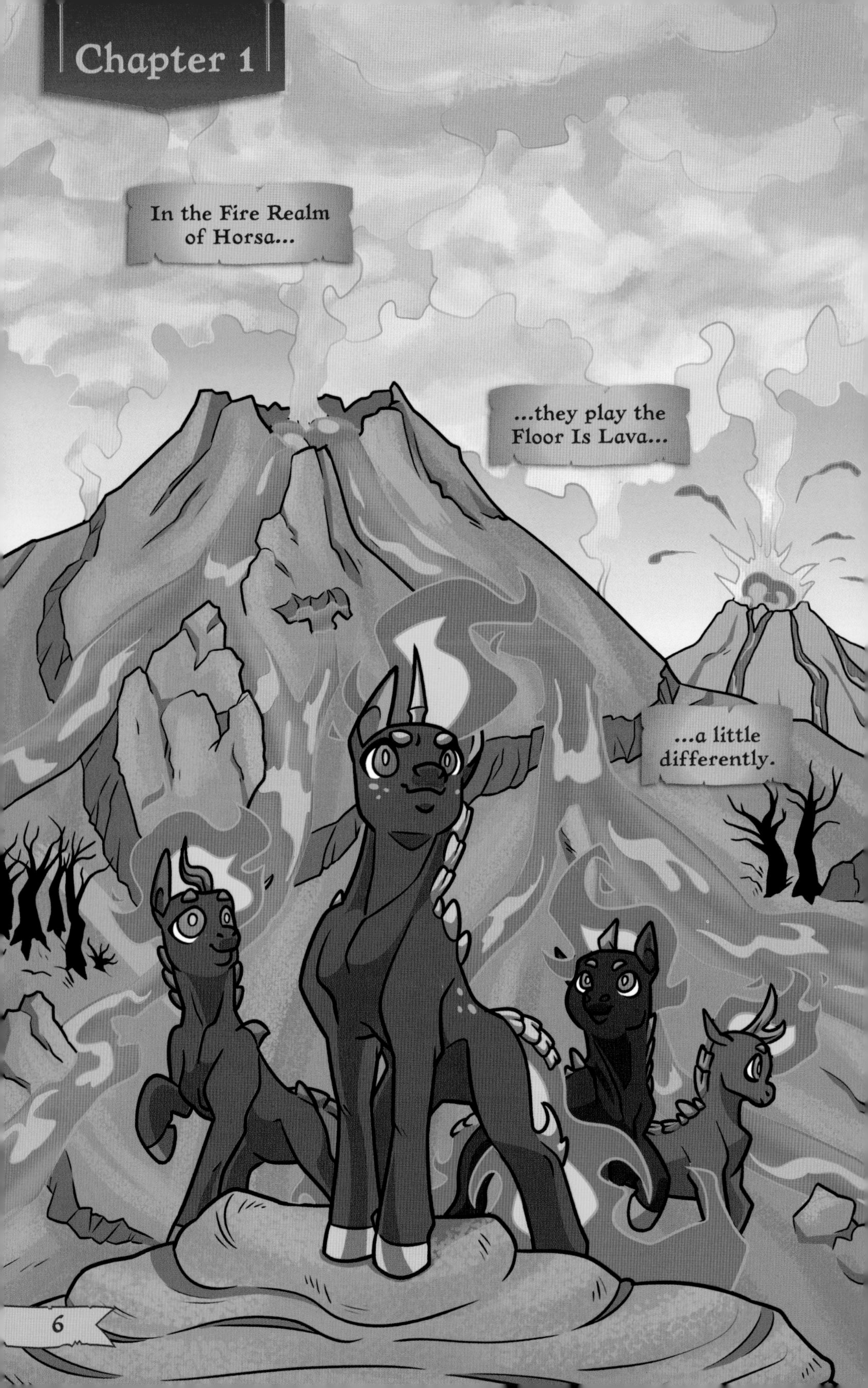
In the Fire Realm of Horsa...
...they play the Floor Is Lava...
...a little differently.

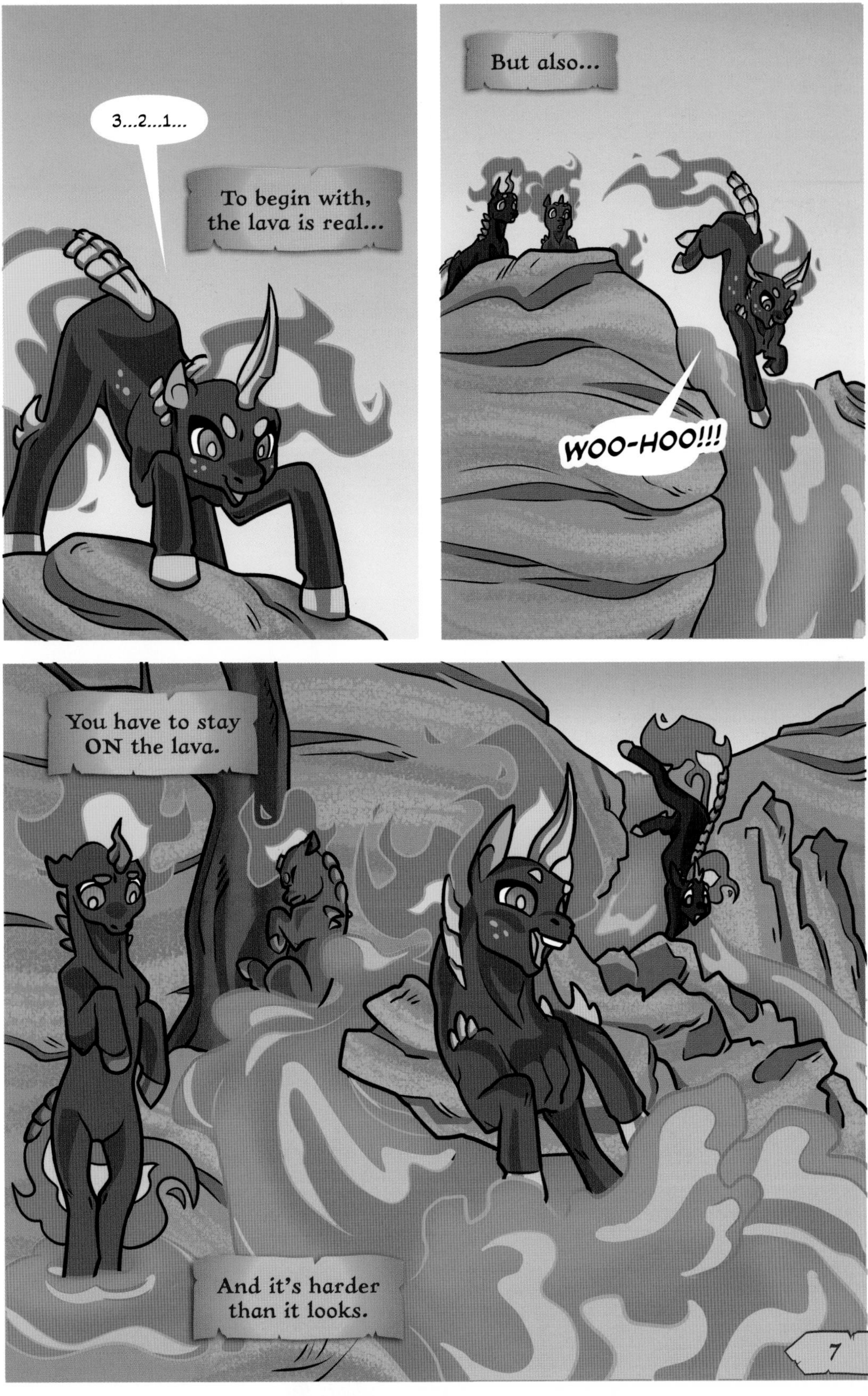
3...2...1...
To begin with, the lava is real...
But also...
WOO-HOO!!!
You have to stay ON the lava.
And it's harder than it looks.

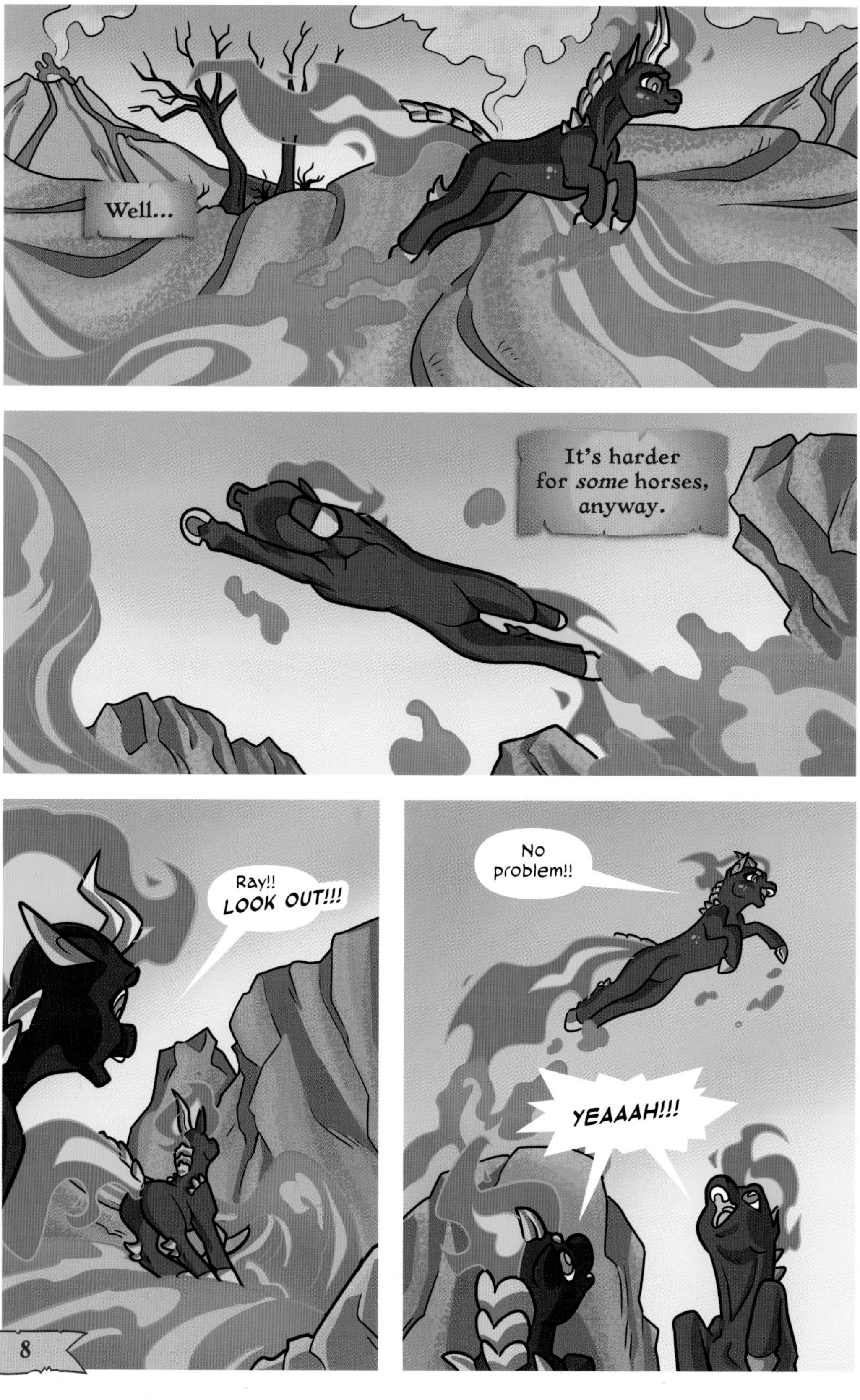
Well...
It's harder for *some* horses, anyway.
Ray!! LOOK OUT!!!
No problem!!
YEAAAH!!!

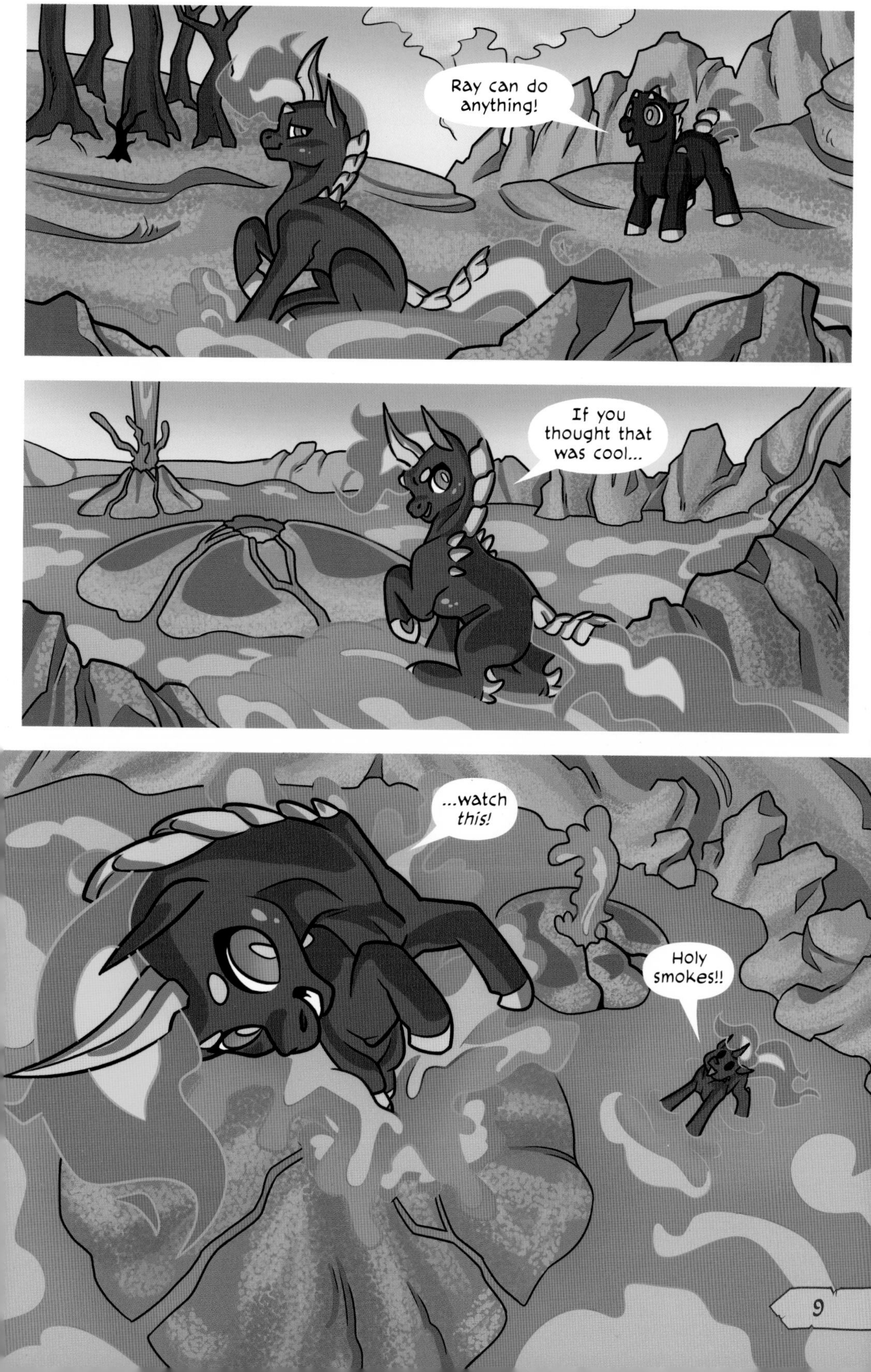

Ray can do anything!
If you thought that was cool...
...watch *this!*
Holy smokes!!

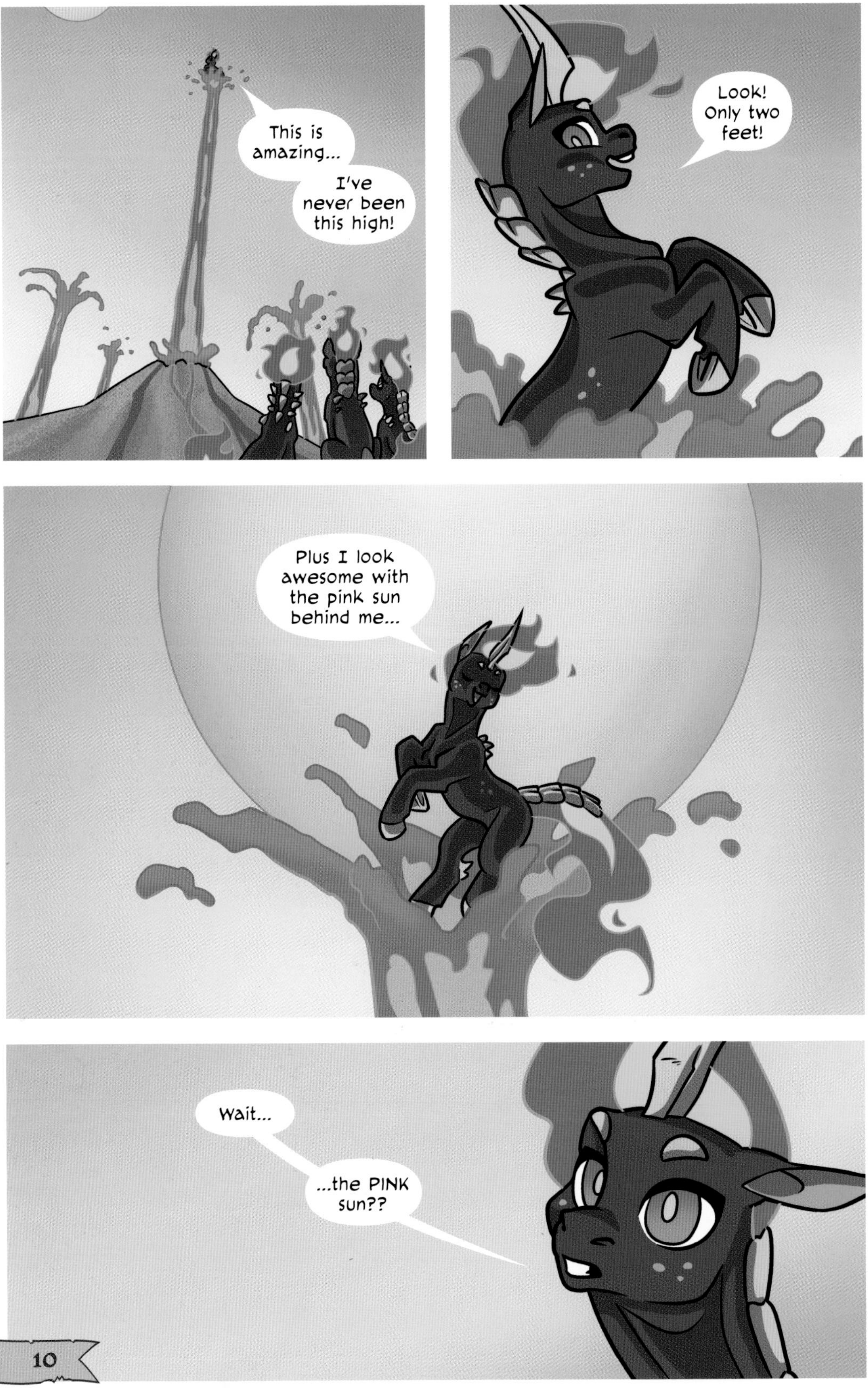
This is amazing...
I've never been this high!
Look! Only two feet!
Plus I look awesome with the pink sun behind me...
Wait...
...the PINK sun??

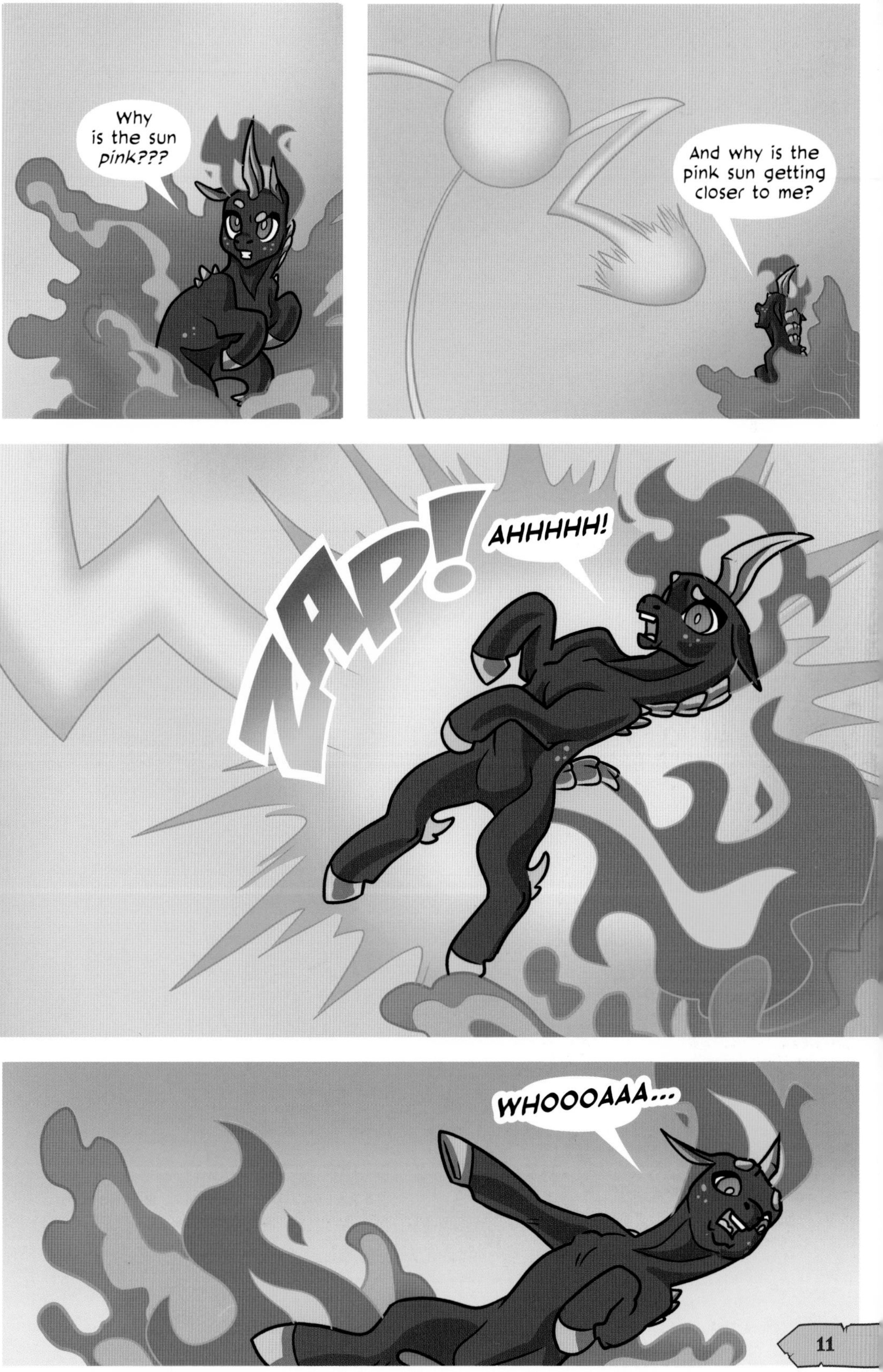
Why is the sun *pink???*
And why is the pink sun getting closer to me?
ZAP!
AHHHHH!
WHOOOAAA...

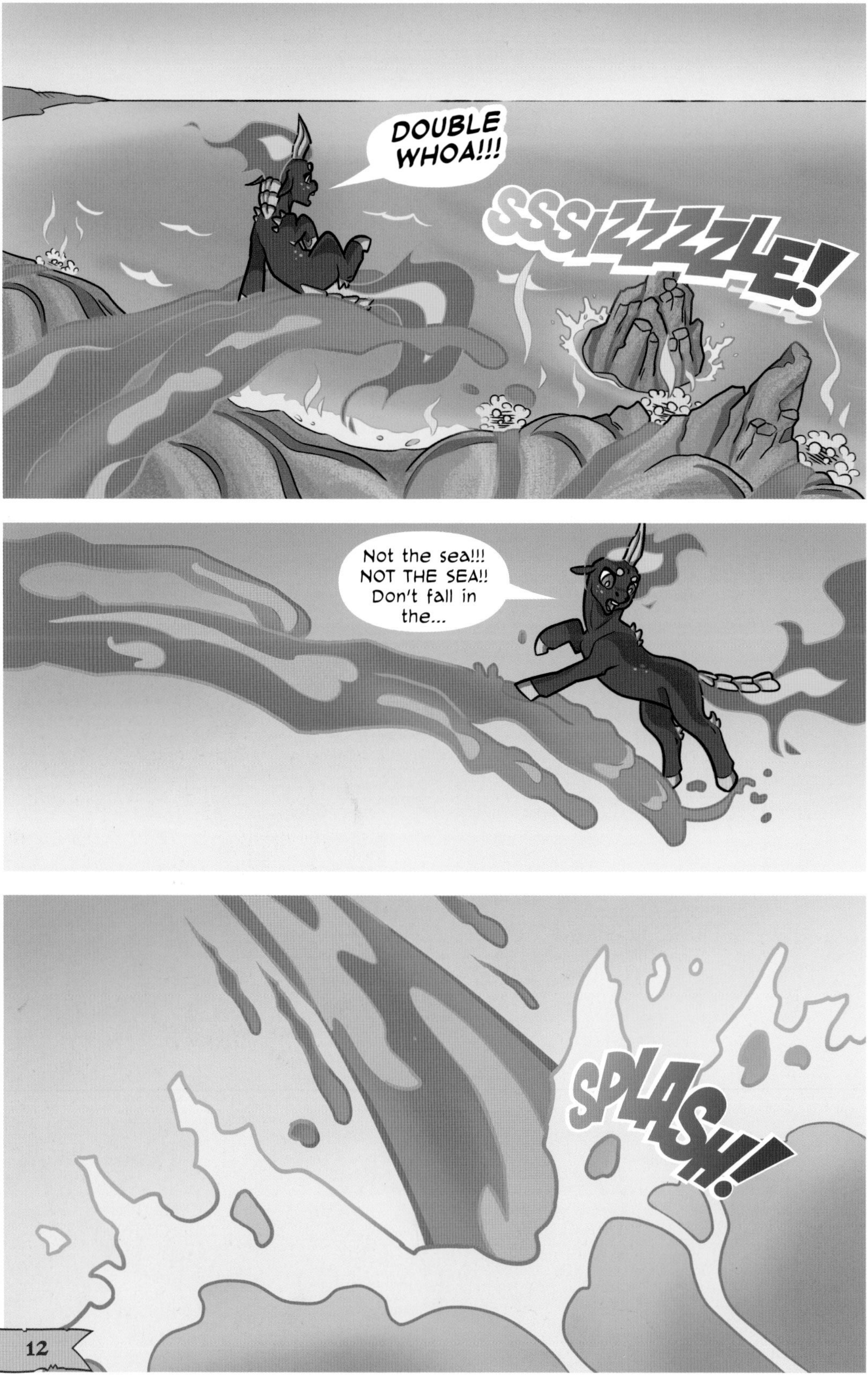
DOUBLE WHOA!!!
SSSIZZZZLE!
Not the sea!!! NOT THE SEA!! Don't fall in the...
SPLASH!

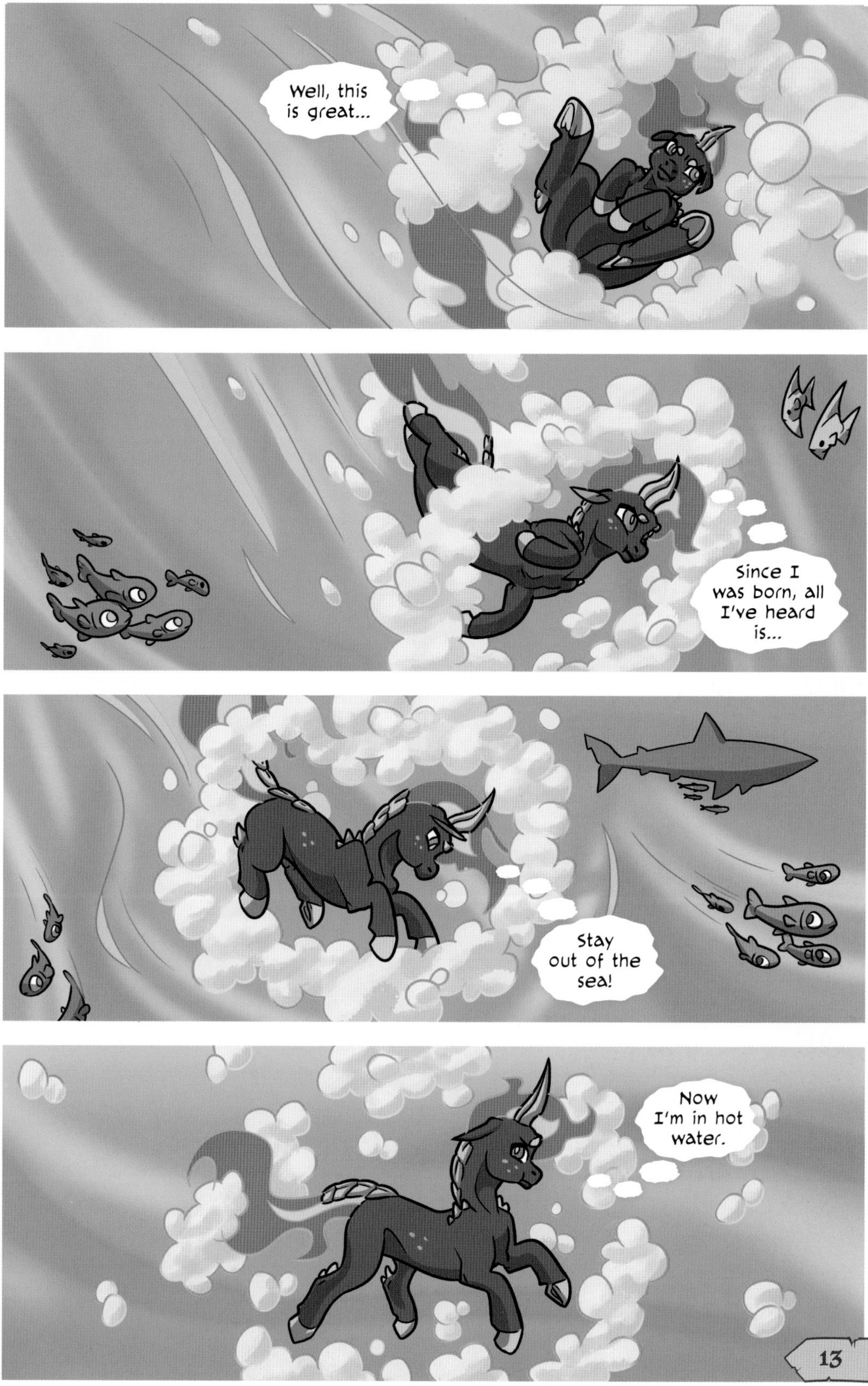
Well, this is great...
Since I was born, all I've heard is...
Stay out of the sea!
Now I'm in hot water.

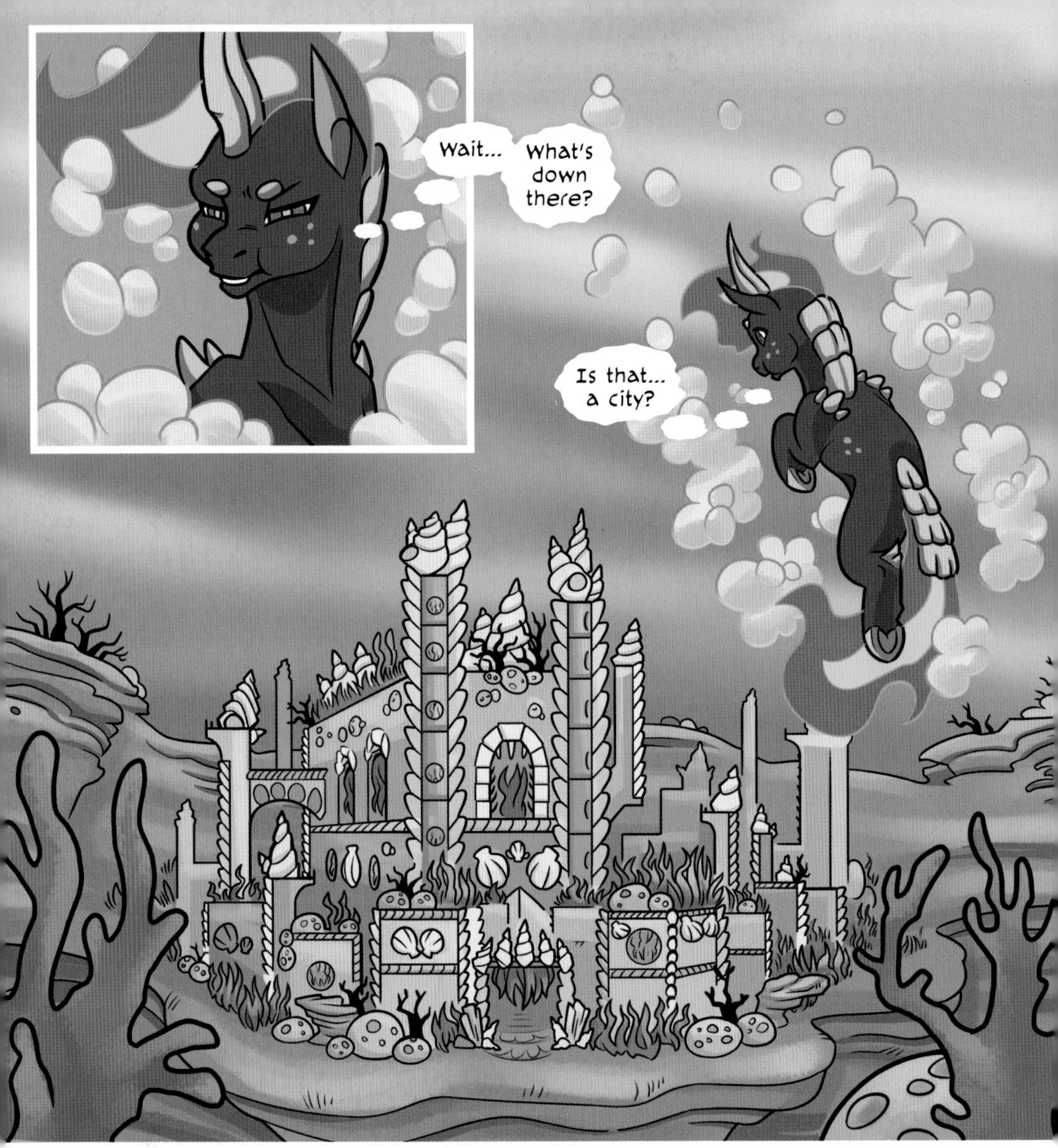
Wait...
What's down there?
Is that... a city?

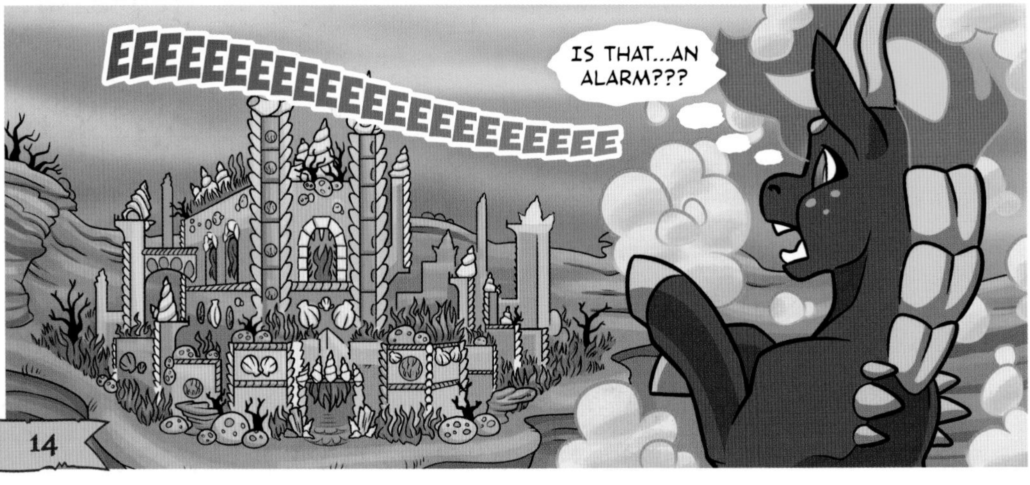
EEEEEEEEEEEEEEEEEEEEEEEE
IS THAT...AN ALARM???

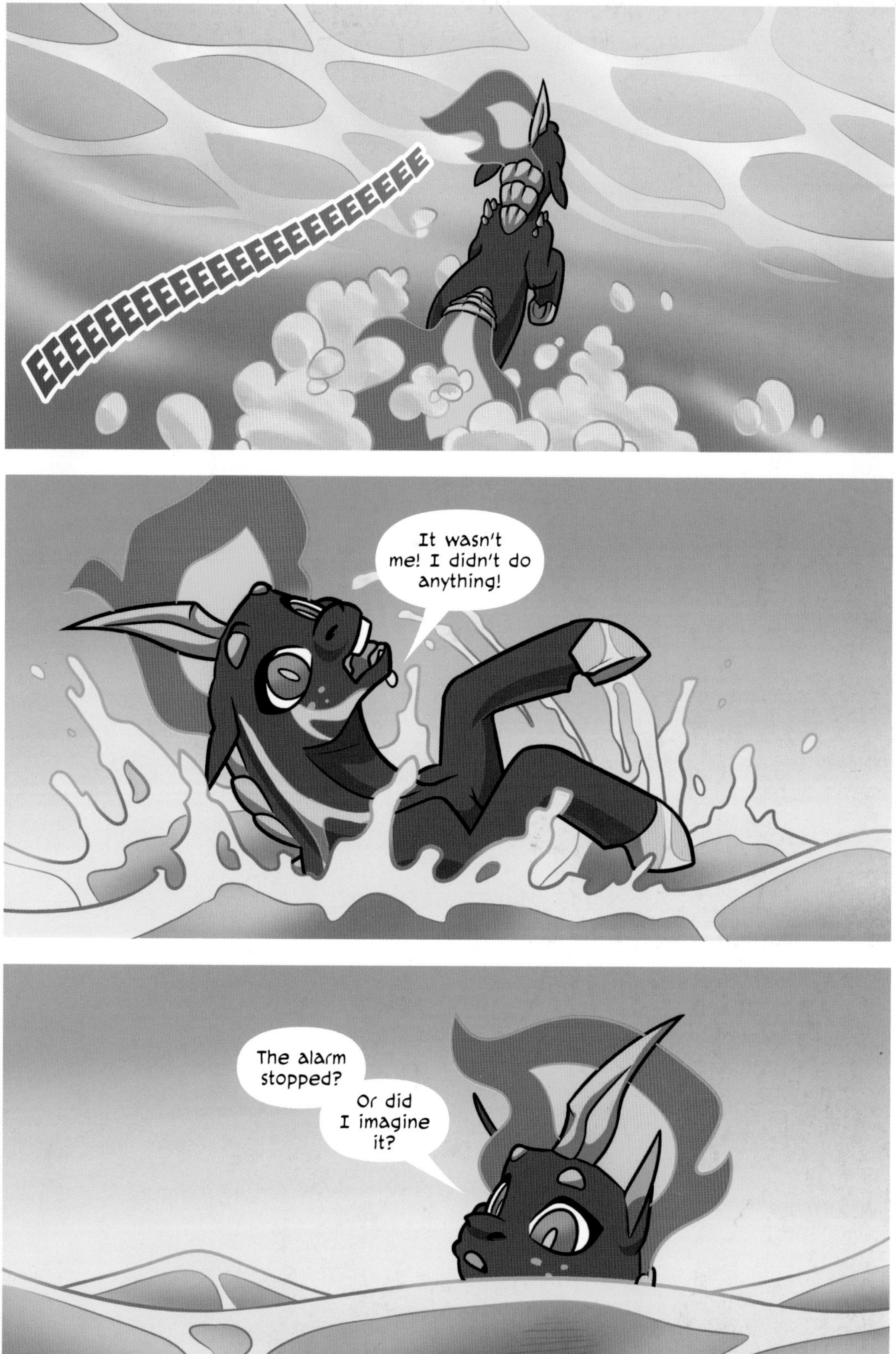
EEEEEEEEEEEEEEEEEEEEEE
It wasn't me! I didn't do anything!
The alarm stopped?
Or did I imagine it?

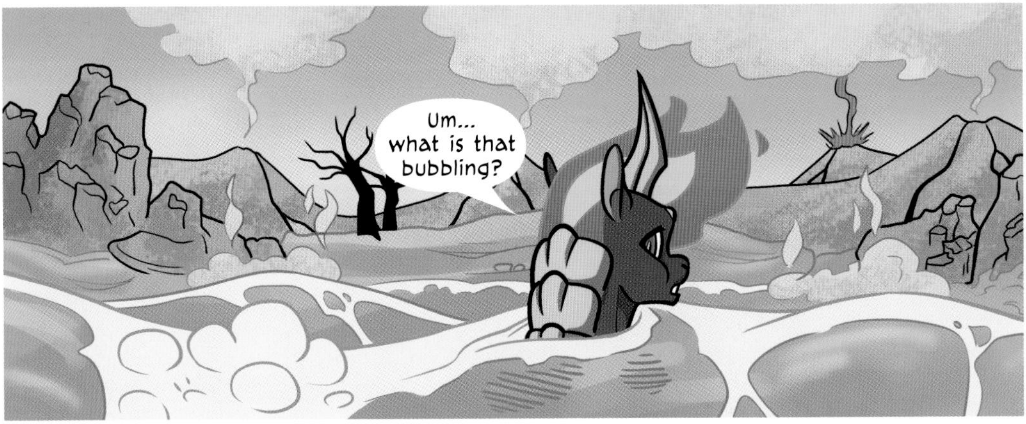
Um...
what is that
bubbling?

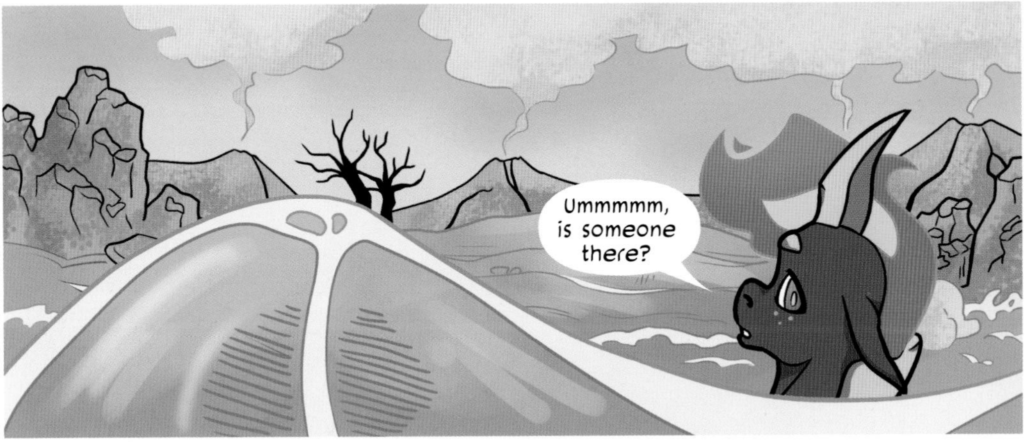
Ummmmm,
is someone
there?

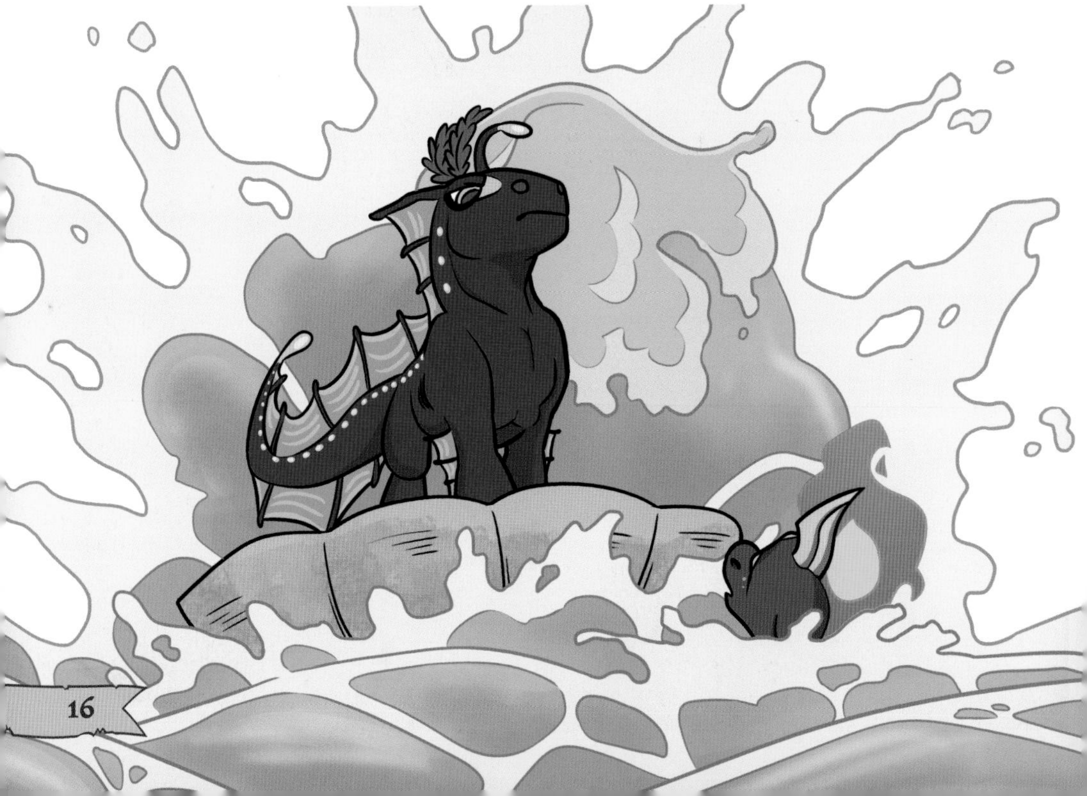

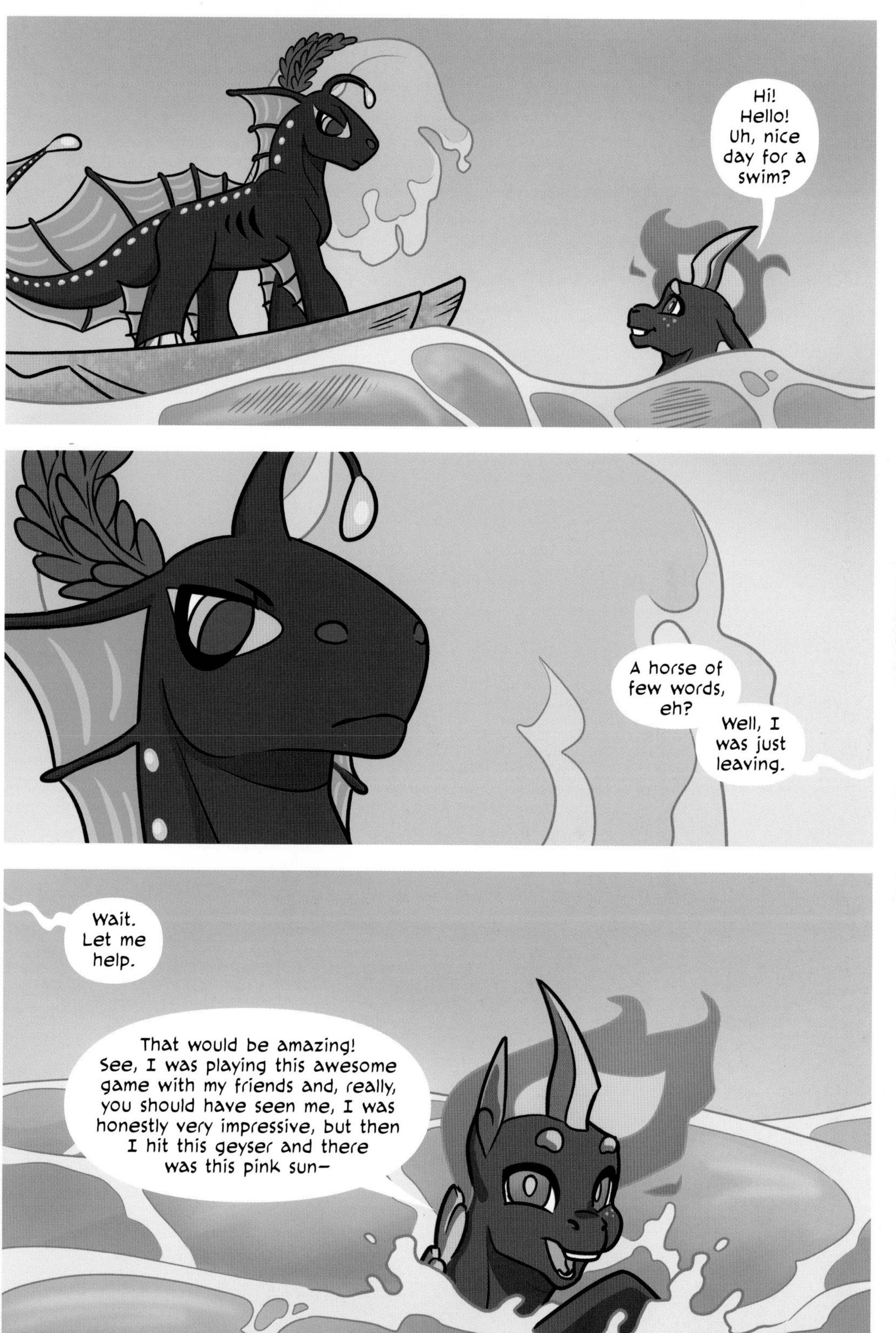
Hi! Hello! Uh, nice day for a swim?
A horse of few words, eh?
Well, I was just leaving.
Wait. Let me help.
That would be amazing! See, I was playing this awesome game with my friends and, really, you should have seen me, I was honestly very impressive, but then I hit this geyser and there was this pink sun–

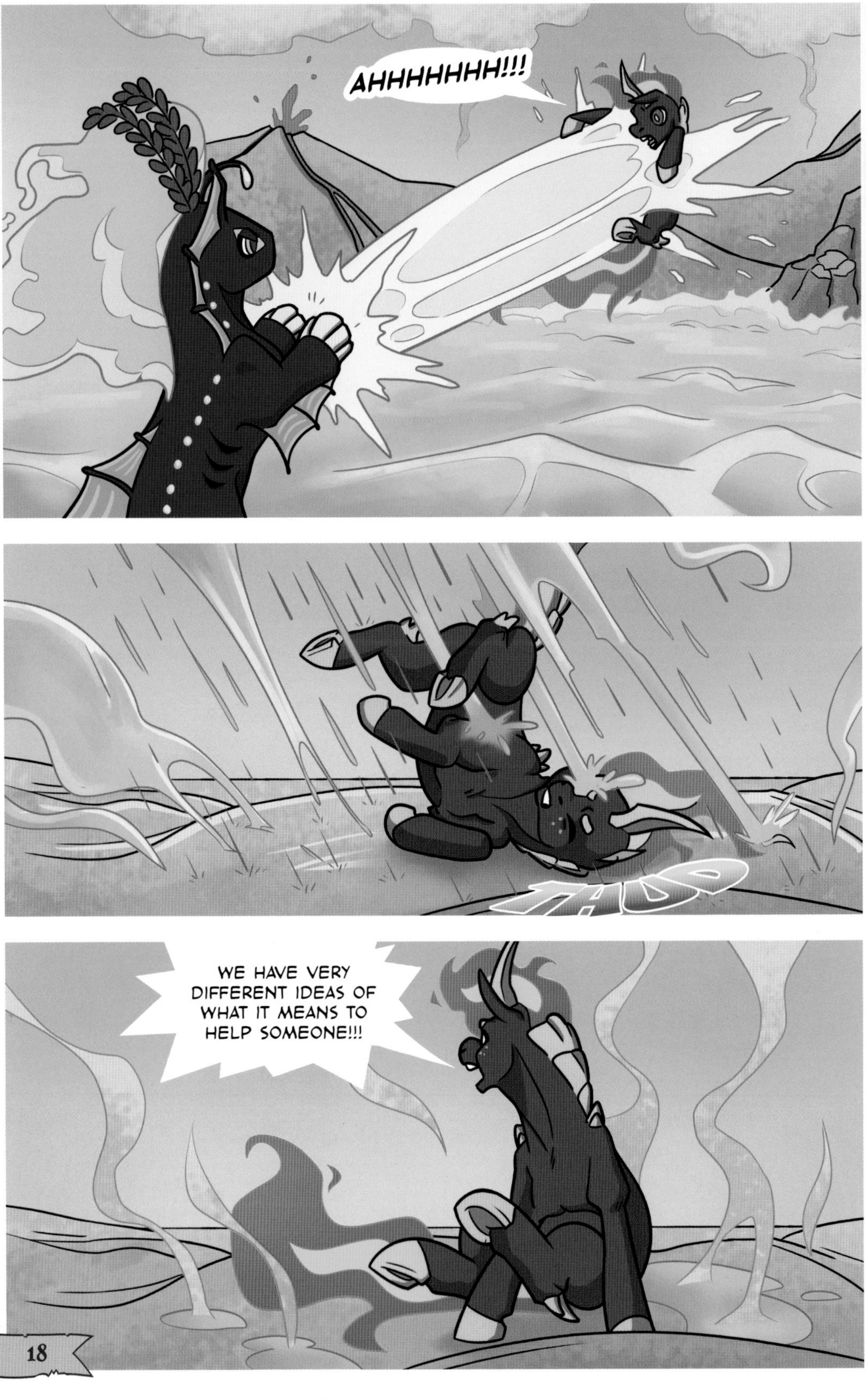
AHHHHHHH!!!
THUD
WE HAVE VERY DIFFERENT IDEAS OF WHAT IT MEANS TO HELP SOMEONE!!!

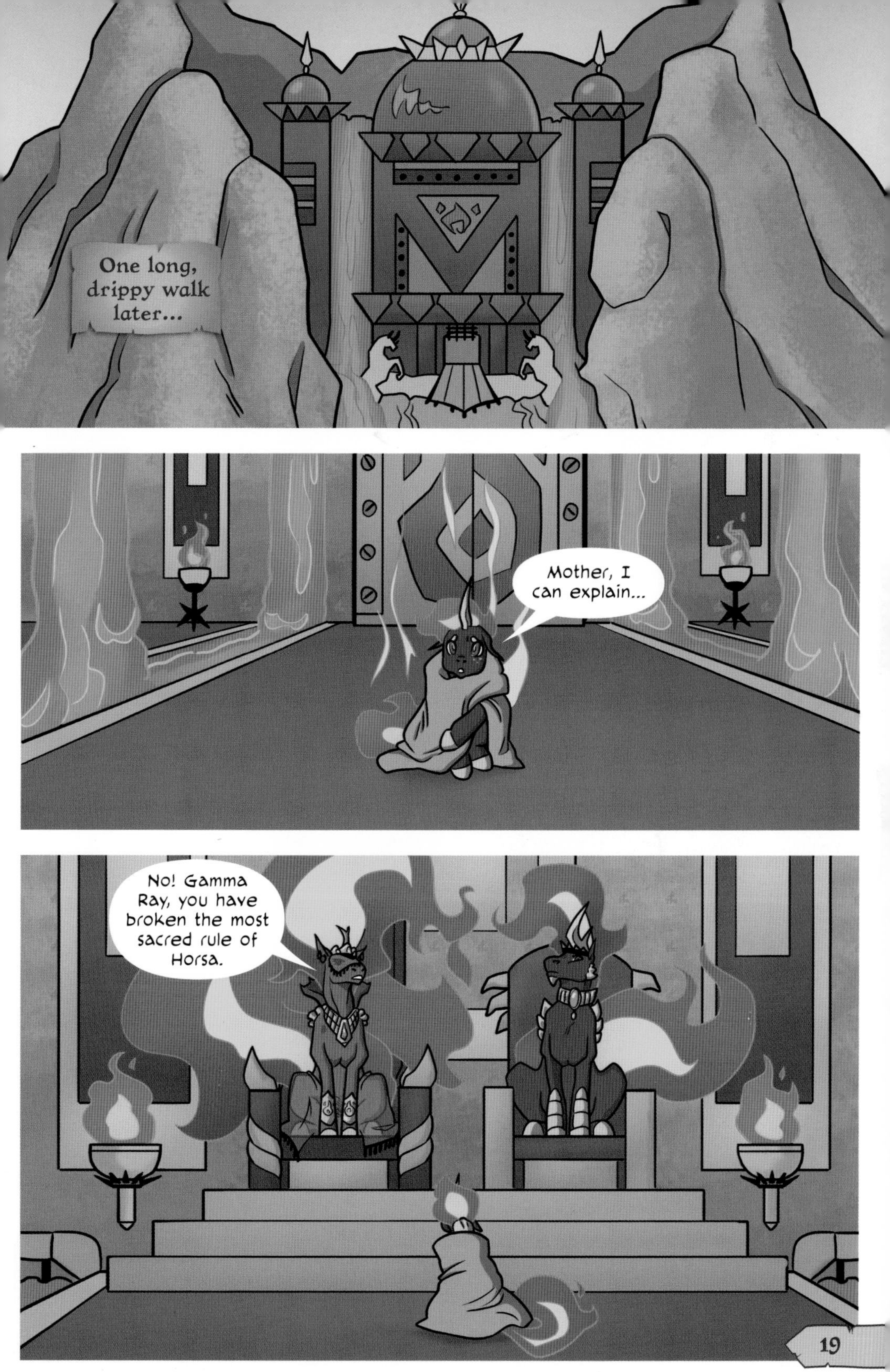
One long, drippy walk later...
Mother, I can explain...
No! Gamma Ray, you have broken the most sacred rule of Horsa.

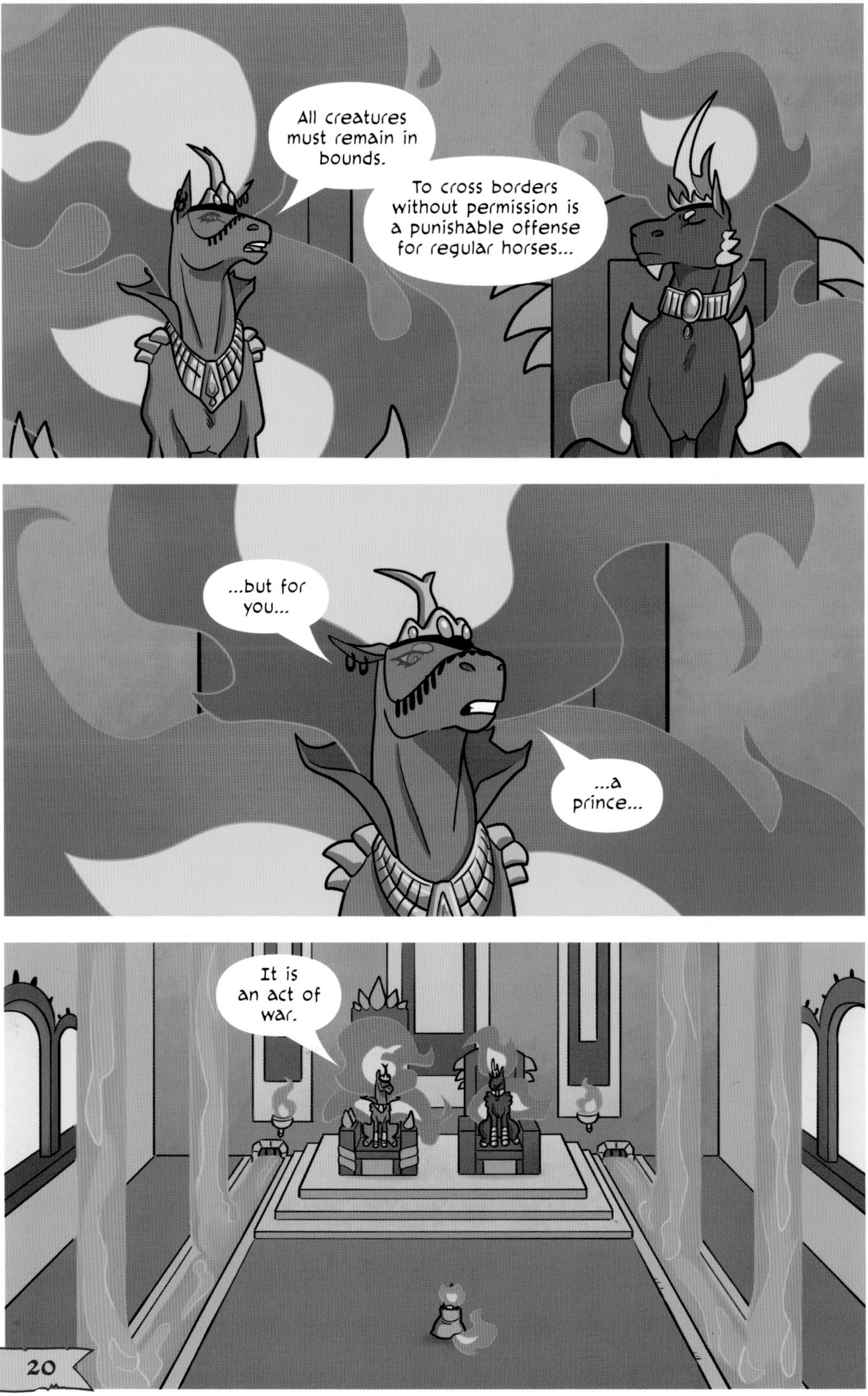
All creatures must remain in bounds.
To cross borders without permission is a punishable offense for regular horses...
...but for you...
...a prince...
It is an act of war.

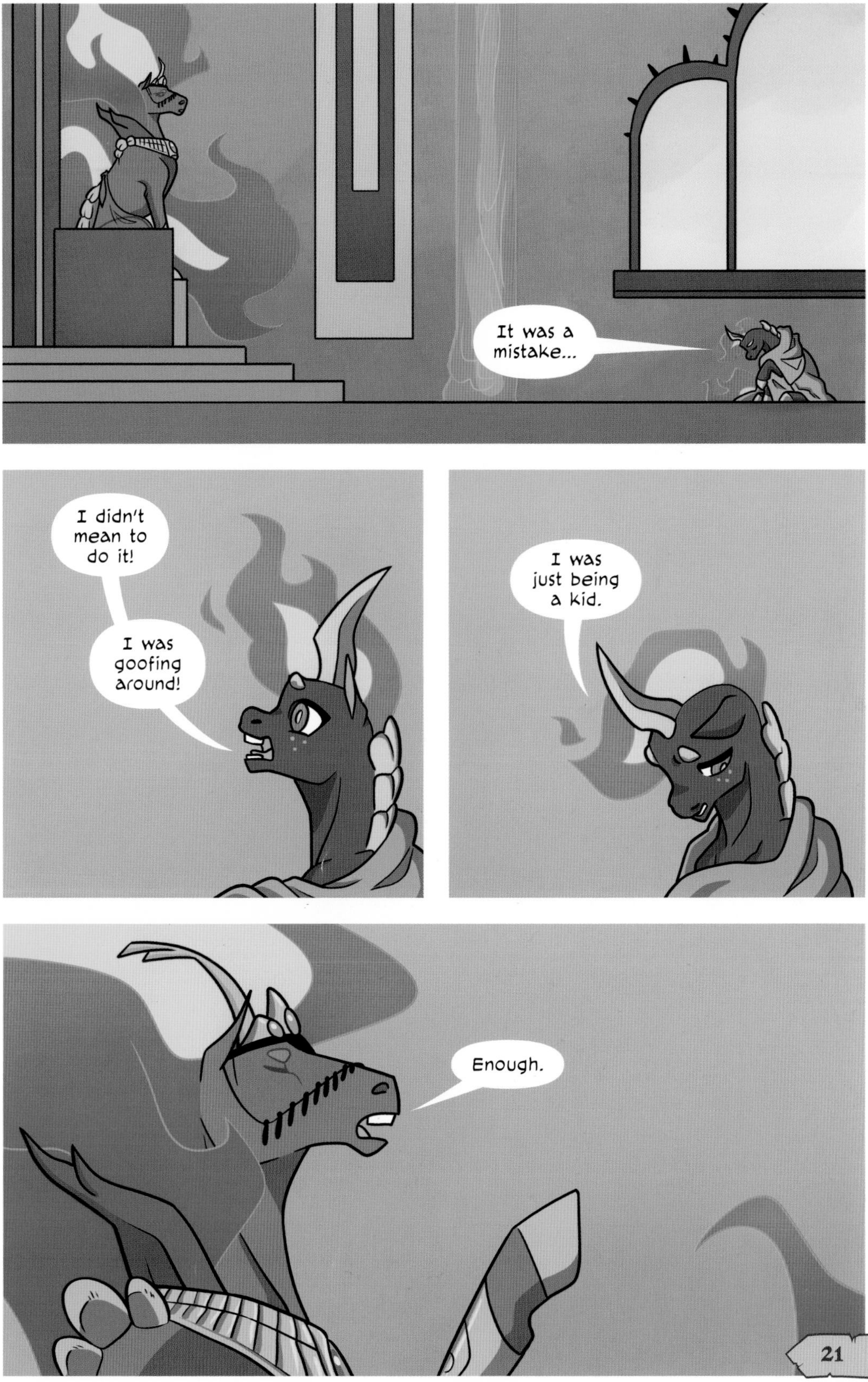
It was a mistake...
I didn't mean to do it!
I was goofing around!
I was just being a kid.
Enough.

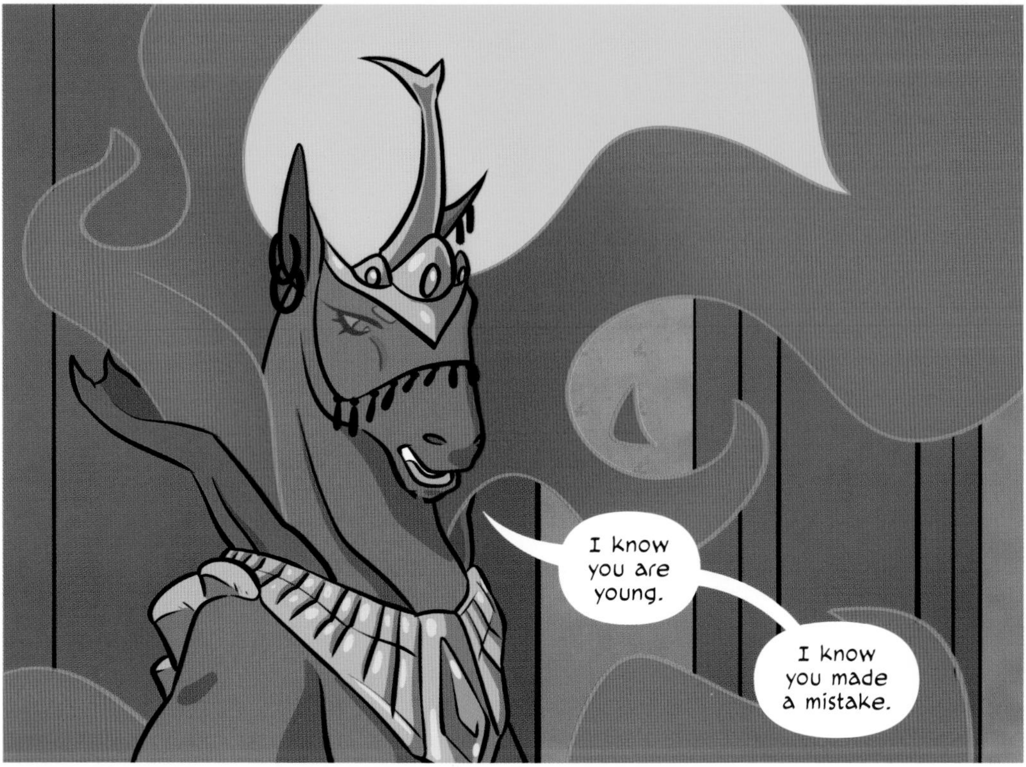
I know you are young.
I know you made a mistake.

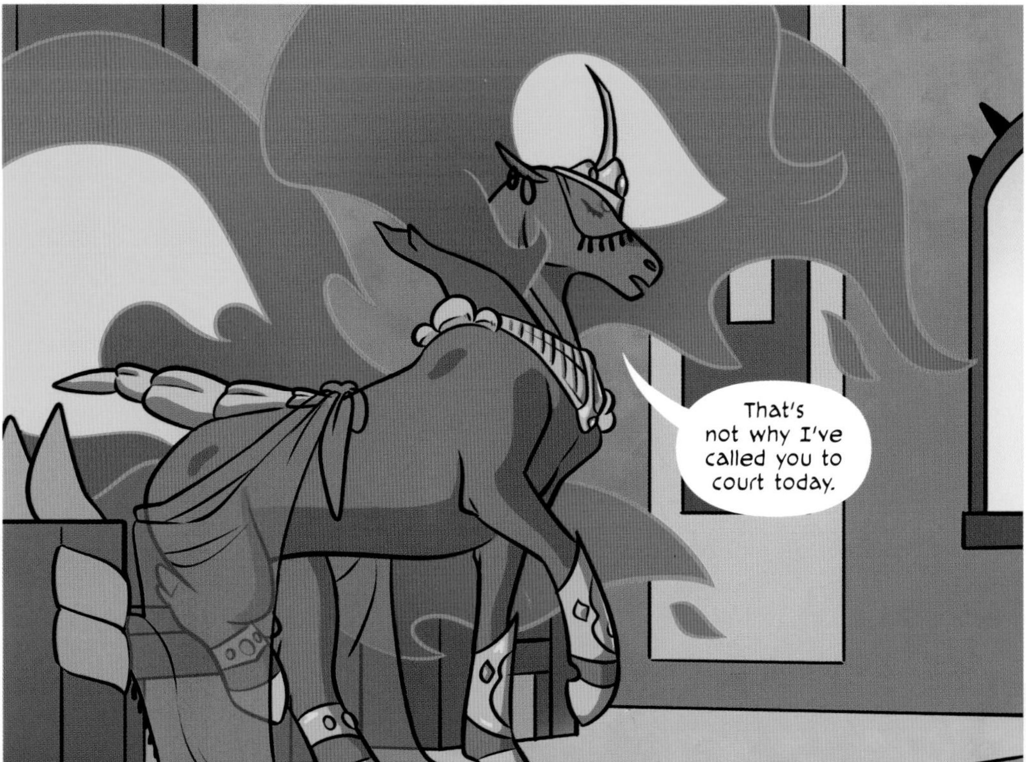
That's not why I've called you to court today.

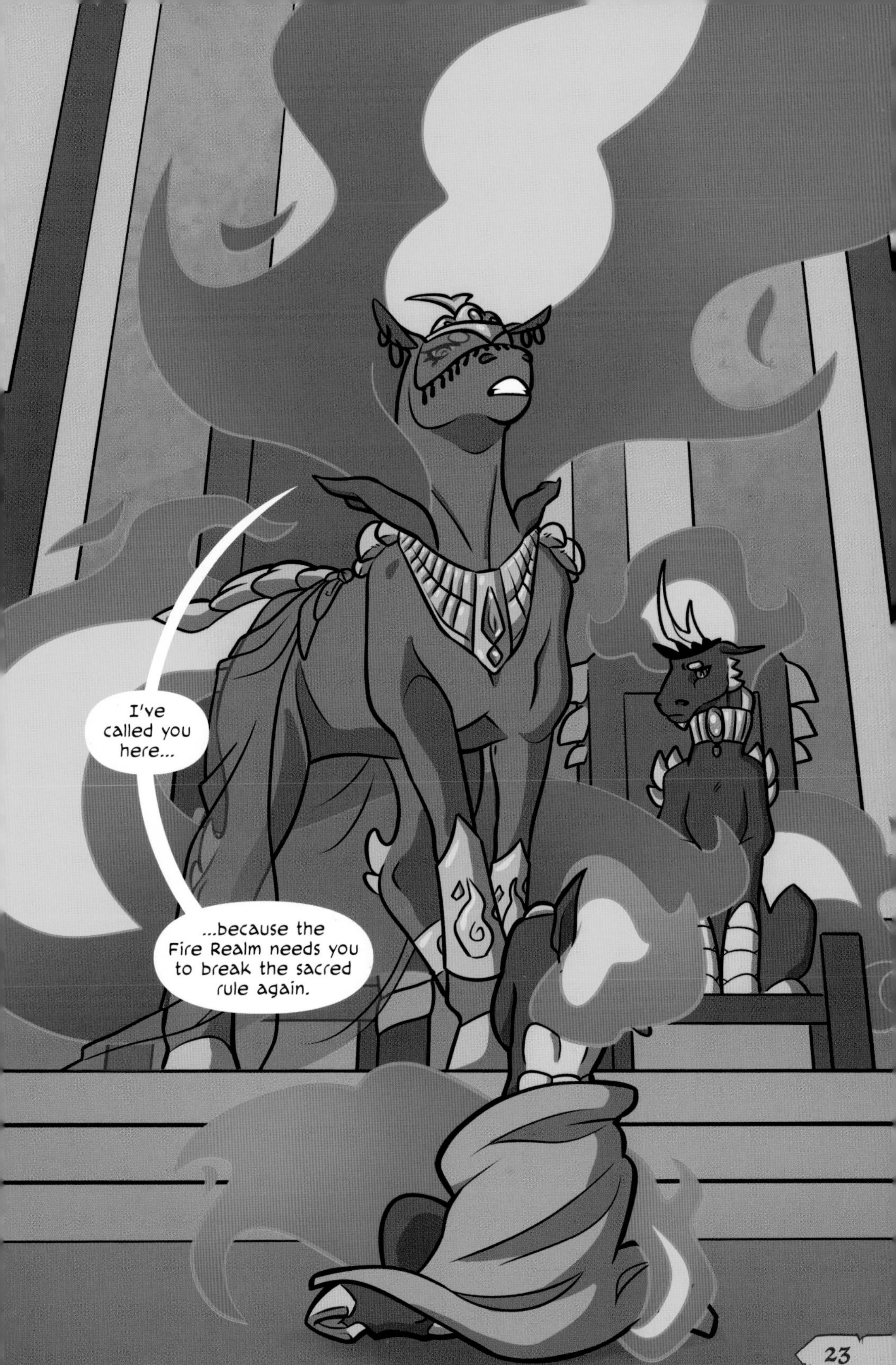
I've called you here...
...because the Fire Realm needs you to break the sacred rule again.

Chapter 2

Meanwhile, in the Sea Scape...

EEEEEEEEEEEEEEEEEEEEEEEEE

The alarm still sounded.

EEEEEEEEEEEEEEEEEEEEEEEE

EEEEEEEEEEEEEEEEEEEEEEEEEE

What IS that pink stuff?

Out of the way!! This is an emergency!!

EEEEEEEEEEEEEEEEEEEEEEEEEE

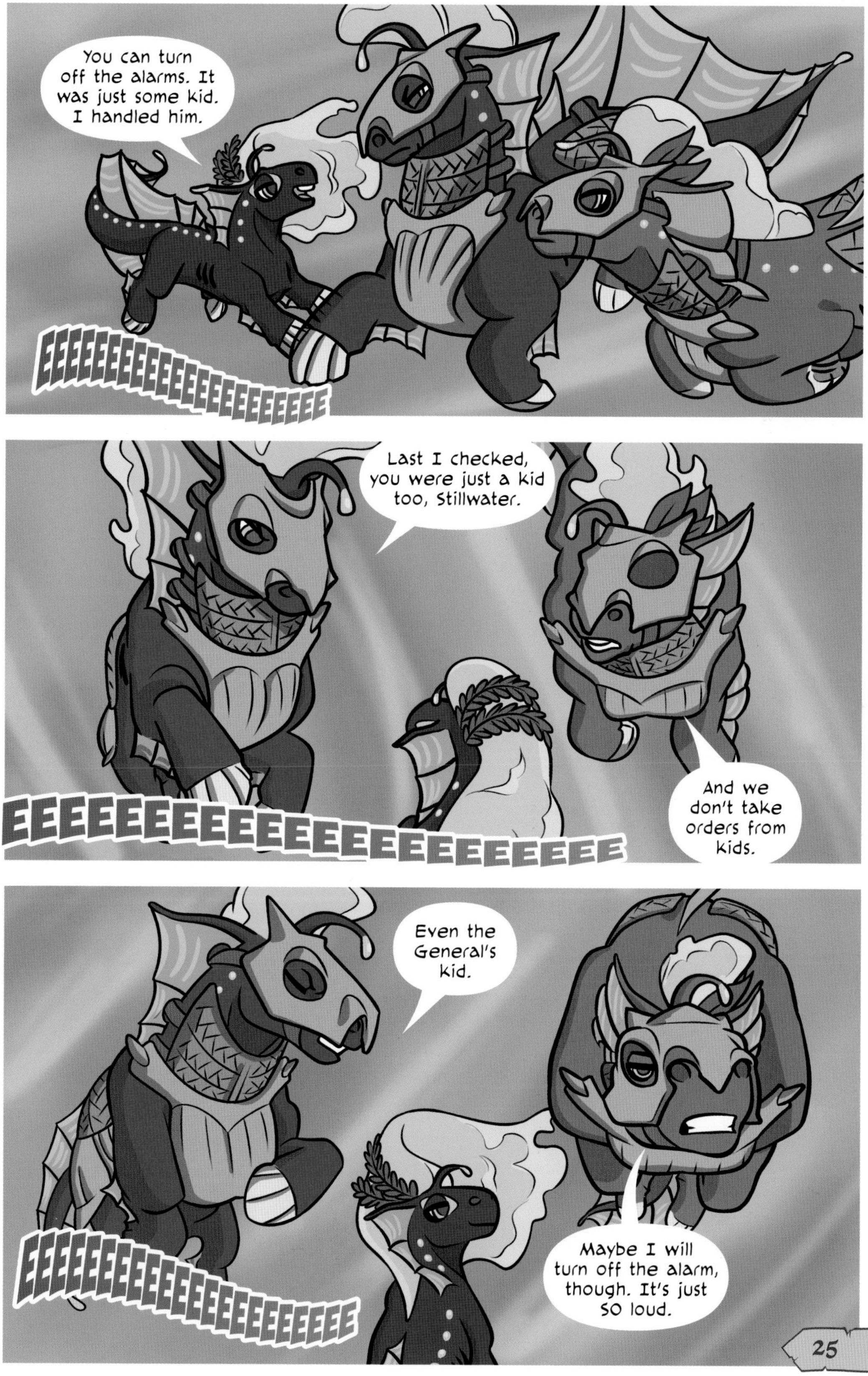
You can turn off the alarms. It was just some kid. I handled him.
EEEEEEEEEEEEEEEEEEEEEEEEE
Last I checked, you were just a kid too, Stillwater.
EEEEEEEEEEEEEEEEEEEEEEE
And we don't take orders from kids.
Even the General's kid.
EEEEEEEEEEEEEEEEEEEEEEEEE
Maybe I will turn off the alarm, though. It's just SO loud.

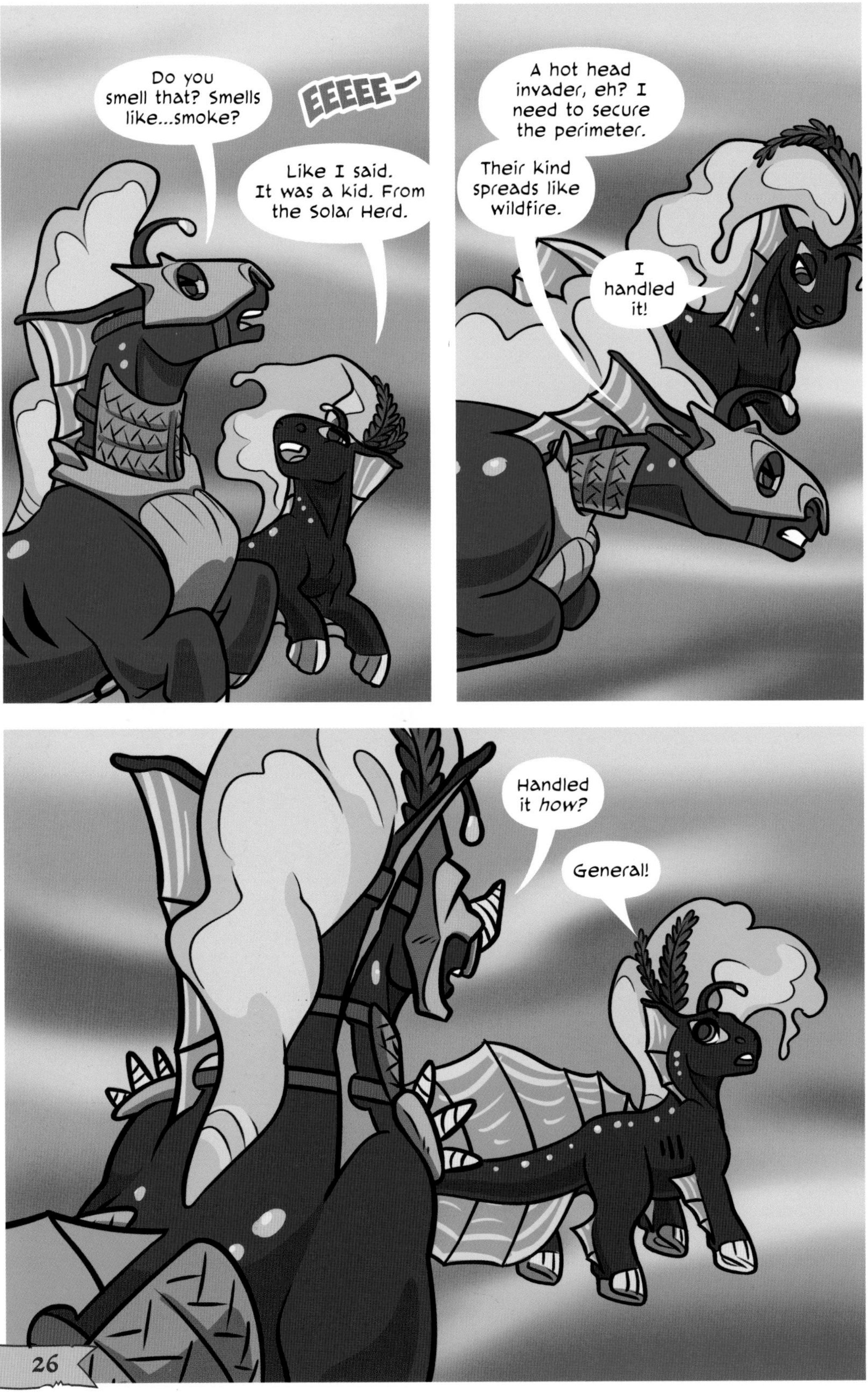
Do you smell that? Smells like...smoke?
EEEEE-
Like I said. It was a kid. From the Solar Herd.
A hot head invader, eh? I need to secure the perimeter.
Their kind spreads like wildfire.
I handled it!
Handled it *how?*
General!

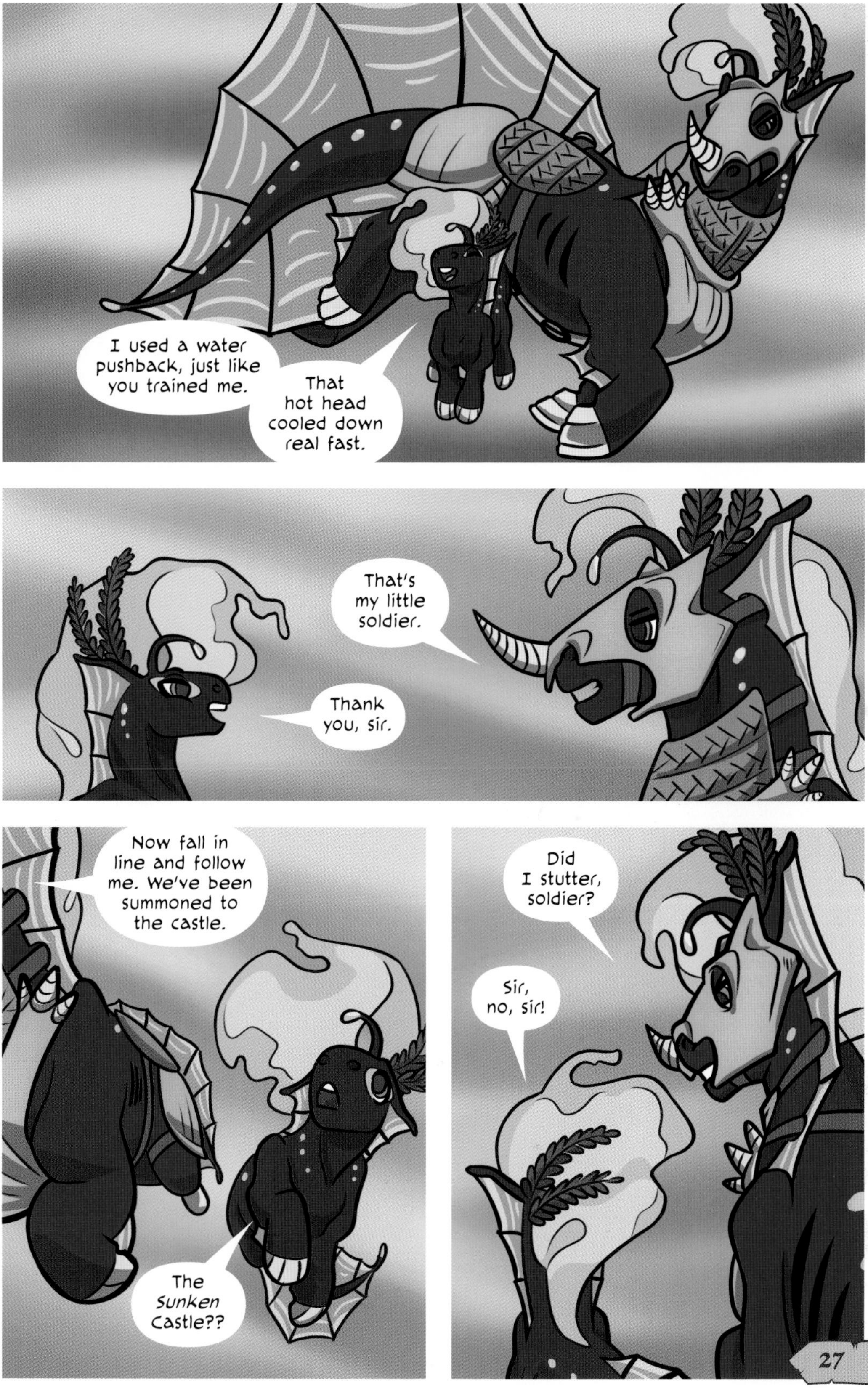
I used a water pushback, just like you trained me.
That hot head cooled down real fast.
That's my little soldier.
Thank you, sir.
Now fall in line and follow me. We've been summoned to the castle.
The Sunken Castle??
Did I stutter, soldier?
Sir, no, sir!

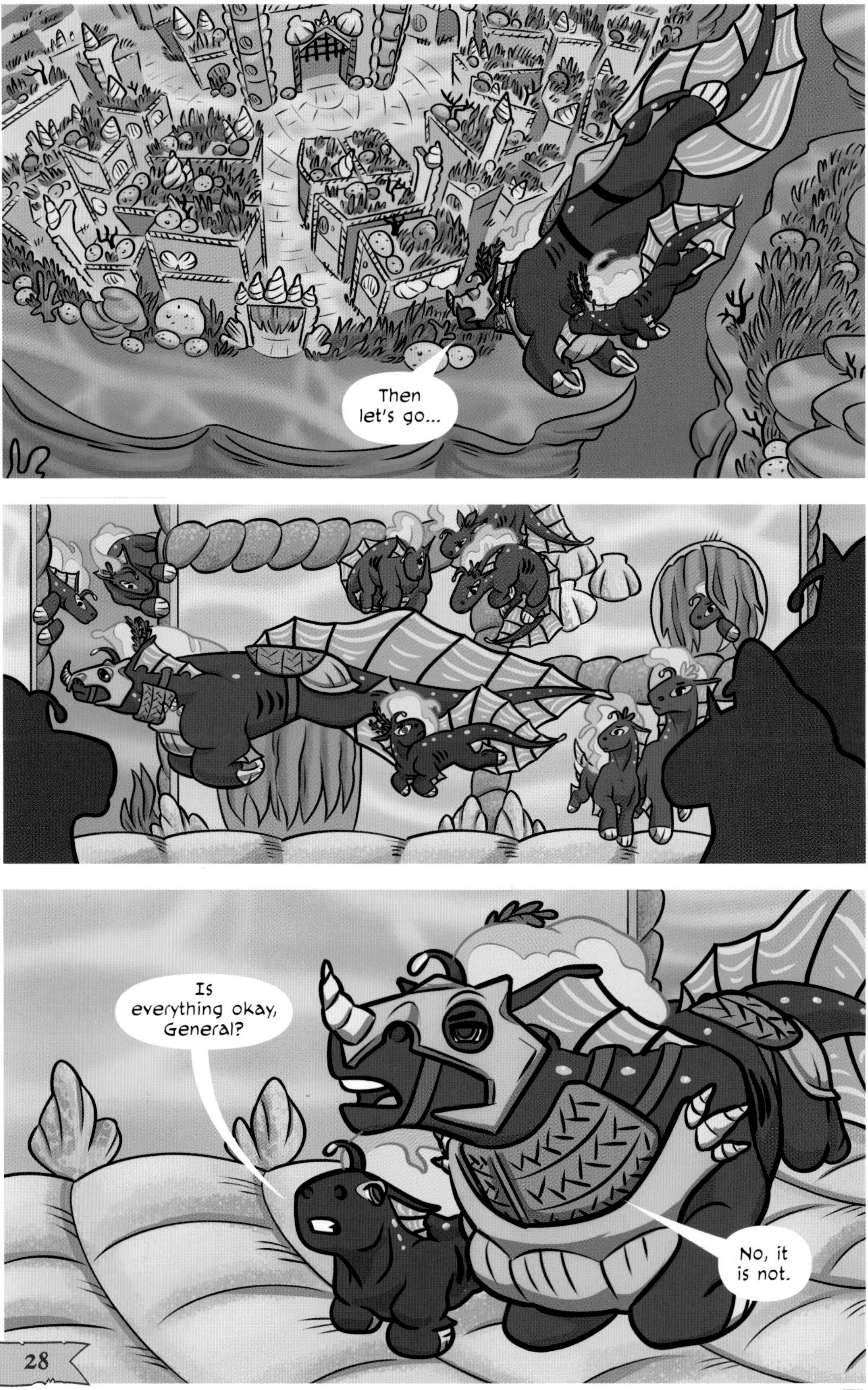
Then let's go...
Is everything okay, General?
No, it is not.

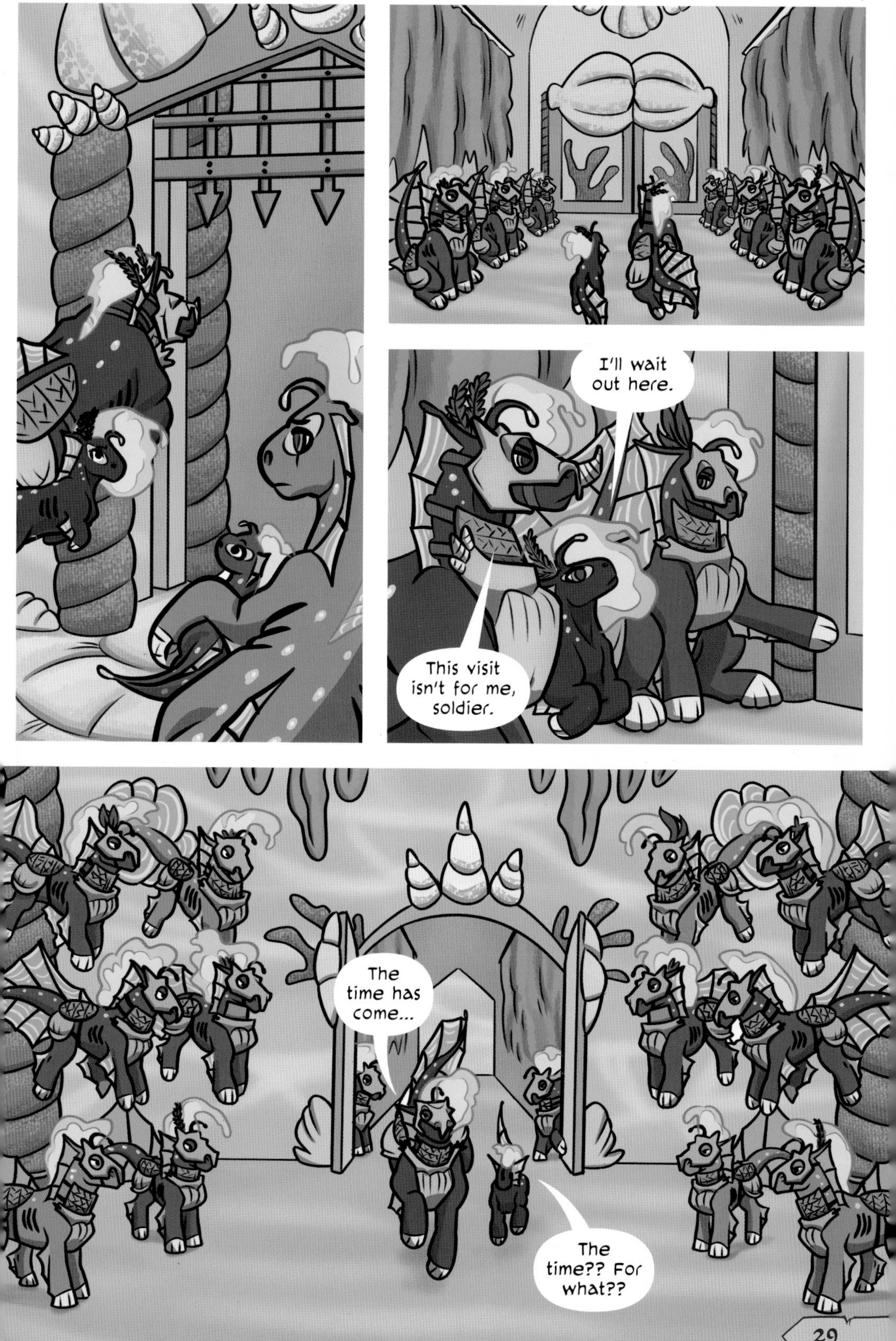
I'll wait out here.
This visit isn't for me, soldier.
The time has come...
The time?? For what??

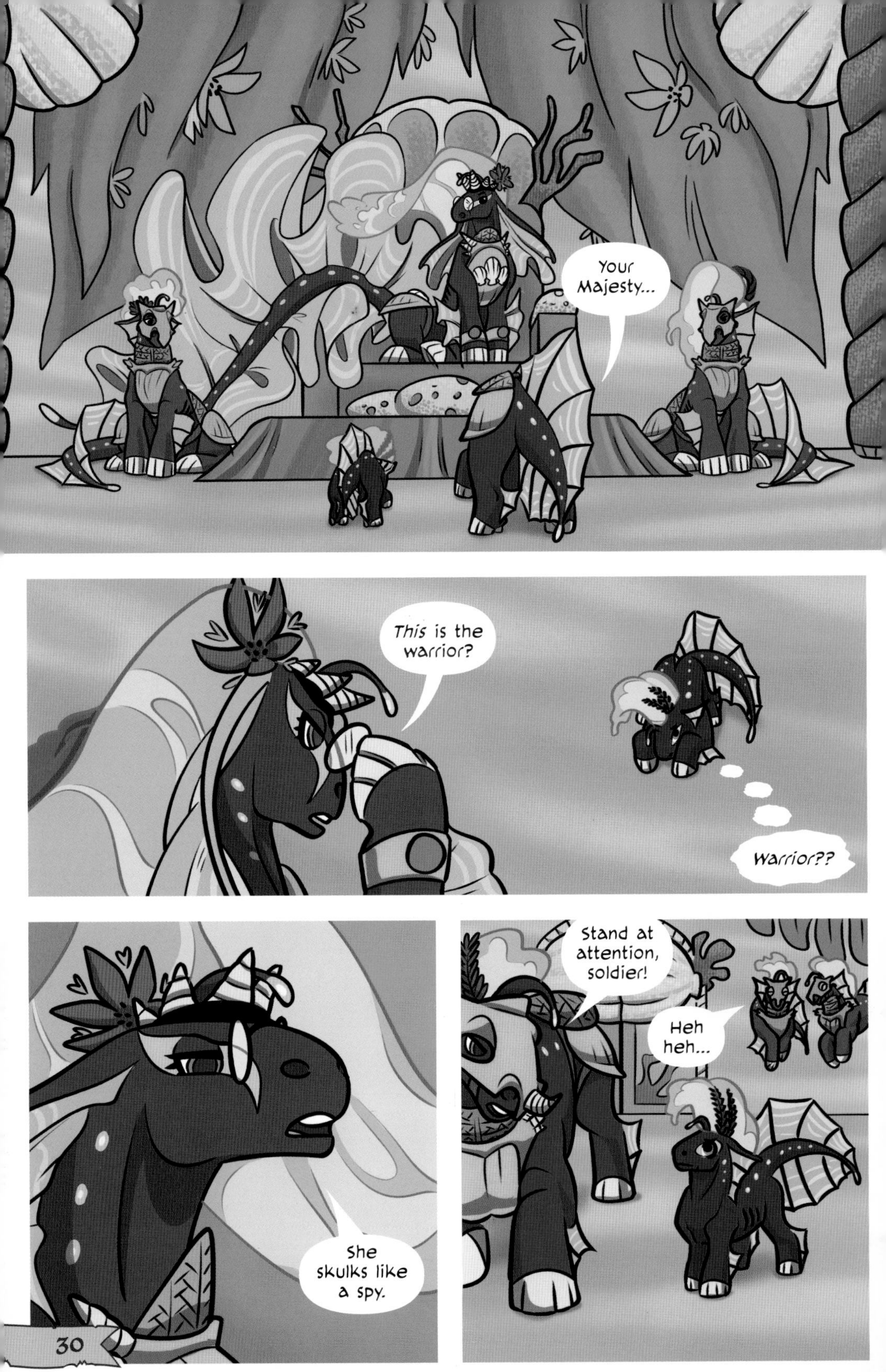

Your Majesty...
This is the warrior?
Warrior??
She skulks like a spy.
Stand at attention, soldier!
Heh heh...

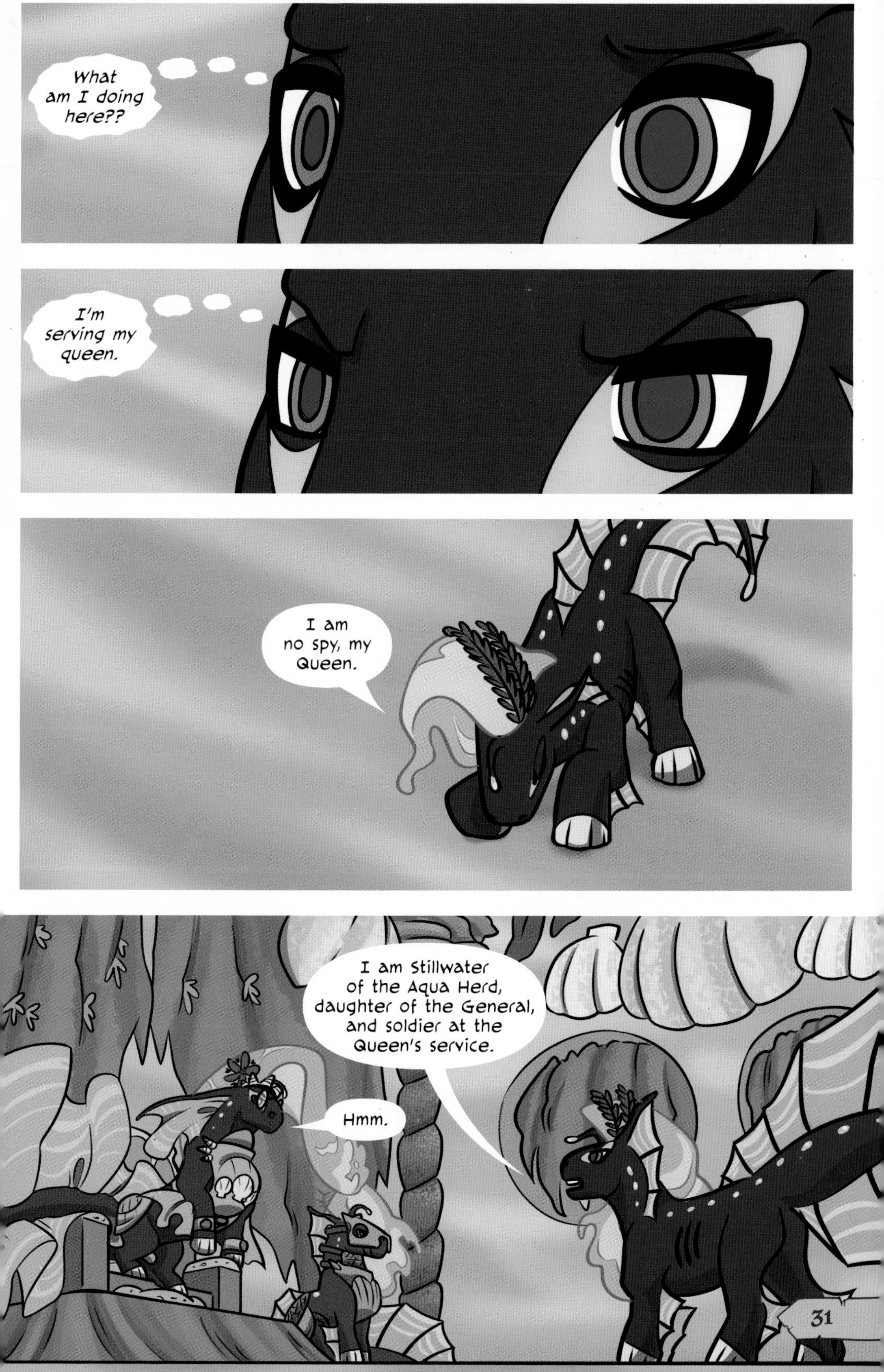
What am I doing here??
I'm serving my queen.
I am no spy, my Queen.
I am Stillwater of the Aqua Herd, daughter of the General, and soldier at the Queen's service.
Hmm.

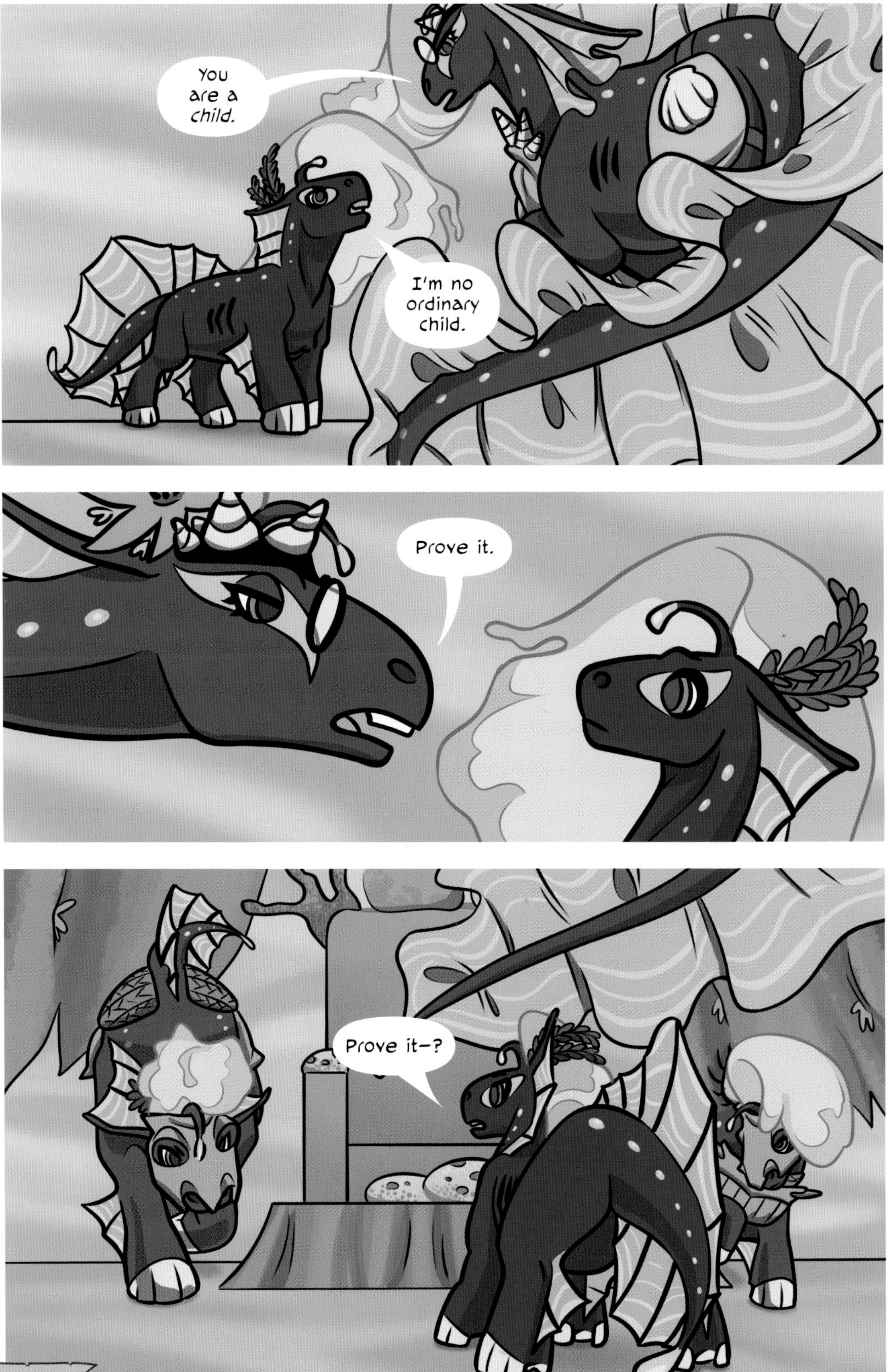
You are a child.
I'm no ordinary child.
Prove it.
Prove it–?

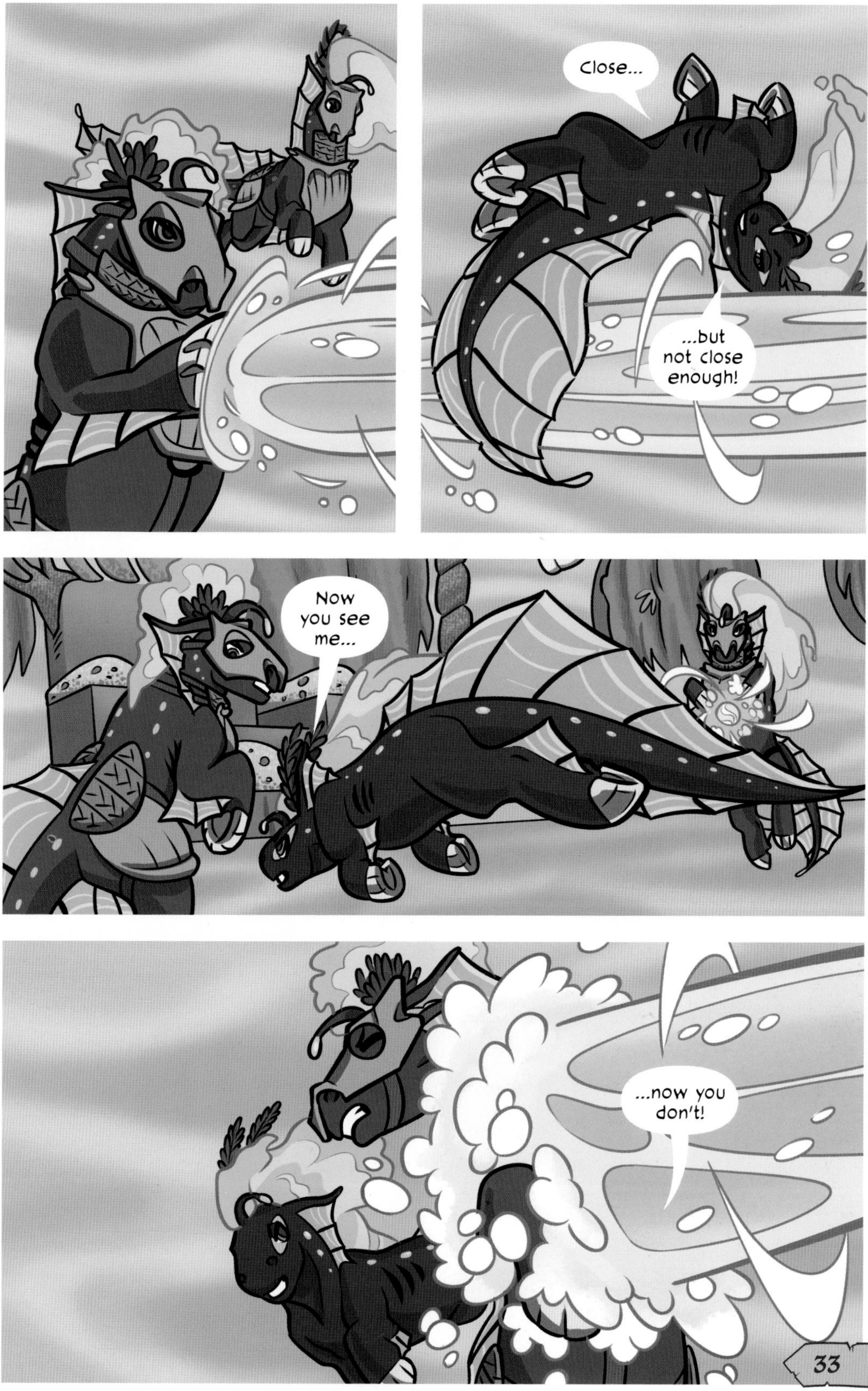
Close...
...but not close enough!
Now you see me...
...now you don't!

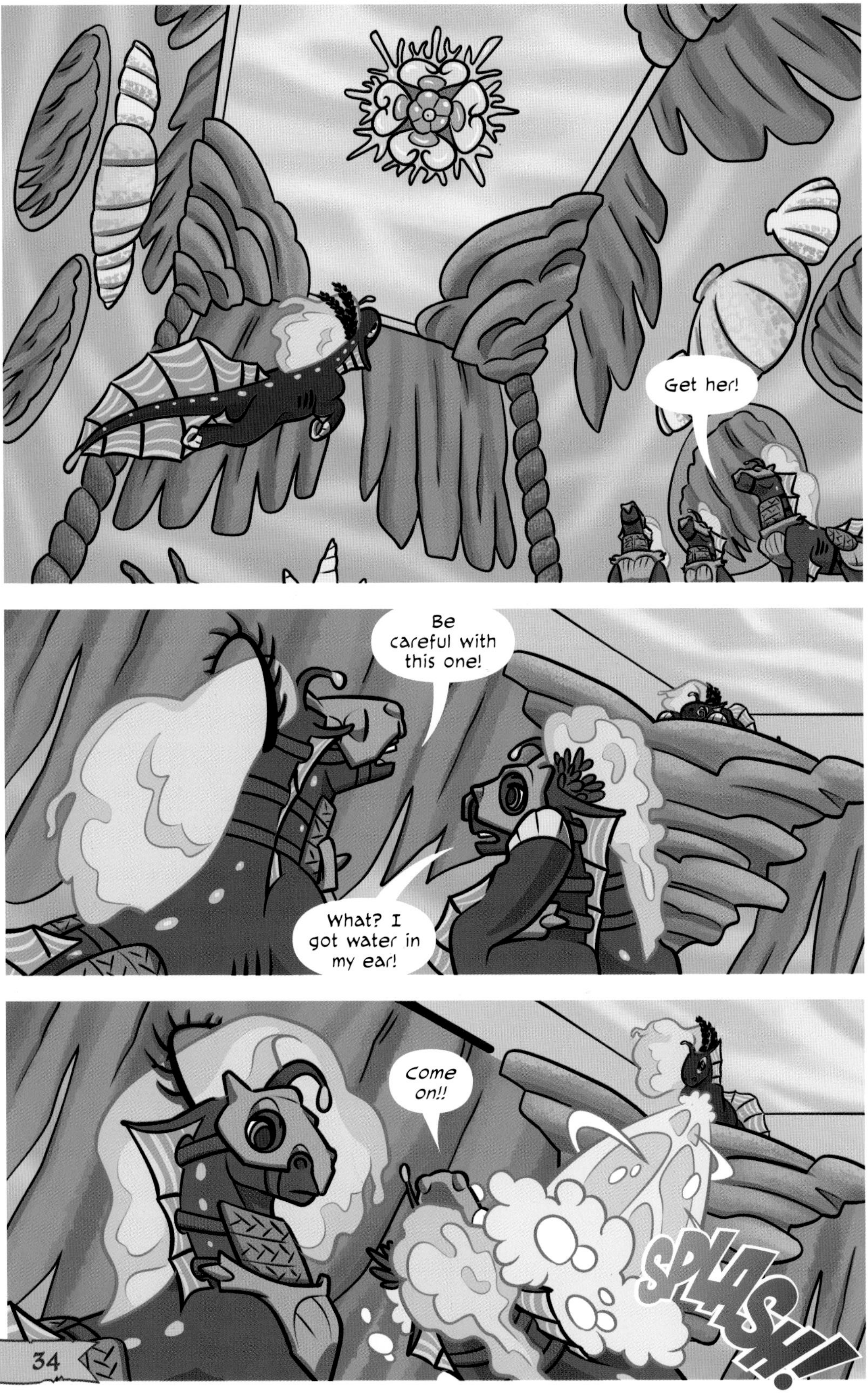
Get her!
Be careful with this one!
What? I got water in my ear!
Come on!!
SPLASH!!

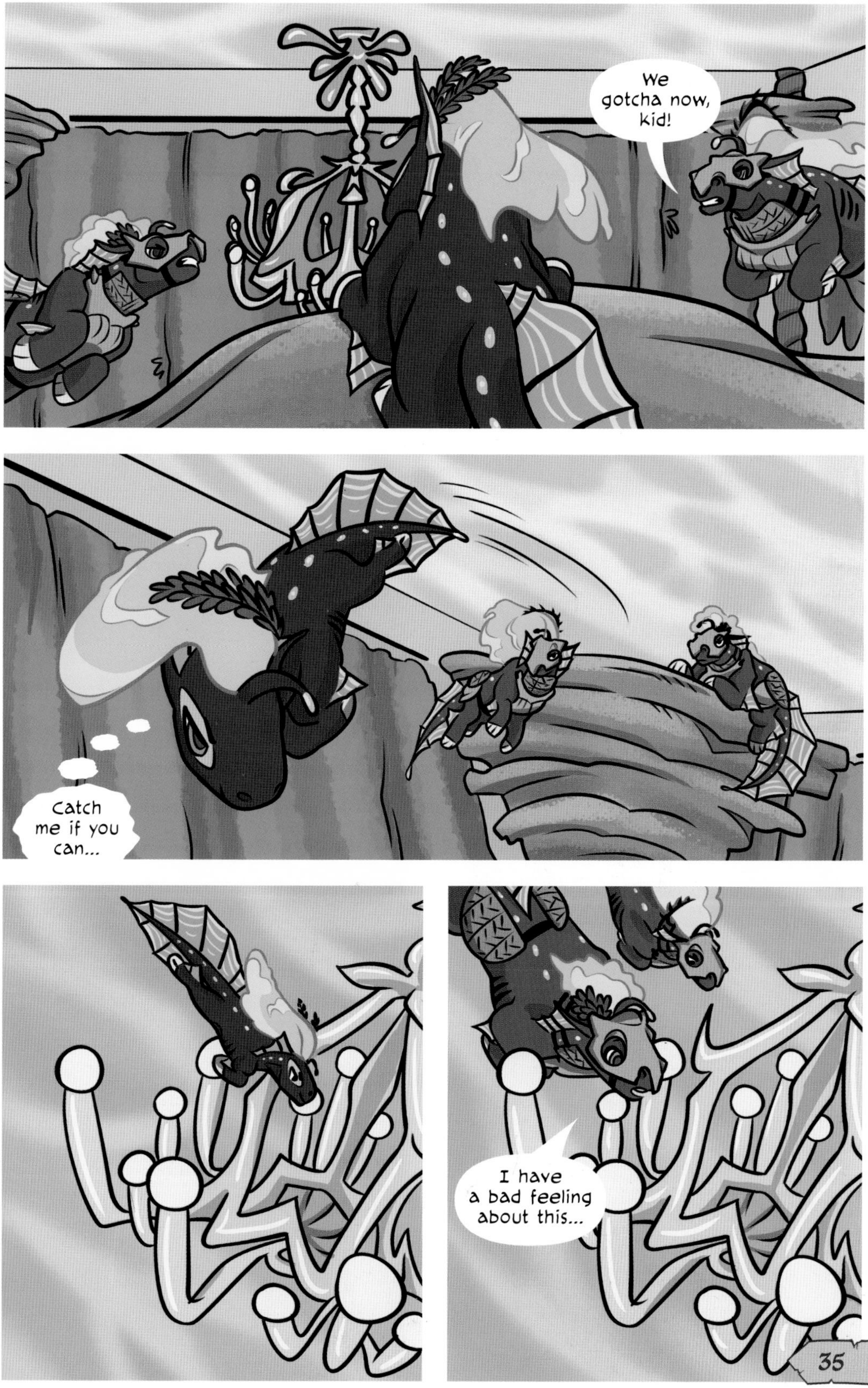
We gotcha now, kid!
Catch me if you can...
I have a bad feeling about this...

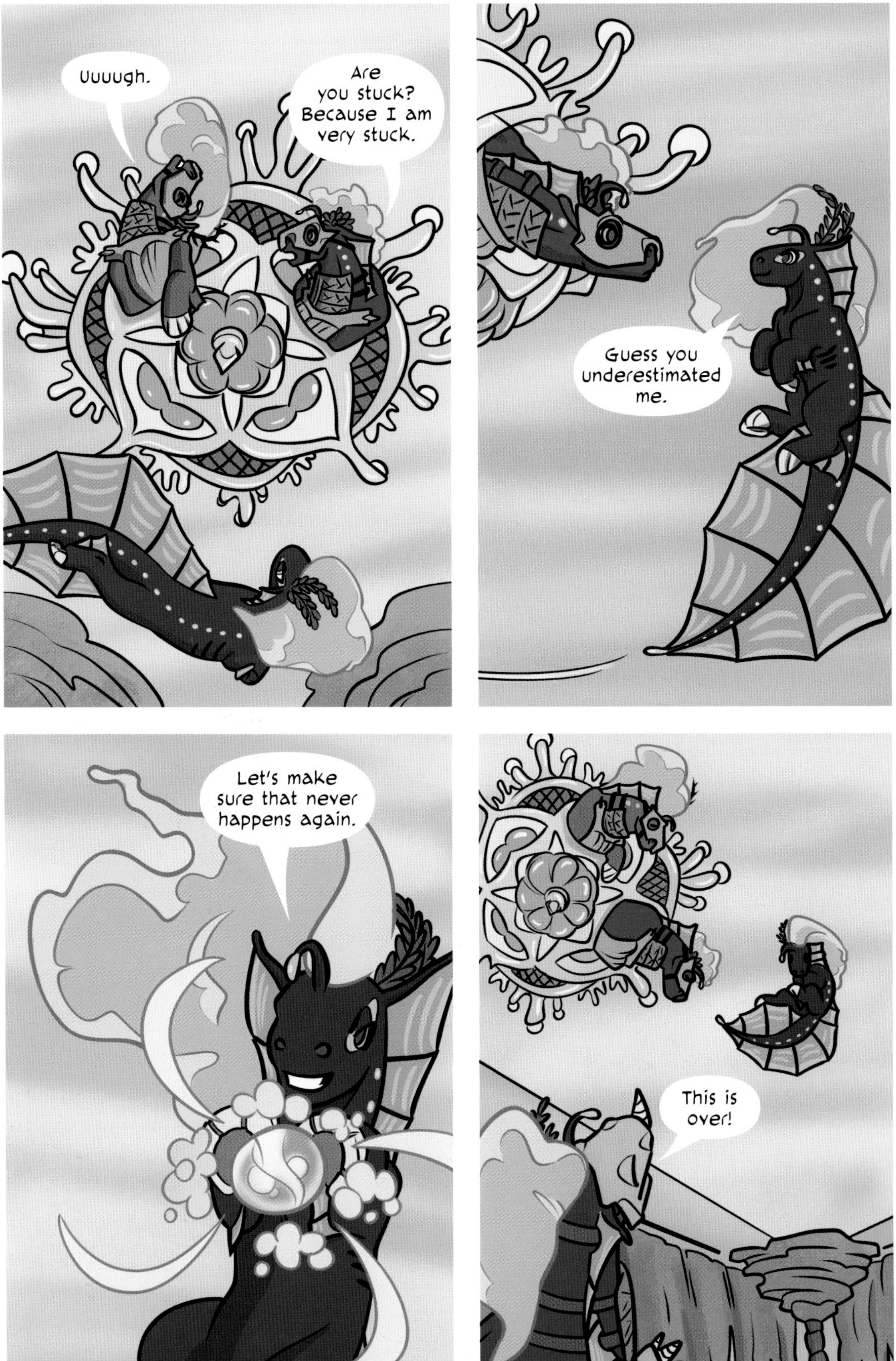
Uuuugh.
Are you stuck? Because I am very stuck.
Guess you underestimated me.
Let's make sure that never happens again.
This is over!

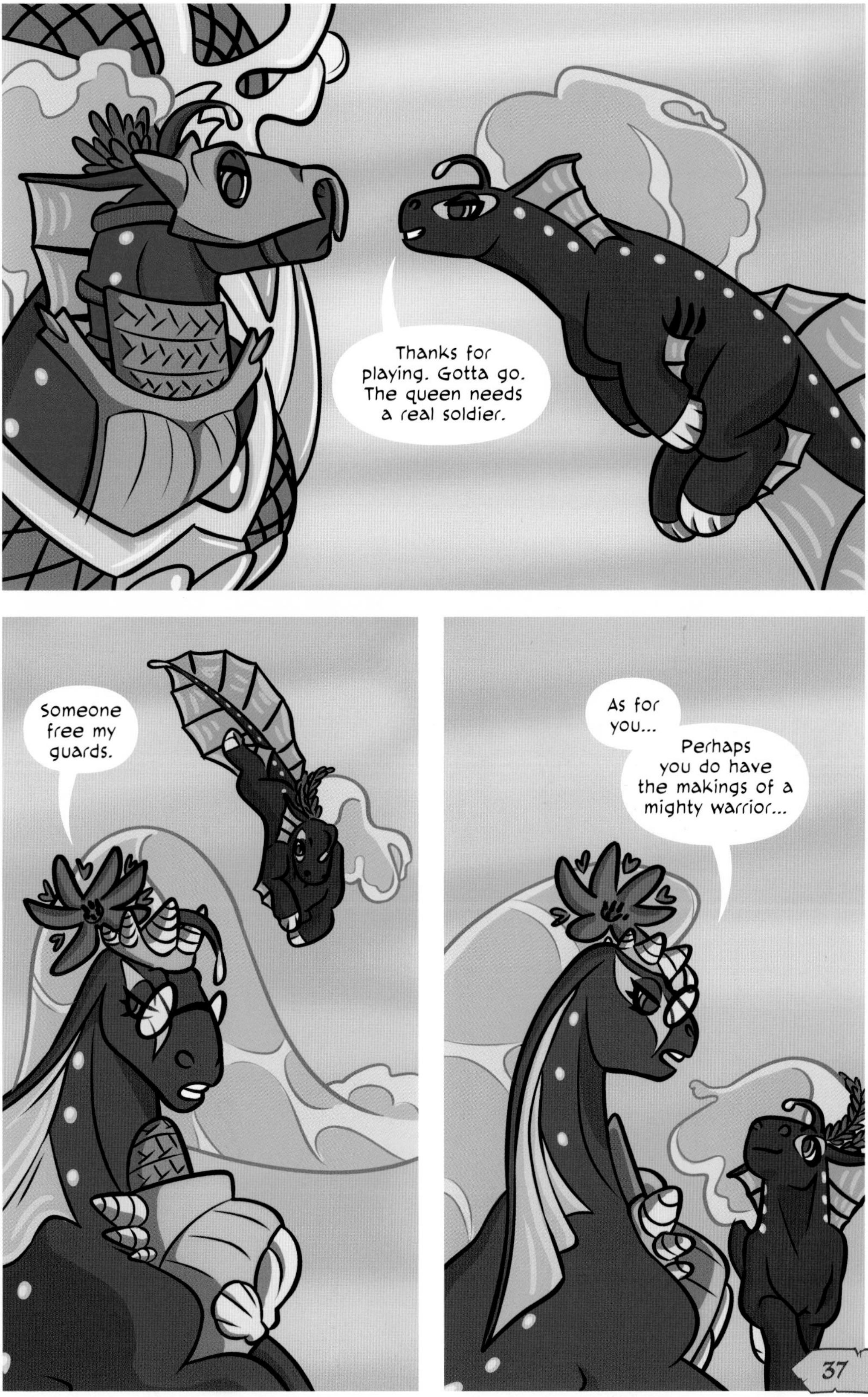
Thanks for playing. Gotta go. The queen needs a real soldier.
Someone free my guards.
As for you...
Perhaps you do have the makings of a mighty warrior...

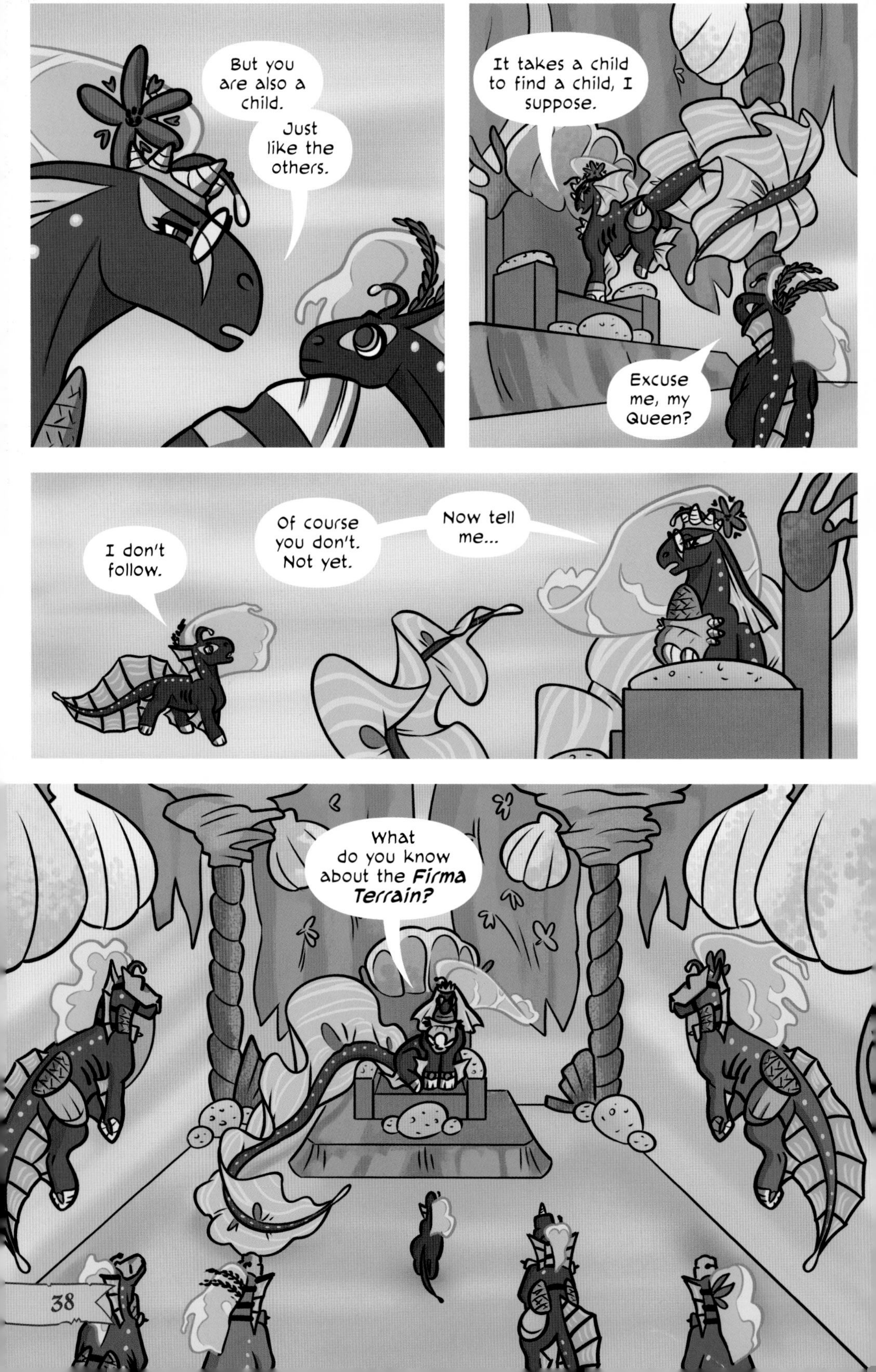
But you are also a child.
Just like the others.
It takes a child to find a child, I suppose.
Excuse me, my Queen?
I don't follow.
Of course you don't. Not yet.
Now tell me...
What do you know about the *Firma Terrain?*

Chapter 3

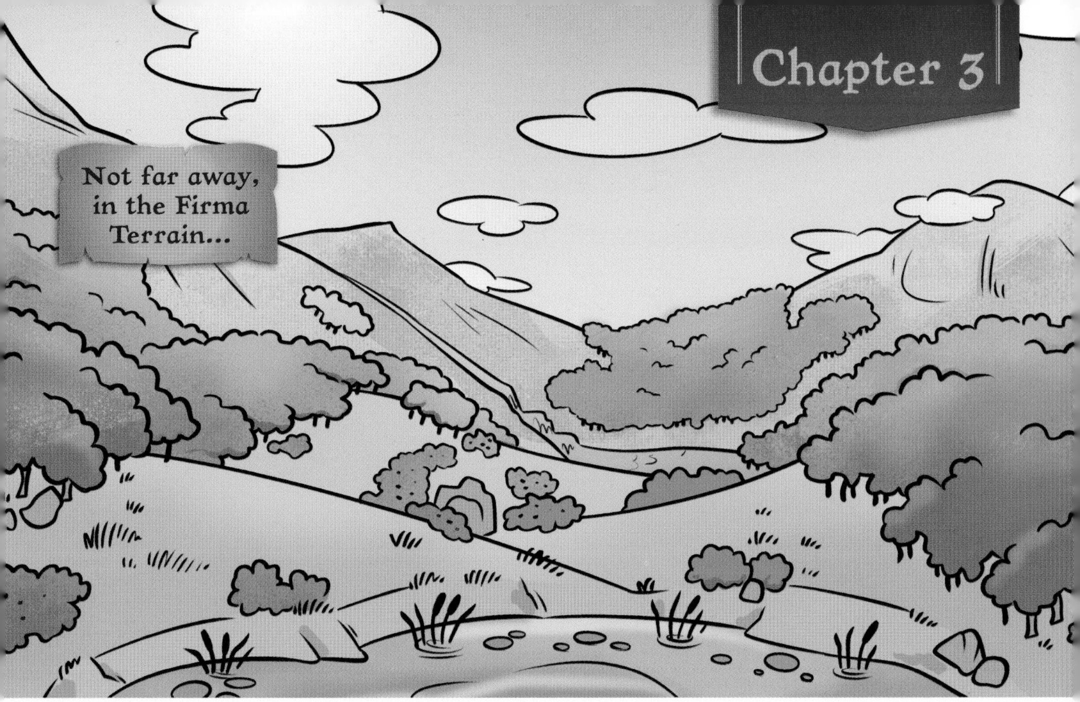
Not far away, in the Firma Terrain...

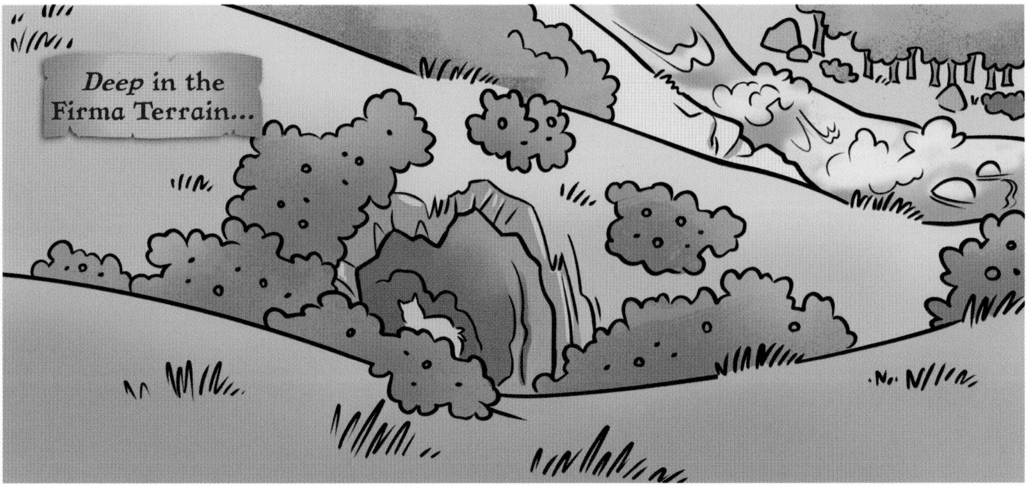
Deep in the Firma Terrain...

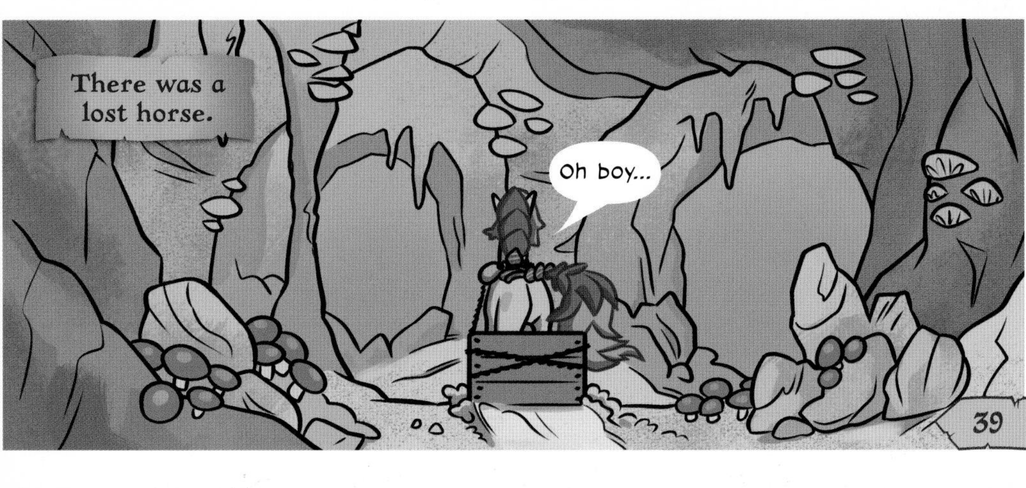
There was a lost horse.
Oh boy...

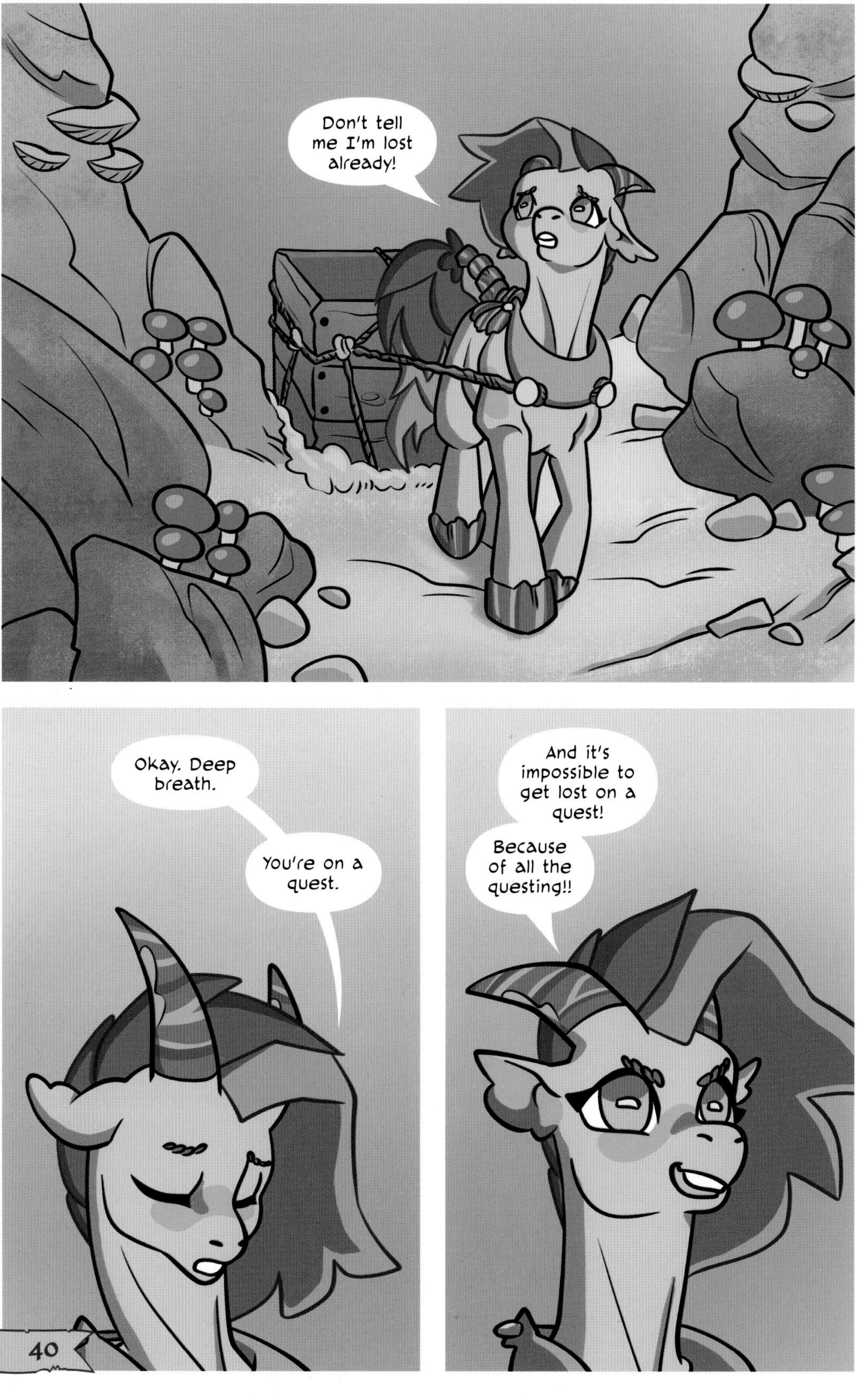
Don't tell me I'm lost already!
Okay. Deep breath.
You're on a quest.
And it's impossible to get lost on a quest!
Because of all the questing!!

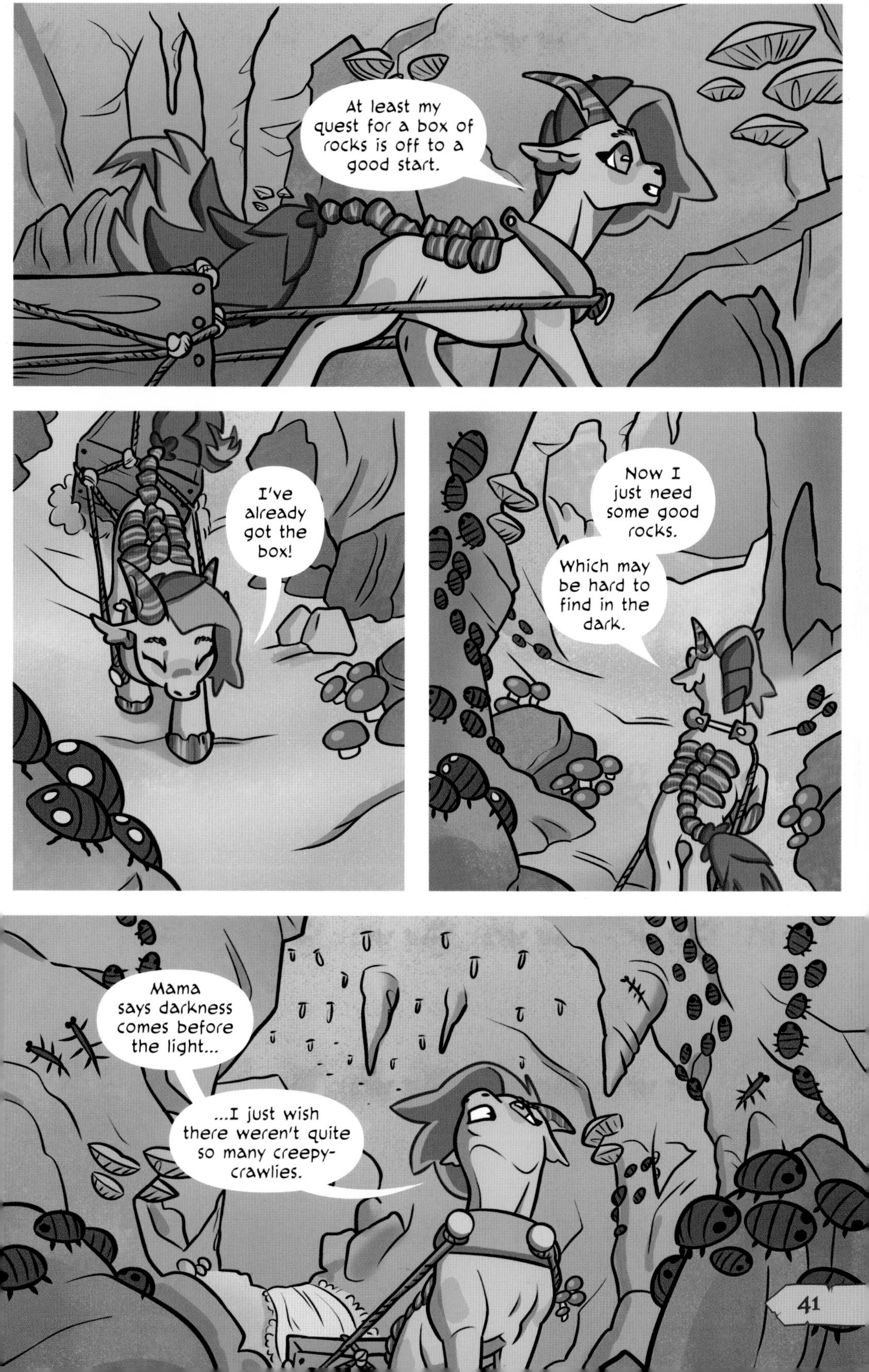
At least my quest for a box of rocks is off to a good start.
I've already got the box!
Now I just need some good rocks.
Which may be hard to find in the dark.
Mama says darkness comes before the light...
...I just wish there weren't quite so many creepy-crawlies.

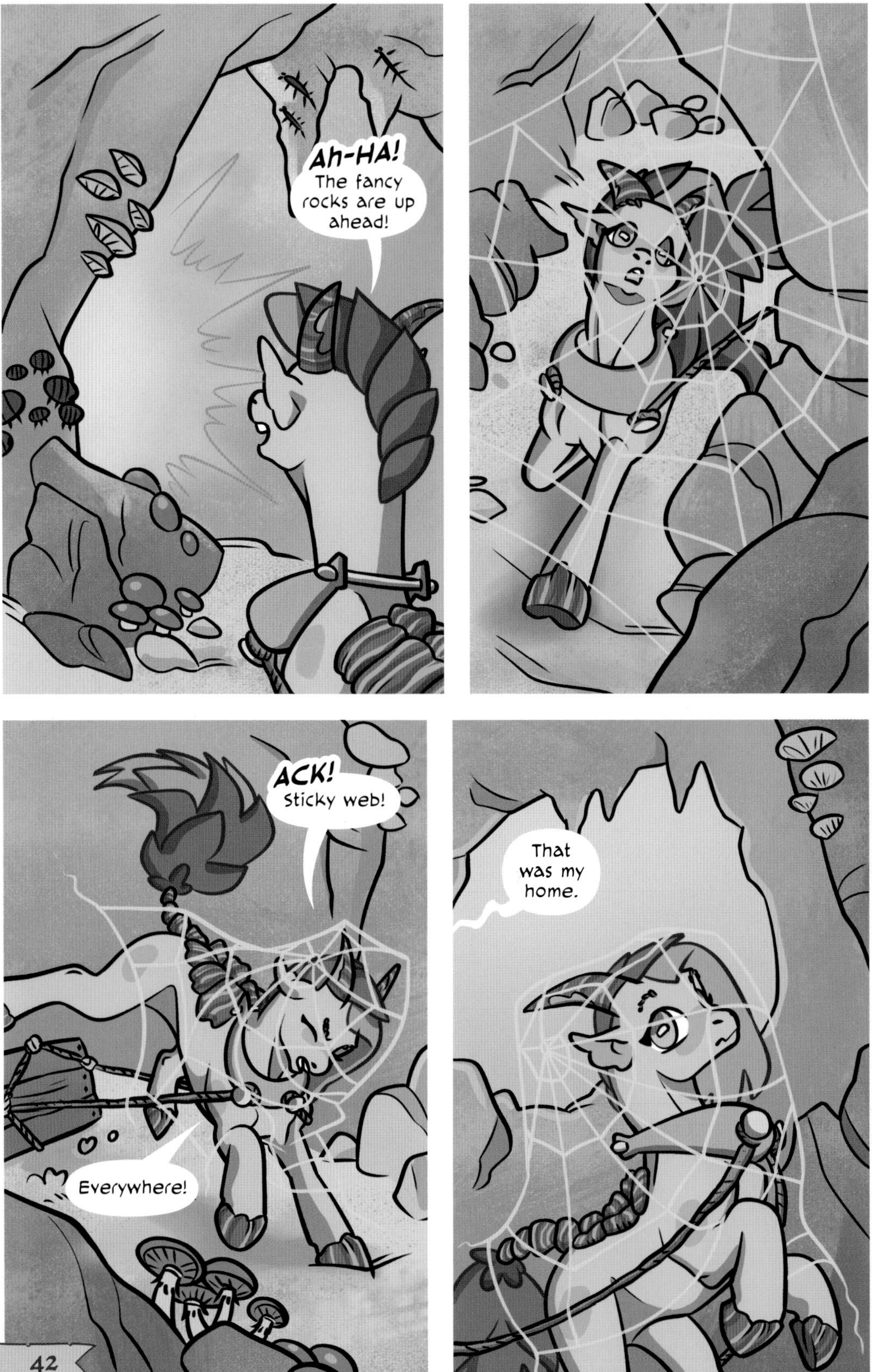
Ah-HA! The fancy rocks are up ahead!
ACK! Sticky web!
Everywhere!
That was my home.

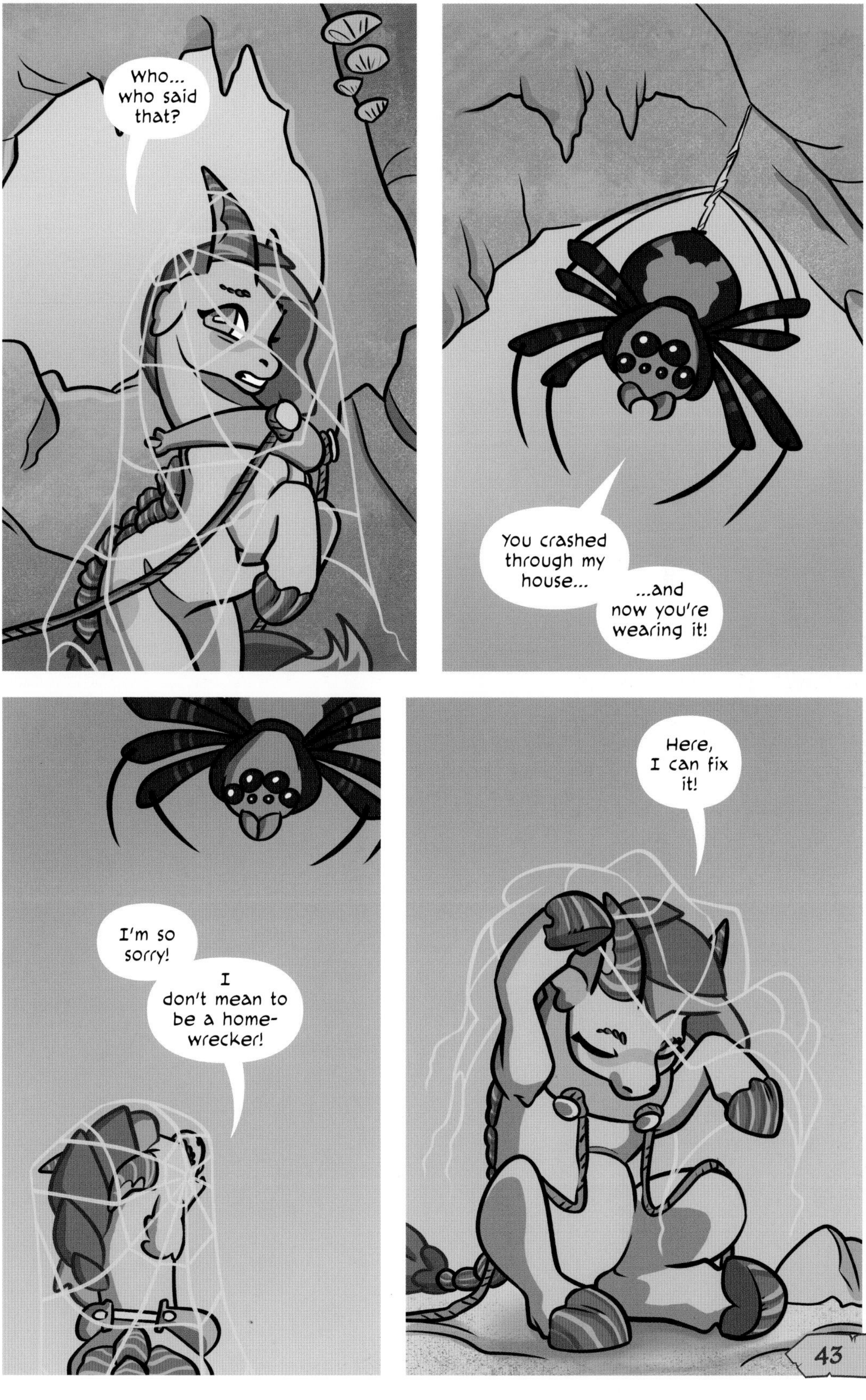
Who... who said that?
You crashed through my house...
...and now you're wearing it!
I'm so sorry!
I don't mean to be a home-wrecker!
Here, I can fix it!

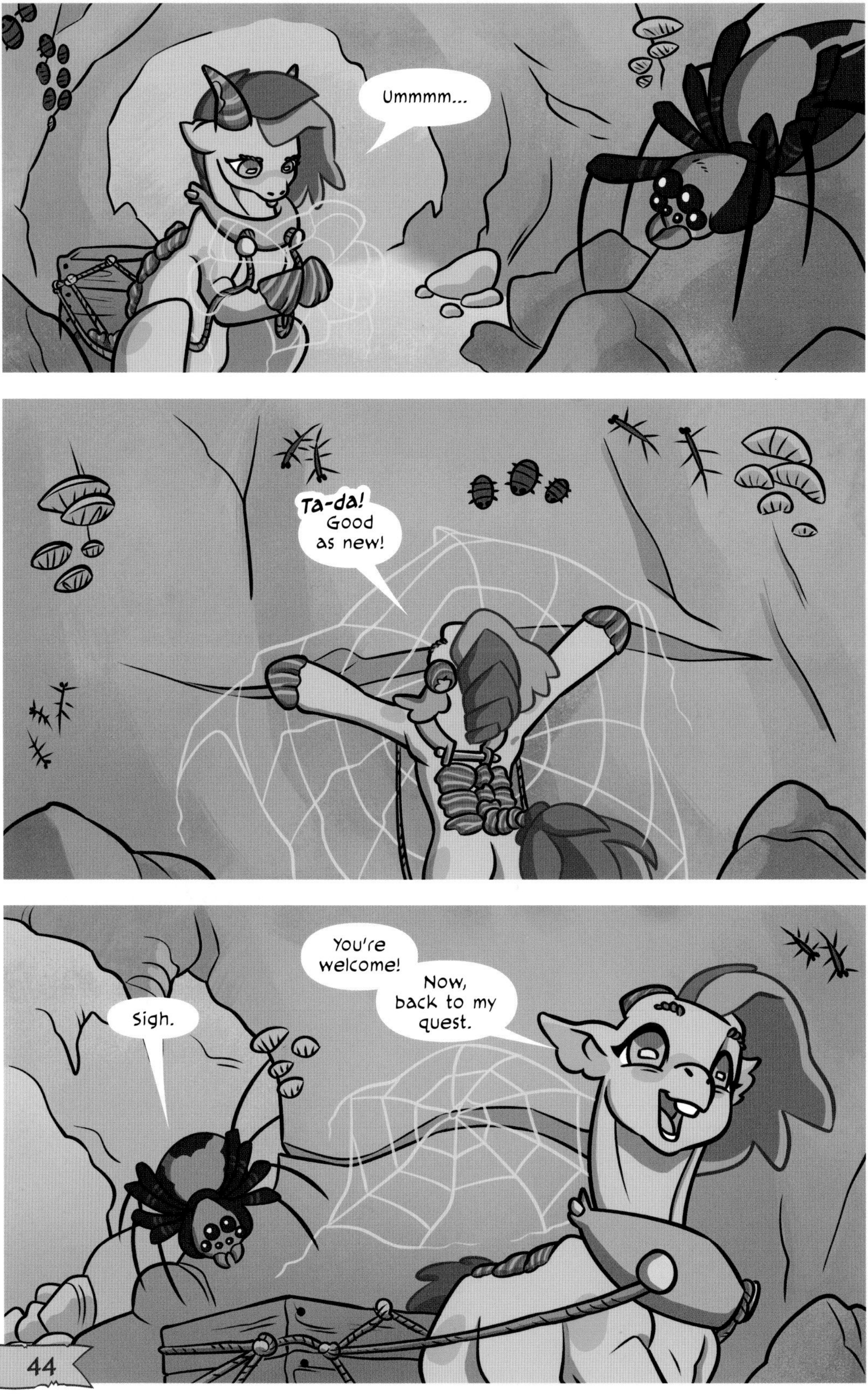
Ummmm...
Ta-da! Good as new!
Sigh.
You're welcome!
Now, back to my quest.

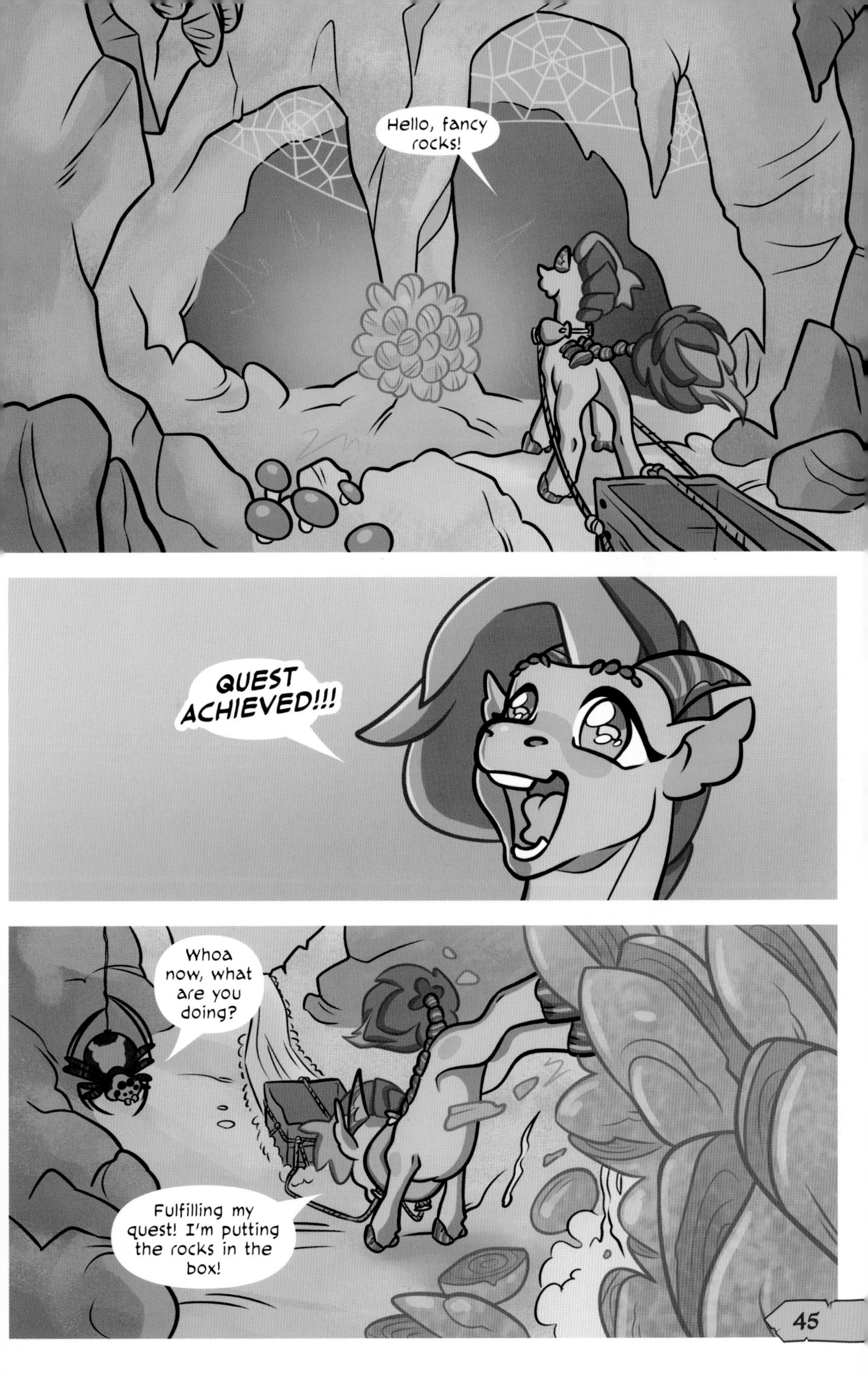
Hello, fancy rocks!
QUEST ACHIEVED!!!
Whoa now, what are you doing?
Fulfilling my quest! I'm putting the rocks in the box!

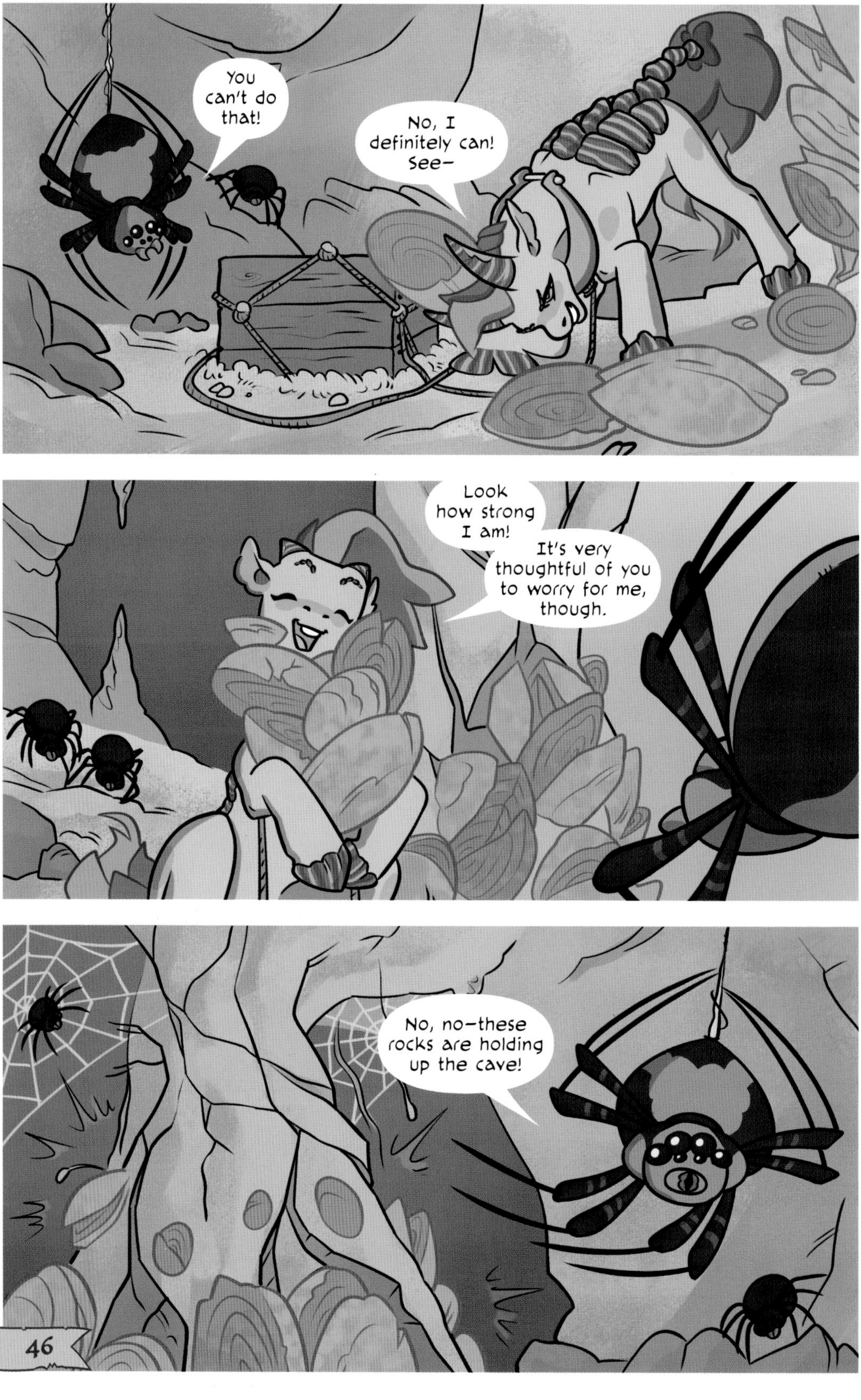
You can't do that!
No, I definitely can! See—
Look how strong I am!
It's very thoughtful of you to worry for me, though.
No, no—these rocks are holding up the cave!

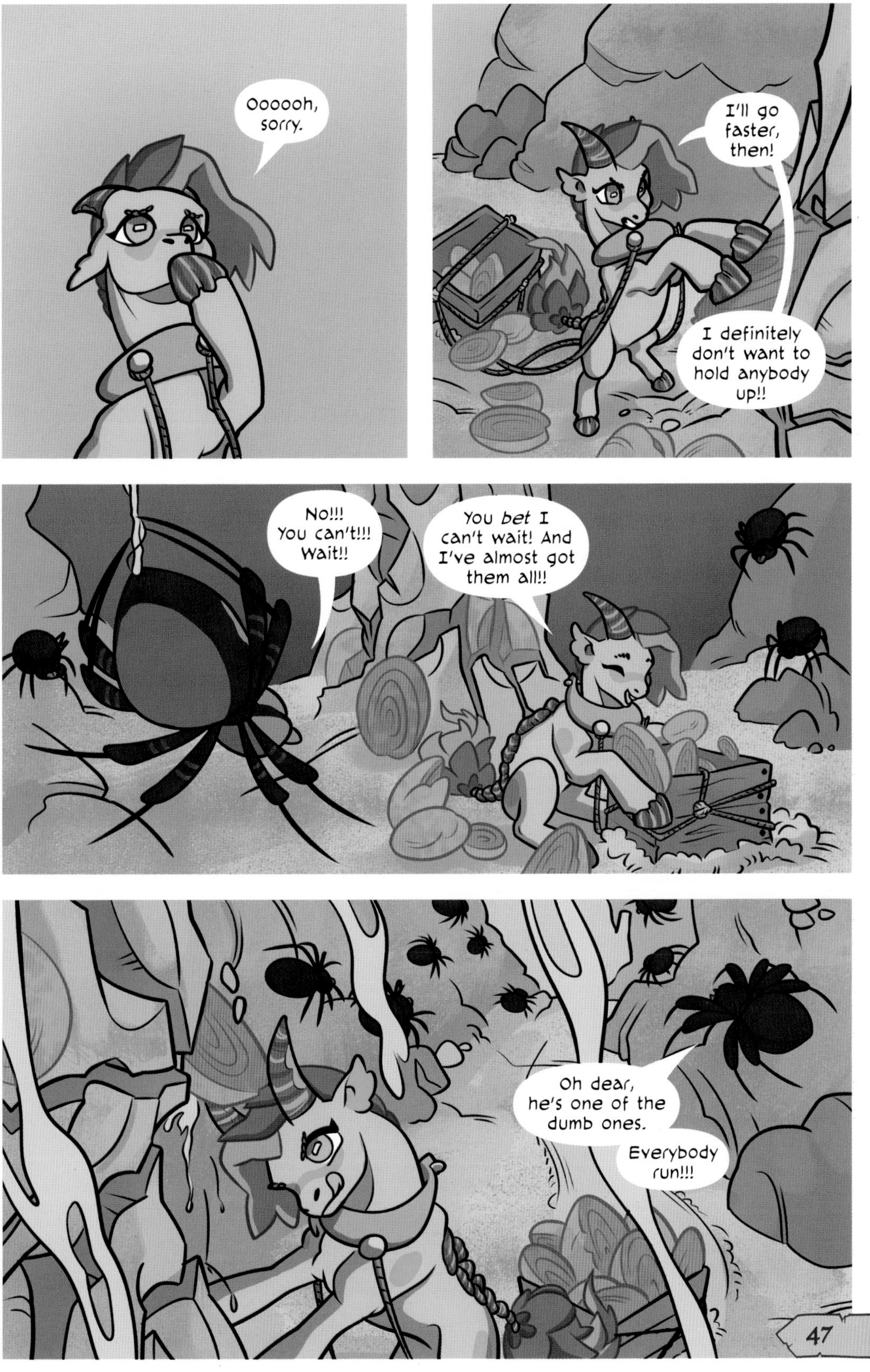
Oooooh, sorry.
I'll go faster, then!
I definitely don't want to hold anybody up!!
No!!! You can't!!! Wait!!
You *bet* I can't wait! And I've almost got them all!!
Oh dear, he's one of the dumb ones.
Everybody run!!!

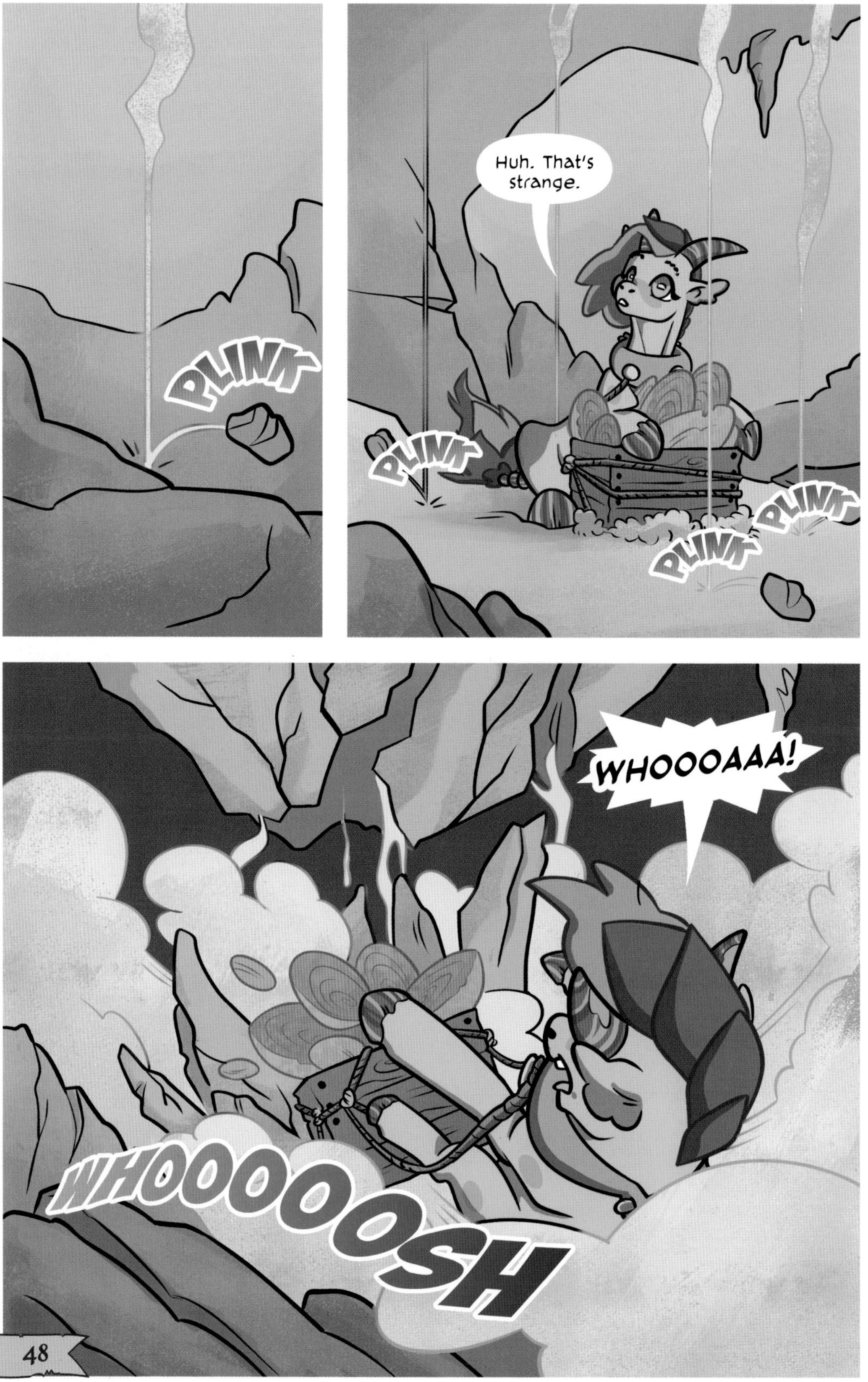
PLINK
Huh. That's strange.
PLINK
PLINK
PLINK
WHOOOAAA!
WHOOOOOOSH

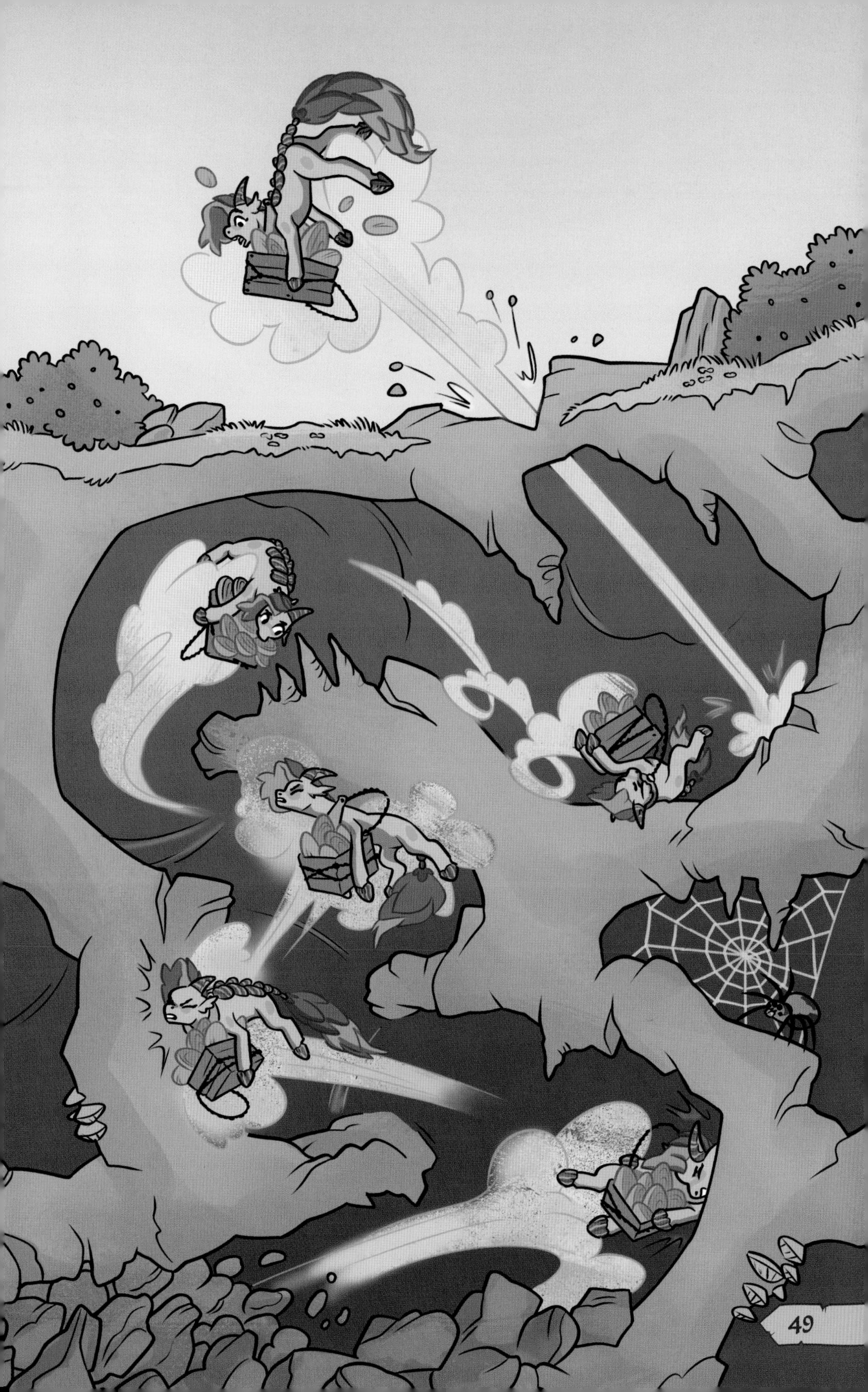

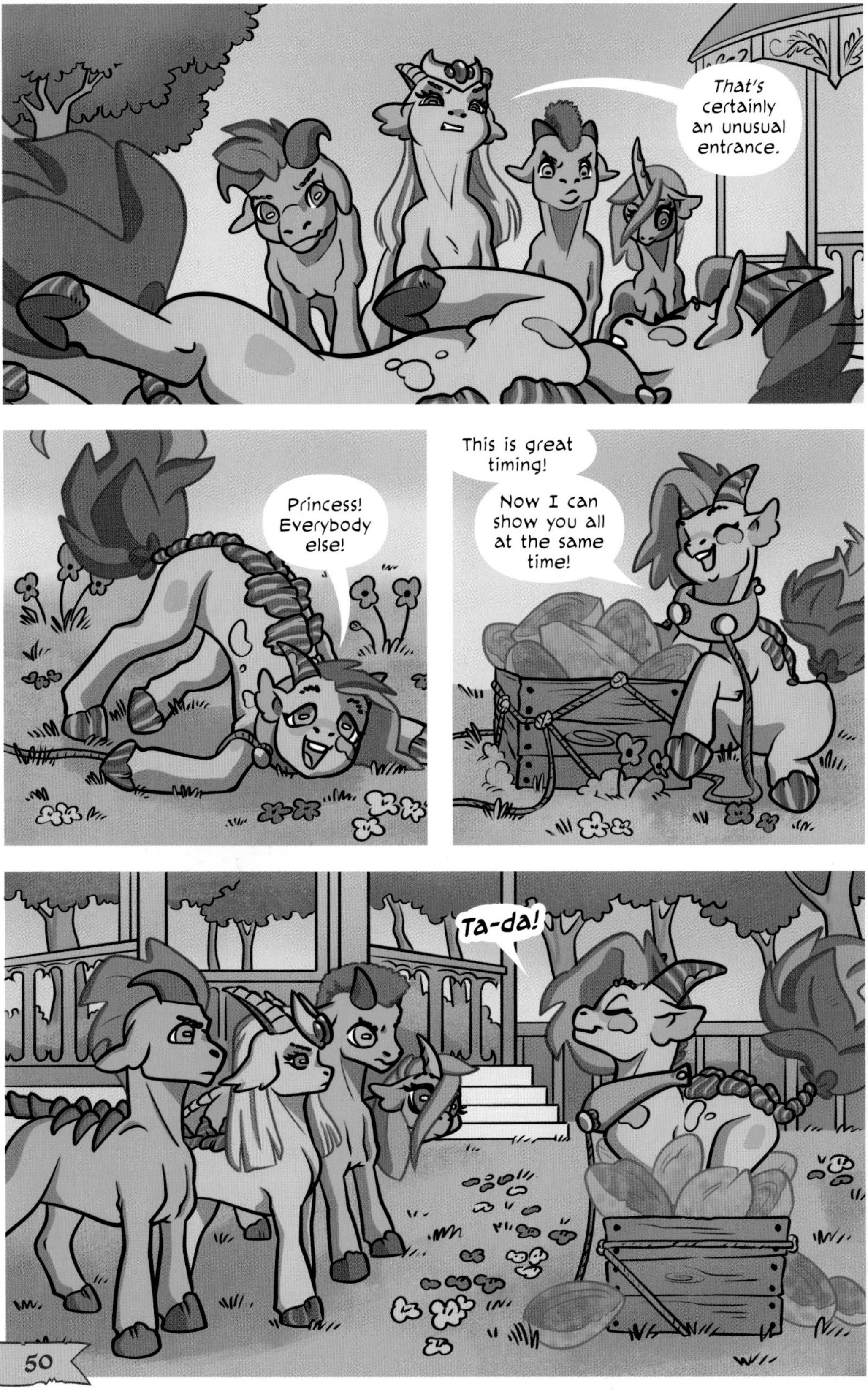
That's certainly an unusual entrance.
Princess! Everybody else!
This is great timing!
Now I can show you all at the same time!
Ta-da!

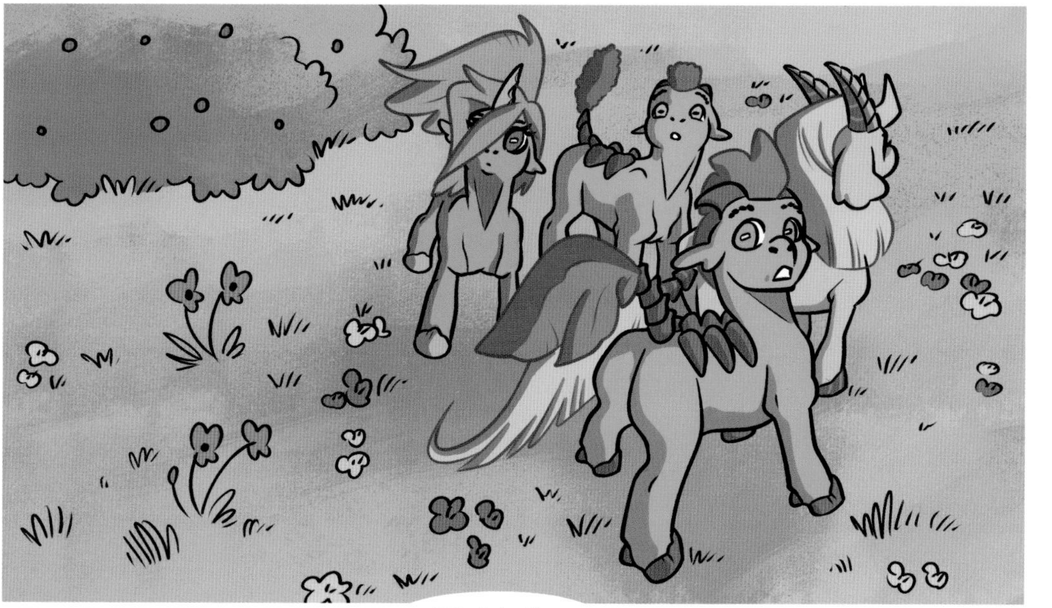

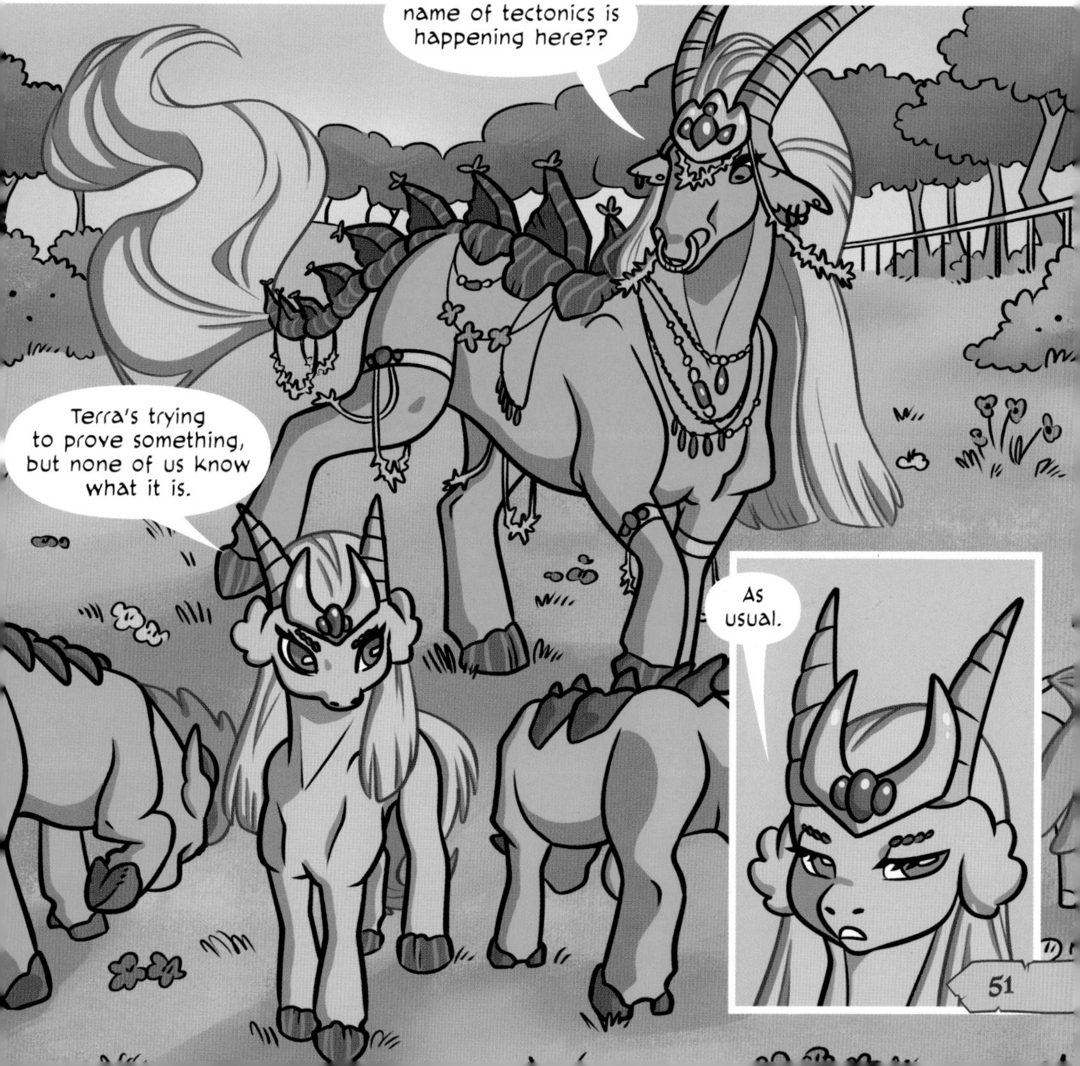
What in the name of tectonics is happening here??
Terra's trying to prove something, but none of us know what it is.
As usual.

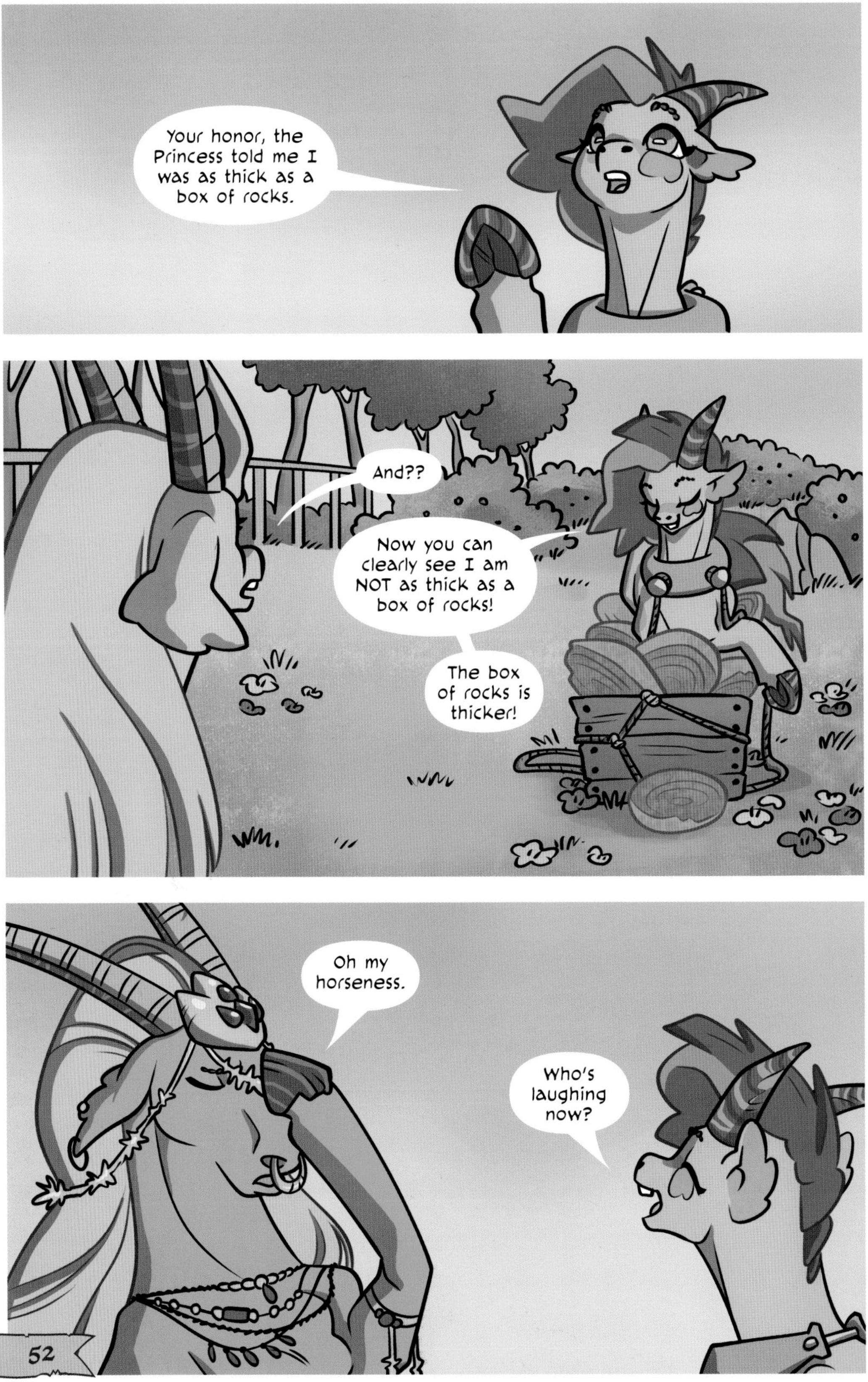
Your honor, the Princess told me I was as thick as a box of rocks.
And??
Now you can clearly see I am NOT as thick as a box of rocks!
The box of rocks is thicker!
Oh my horseness.
Who's laughing now?

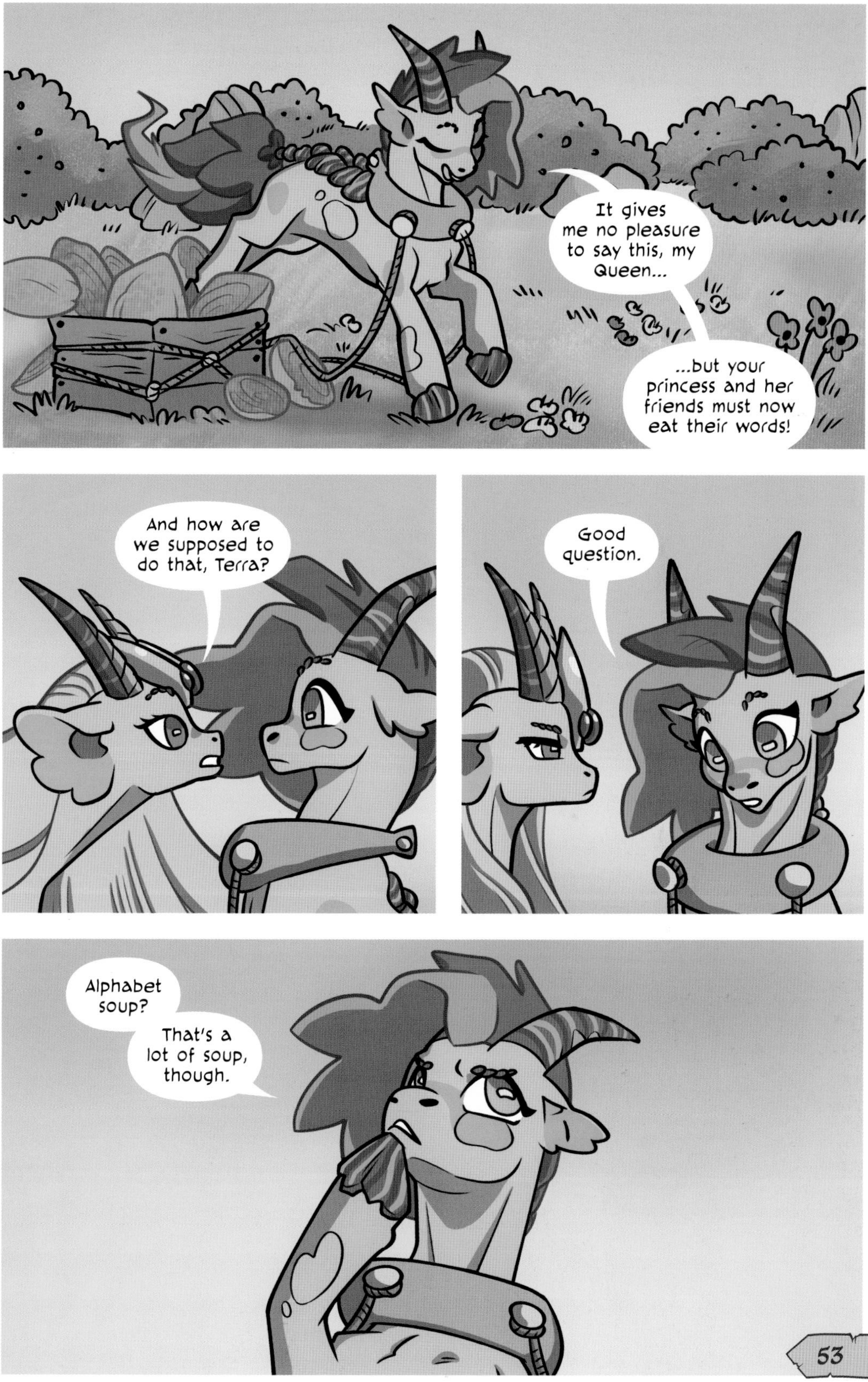
It gives me no pleasure to say this, my Queen...
...but your princess and her friends must now eat their words!
And how are we supposed to do that, Terra?
Good question.
Alphabet soup?
That's a lot of soup, though.

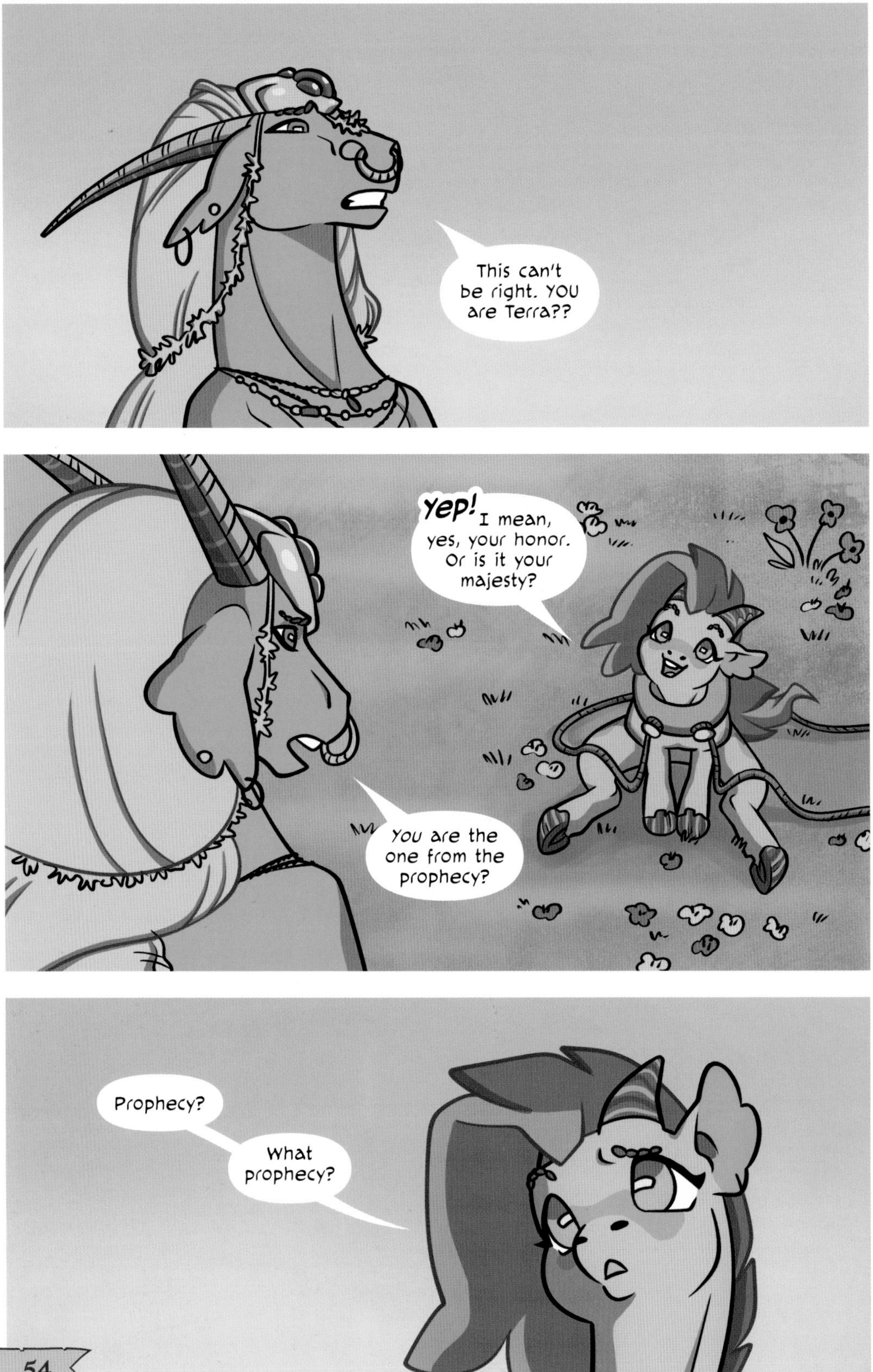
This can't be right. YOU are Terra??
YEP! I mean, yes, your honor. Or is it your majesty?
You are the one from the prophecy?
Prophecy?
What prophecy?

Chapter 4

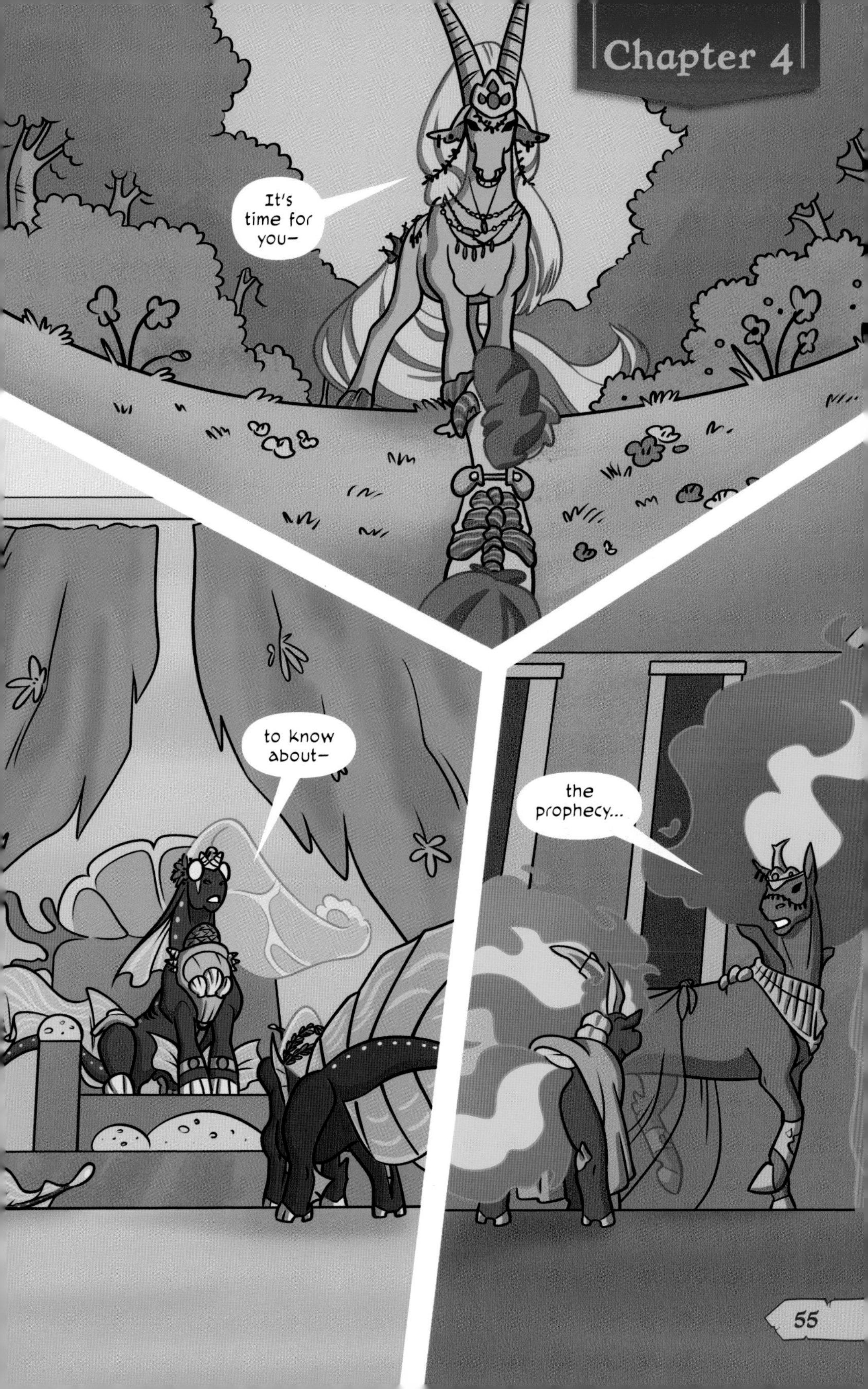

It's time for you-
to know about-
the prophecy...

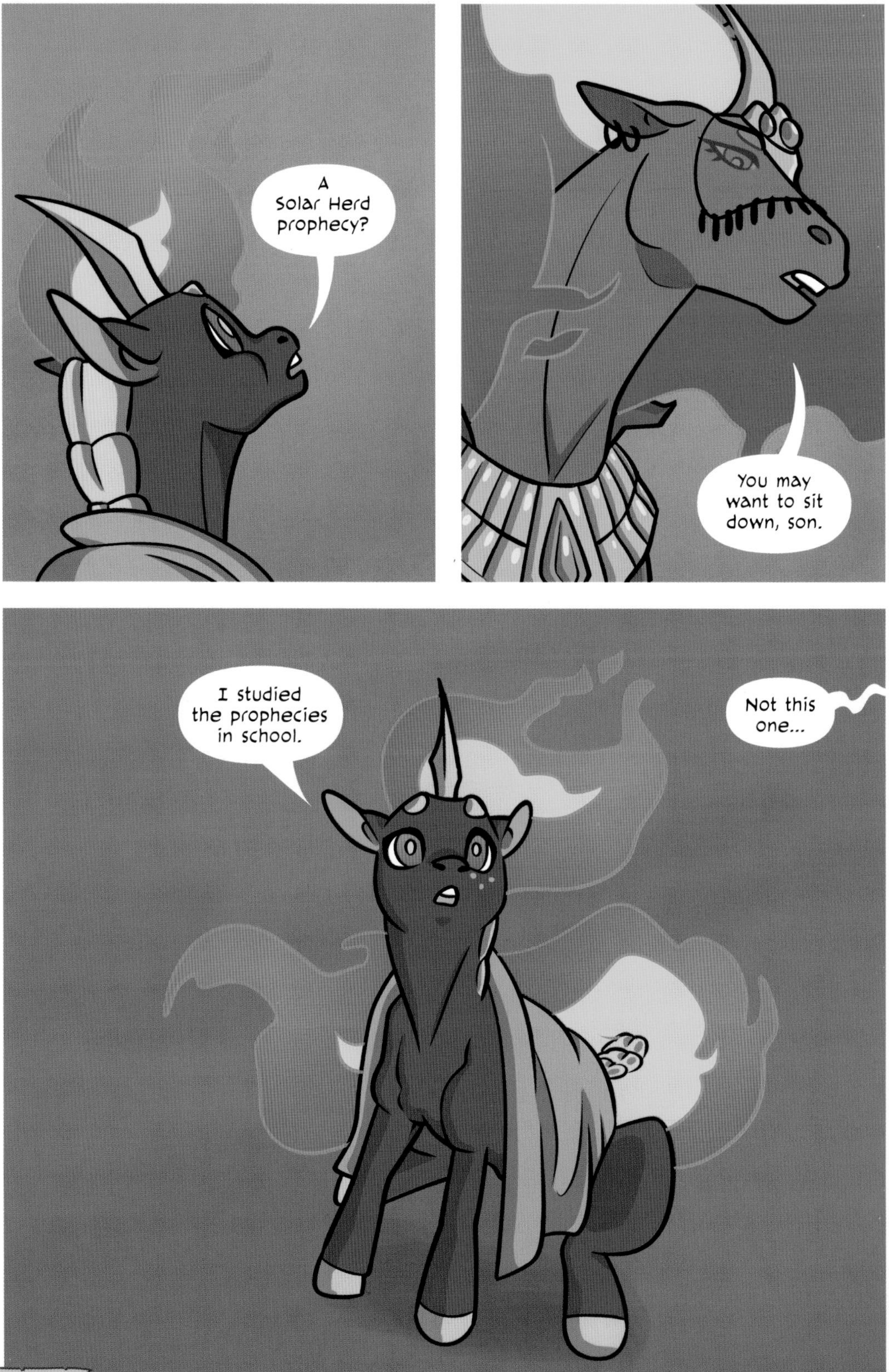
A Solar Herd prophecy?
You may want to sit down, son.
I studied the prophecies in school.
Not this one...

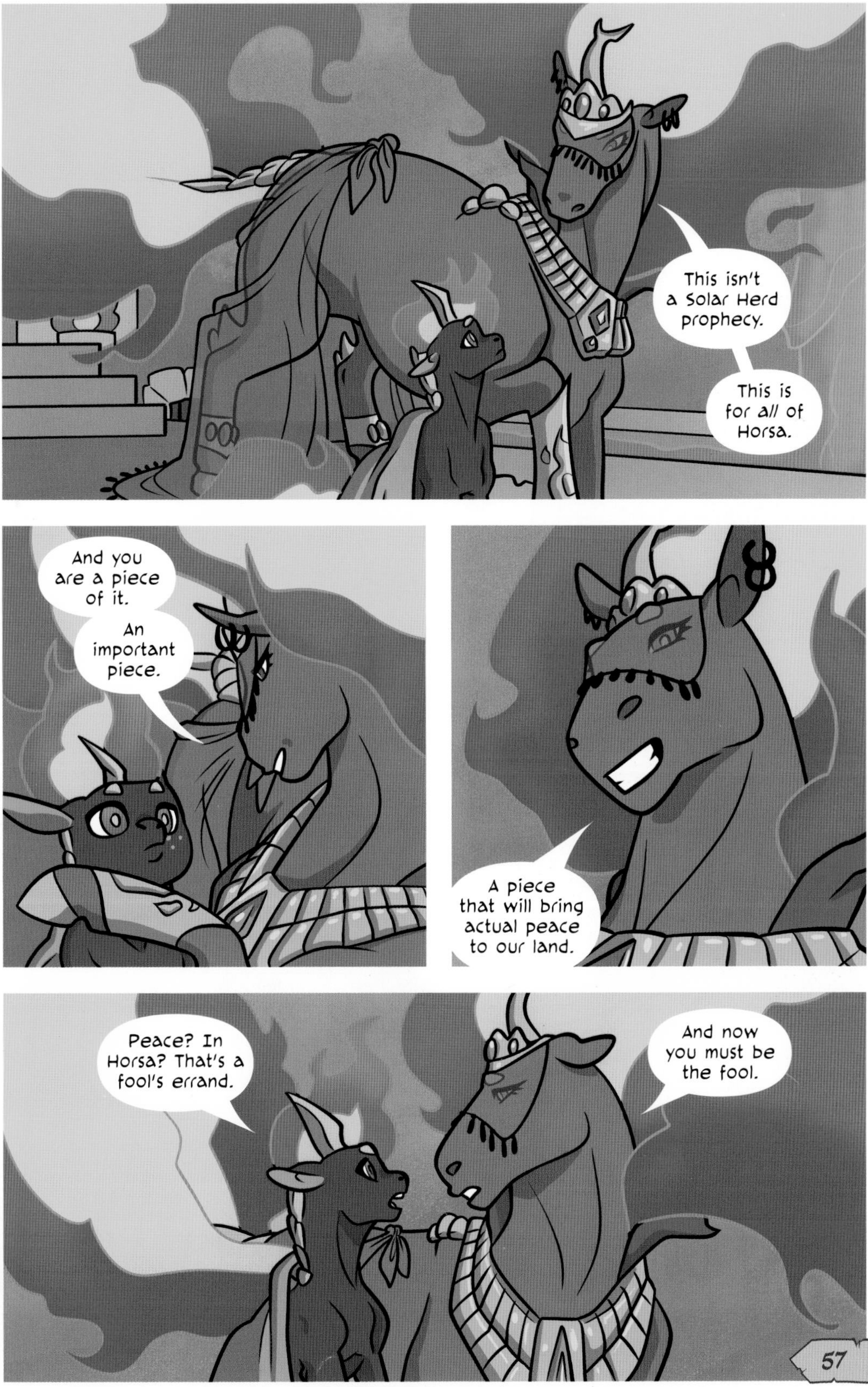
This isn't a Solar Herd prophecy.
This is for *all* of Horsa.
And you are a piece of it.
An important piece.
A piece that will bring actual peace to our land.
Peace? In Horsa? That's a fool's errand.
And now you must be the fool.

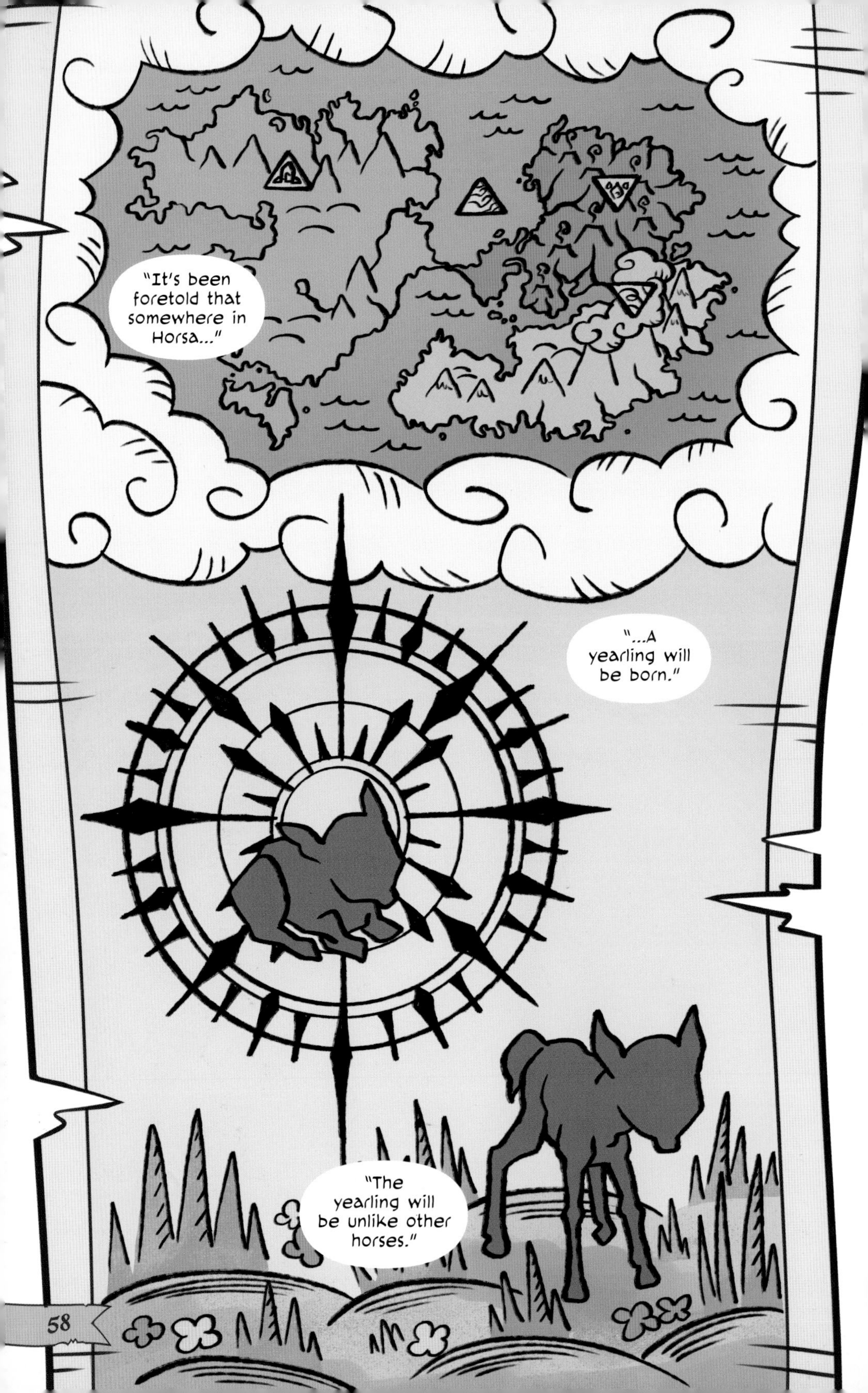
"It's been foretold that somewhere in Horsa..."
"...A yearling will be born."
"The yearling will be unlike other horses."

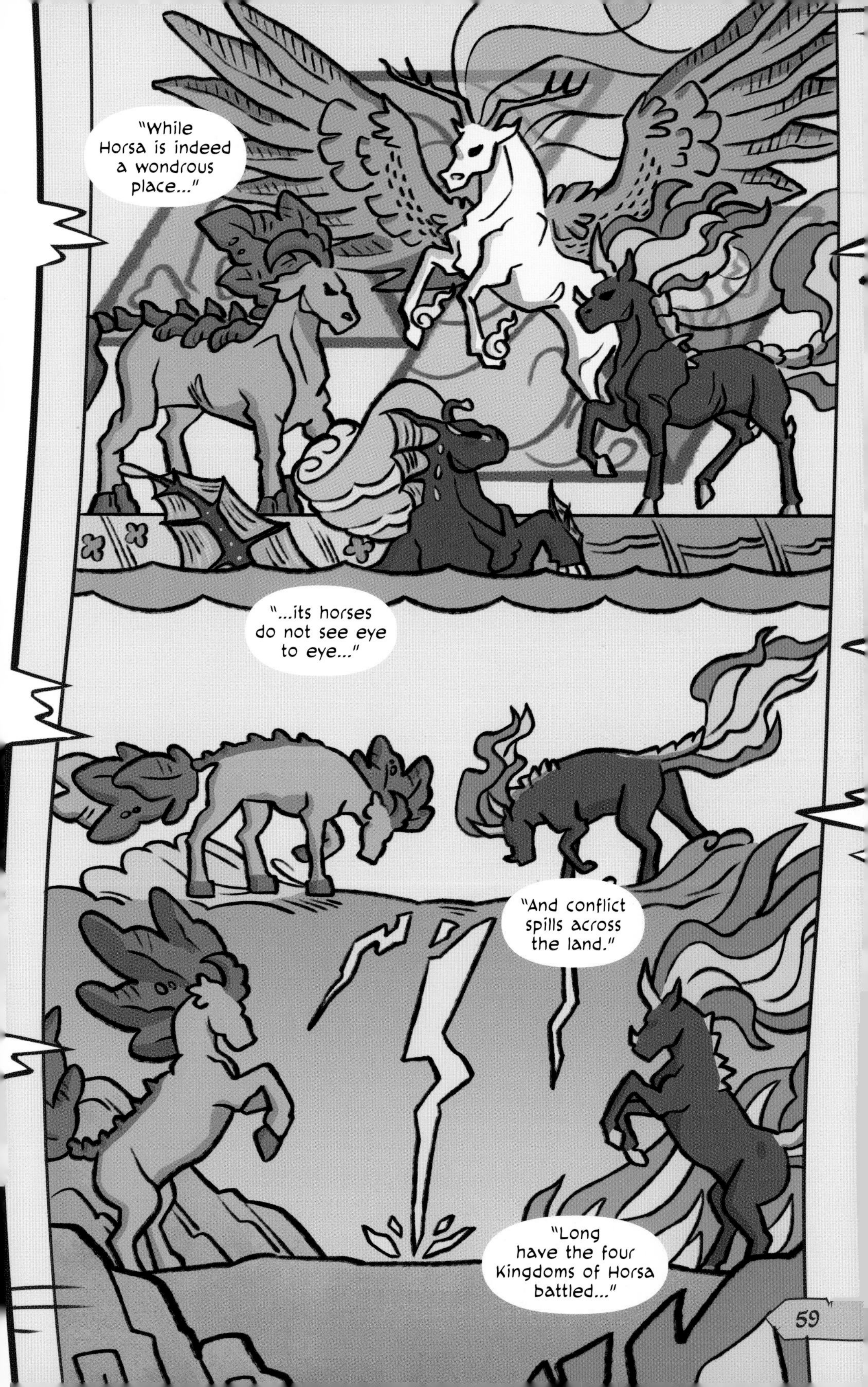
"While Horsa is indeed a wondrous place..."
"...its horses do not see eye to eye..."
"And conflict spills across the land."
"Long have the four Kingdoms of Horsa battled..."

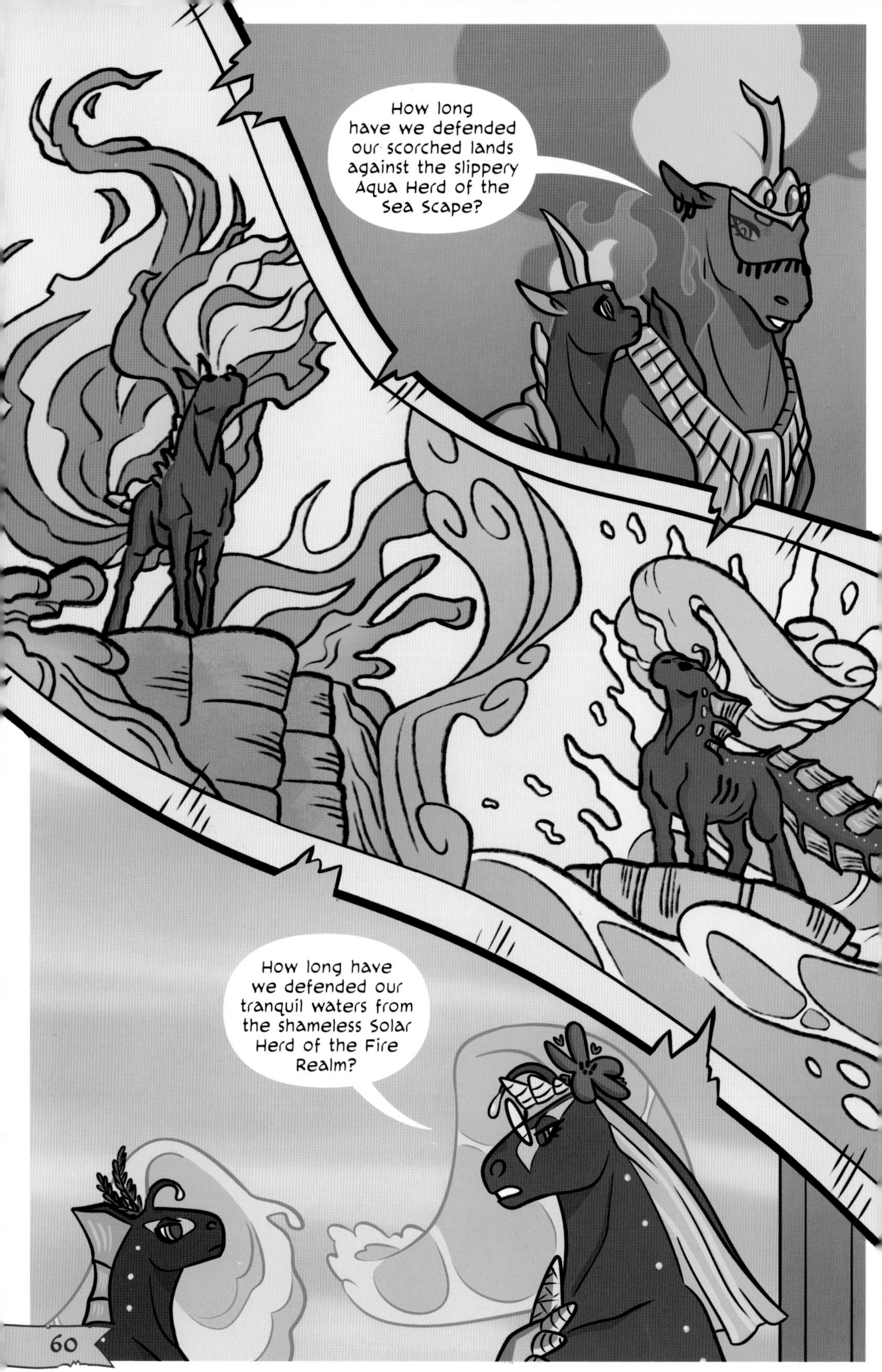
How long have we defended our scorched lands against the slippery Aqua Herd of the Sea Scape?
How long have we defended our tranquil waters from the shameless Solar Herd of the Fire Realm?

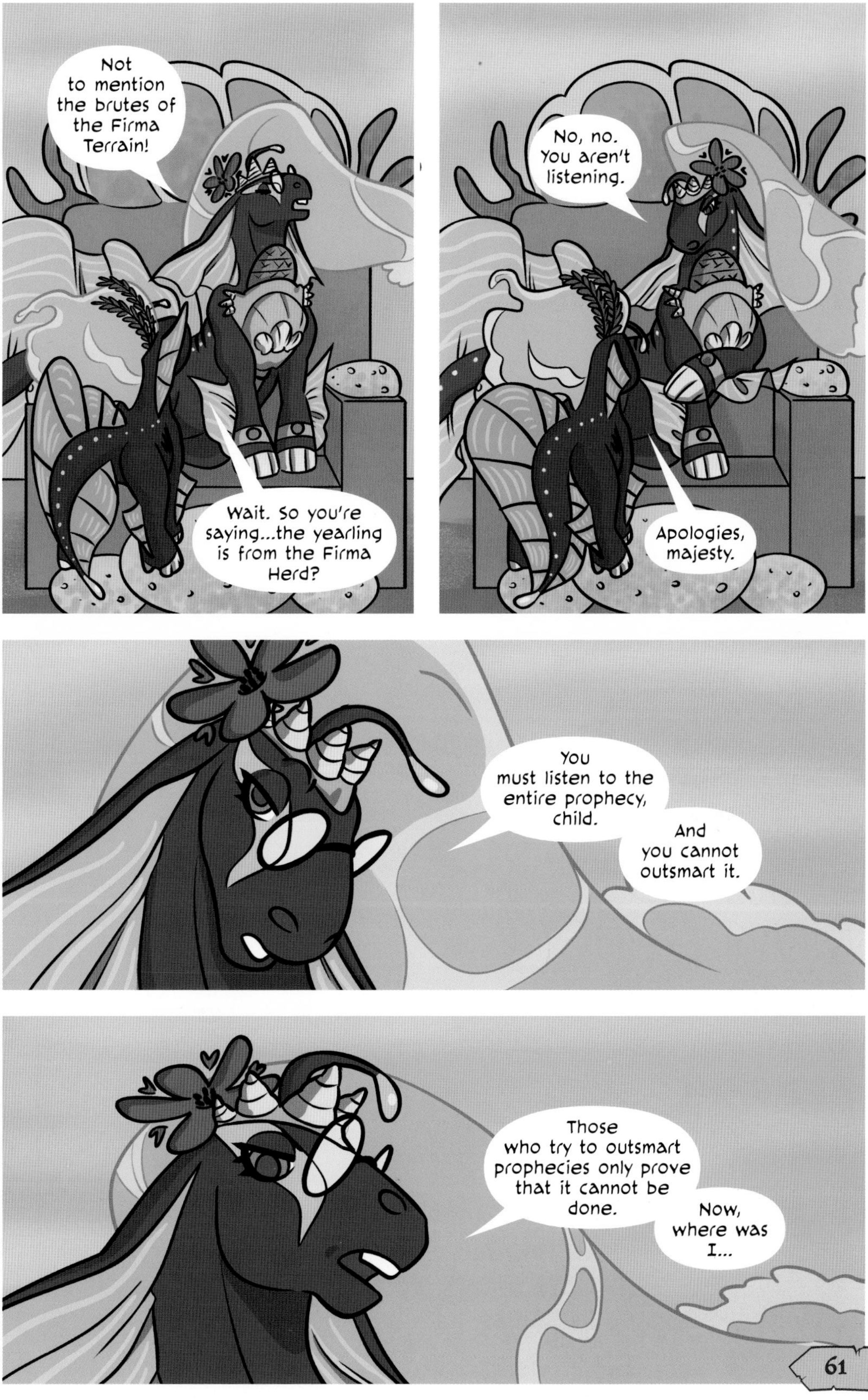
Not to mention the brutes of the Firma Terrain!
Wait. So you're saying...the yearling is from the Firma Herd?
No, no. You aren't listening.
Apologies, majesty.
You must listen to the entire prophecy, child.
And you cannot outsmart it.
Those who try to outsmart prophecies only prove that it cannot be done.
Now, where was I...

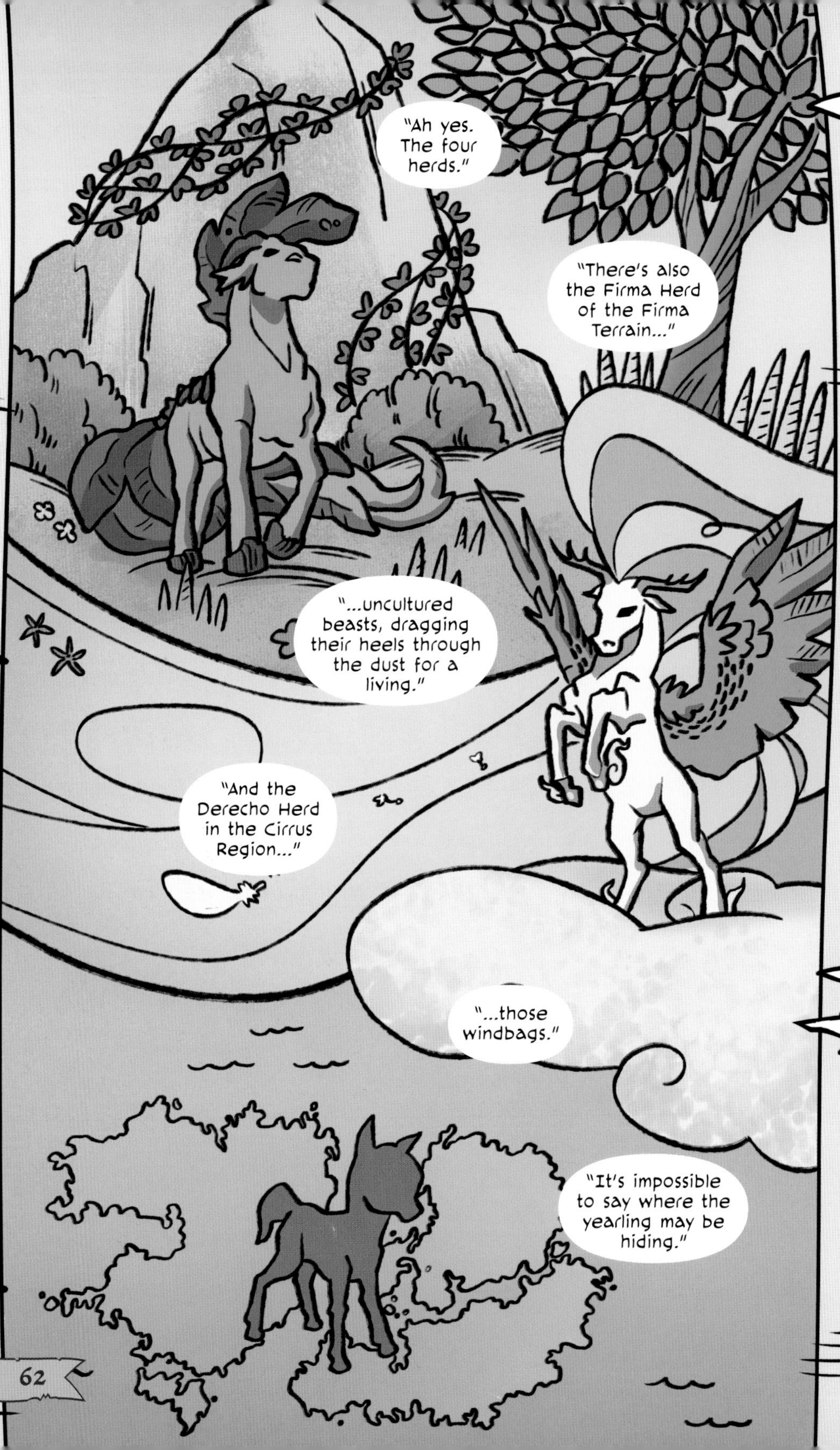
"Ah yes. The four herds."
"There's also the Firma Herd of the Firma Terrain..."
"...uncultured beasts, dragging their heels through the dust for a living."
"And the Derecho Herd in the Cirrus Region..."
"...those windbags."
"It's impossible to say where the yearling may be hiding."

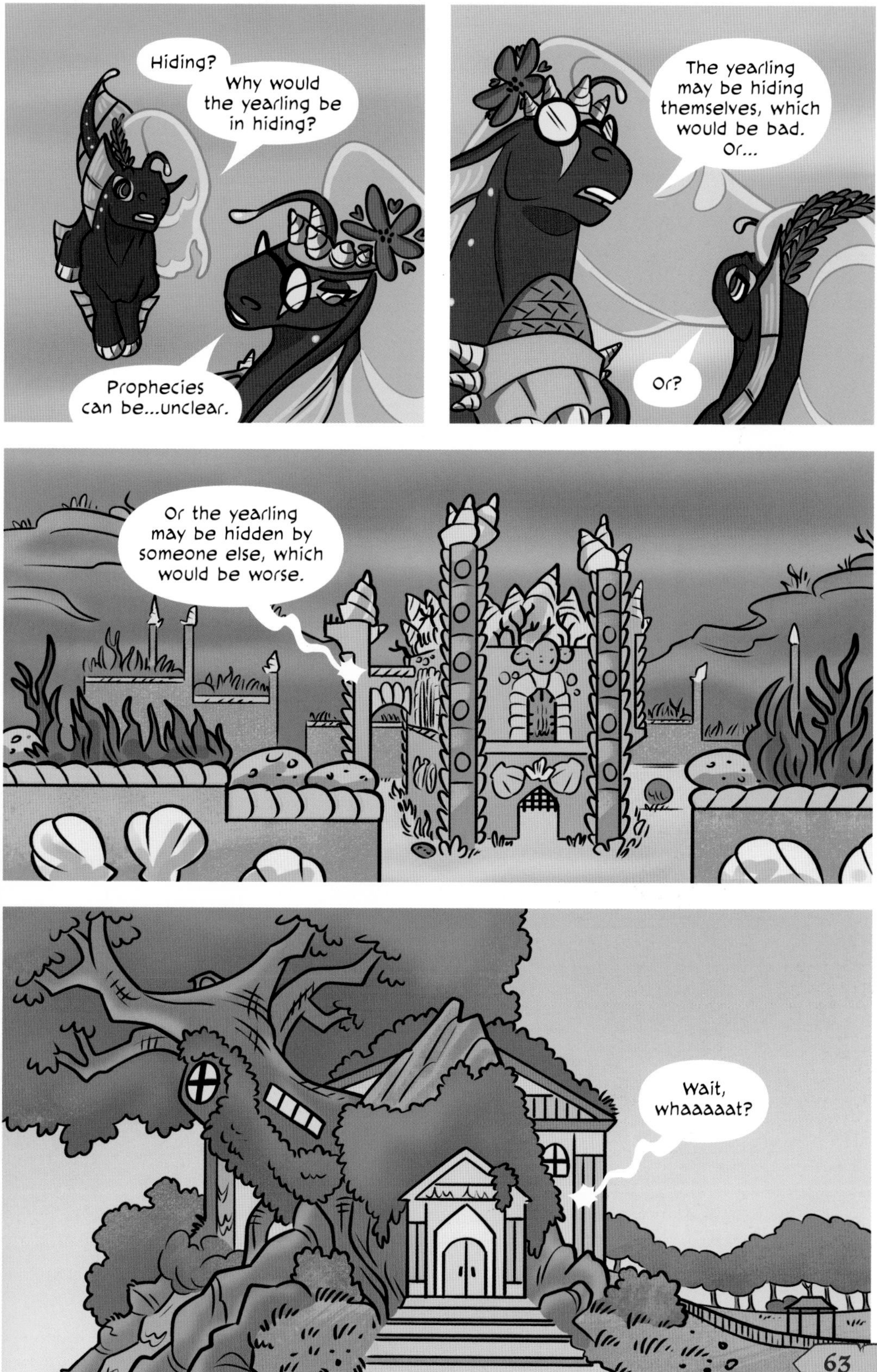
Hiding?
Why would the yearling be in hiding?
Prophecies can be...unclear.
The yearling may be hiding themselves, which would be bad. Or...
Or?
Or the yearling may be hidden by someone else, which would be worse.
Wait, whaaaaat?

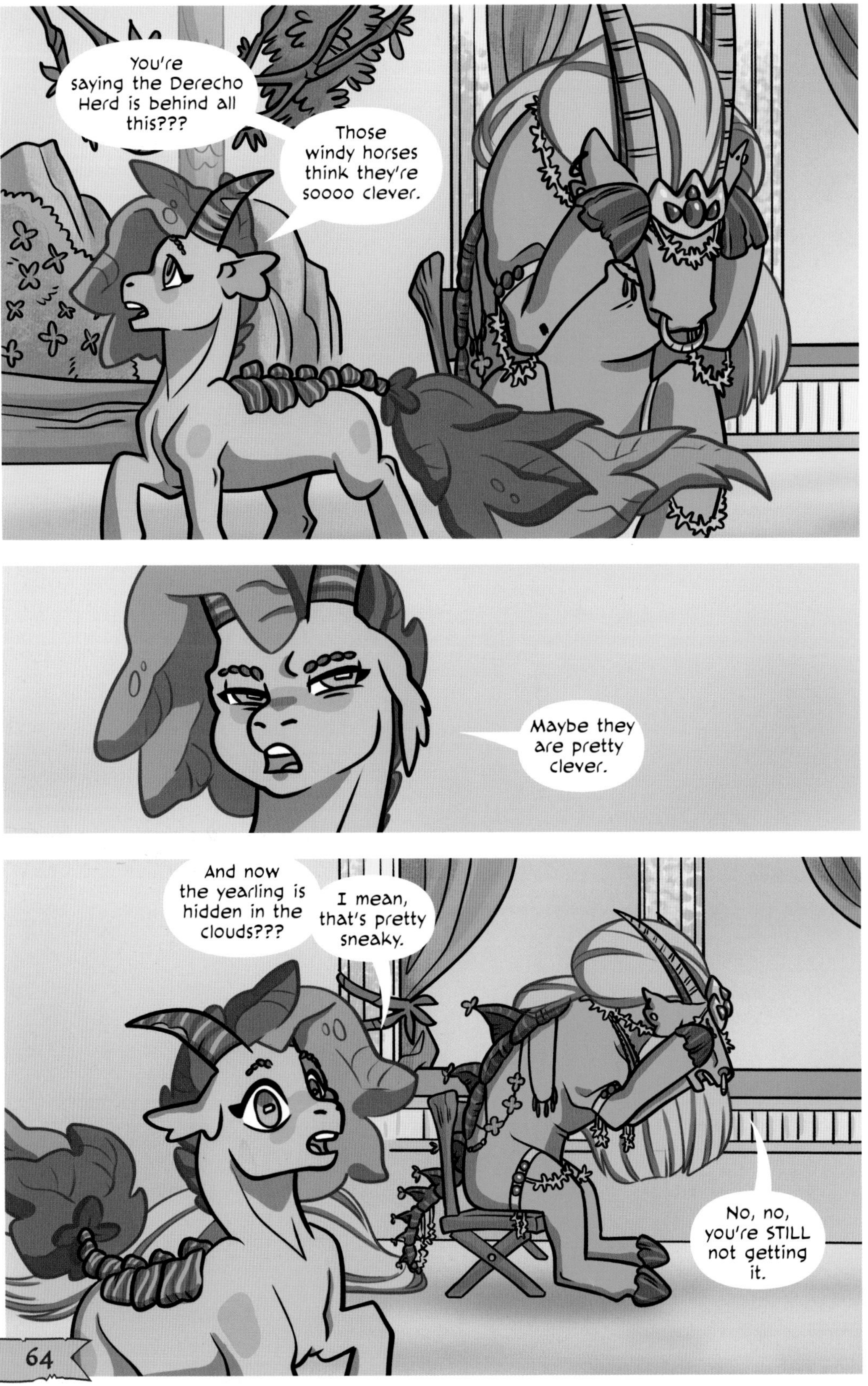
You're saying the Derecho Herd is behind all this???
Those windy horses think they're soooo clever.
Maybe they are pretty clever.
And now the yearling is hidden in the clouds???
I mean, that's pretty sneaky.
No, no, you're STILL not getting it.

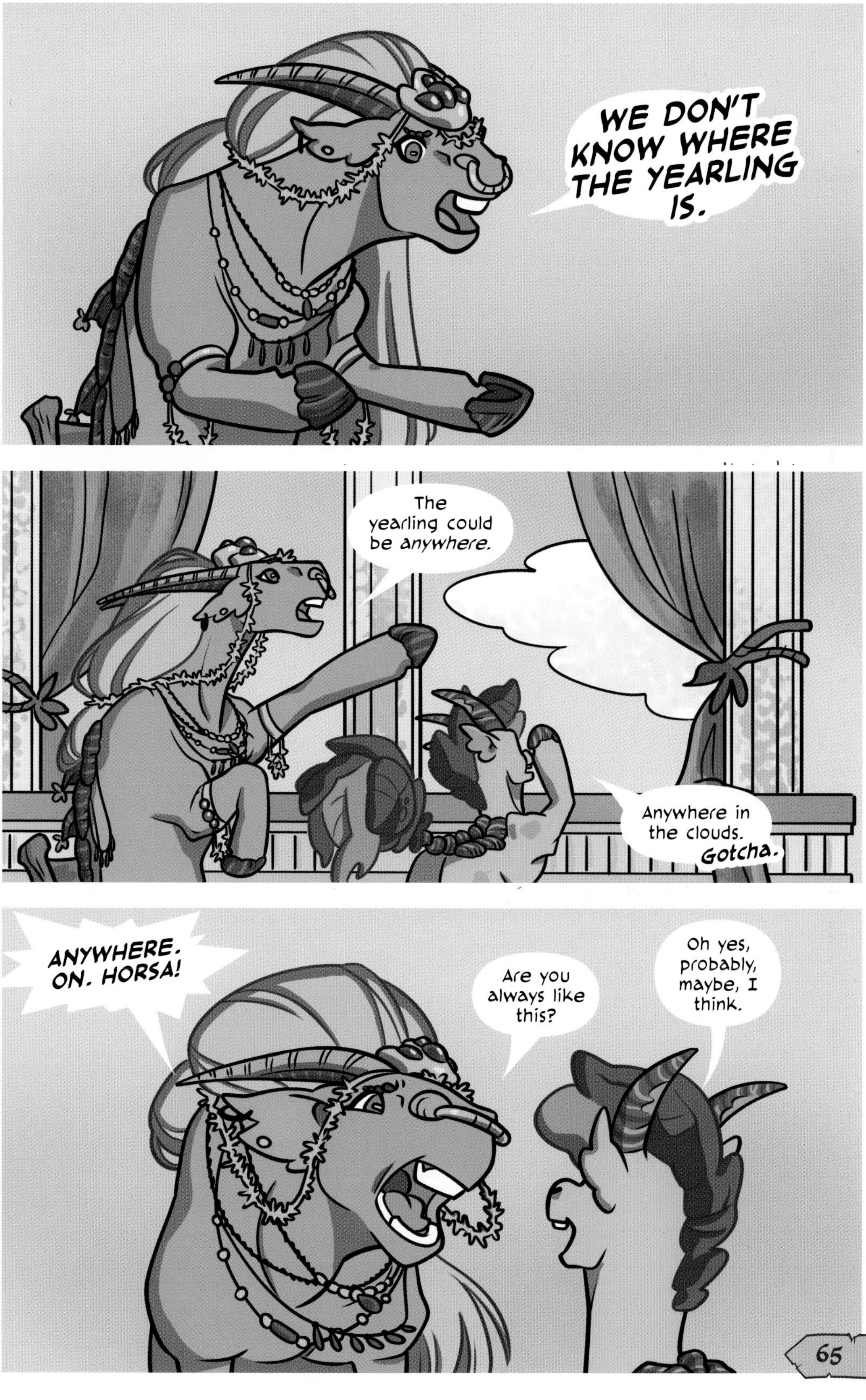
WE DON'T KNOW WHERE THE YEARLING IS.
The yearling could be *anywhere.*
Anywhere in the clouds. *Gotcha.*
ANYWHERE. ON. HORSA!
Are you always like this?
Oh yes, probably, maybe, I think.

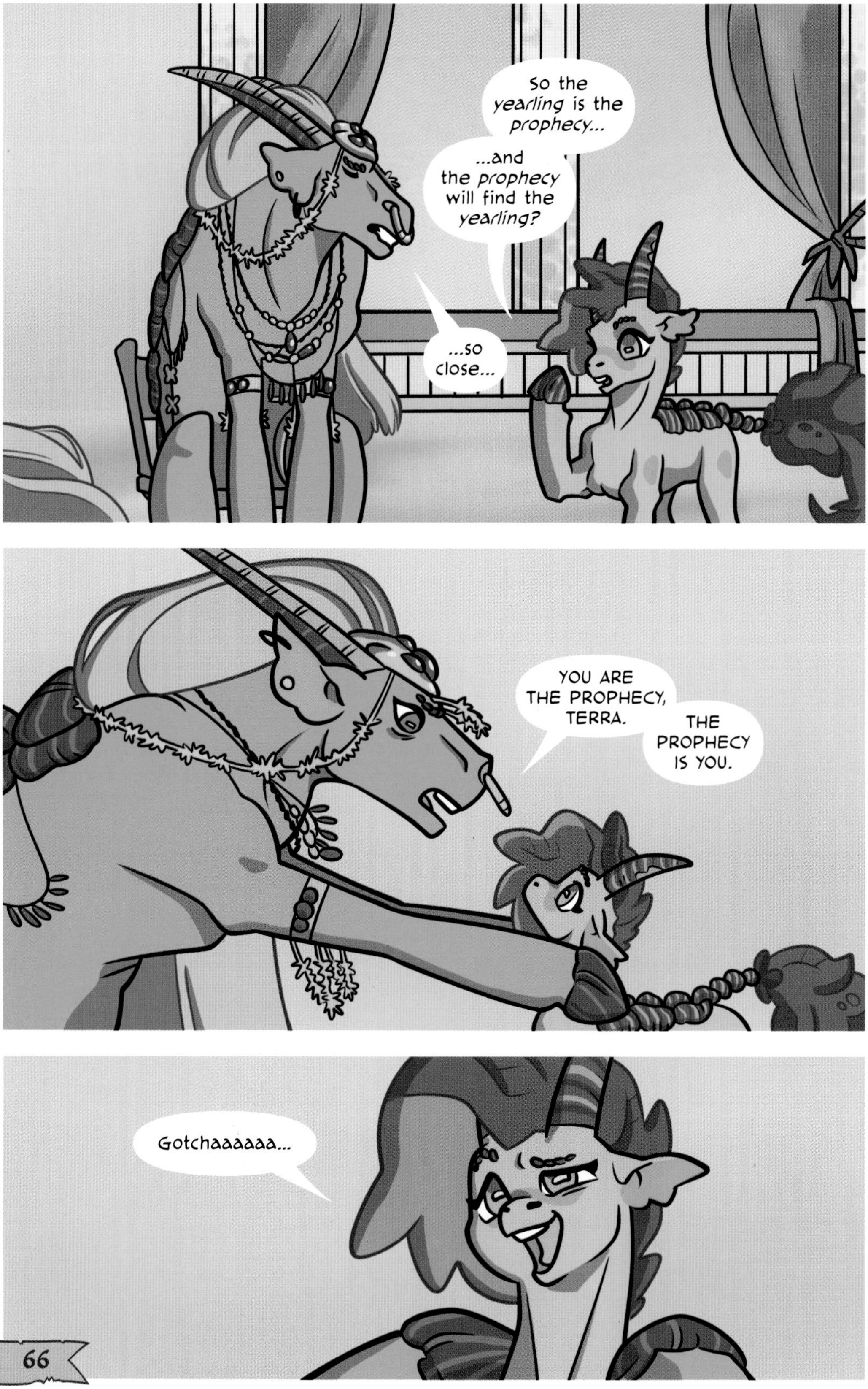
So the *yearling* is the *prophecy*...
...and the *prophecy* will find the *yearling*?
...so close...
YOU ARE THE PROPHECY, TERRA.
THE PROPHECY IS YOU.
Gotchaaaaaaa...

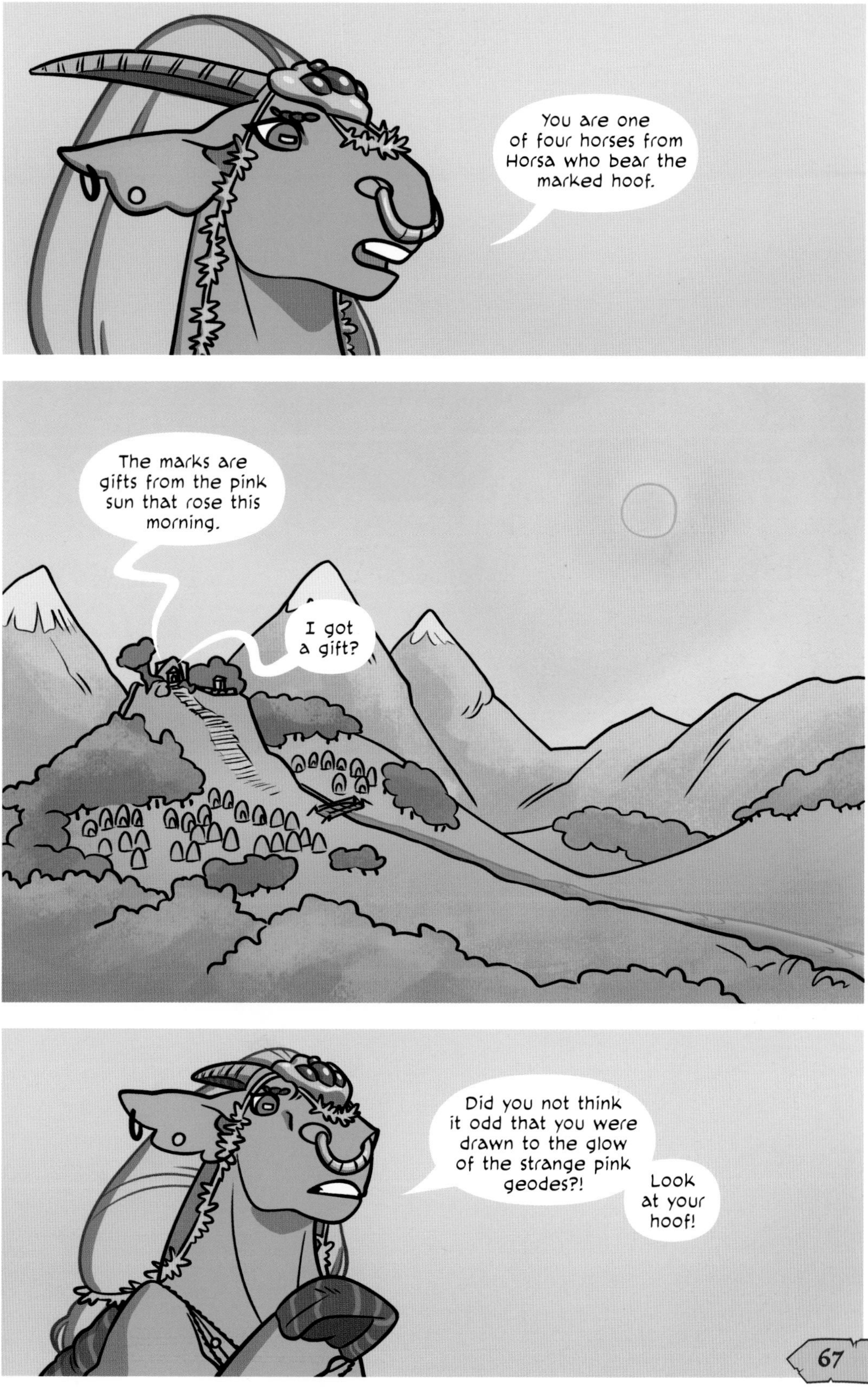
You are one of four horses from Horsa who bear the marked hoof.
The marks are gifts from the pink sun that rose this morning.
I got a gift?
Did you not think it odd that you were drawn to the glow of the strange pink geodes?!
Look at your hoof!

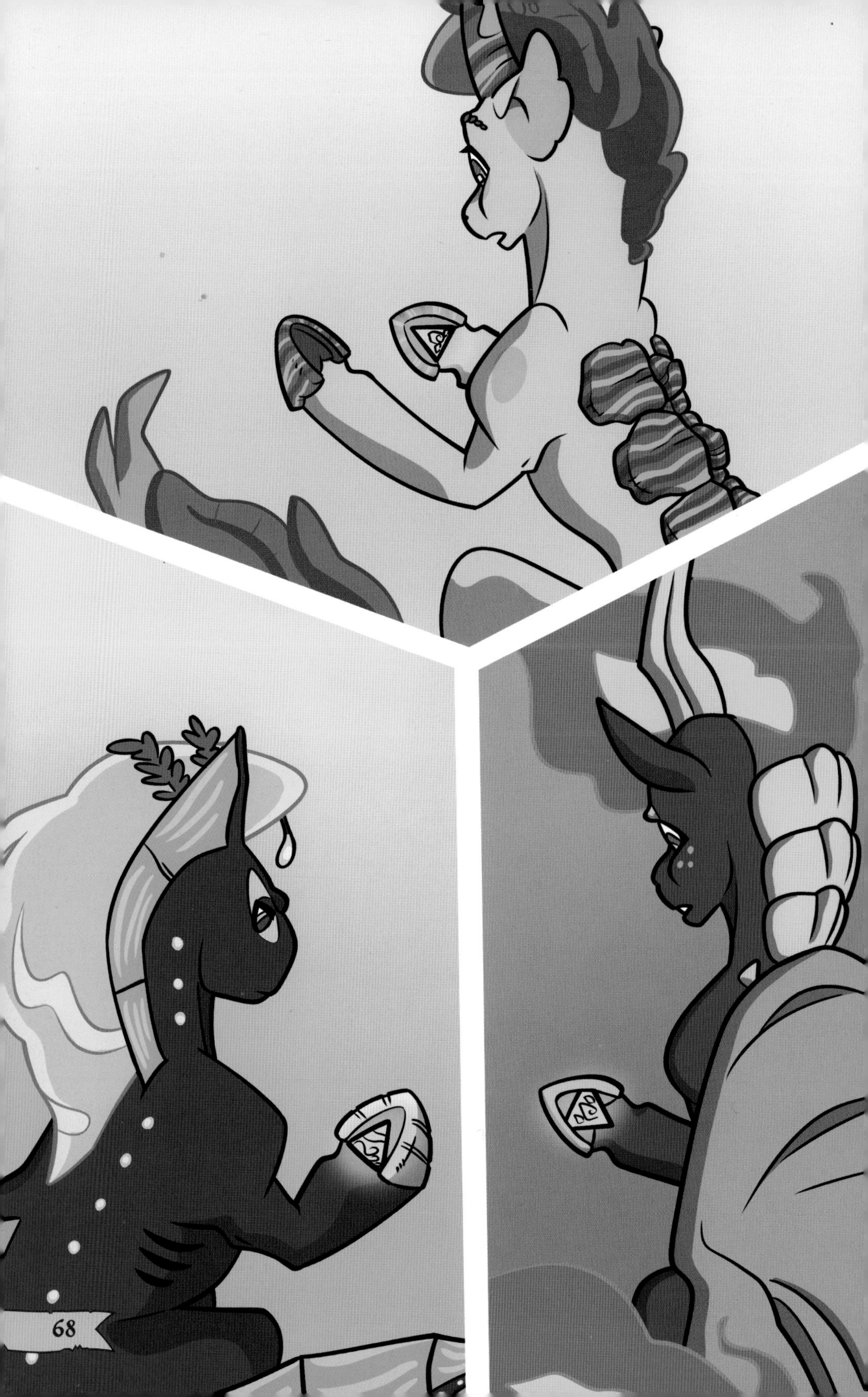

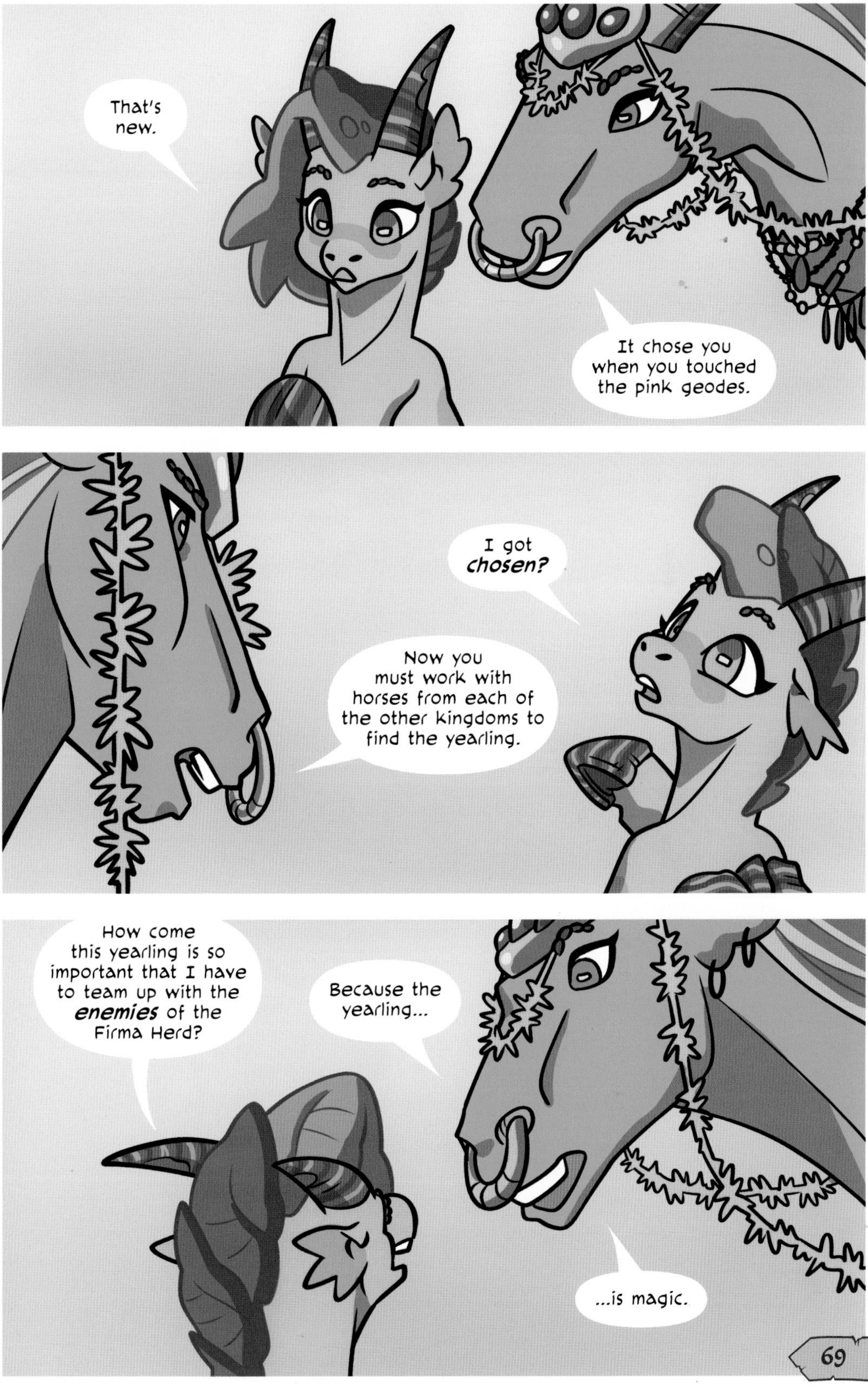
That's new.
It chose you when you touched the pink geodes.
I got *chosen?*
Now you must work with horses from each of the other kingdoms to find the yearling.
How come this yearling is so important that I have to team up with the *enemies* of the Firma Herd?
Because the yearling...
...is magic.

Chapter 5

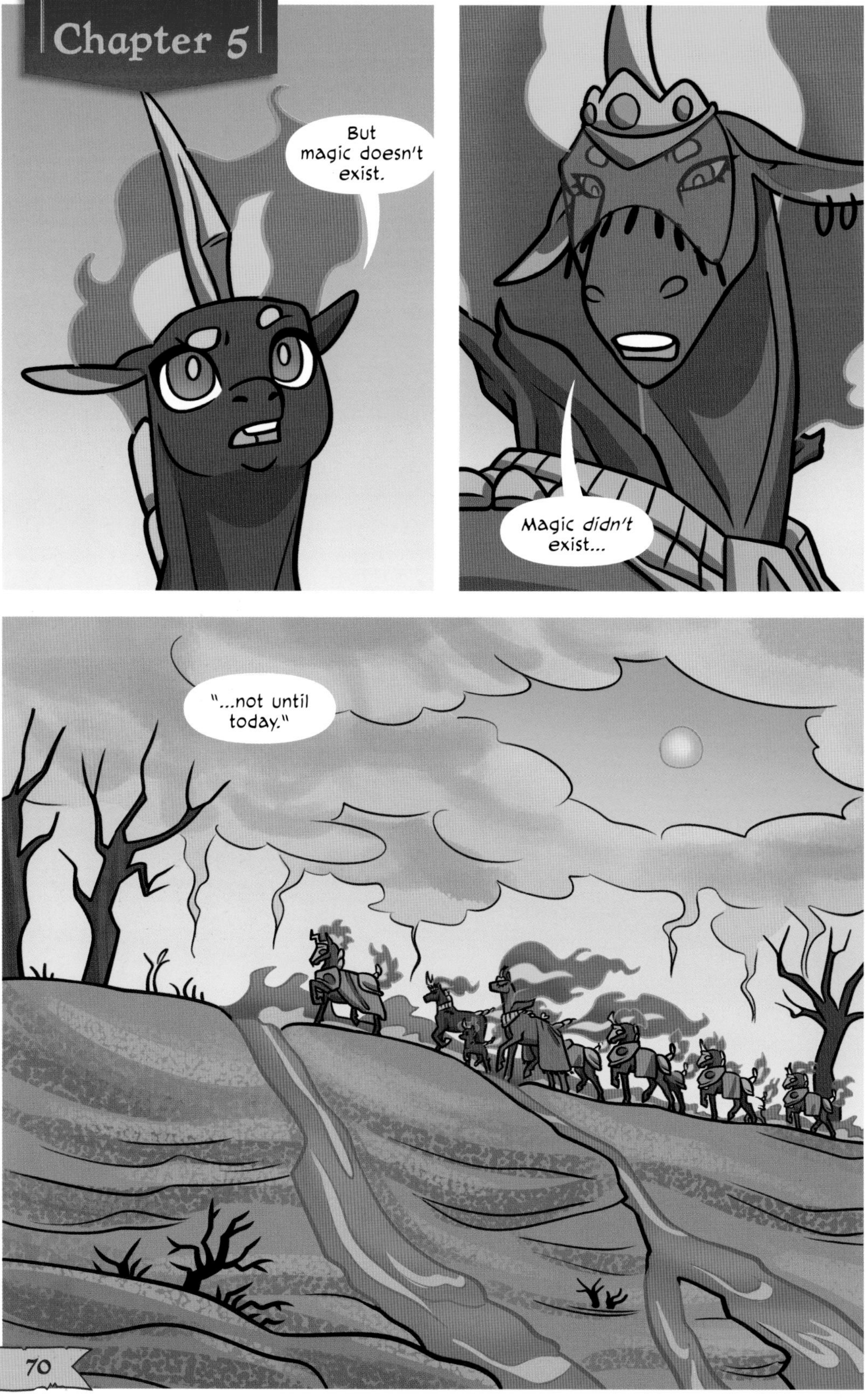
But magic doesn't exist.
Magic didn't exist...
"...not until today."

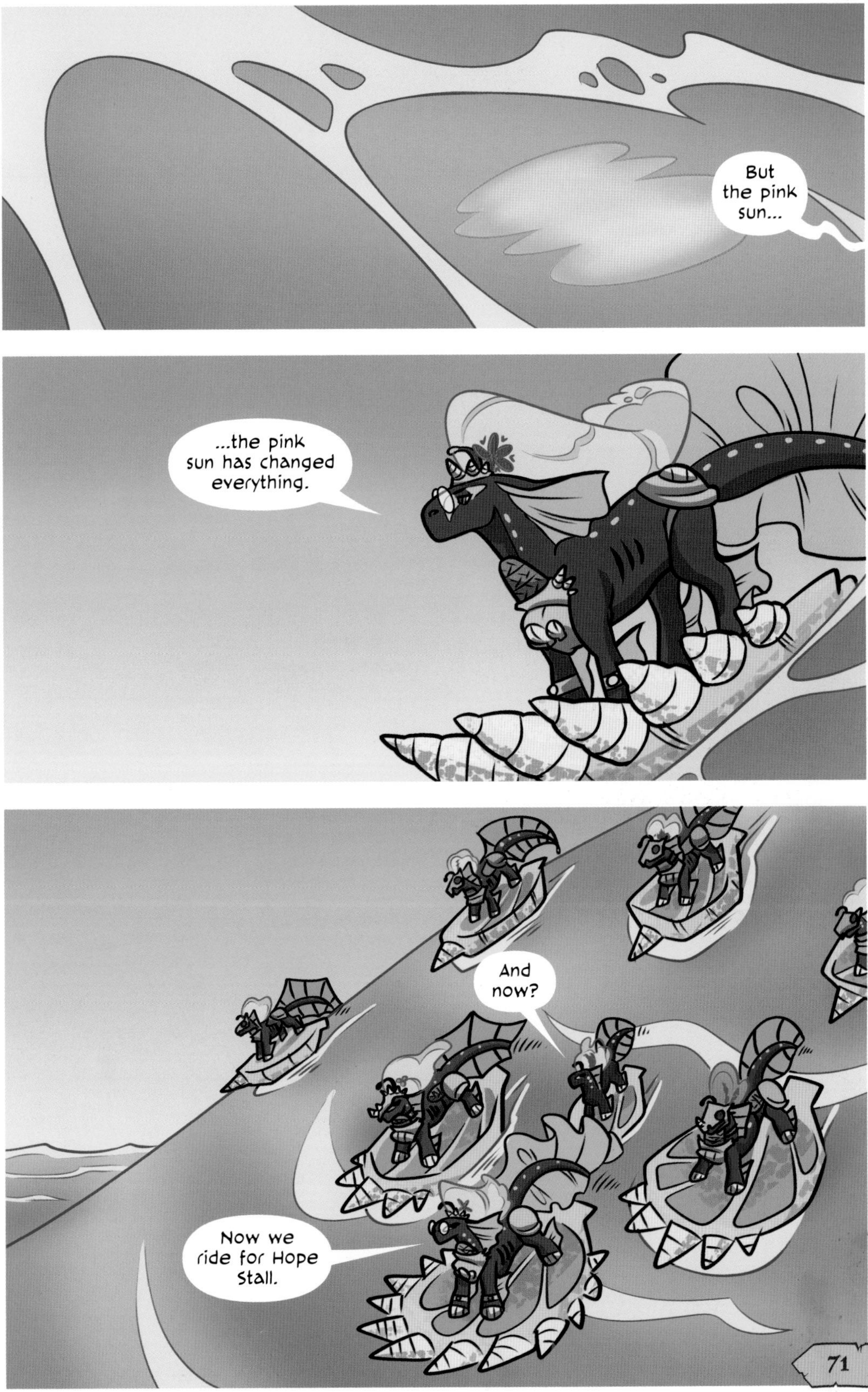
But the pink sun...
...the pink sun has changed everything.
And now?
Now we ride for Hope Stall.

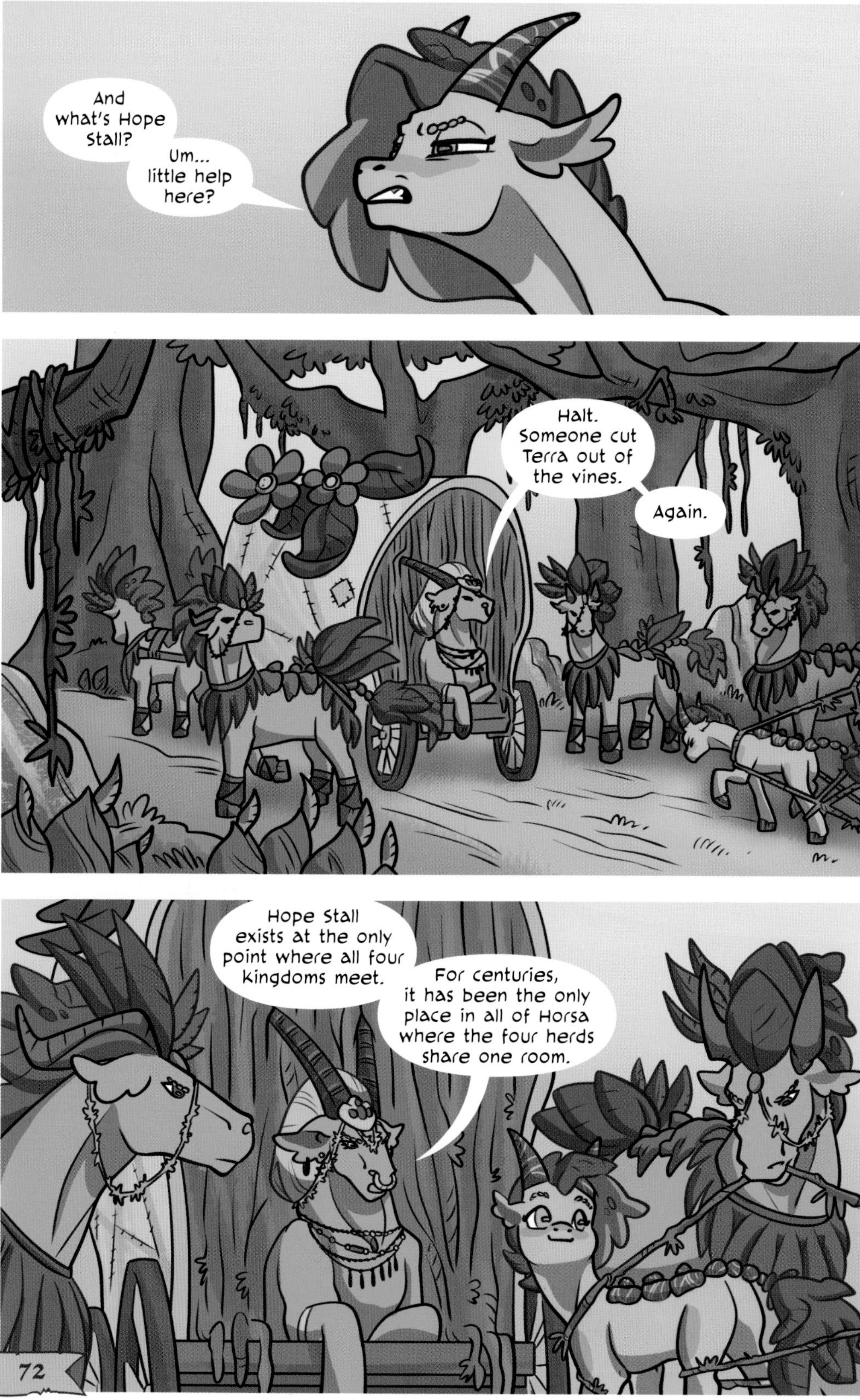
And what's Hope Stall?
Um... little help here?
Halt. Someone cut Terra out of the vines.
Again.
Hope Stall exists at the only point where all four kingdoms meet.
For centuries, it has been the only place in all of Horsa where the four herds share one room.

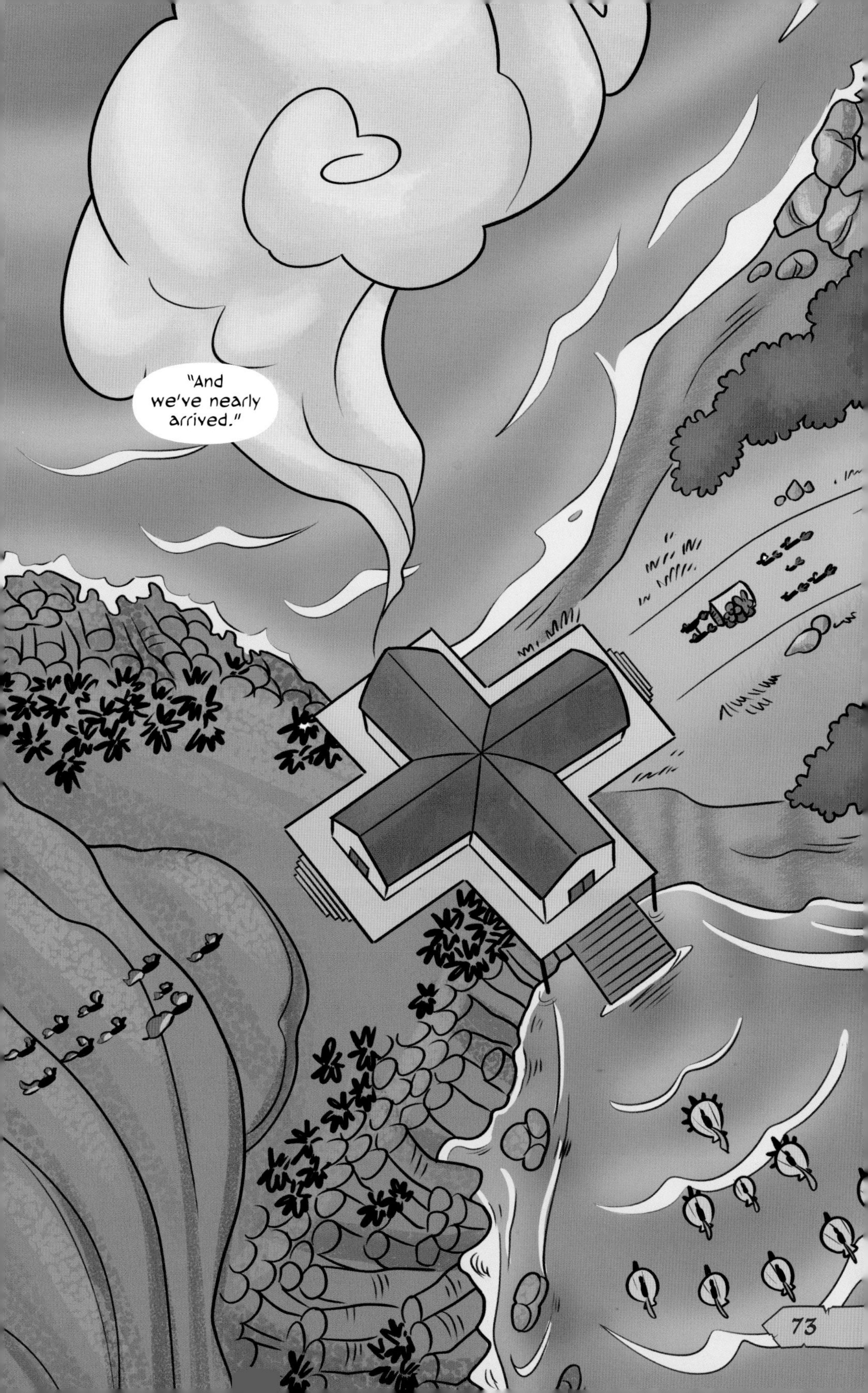
"And we've nearly arrived."

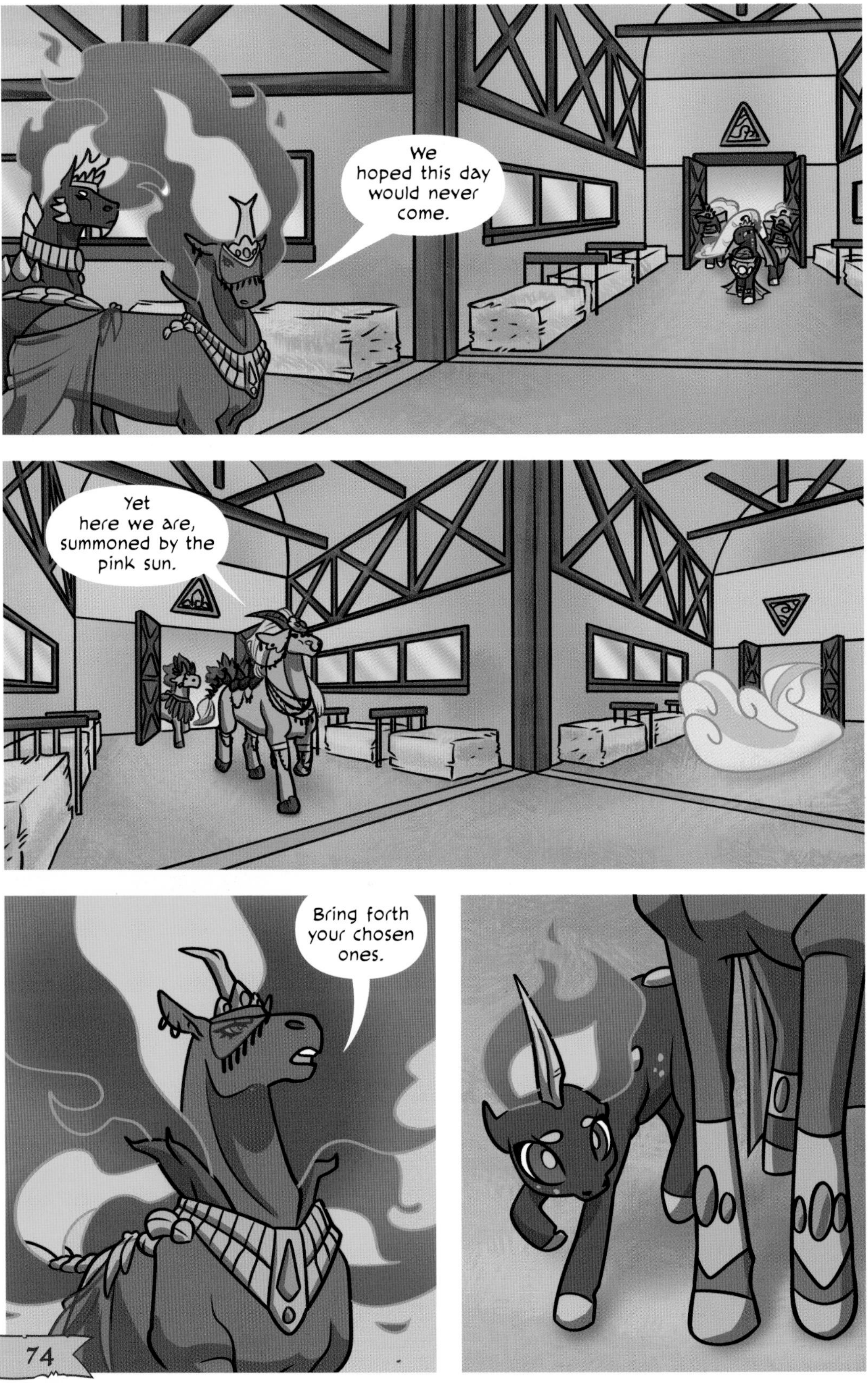
We hoped this day would never come.
Yet here we are, summoned by the pink sun.
Bring forth your chosen ones.

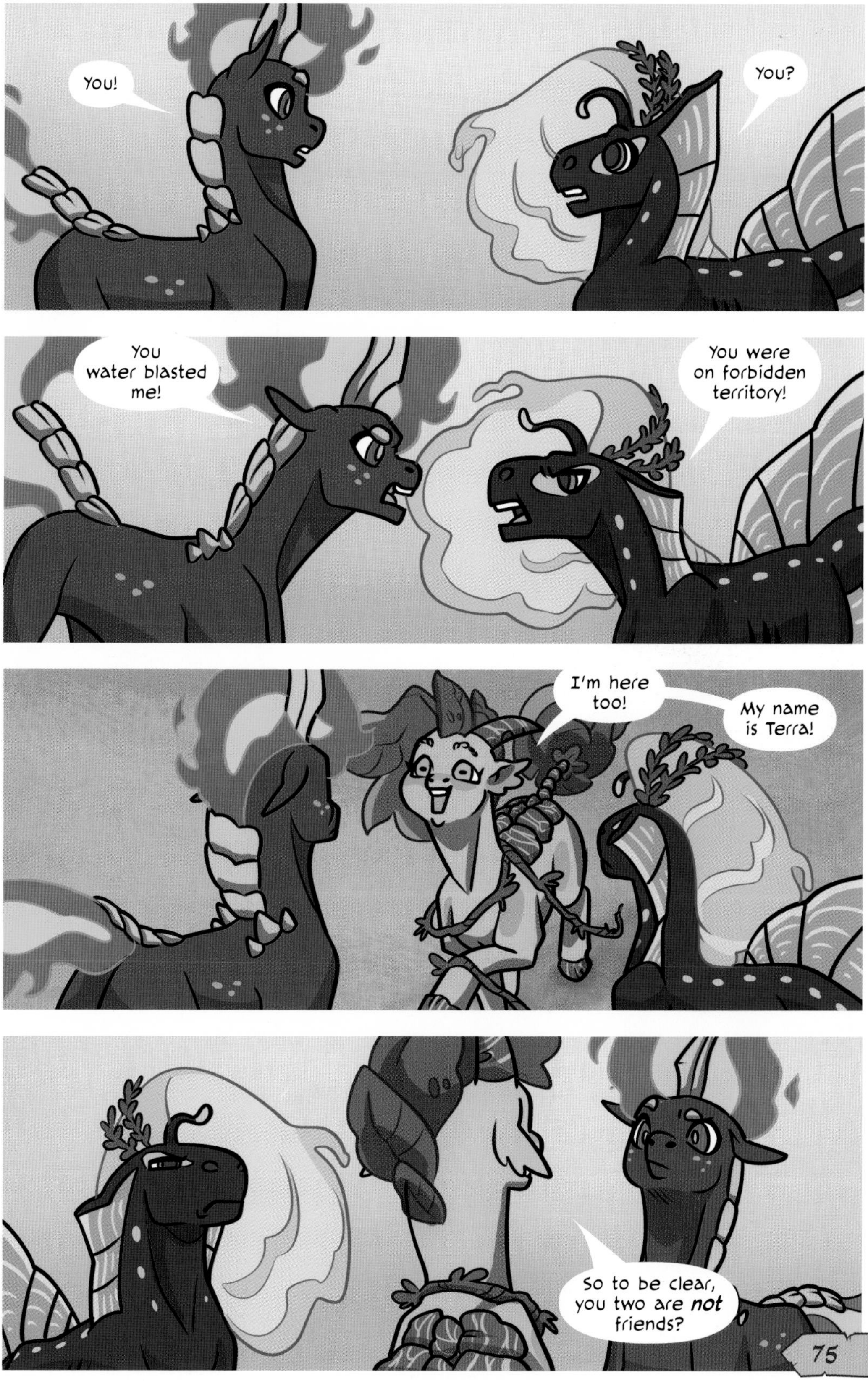
You!
You?
You water blasted me!
You were on forbidden territory!
I'm here too!
My name is Terra!
So to be clear, you two are ***not*** friends?

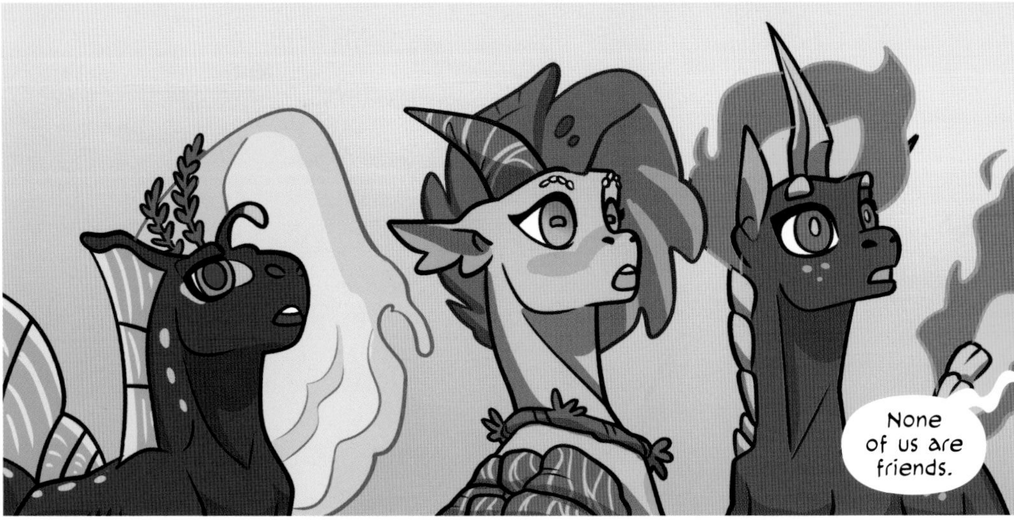
None of us are friends.

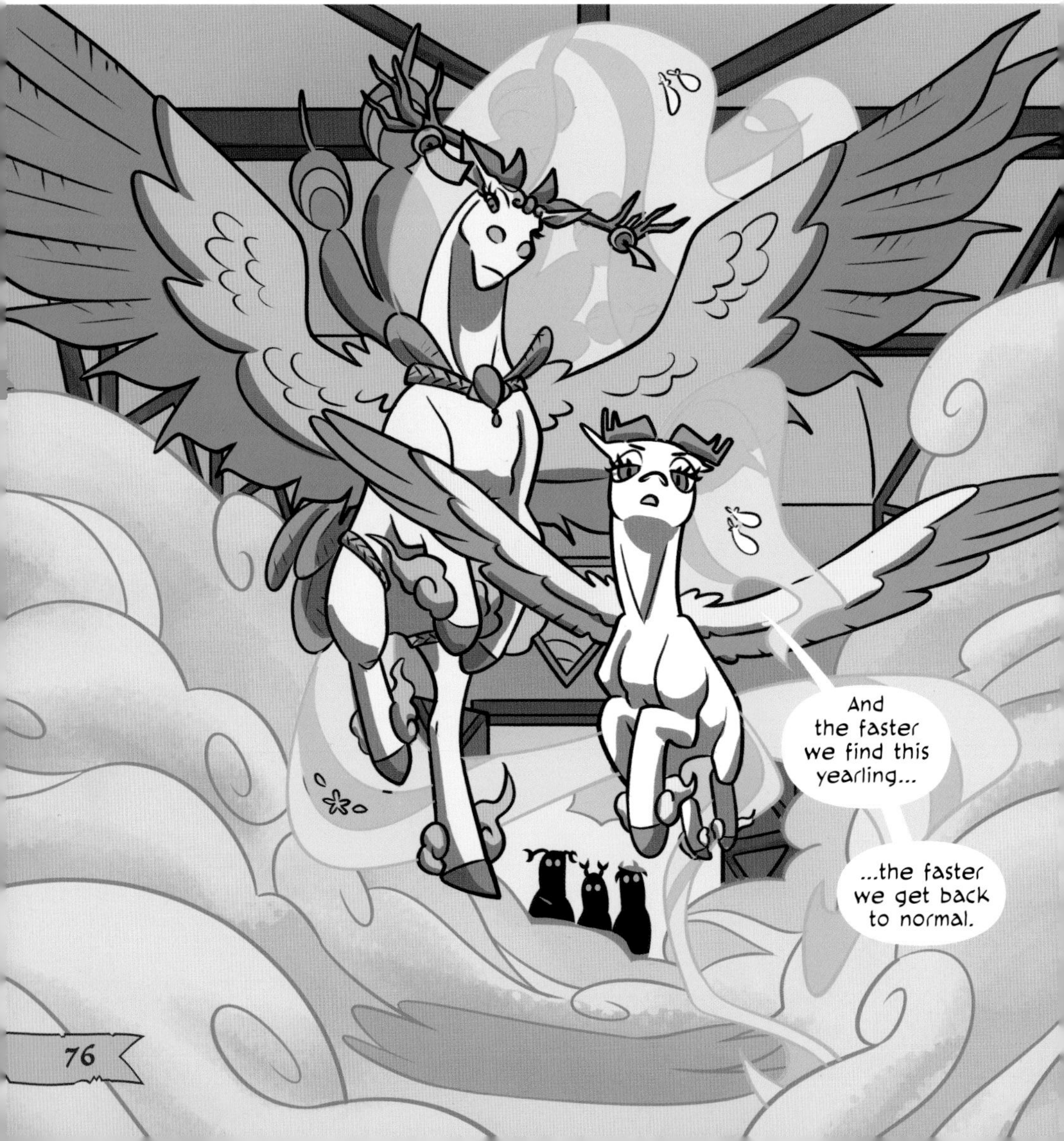
And the faster we find this yearling...
...the faster we get back to normal.

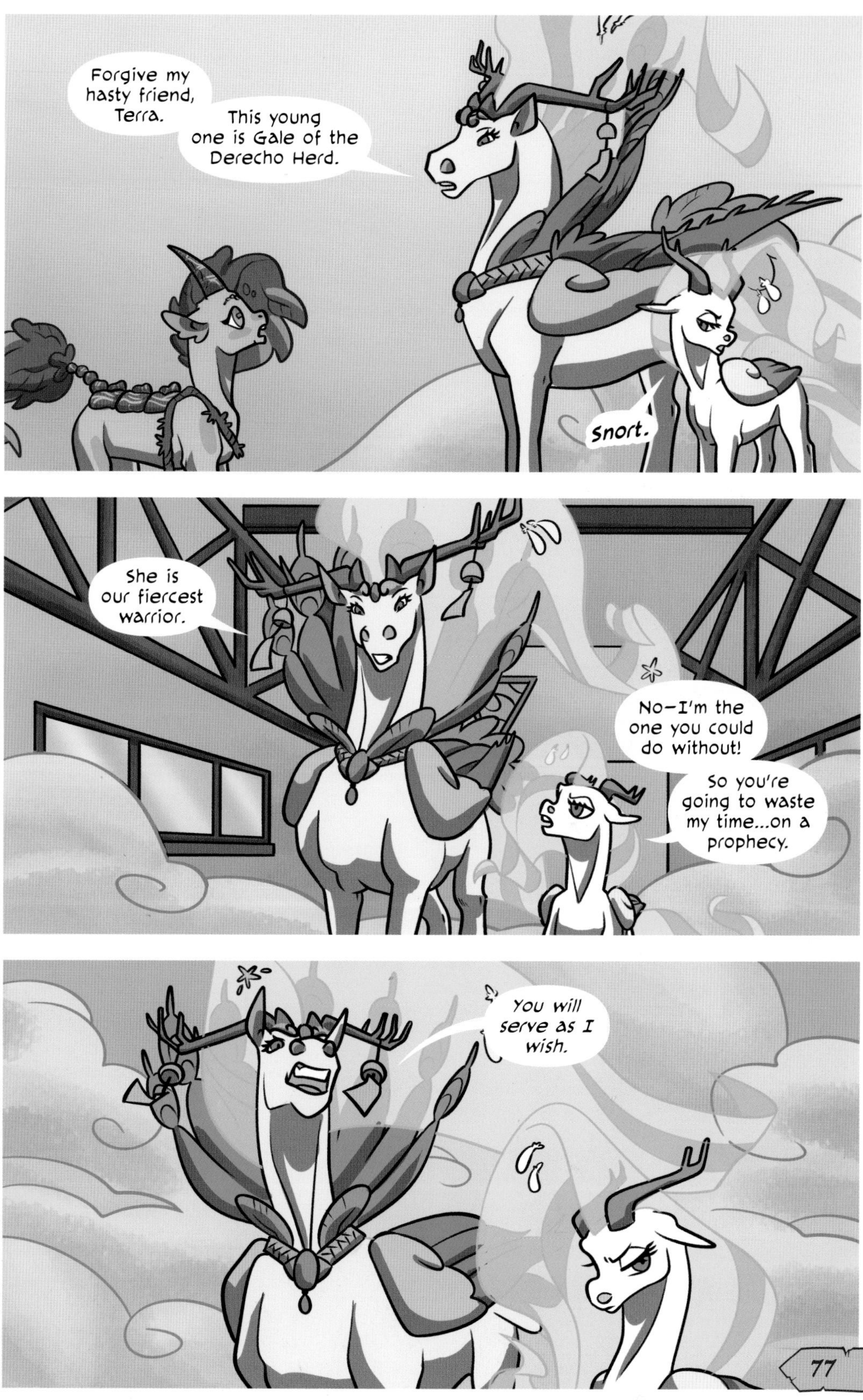
Forgive my hasty friend, Terra.
This young one is Gale of the Derecho Herd.
Snort.
She is our fiercest warrior.
No—I'm the one you could do without!
So you're going to waste my time...on a prophecy.
You will serve as I wish.

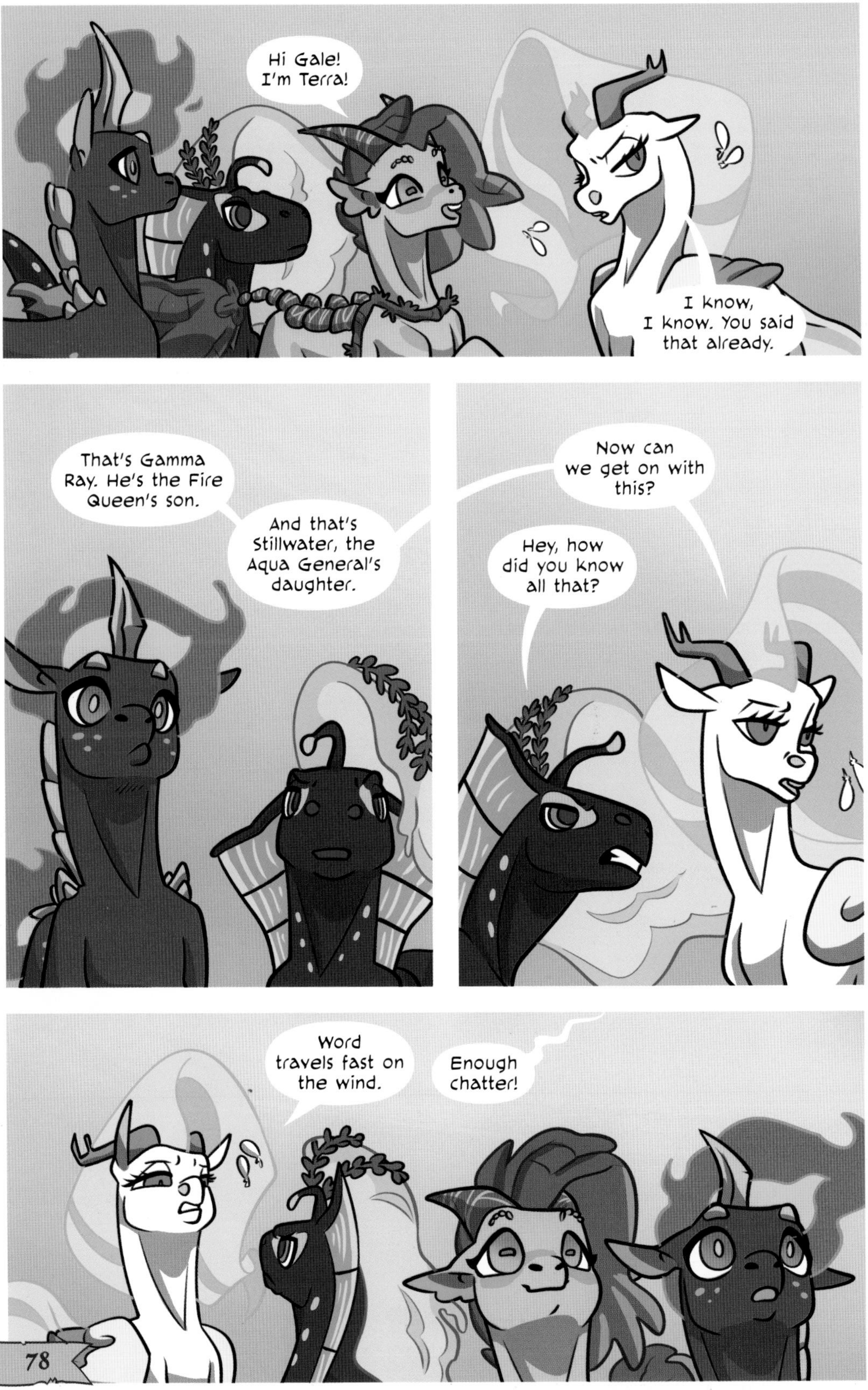
Hi Gale! I'm Terra!
I know, I know. You said that already.
That's Gamma Ray. He's the Fire Queen's son.
And that's Stillwater, the Aqua General's daughter.
Now can we get on with this?
Hey, how did you know all that?
Word travels fast on the wind.
Enough chatter!

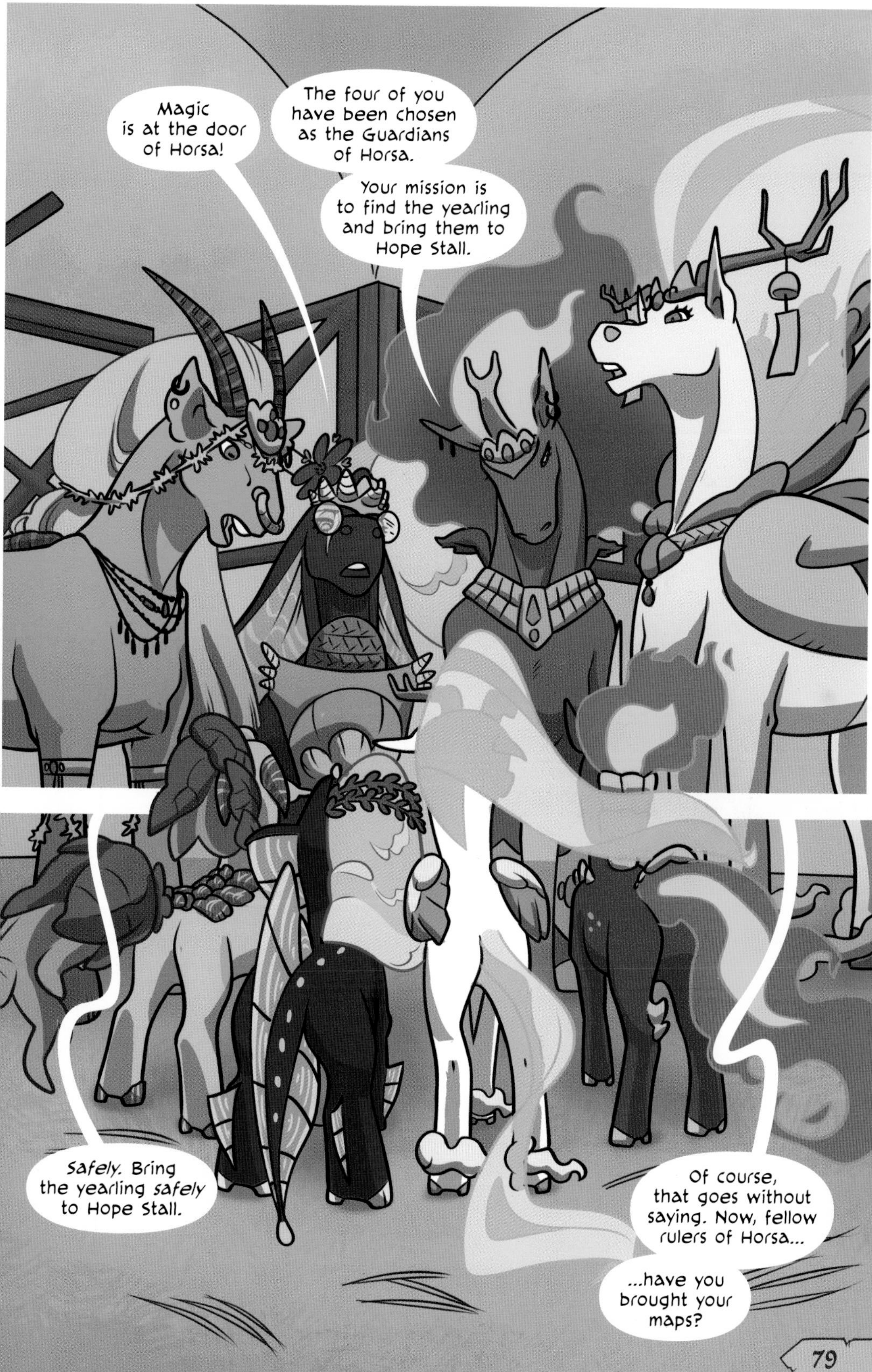
Magic is at the door of Horsa!
The four of you have been chosen as the Guardians of Horsa.
Your mission is to find the yearling and bring them to Hope Stall.
Safely. Bring the yearling *safely* to Hope Stall.
Of course, that goes without saying. Now, fellow rulers of Horsa...
...have you brought your maps?

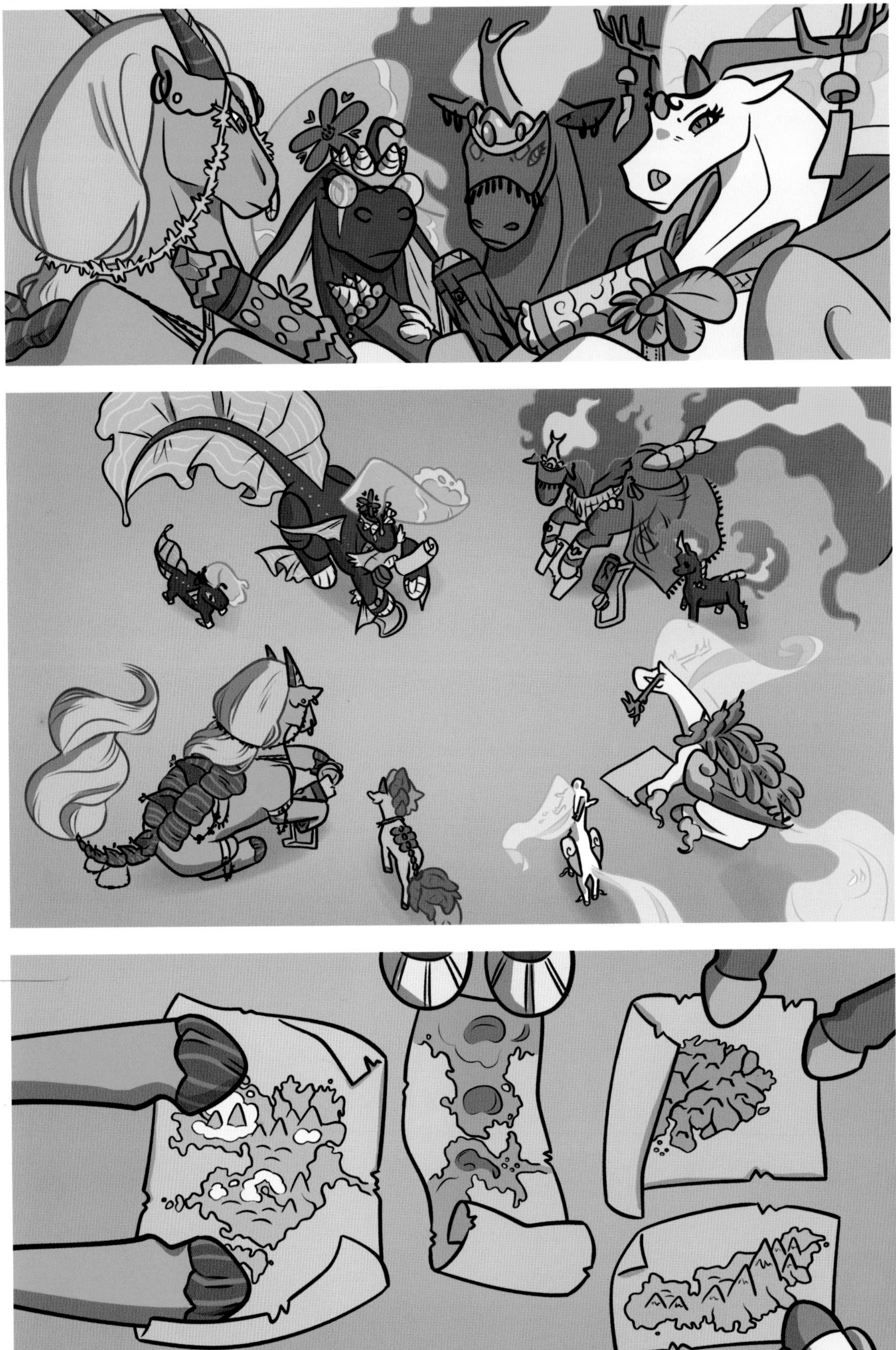

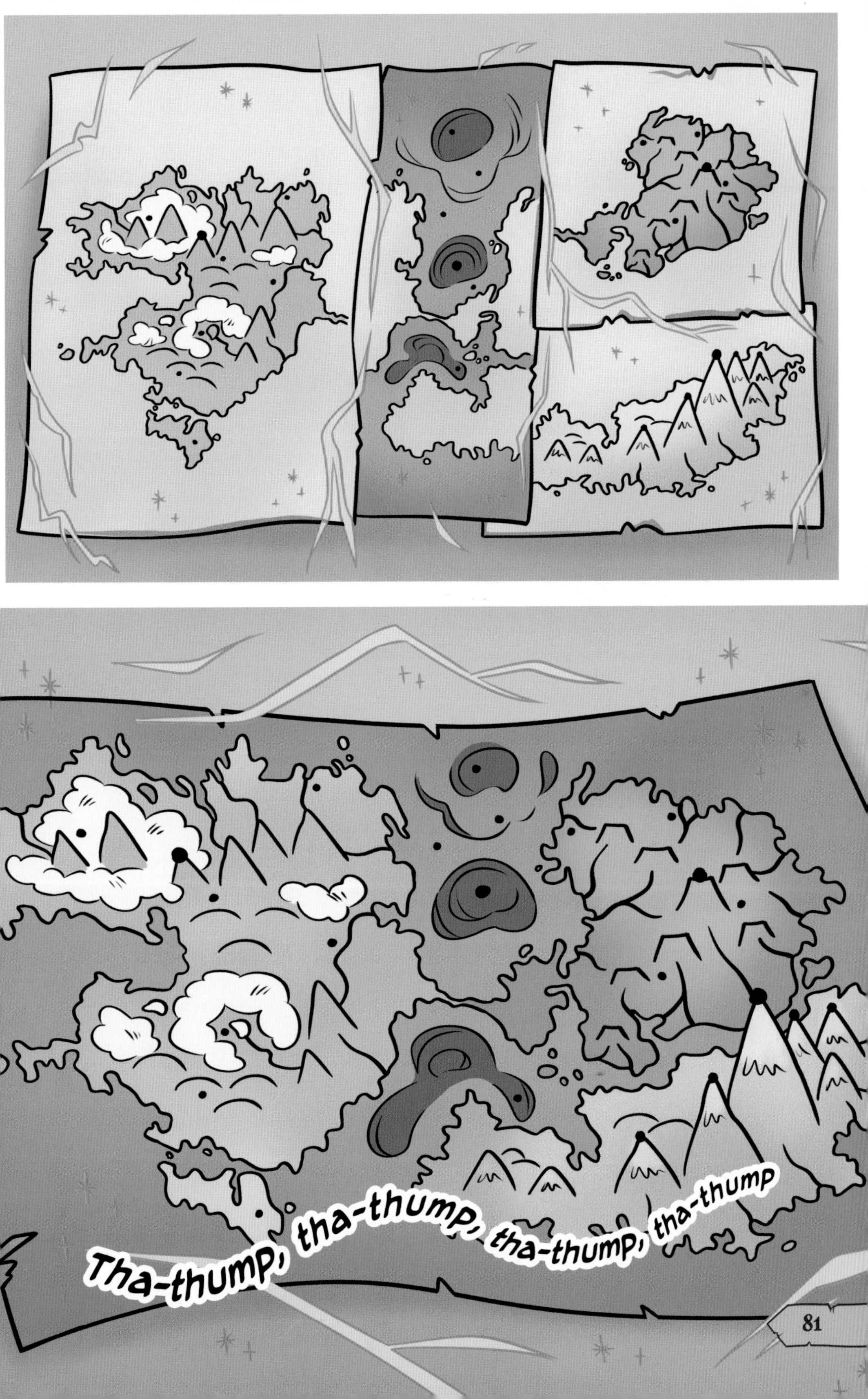
Tha-thump, tha-thump, tha-thump, tha-thump

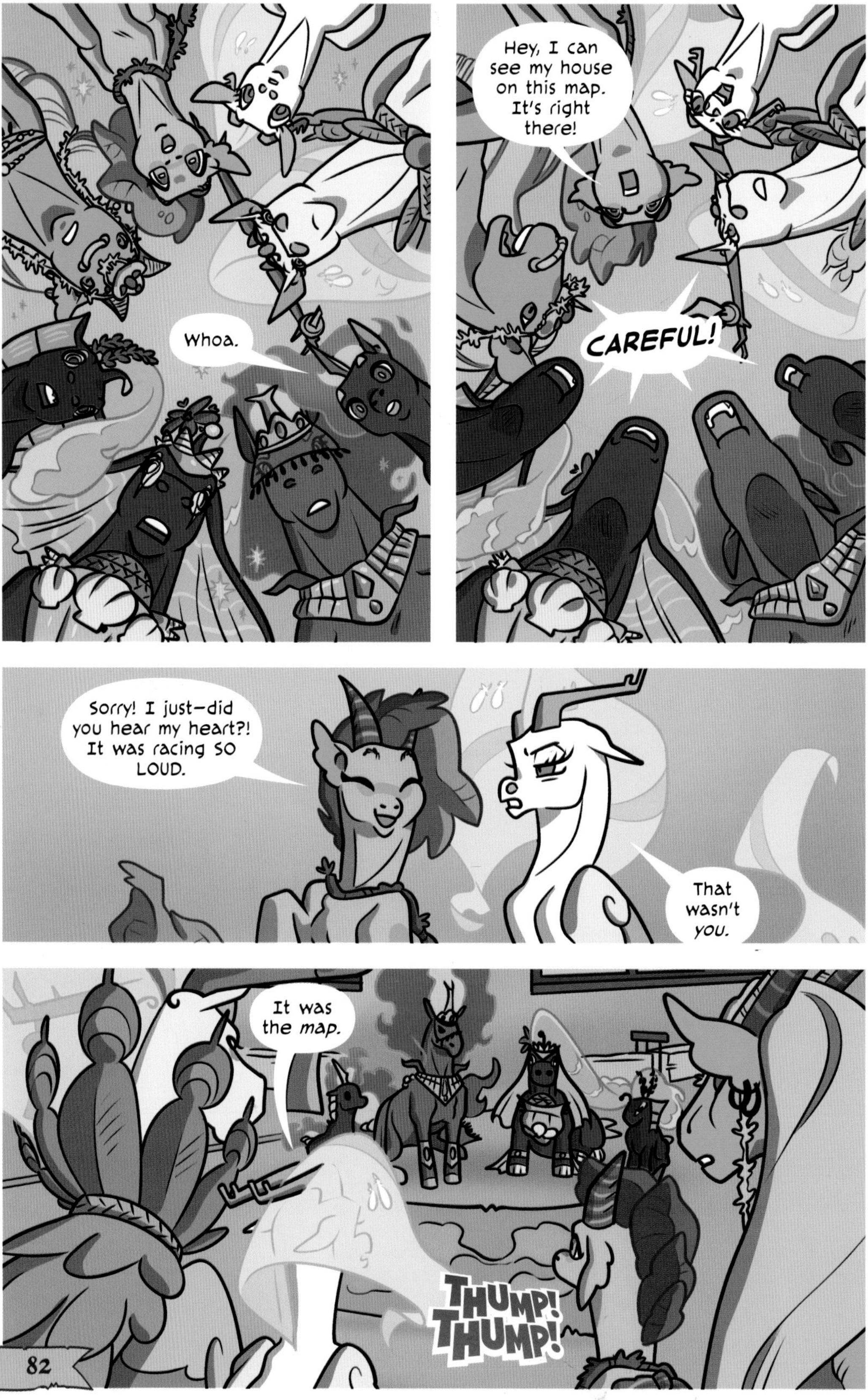
Whoa.
Hey, I can see my house on this map. It's right there!
CAREFUL!
Sorry! I just—did you hear my heart?! It was racing SO LOUD.
That wasn't *you.*
It was the *map.*
THUMP! THUMP!

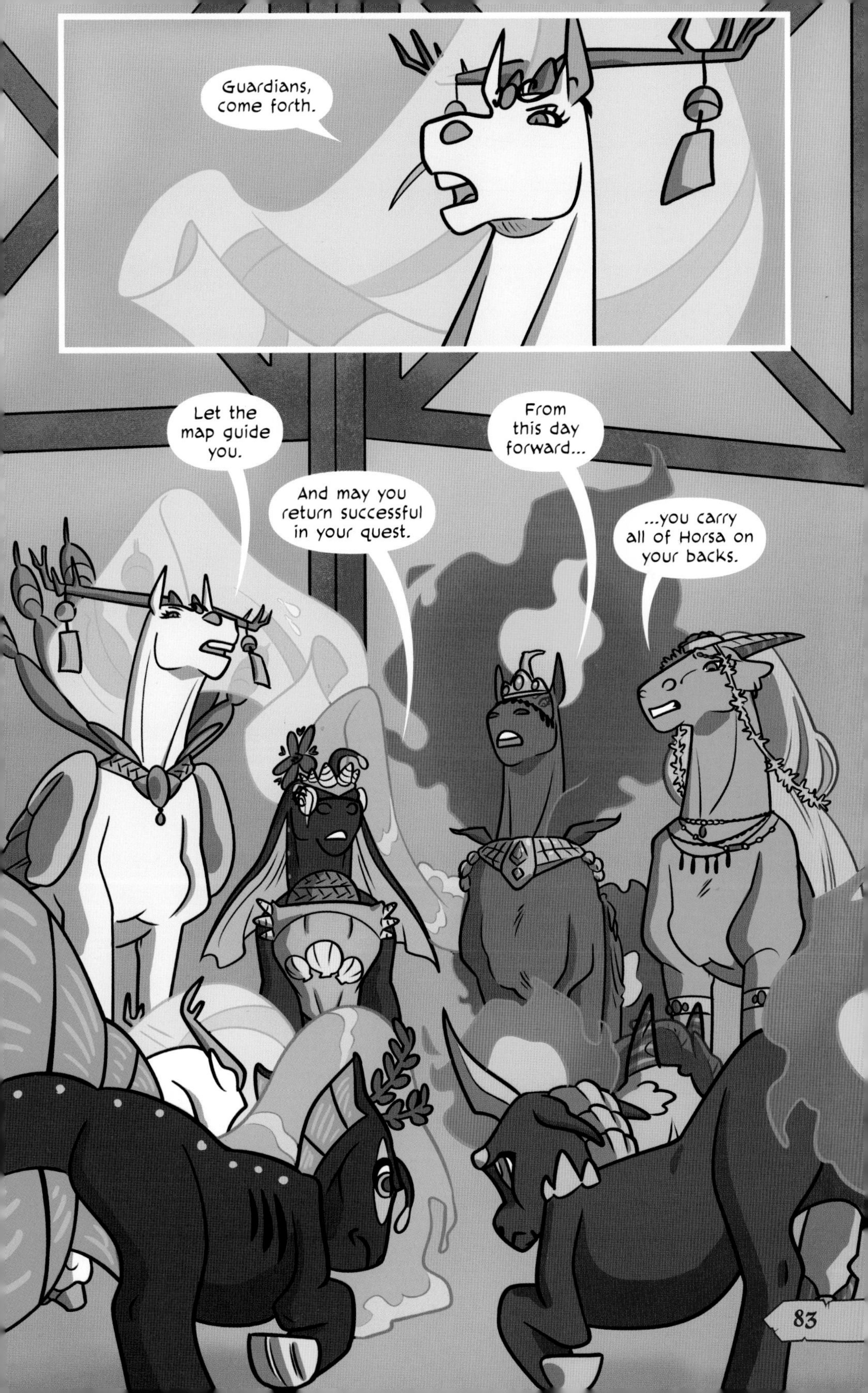
Guardians, come forth.
Let the map guide you.
And may you return successful in your quest.
From this day forward...
...you carry all of Horsa on your backs.

Chapter 6

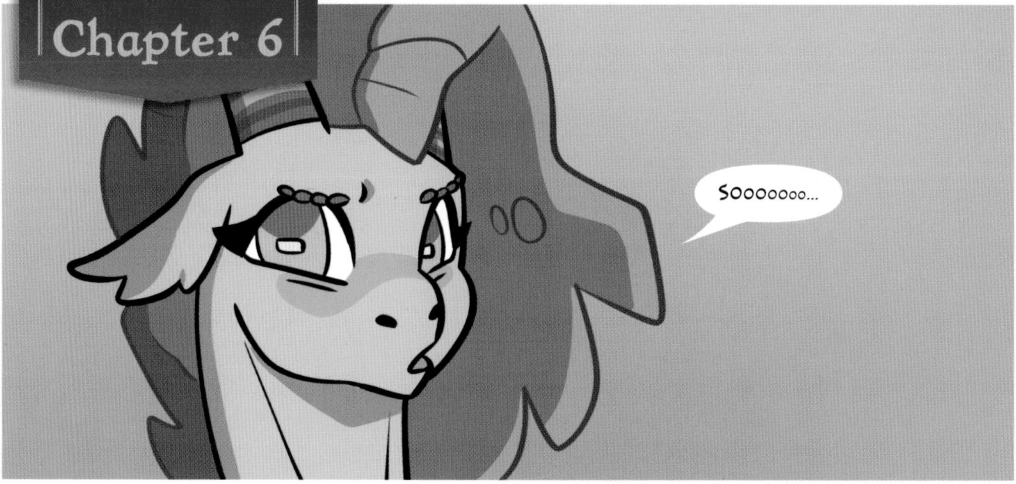
Soooooooo...

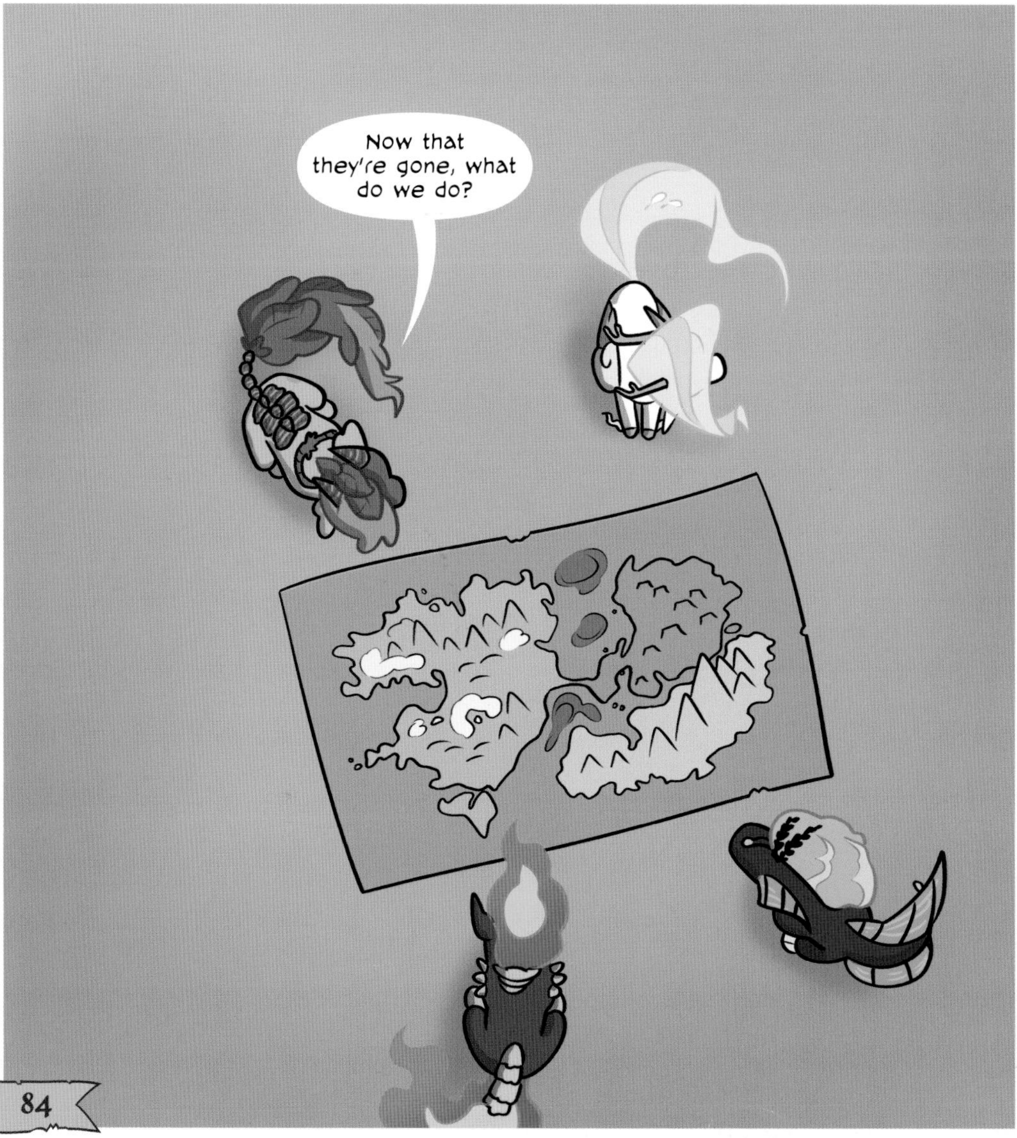
Now that they're gone, what do we do?

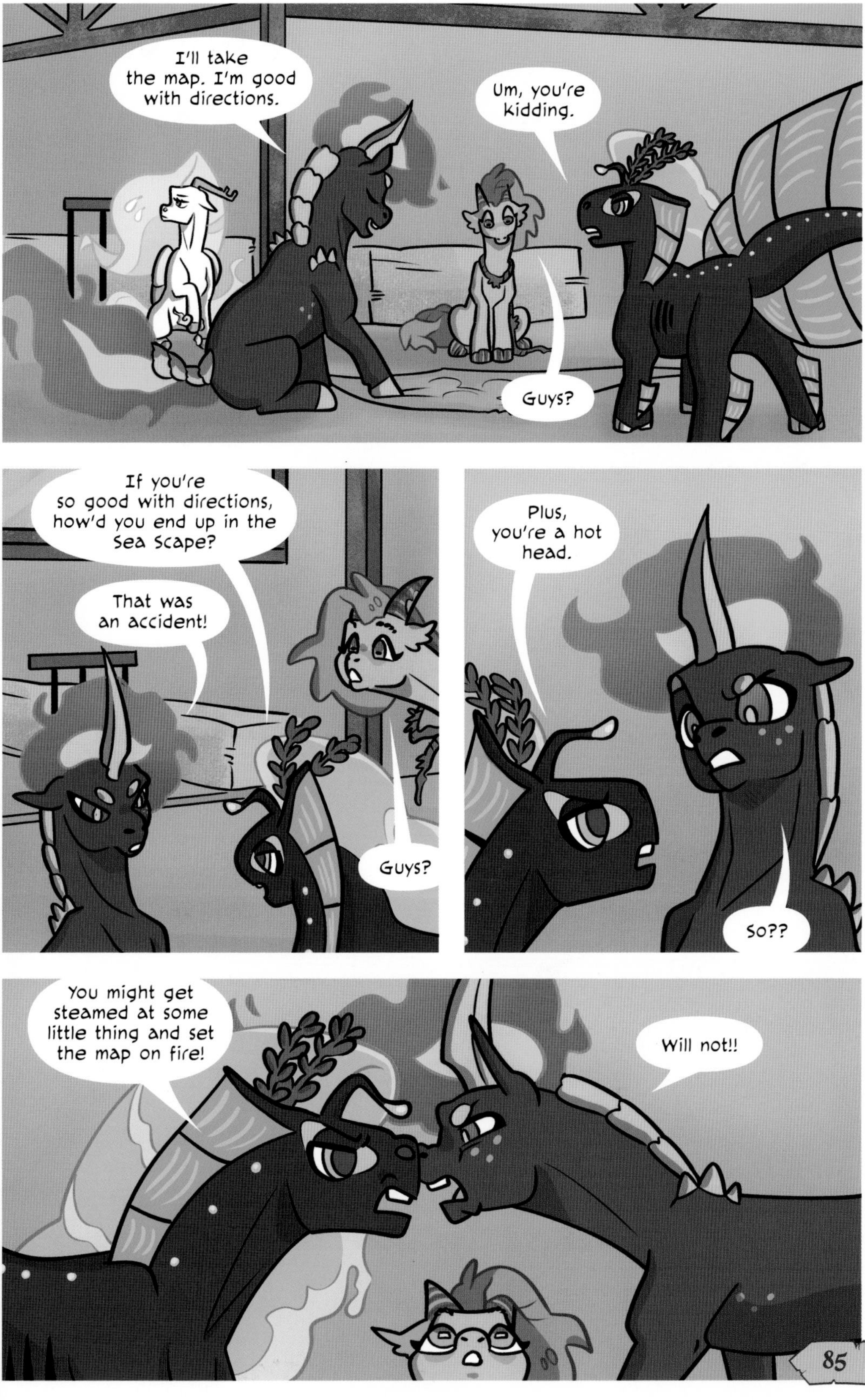
I'll take the map. I'm good with directions.
Um, you're kidding.
Guys?
If you're so good with directions, how'd you end up in the Sea Scape?
That was an accident!
Guys?
Plus, you're a hot head.
So??
You might get steamed at some little thing and set the map on fire!
Will not!!

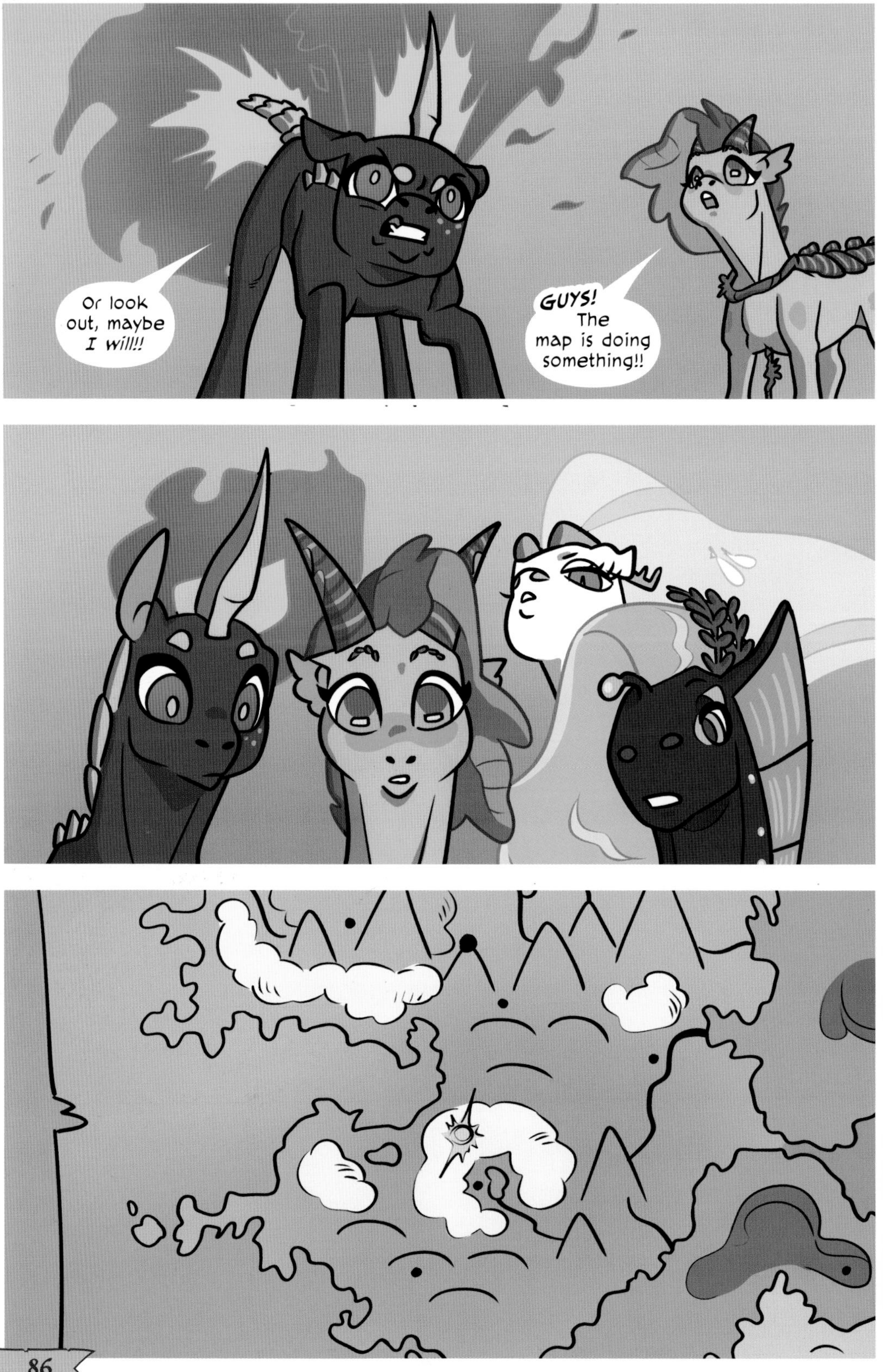
Or look out, maybe I will!!
GUYS! The map is doing something!!

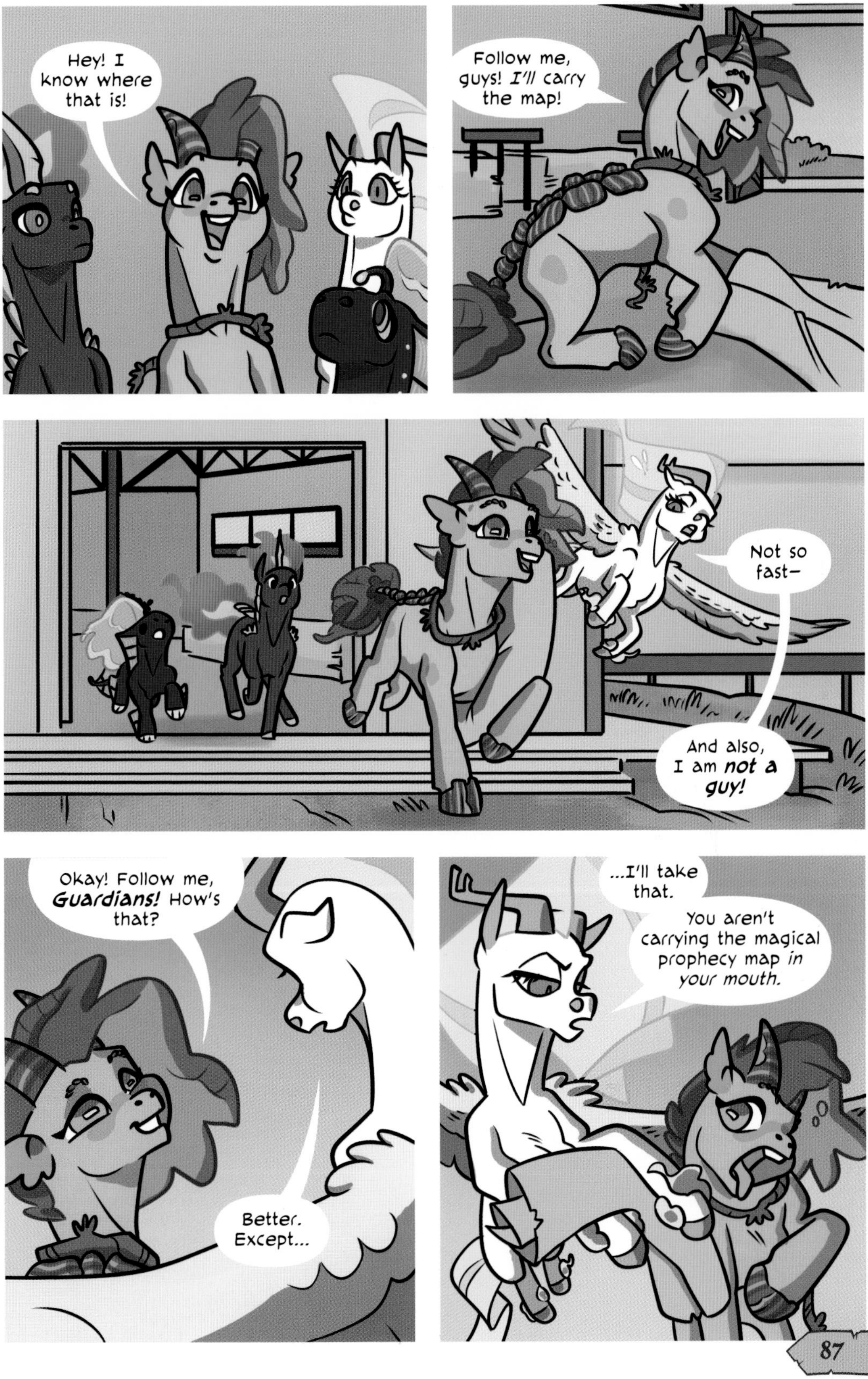
Hey! I know where that is!
Follow me, guys! *I'll* carry the map!
Not so fast–
And also, I am ***not a guy!***
Okay! Follow me, ***Guardians!*** How's that?
Better. Except...
...I'll take that.
You aren't carrying the magical prophecy map *in your mouth.*

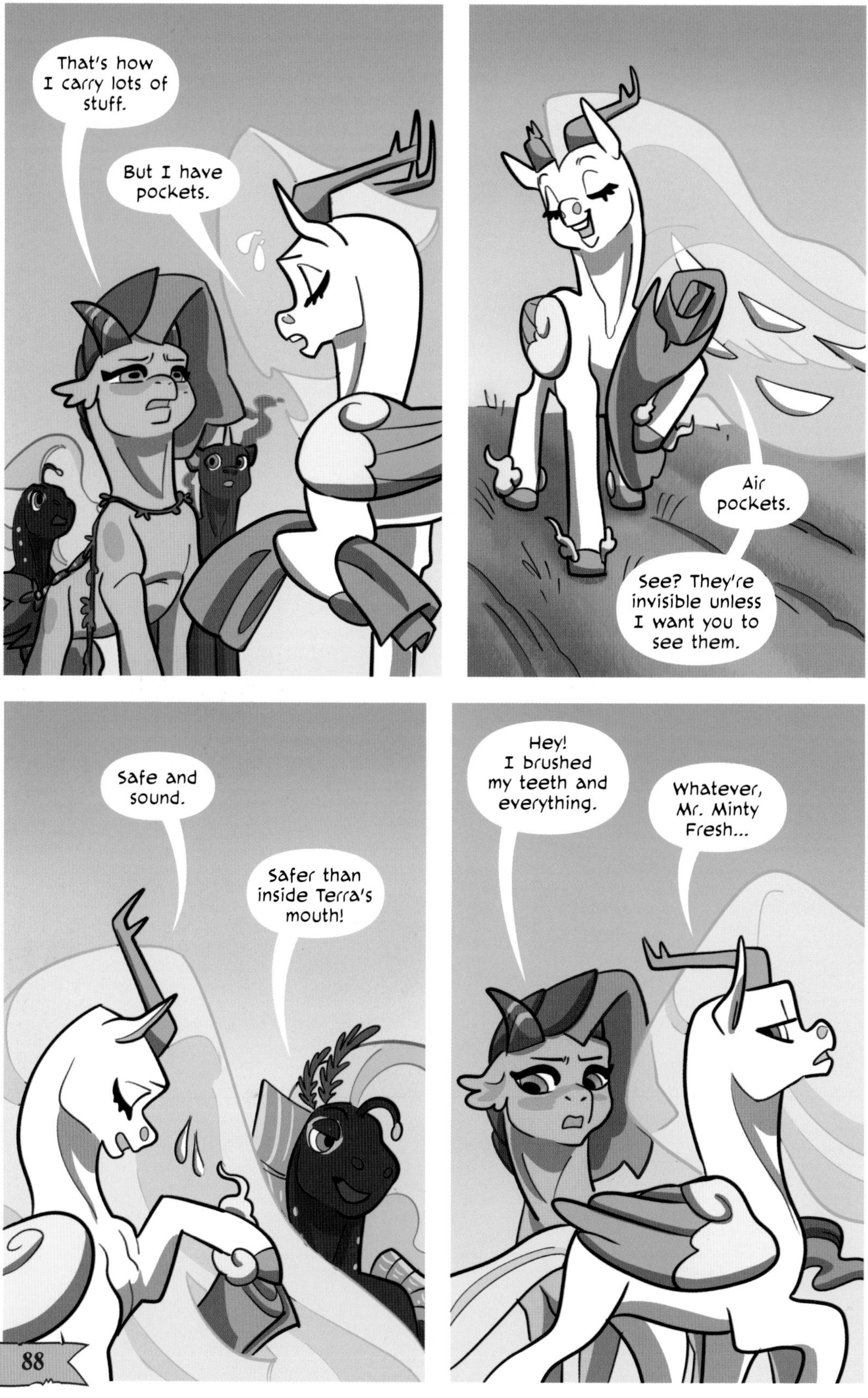
That's how I carry lots of stuff.
But I have pockets.
Air pockets.
See? They're invisible unless I want you to see them.
Safe and sound.
Safer than inside Terra's mouth!
Hey! I brushed my teeth and everything.
Whatever, Mr. Minty Fresh...

Let's see if you can keep up!

Coming!

Right behind you— but not for long!

That's pretty cool.

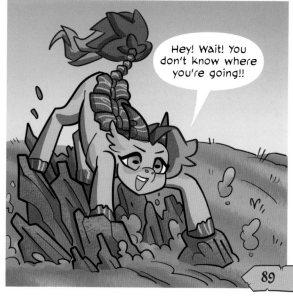

Hey! Wait! You don't know where you're going!!

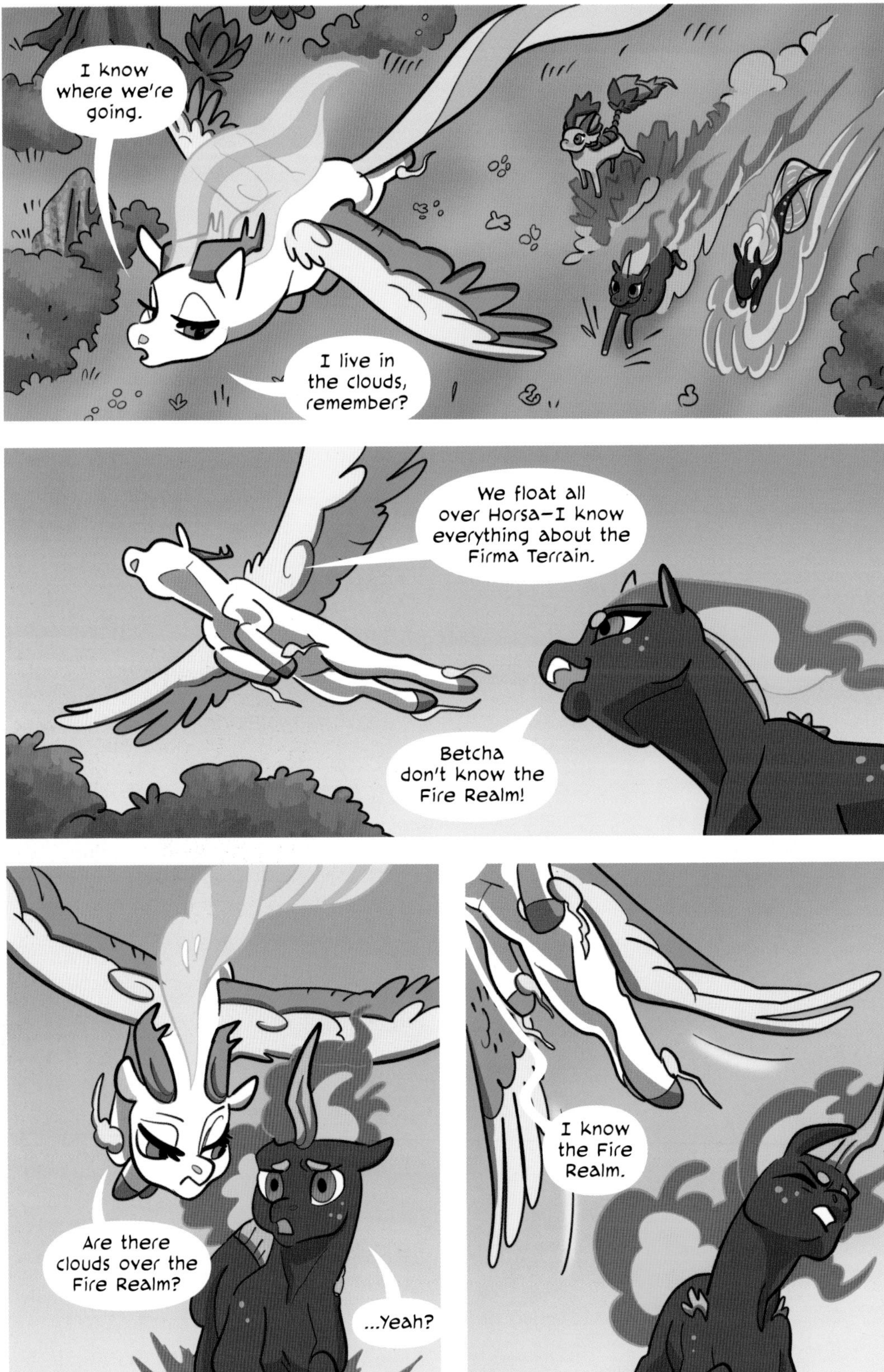

I know where we're going.
I live in the clouds, remember?
We float all over Horsa—I know everything about the Firma Terrain.
Betcha don't know the Fire Realm!
Are there clouds over the Fire Realm?
...Yeah?
I know the Fire Realm.

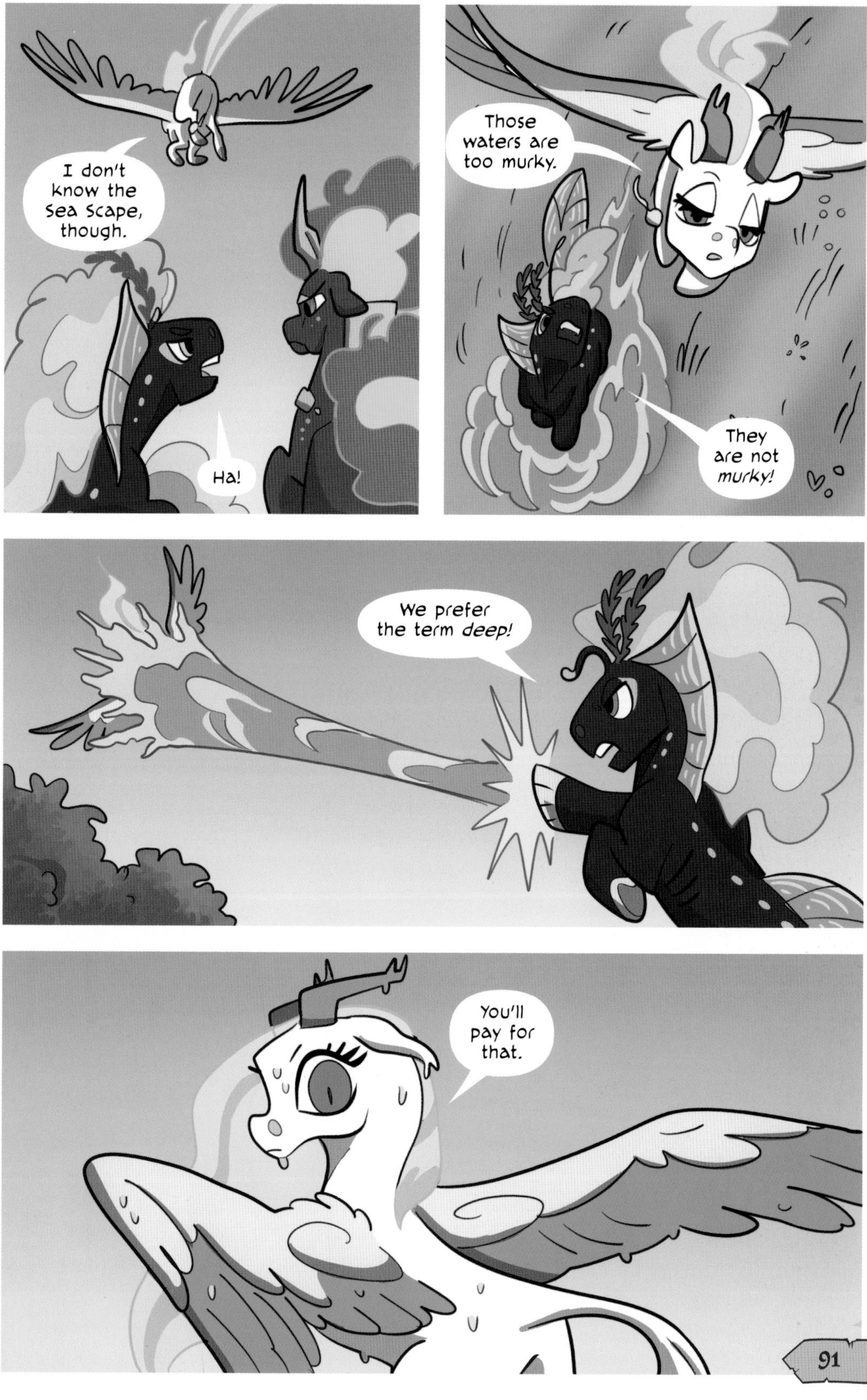
I don't know the Sea Scape, though.
Ha!
Those waters are too murky.
They are not *murky!*
We prefer the term *deep!*
You'll pay for that.

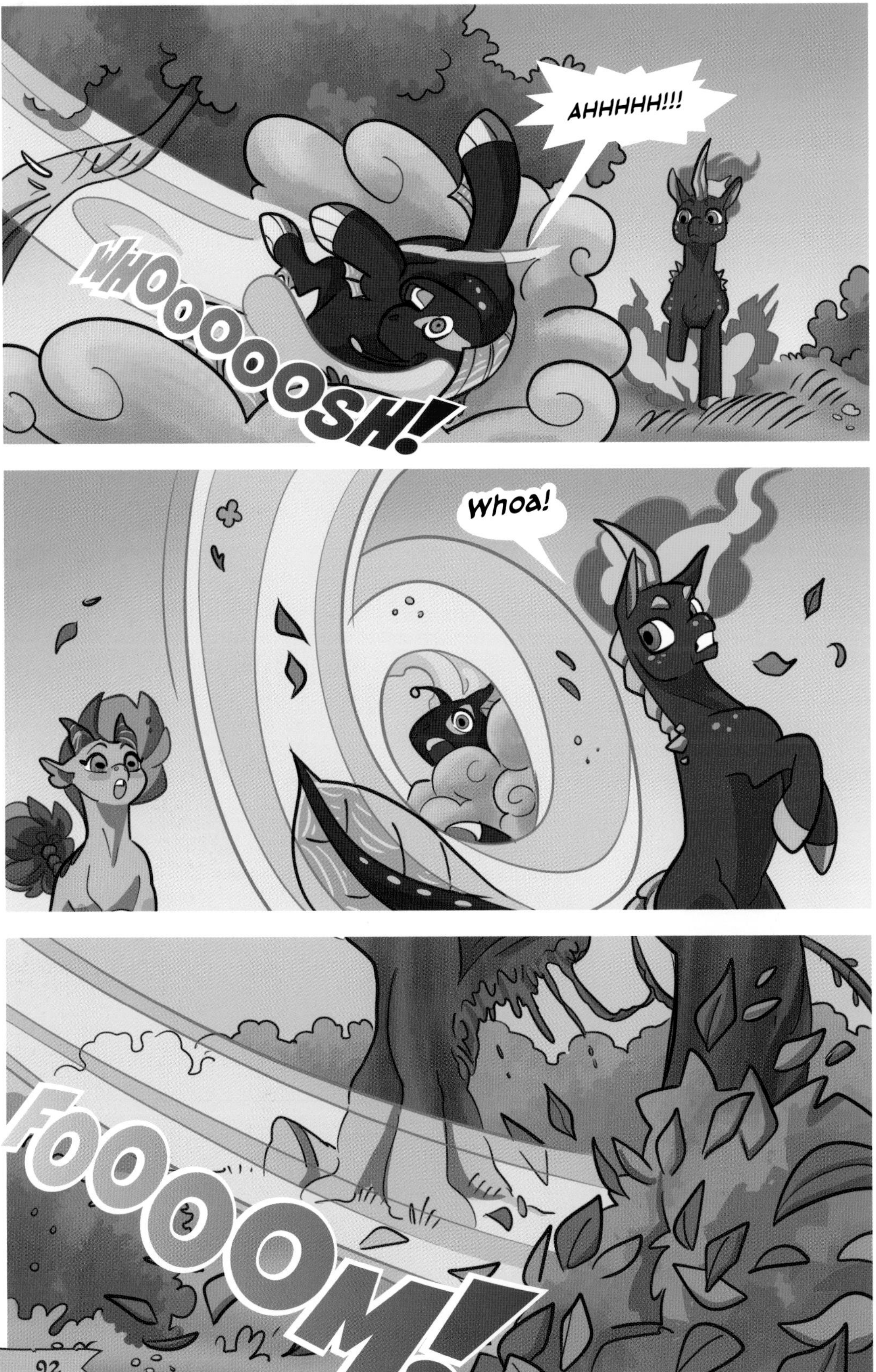
AHHHHH!!!
WHOOOOOOSH!
Whoa!
FOOOOM!

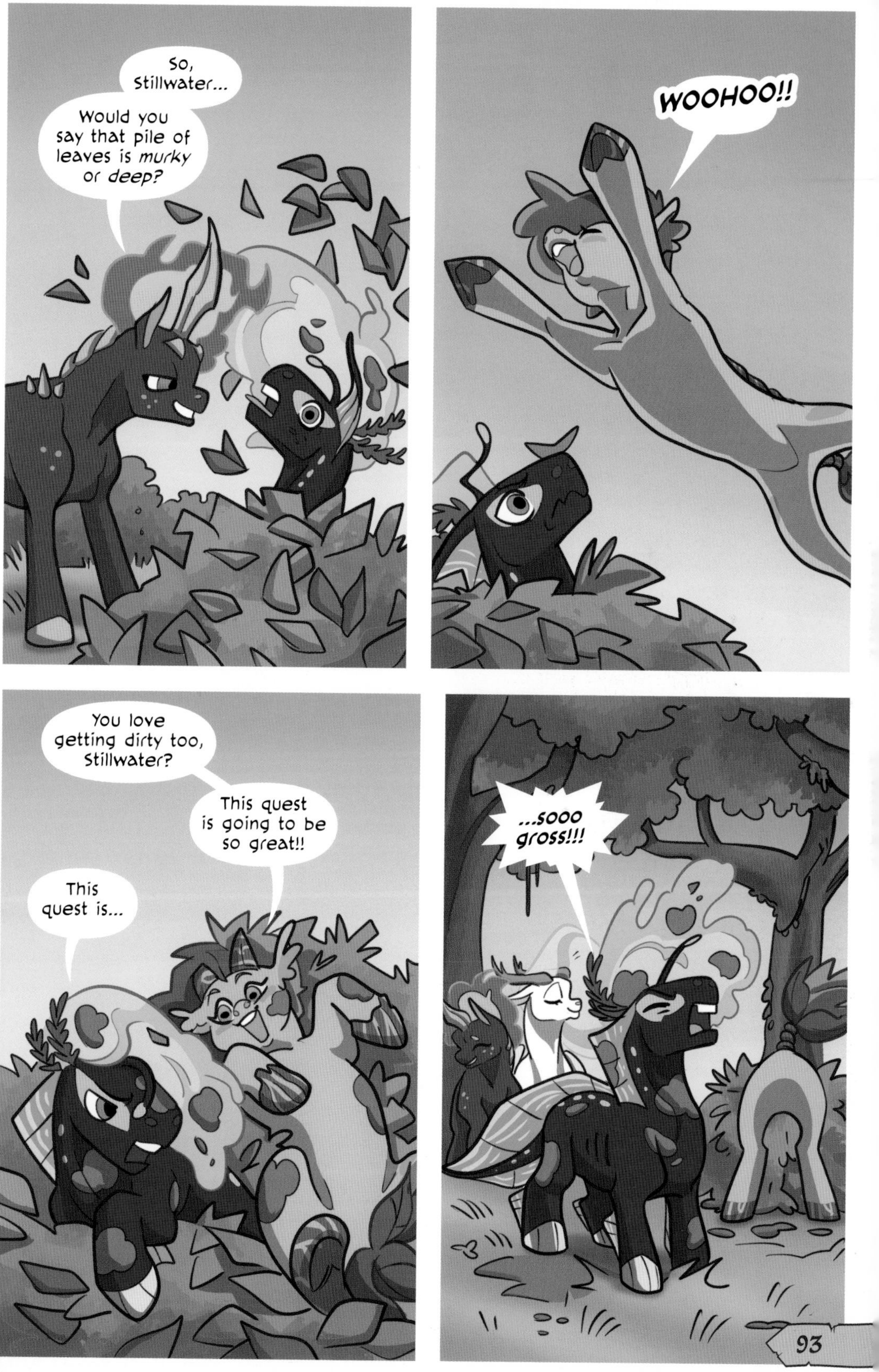
So, Stillwater...
Would you say that pile of leaves is *murky* or *deep*?
WOOHOO!!
You love getting dirty too, Stillwater?
This quest is going to be so great!!
This quest is...
...sooo gross!!!

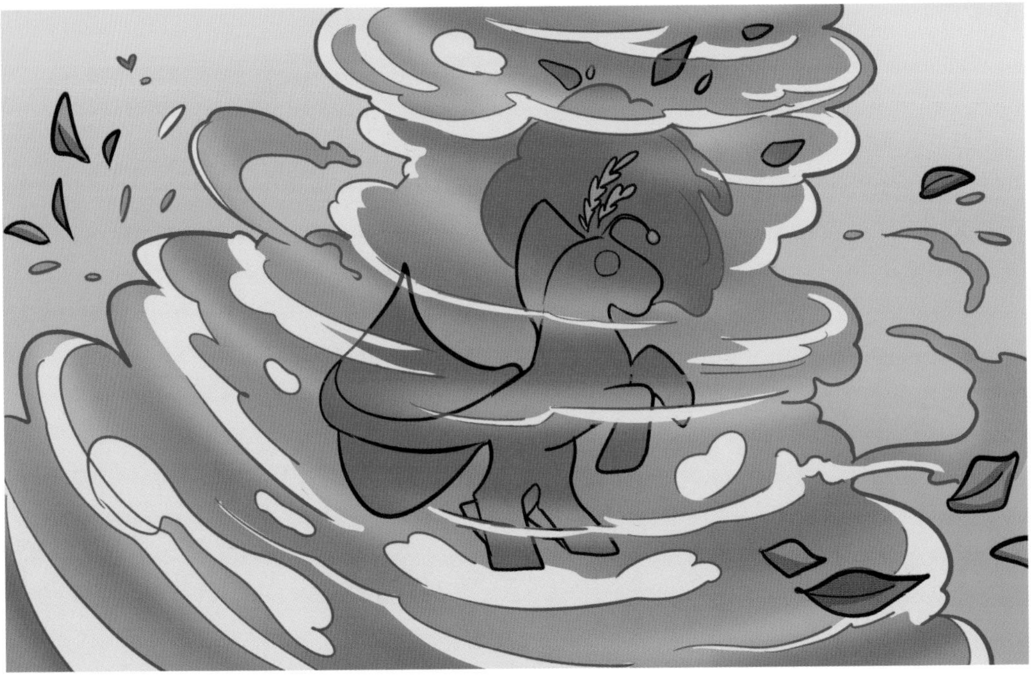

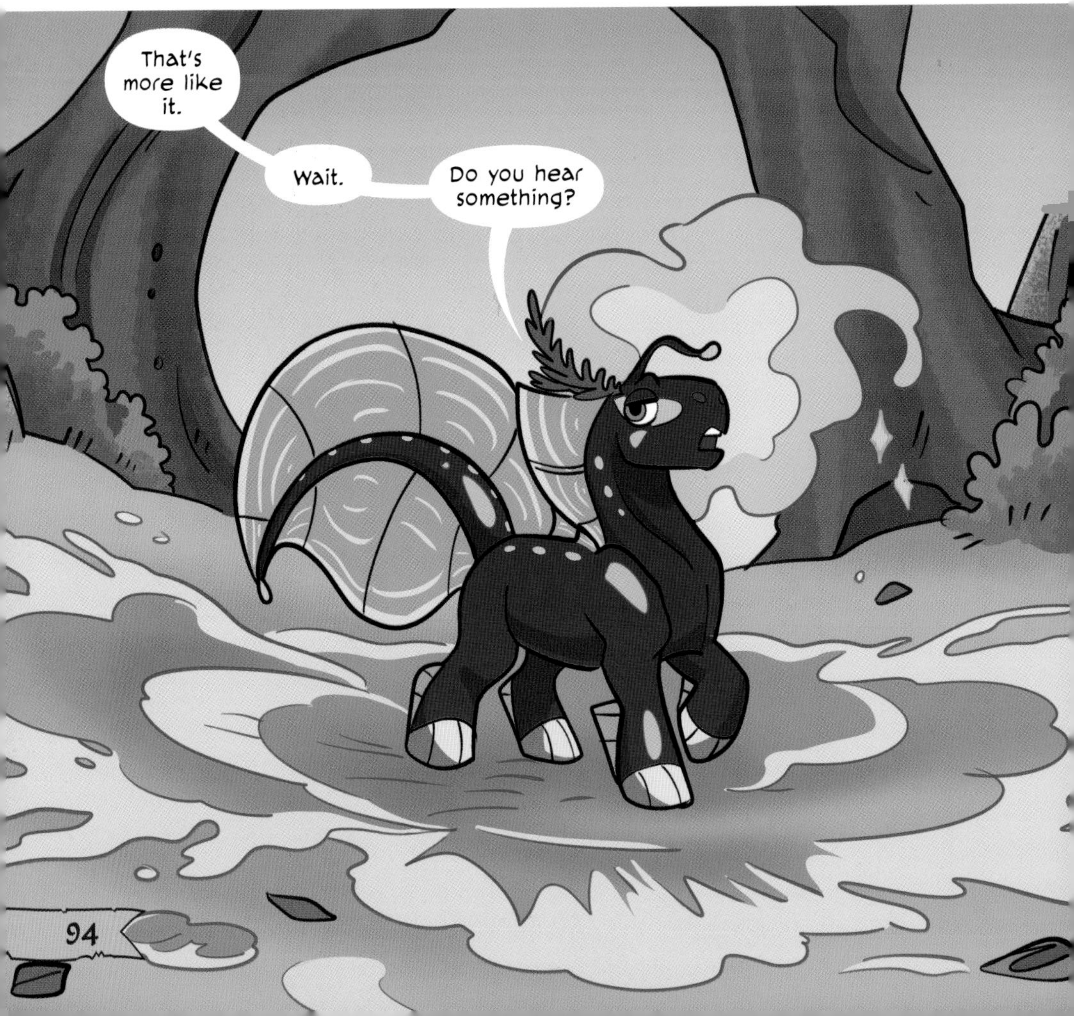
That's more like it.
Wait.
Do you hear something?

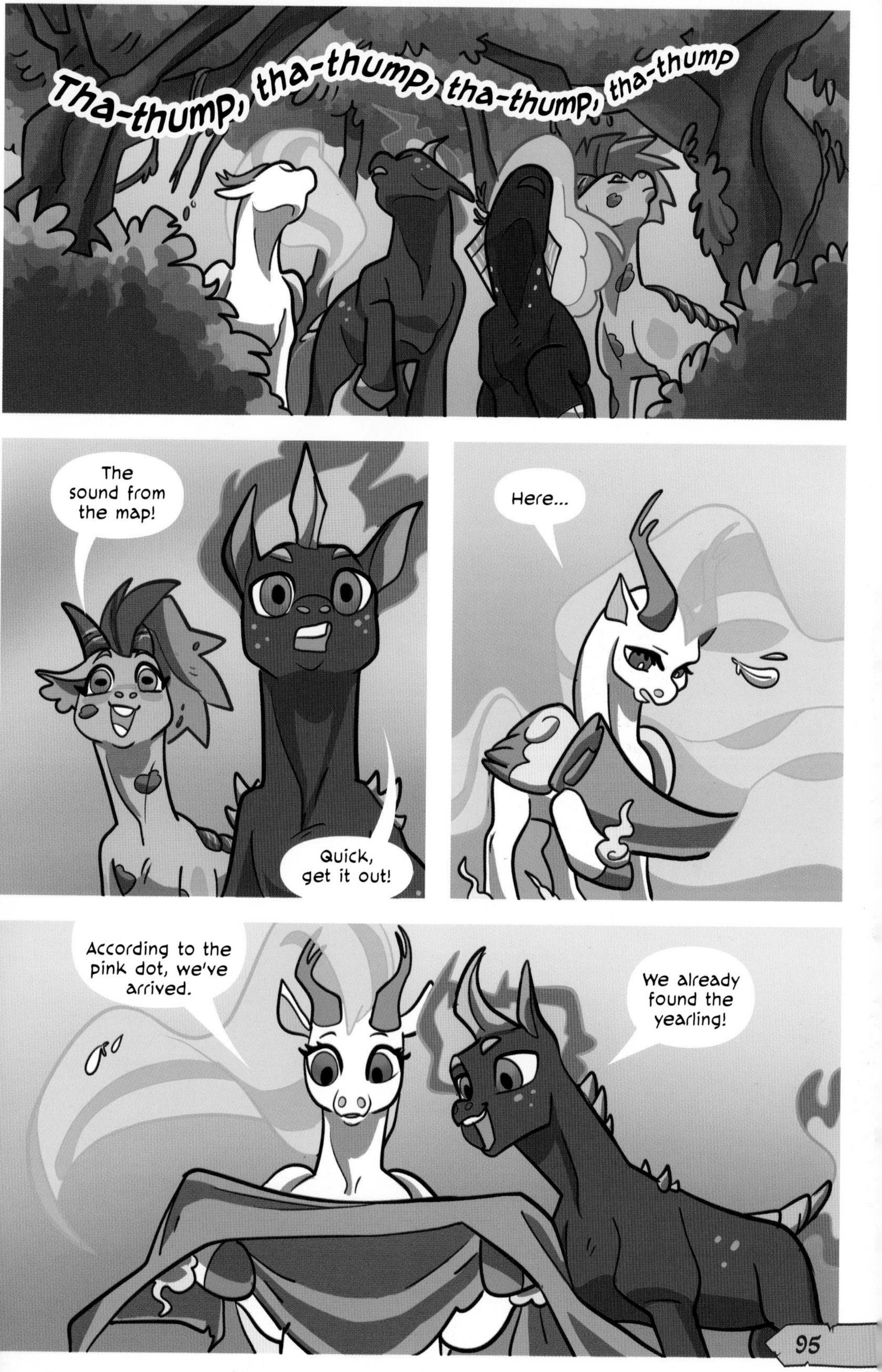
Tha-thump, tha-thump, tha-thump, tha-thump
The sound from the map!
Quick, get it out!
Here...
According to the pink dot, we've arrived.
We already found the yearling!

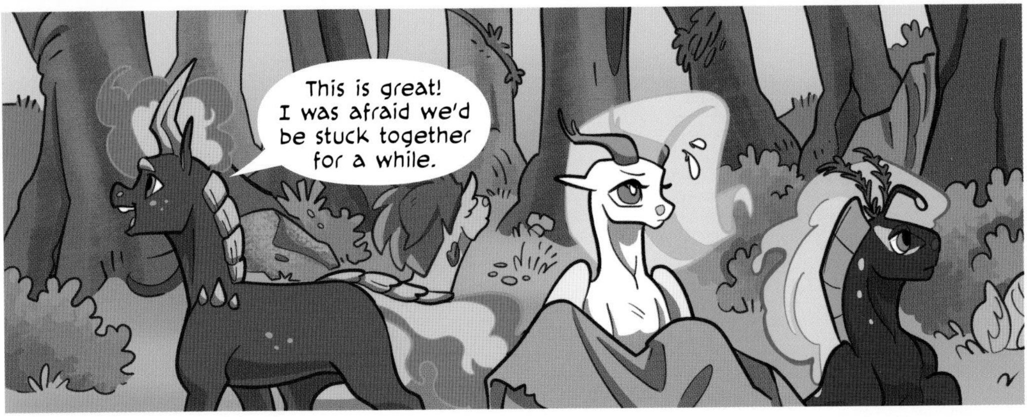
This is great! I was afraid we'd be stuck together for a while.

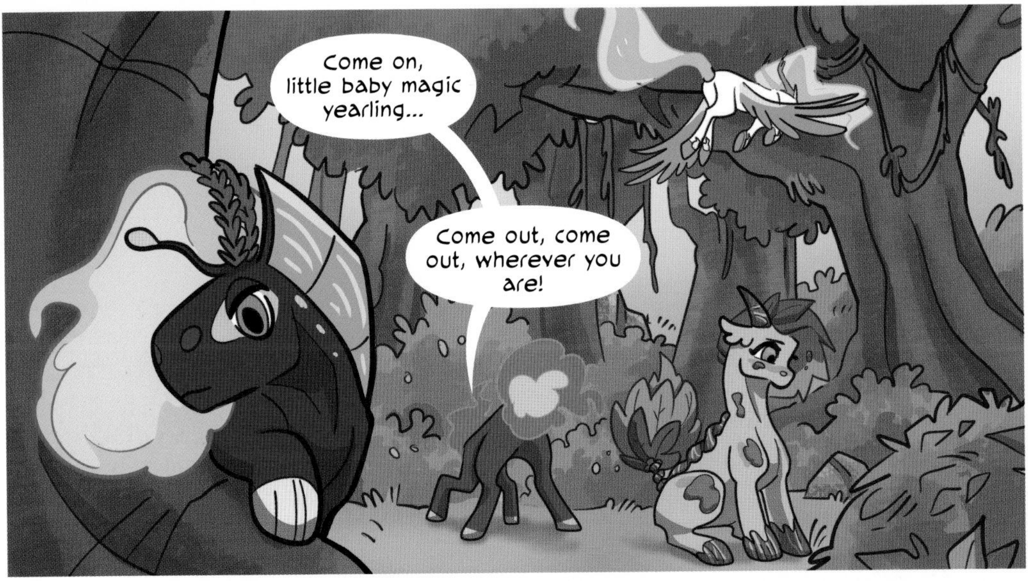
Come on, little baby magic yearling...
Come out, come out, wherever you are!

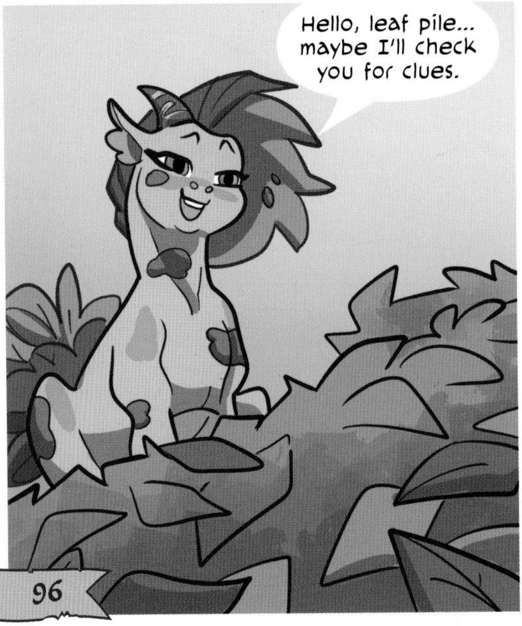
Hello, leaf pile... maybe I'll check you for clues.

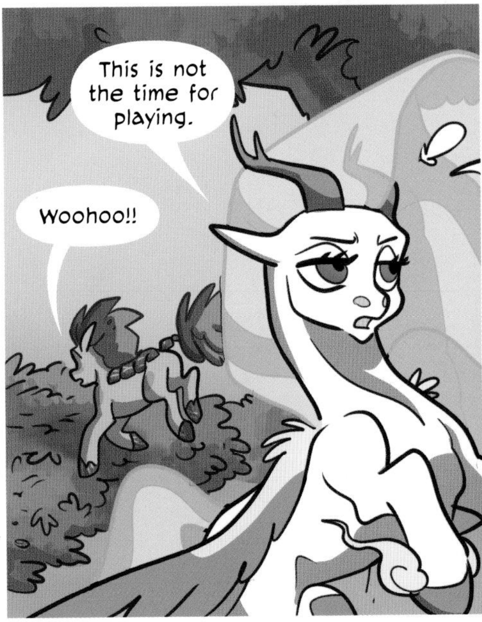
This is not the time for playing.
Woohoo!!

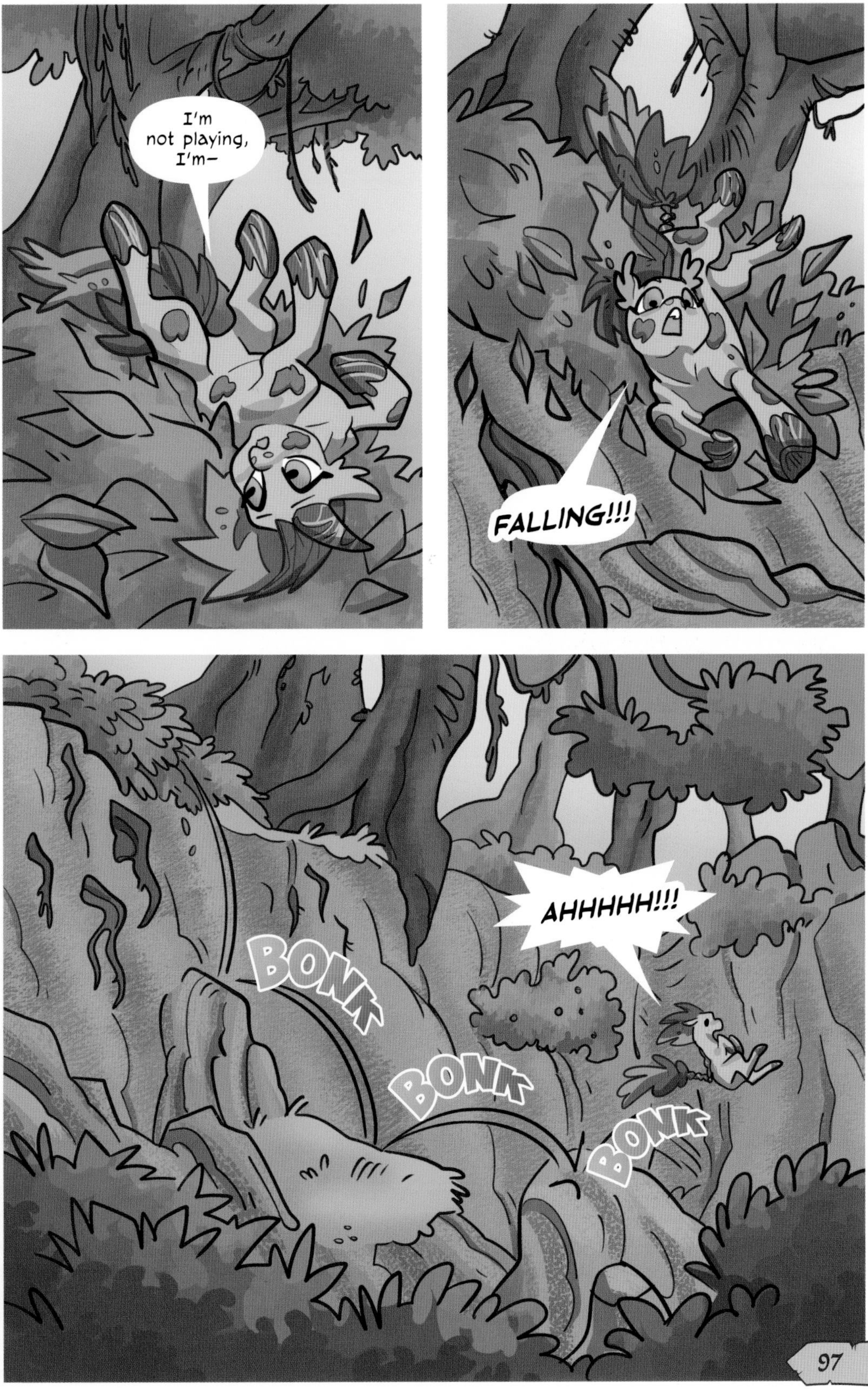
I'm not playing, I'm–
FALLING!!!
AHHHHH!!!
BONK
BONK
BONK

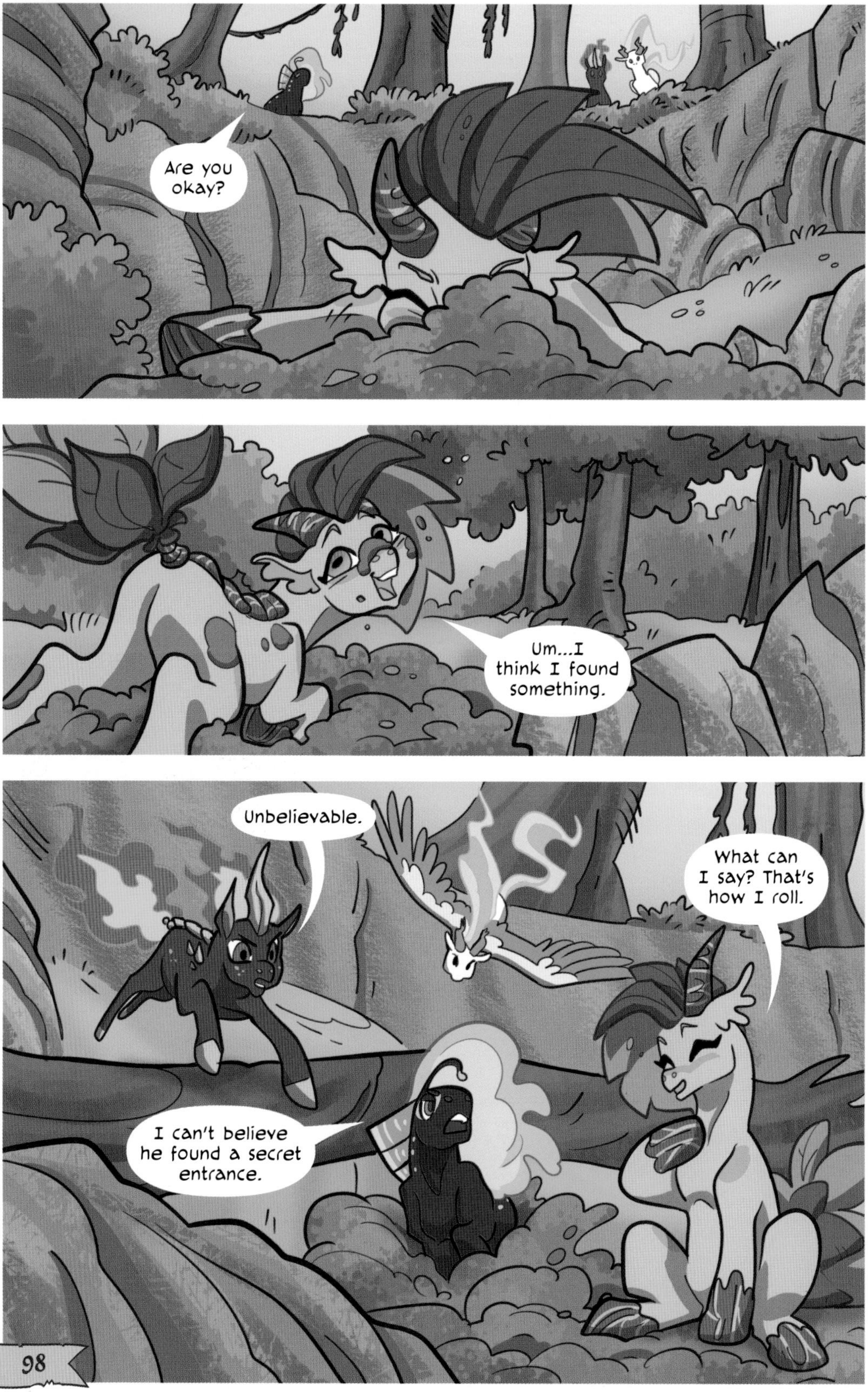
Are you okay?
Um...I think I found something.
Unbelievable.
What can I say? That's how I roll.
I can't believe he found a secret entrance.

Chapter 7

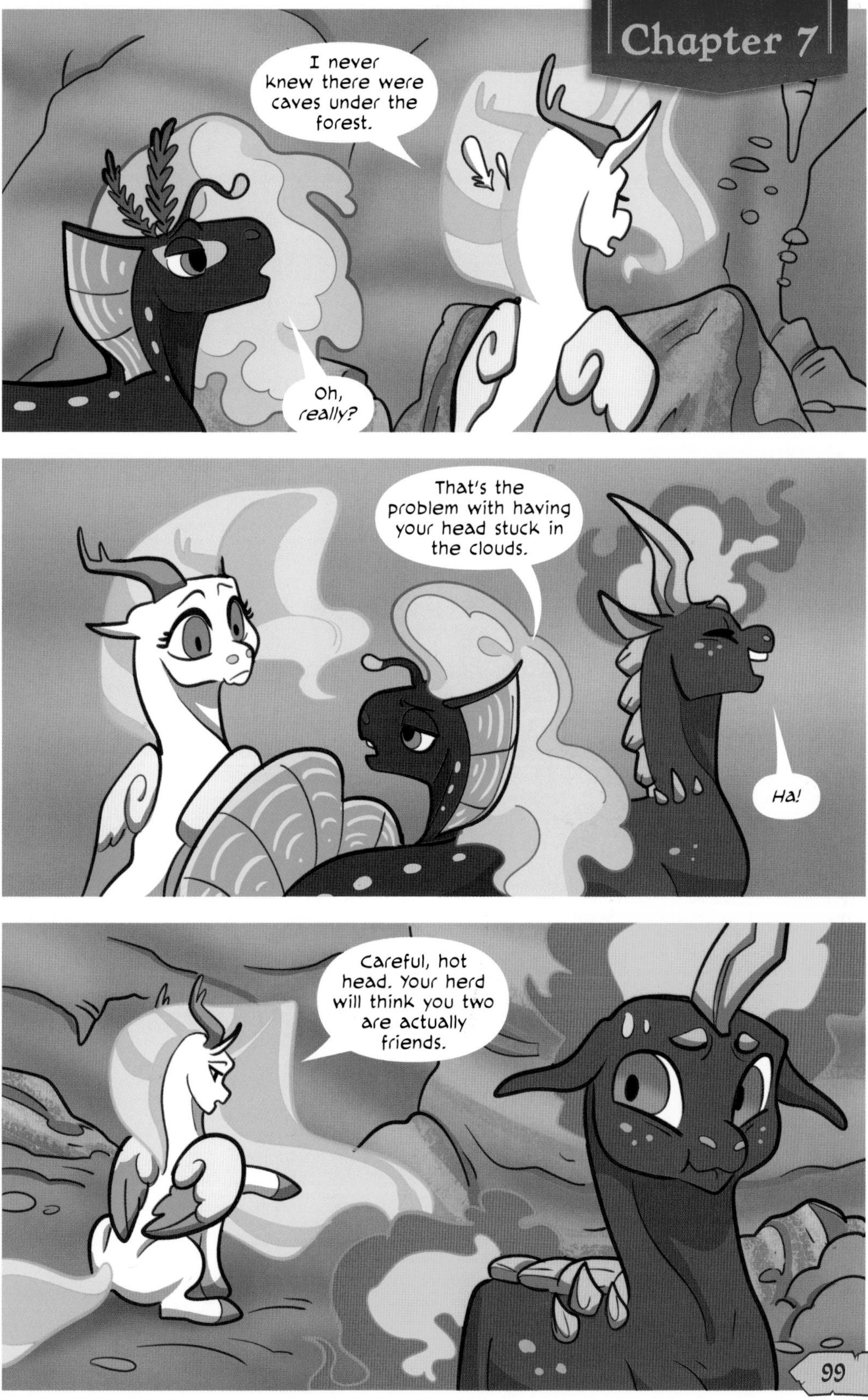

I never knew there were caves under the forest.
Oh, *really?*
That's the problem with having your head stuck in the clouds.
Ha!
Careful, hot head. Your herd will think you two are actually friends.

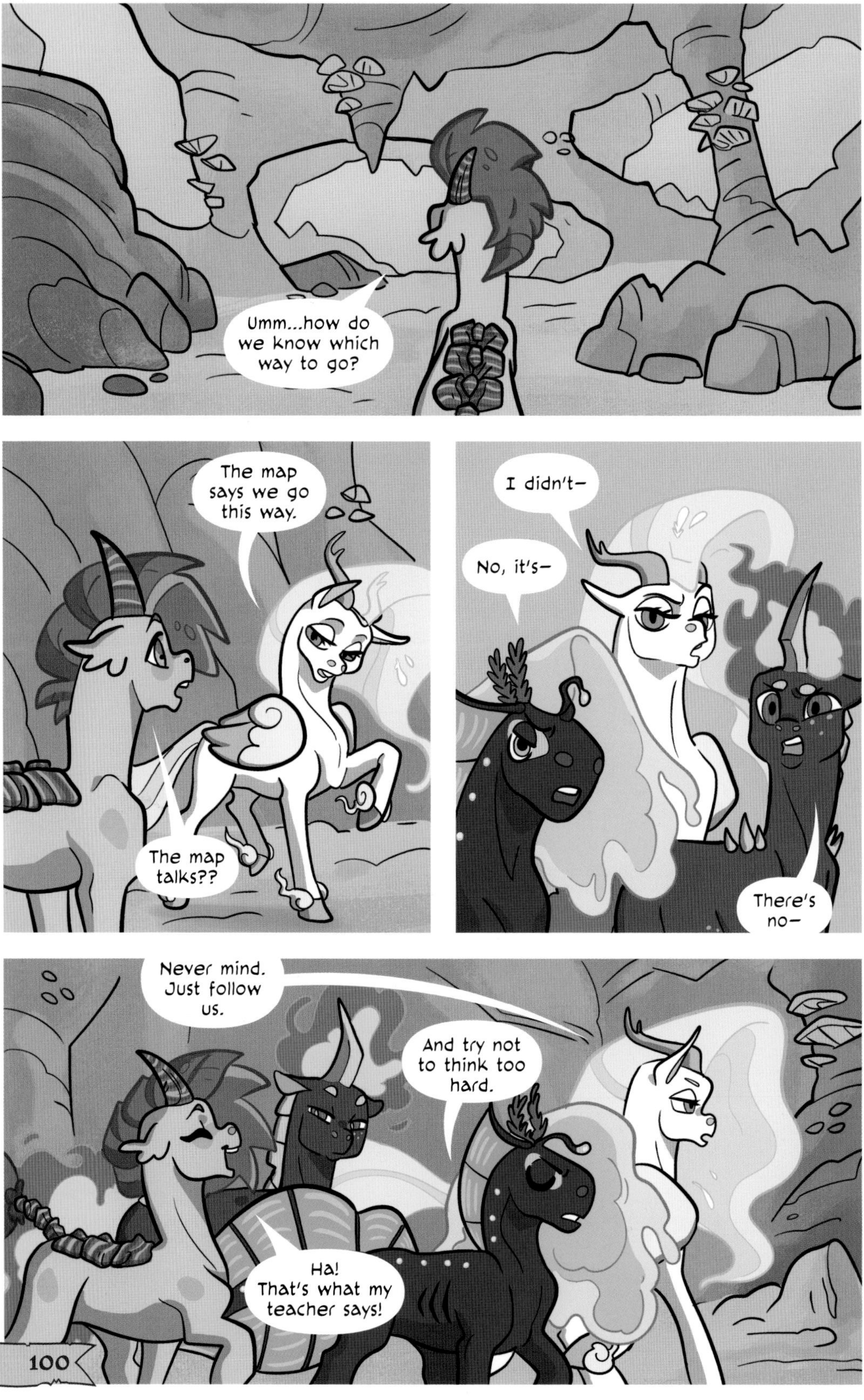
Umm...how do we know which way to go?
The map says we go this way.
The map talks??
I didn't—
No, it's—
There's no—
Never mind. Just follow us.
And try not to think too hard.
Ha! That's what my teacher says!

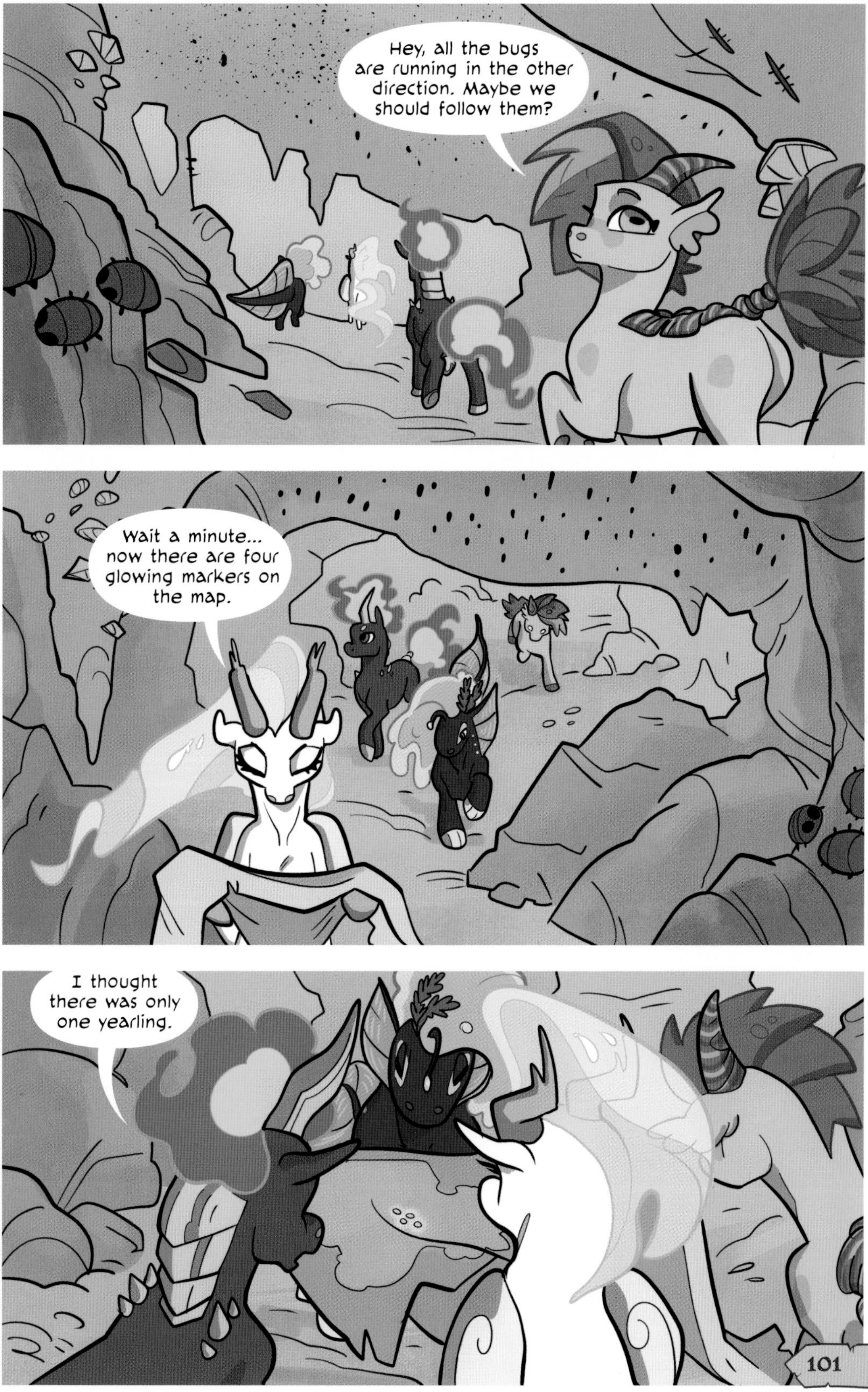
Hey, all the bugs are running in the other direction. Maybe we should follow them?
Wait a minute... now there are four glowing markers on the map.
I thought there was only one yearling.

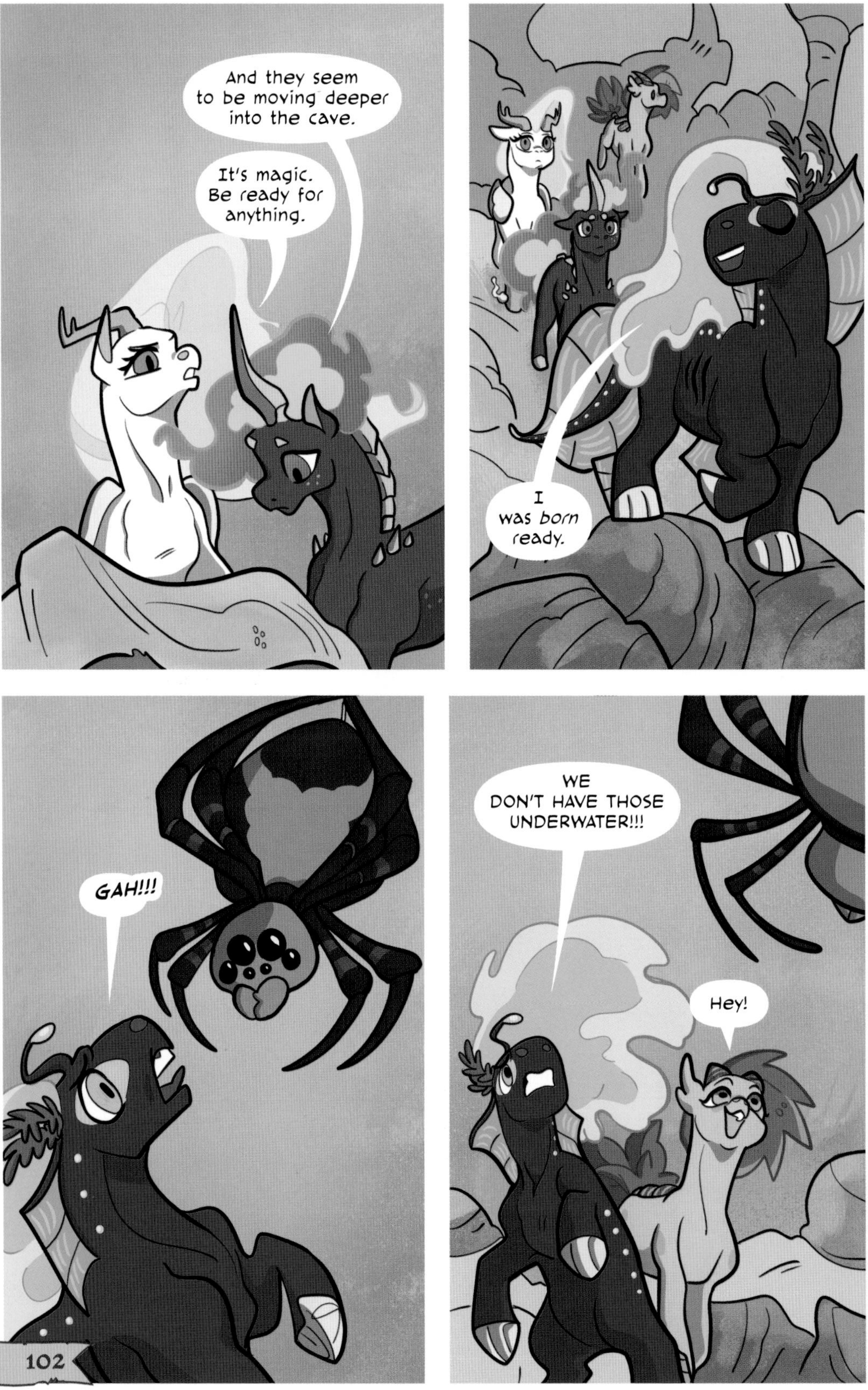
And they seem to be moving deeper into the cave.
It's magic. Be ready for anything.
I was *born* ready.
GAH!!!
WE DON'T HAVE THOSE UNDERWATER!!!
Hey!

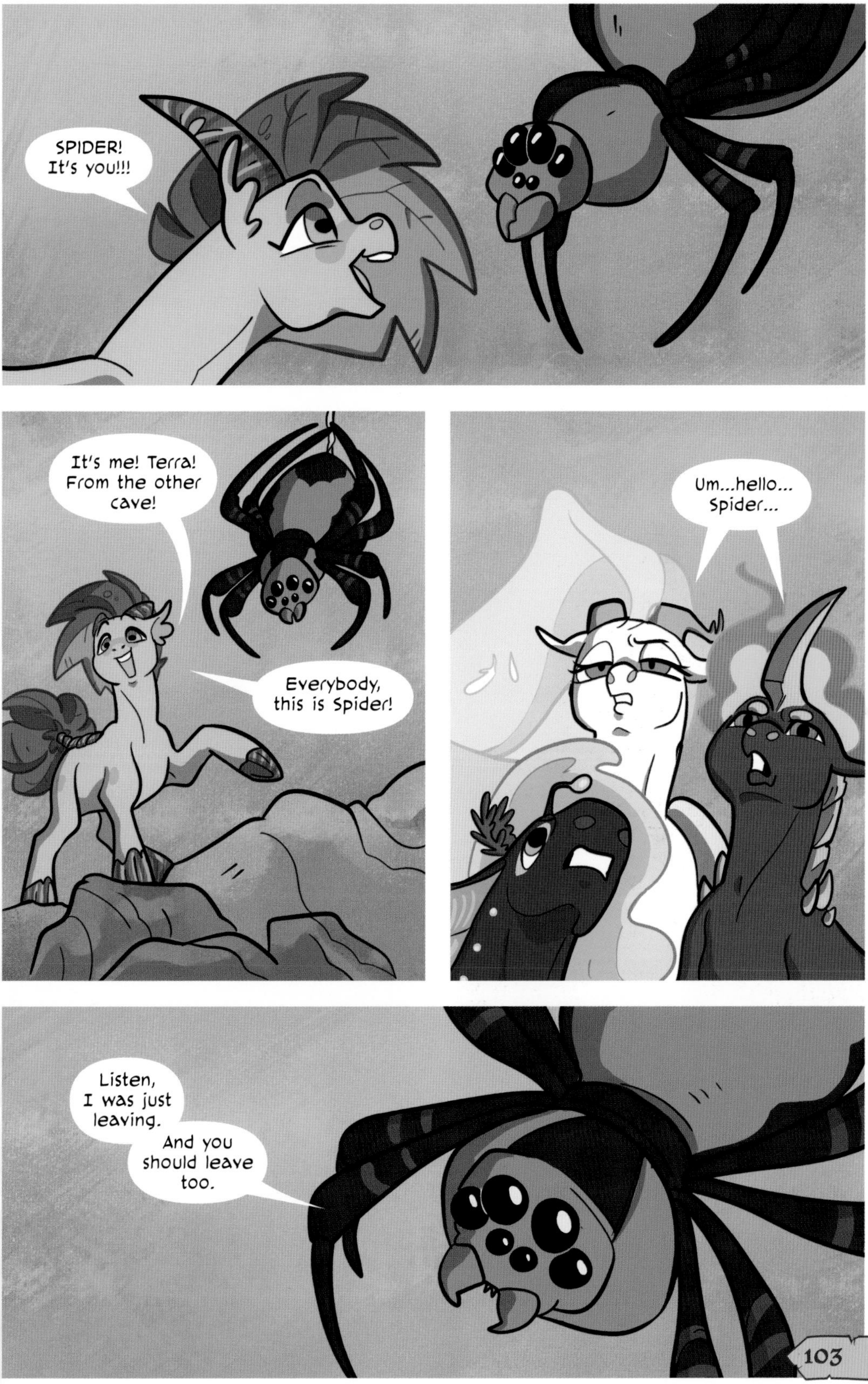
SPIDER! It's you!!!
It's me! Terra! From the other cave!
Everybody, this is Spider!
Um...hello... Spider...
Listen, I was just leaving.
And you should leave too.

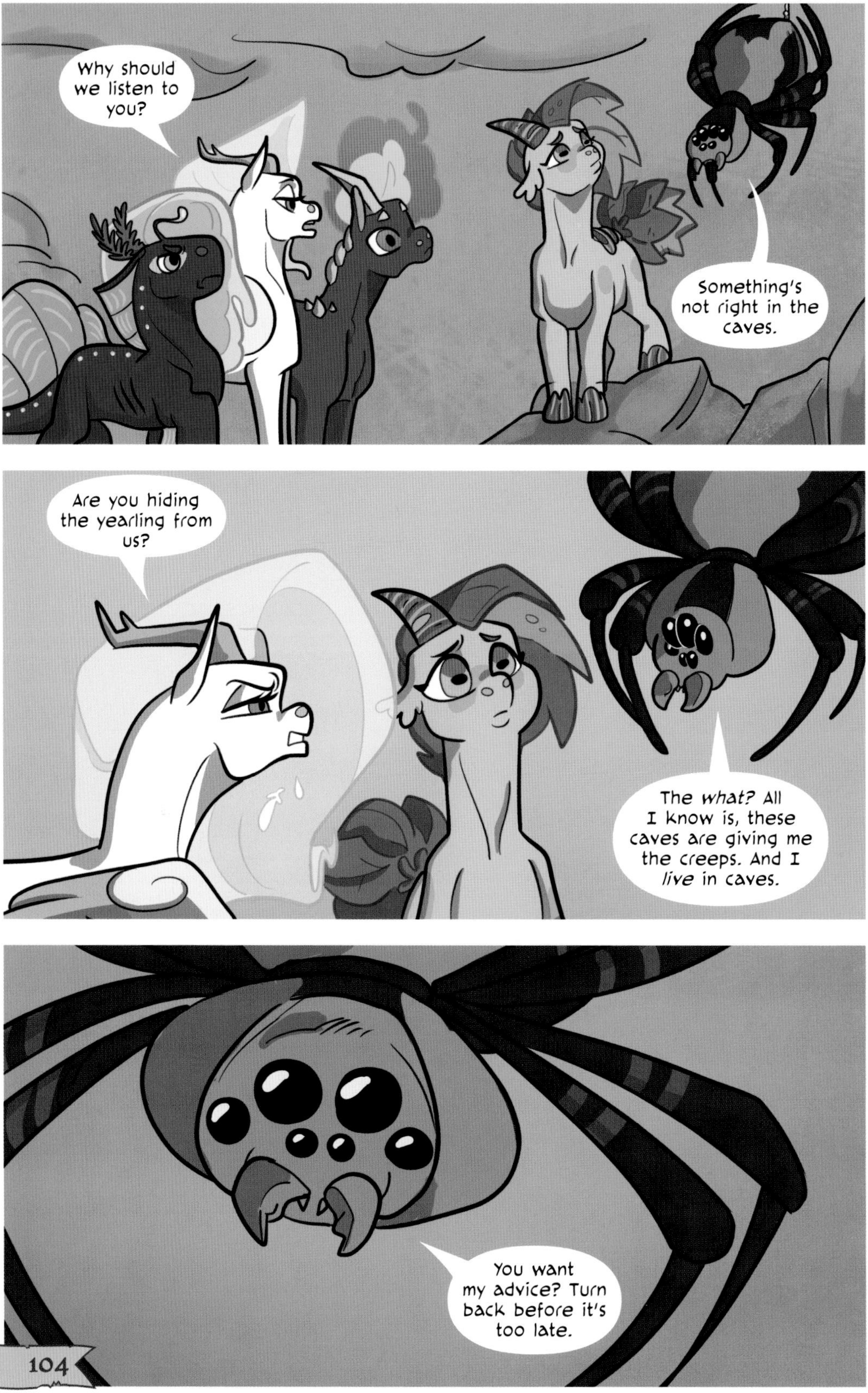
Why should we listen to you?
Something's not right in the caves.
Are you hiding the yearling from us?
The *what?* All I know is, these caves are giving me the creeps. And I *live* in caves.
You want my advice? Turn back before it's too late.

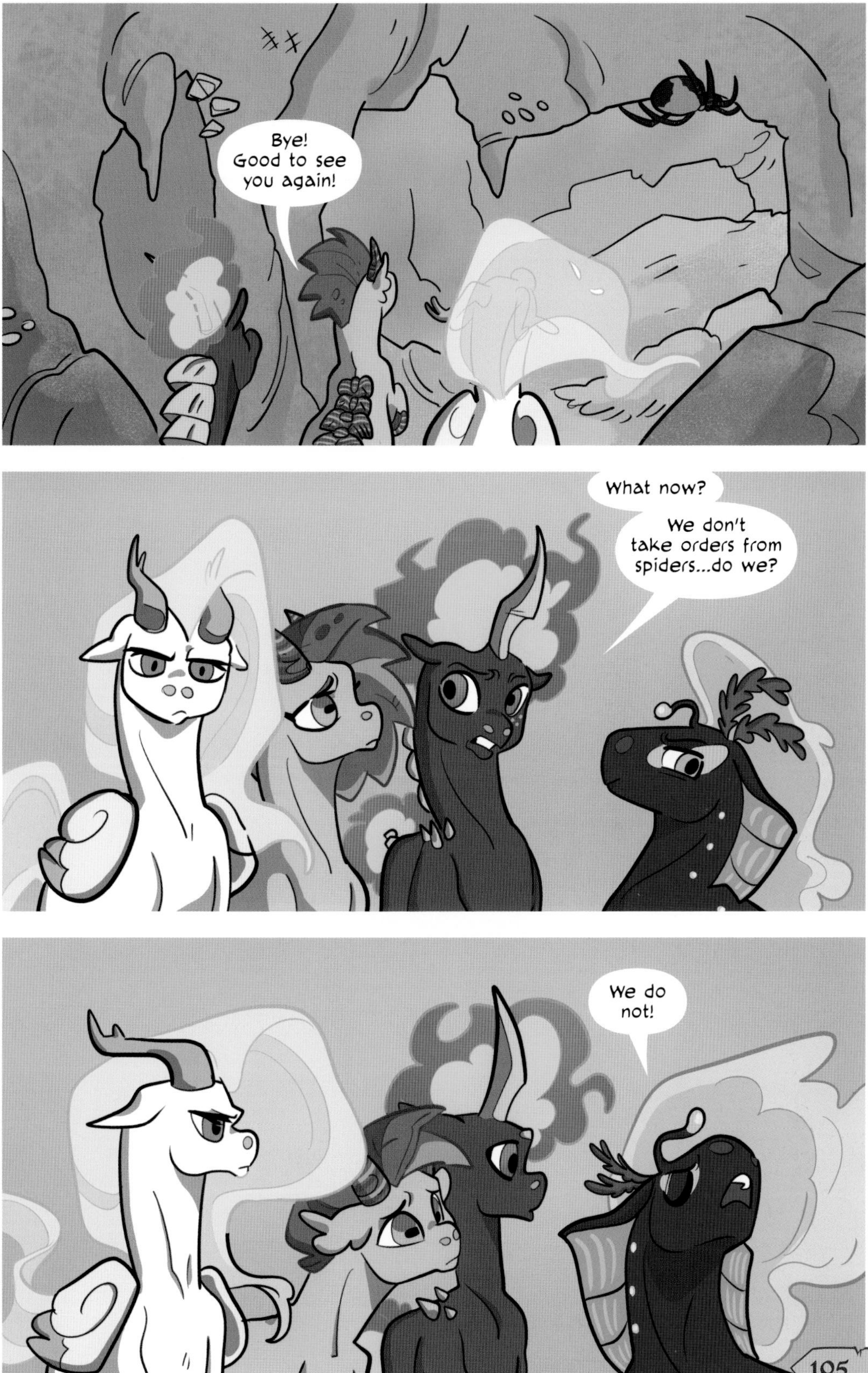
Bye! Good to see you again!
What now?
We don't take orders from spiders...do we?
We do not!

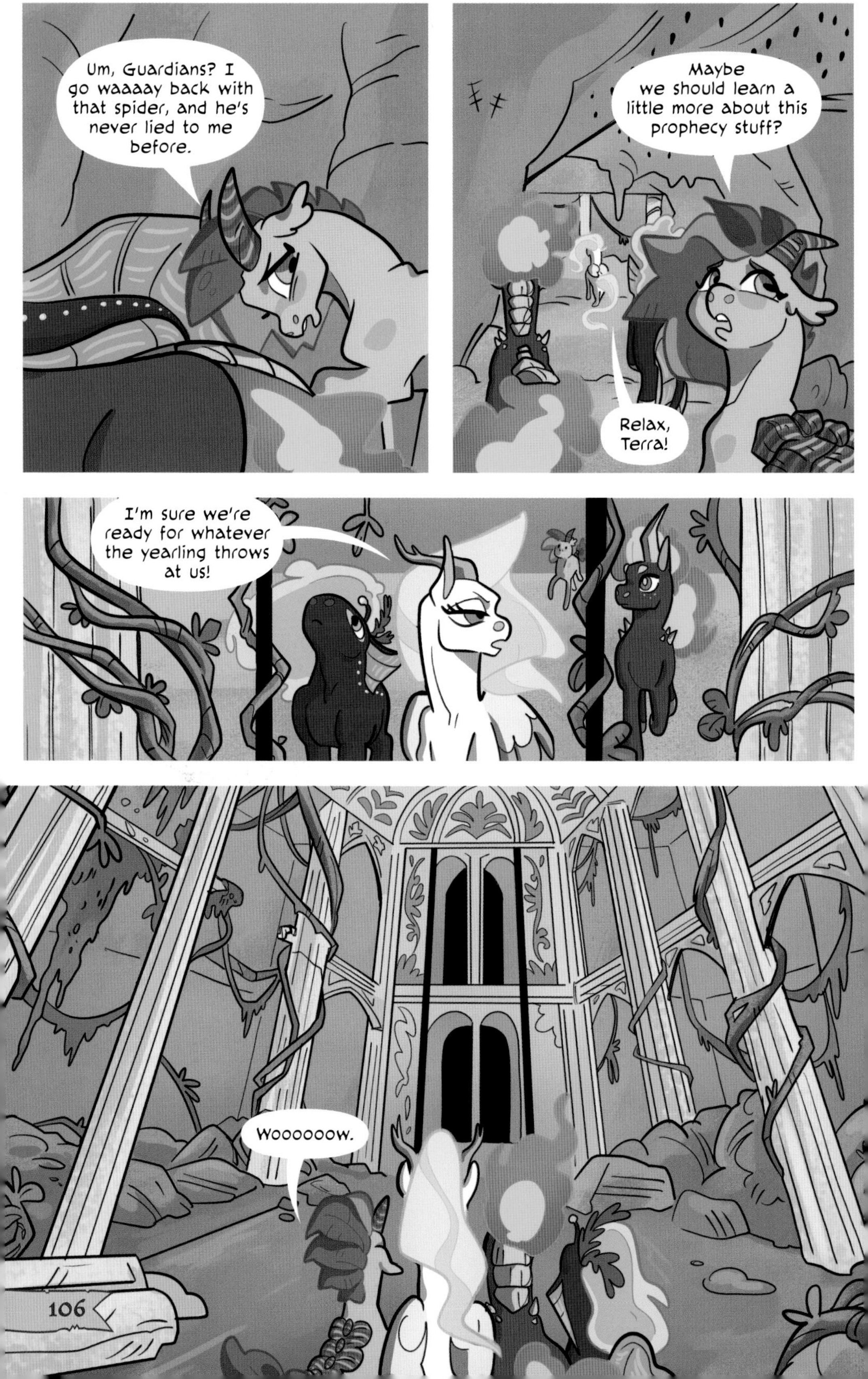
Um, Guardians? I go waaaay back with that spider, and he's never lied to me before.
Maybe we should learn a little more about this prophecy stuff?
Relax, Terra!
I'm sure we're ready for whatever the yearling throws at us!
Woooooow.

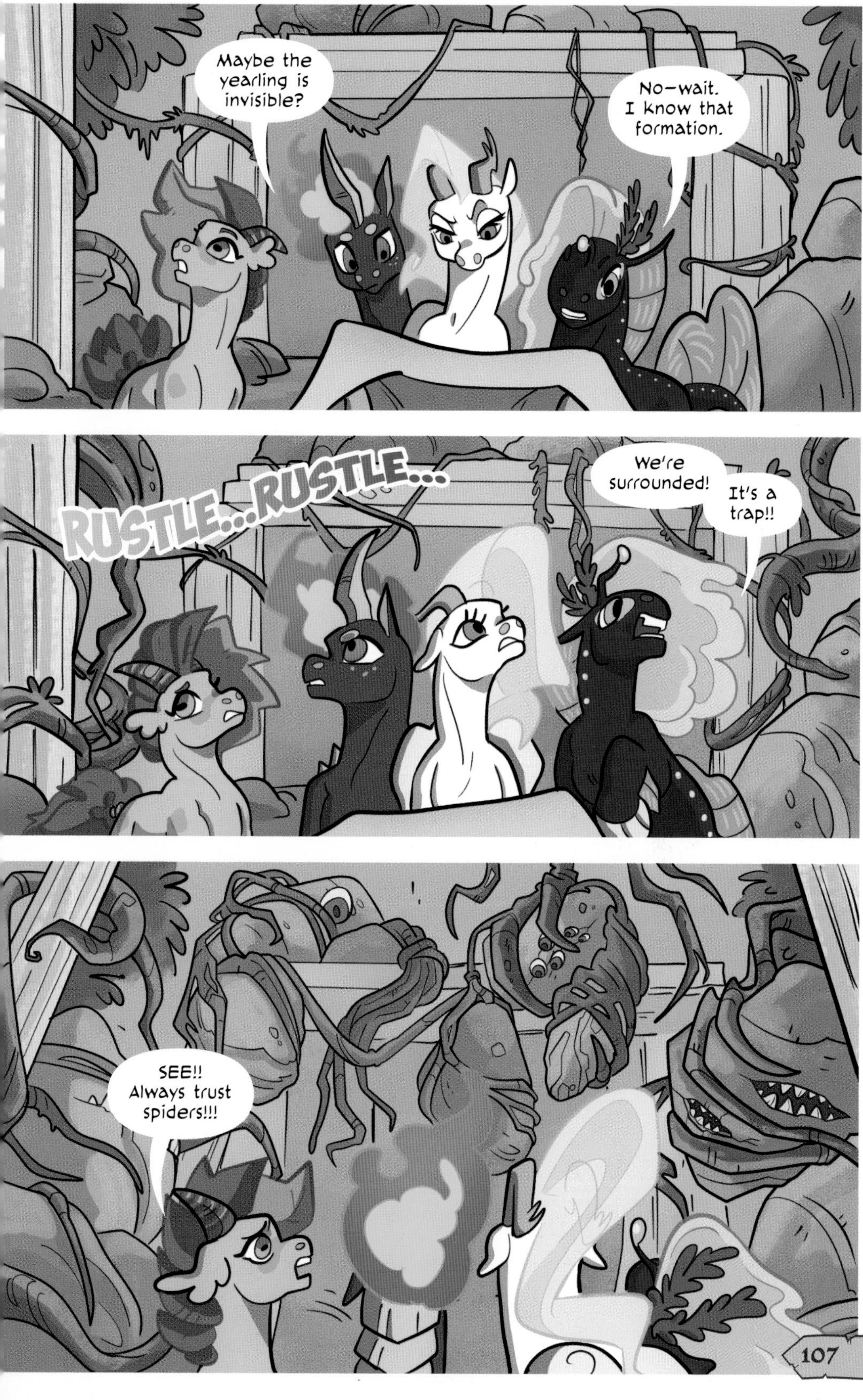

Maybe the yearling is invisible?
No—wait. I know that formation.
RUSTLE...RUSTLE...
We're surrounded!
It's a trap!!
SEE!! Always trust spiders!!!

Chapter 8

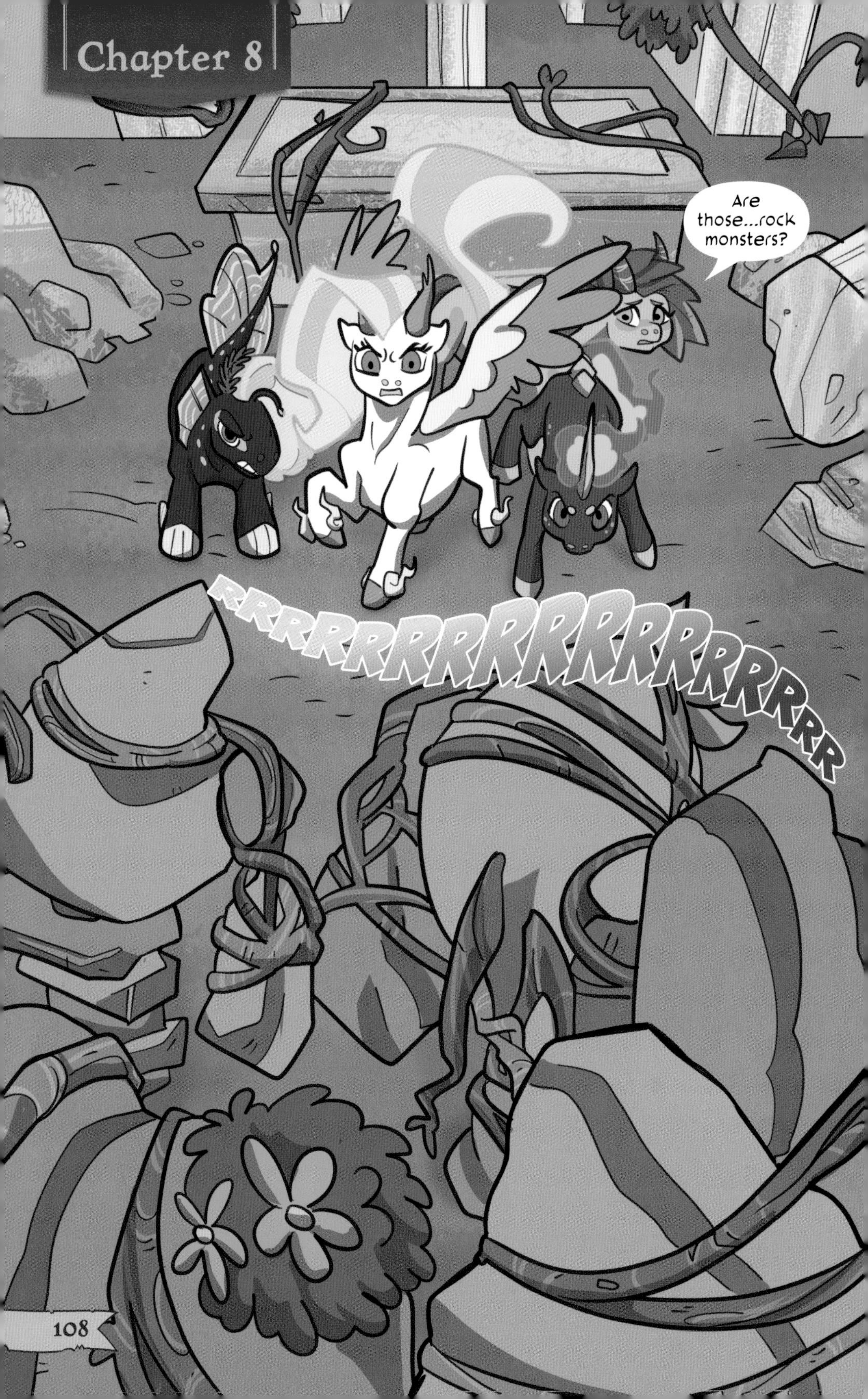
Are those...rock monsters?
RRRRRRRRRRRRRRRRR

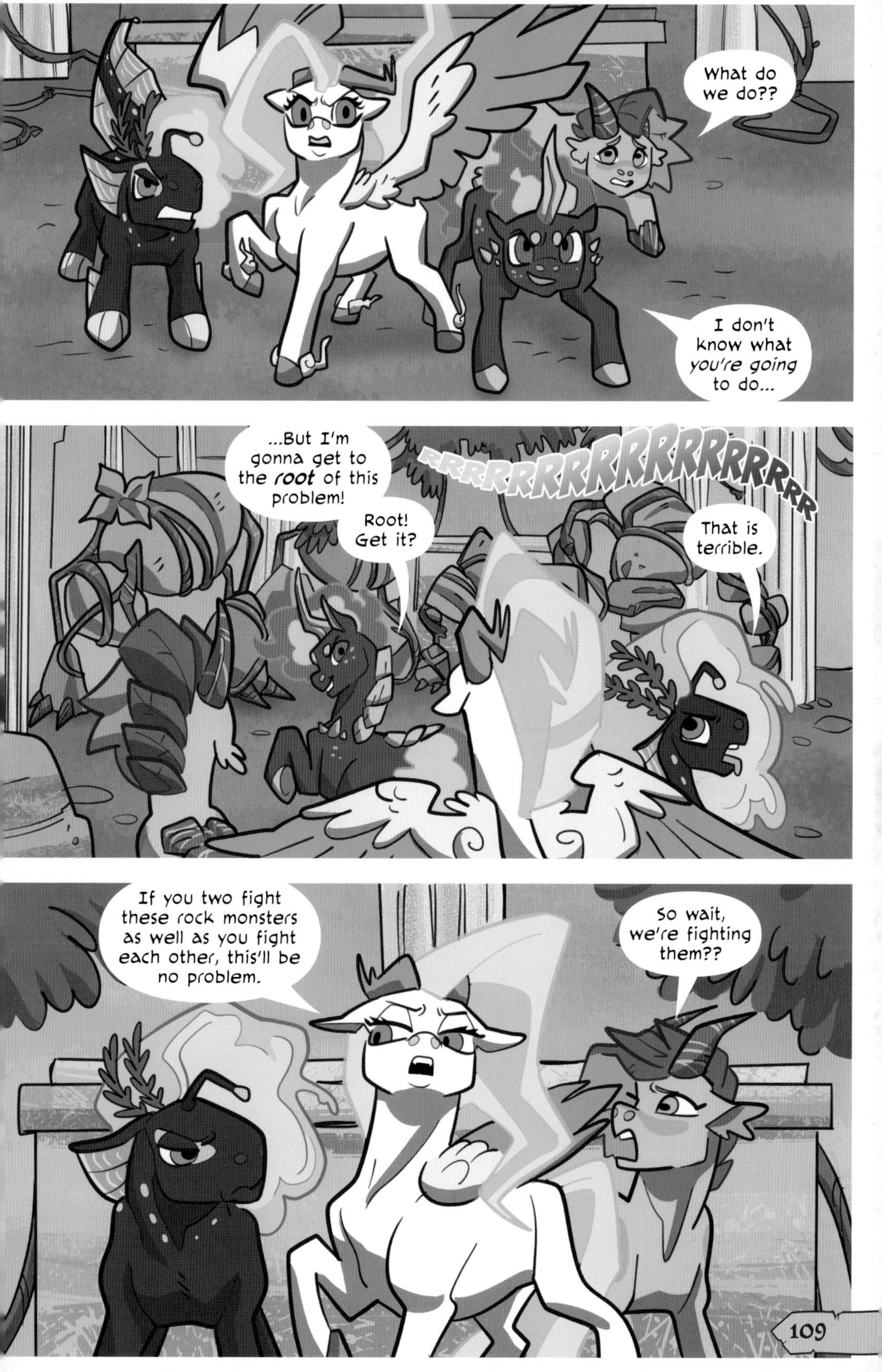
What do we do??
I don't know what *you're going* to do...
...But I'm gonna get to the *root* of this problem!
RRRRRRRRRRRRRRRRRRRR
Root! Get it?
That is terrible.
If you two fight these rock monsters as well as you fight each other, this'll be no problem.
So wait, we're fighting them??

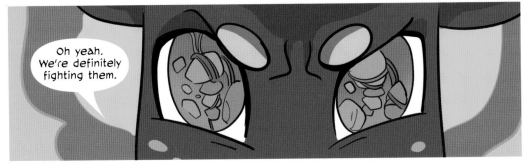

Oh yeah. We're definitely fighting them.

Hey, you big plant!

Try to catch something that's too hot to hold!

Missed me!

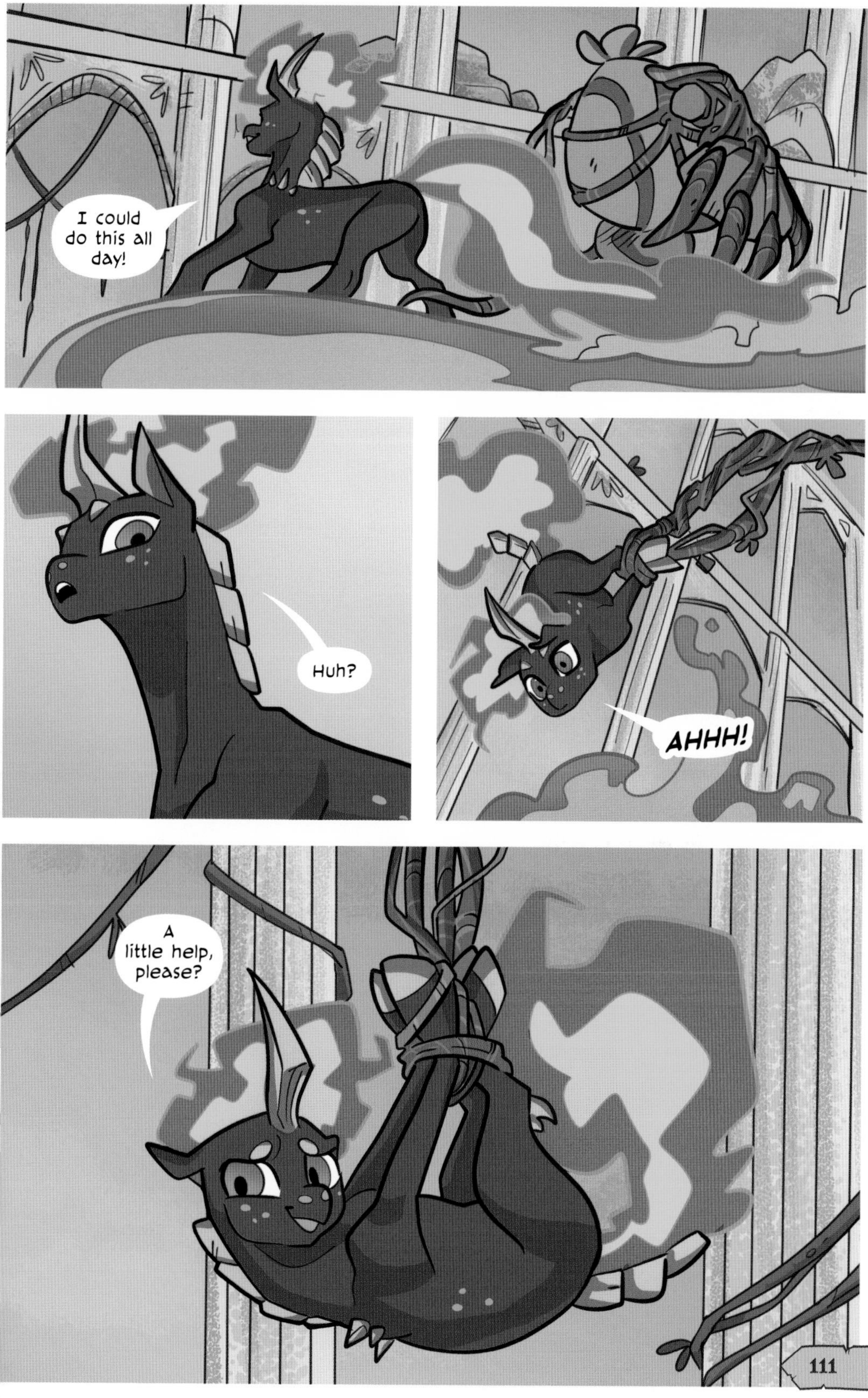
I could do this all day!
Huh?
AHHH!
A little help, please?

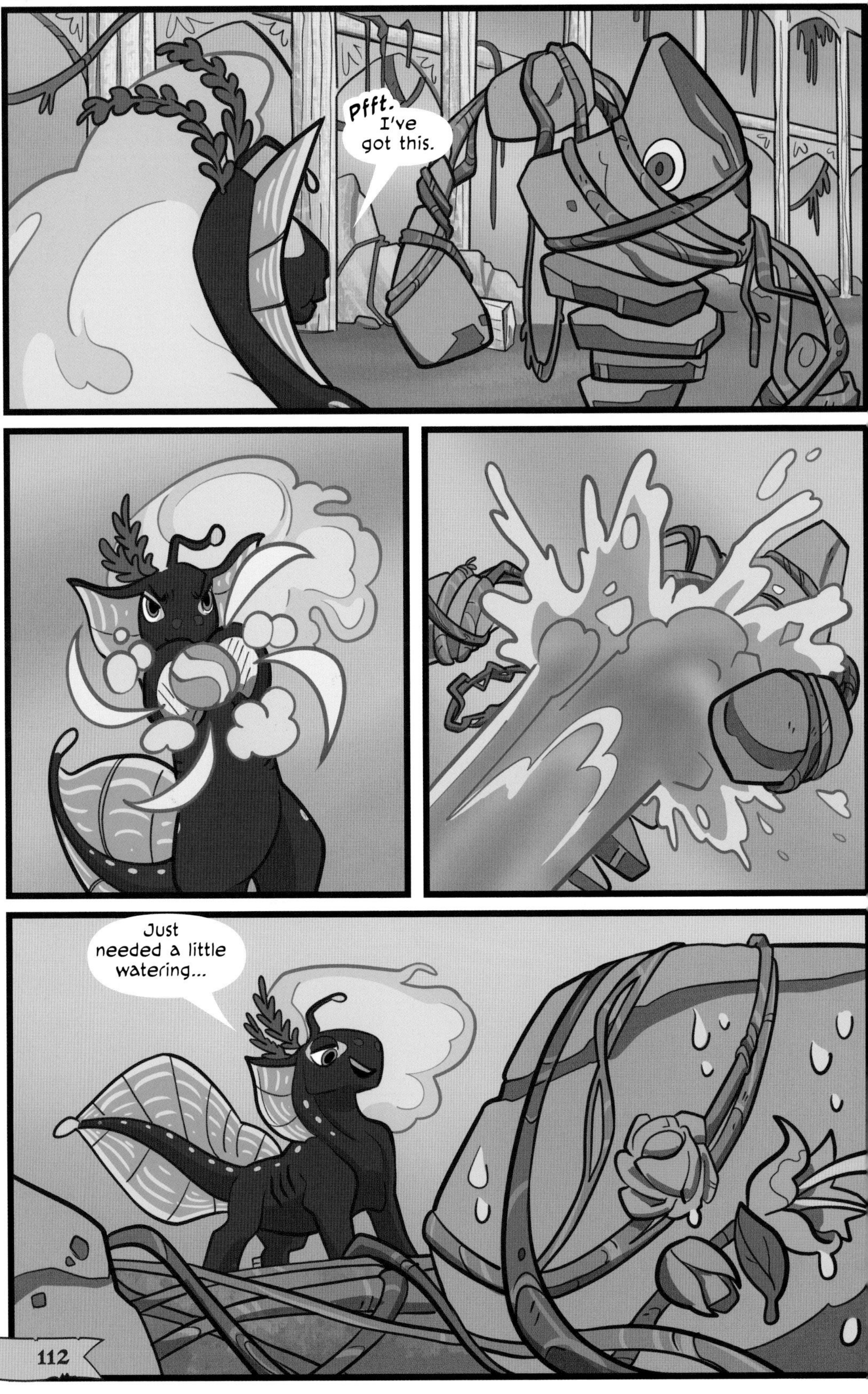
Pfft. I've got this.
Just needed a little watering...

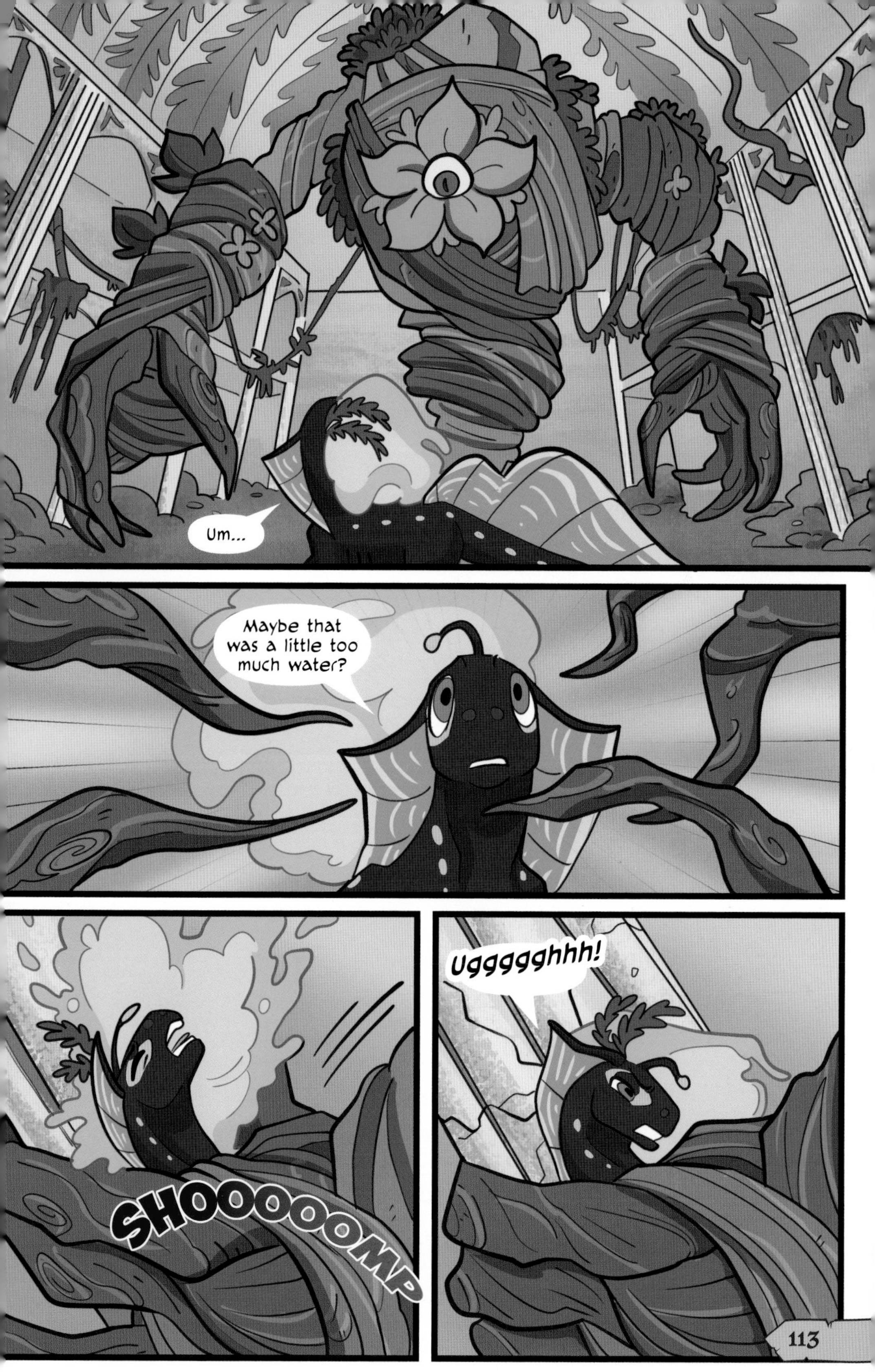
Um...
Maybe that was a little too much water?
SHOOOOOOMP
Uggggghhh!

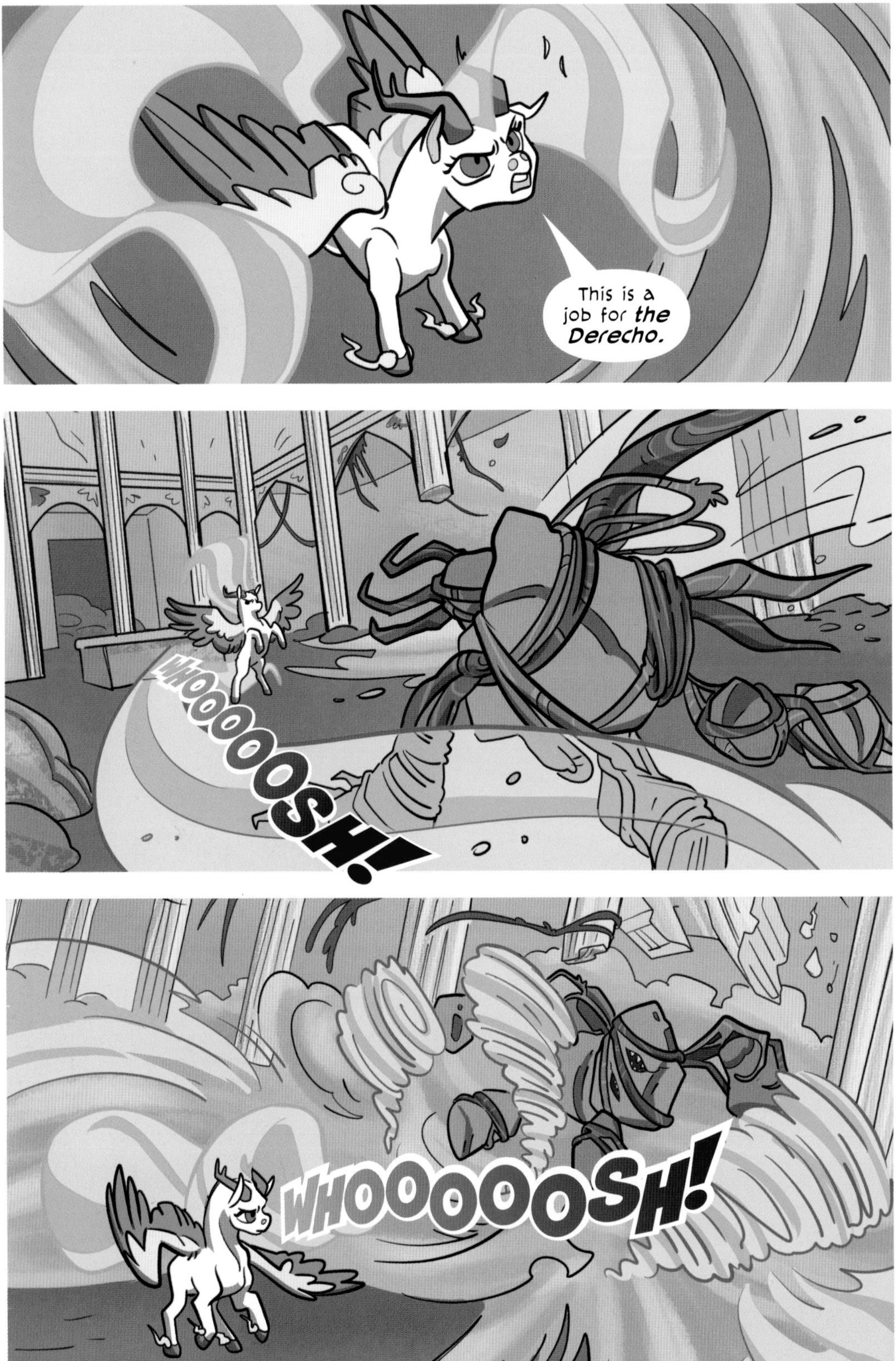
This is a job for the Derecho.
WHOOOOOSH!
WHOOOOOOOSH!

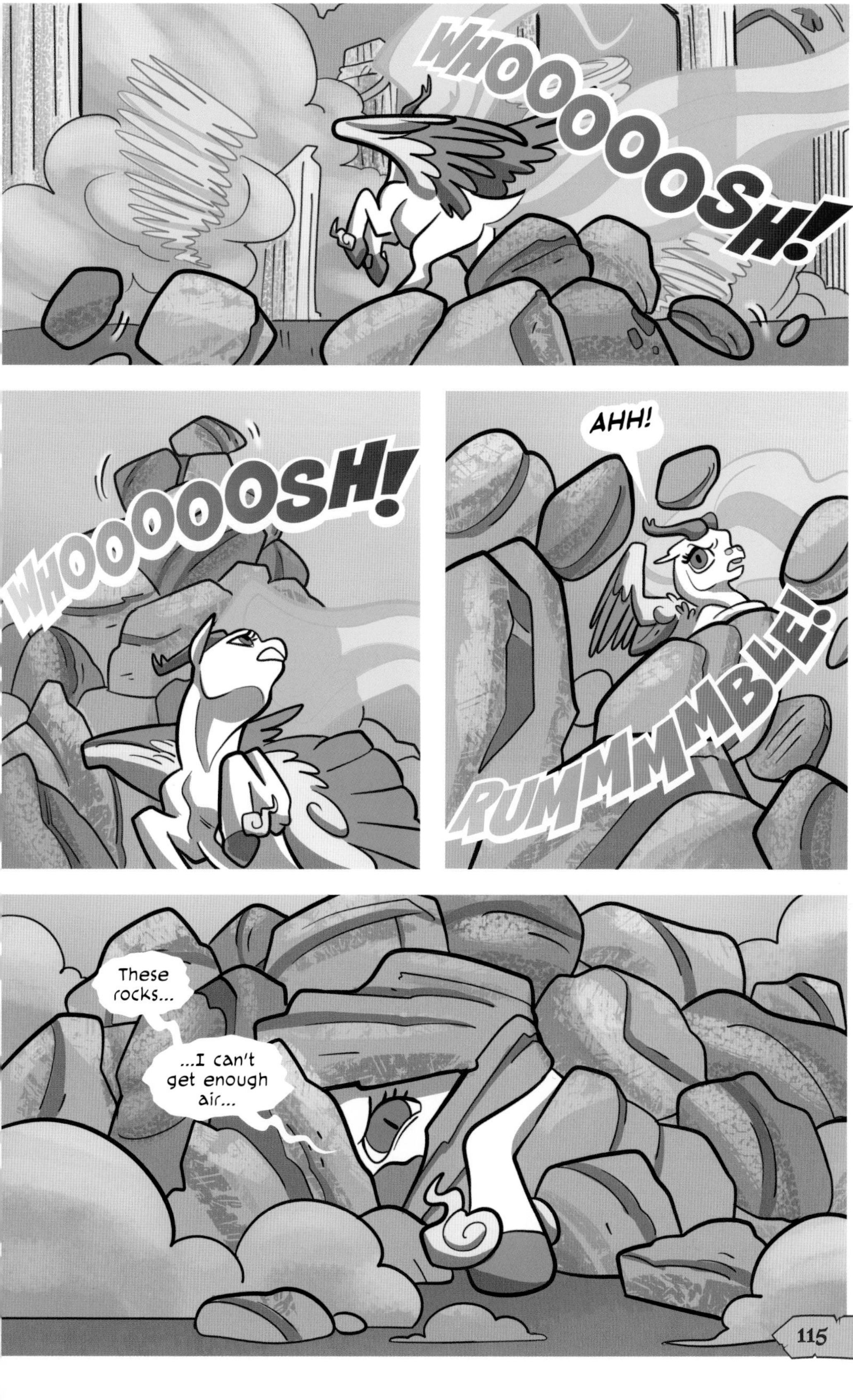
WHOOOOOOSH!
WHOOOOOOSH!
AHH!
RUMMMMBLE!
These rocks...
...I can't get enough air...

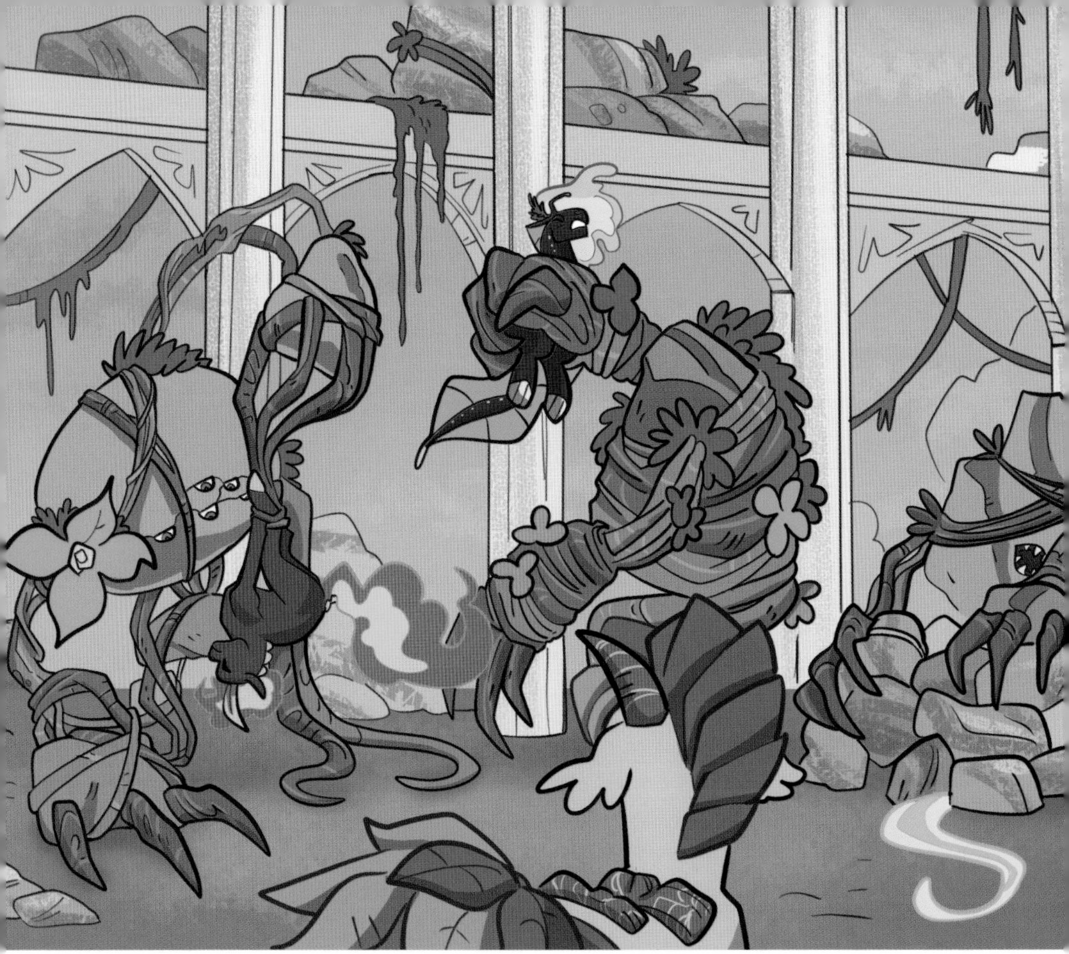

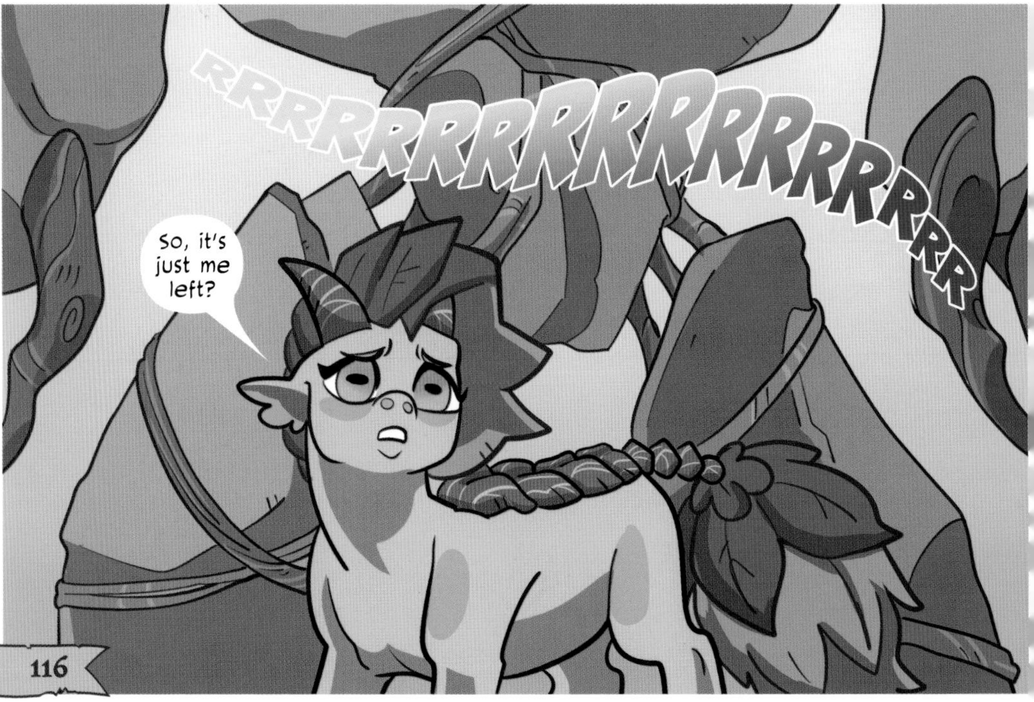
RRRRRRRRRRRRRRRRR
So, it's just me left?

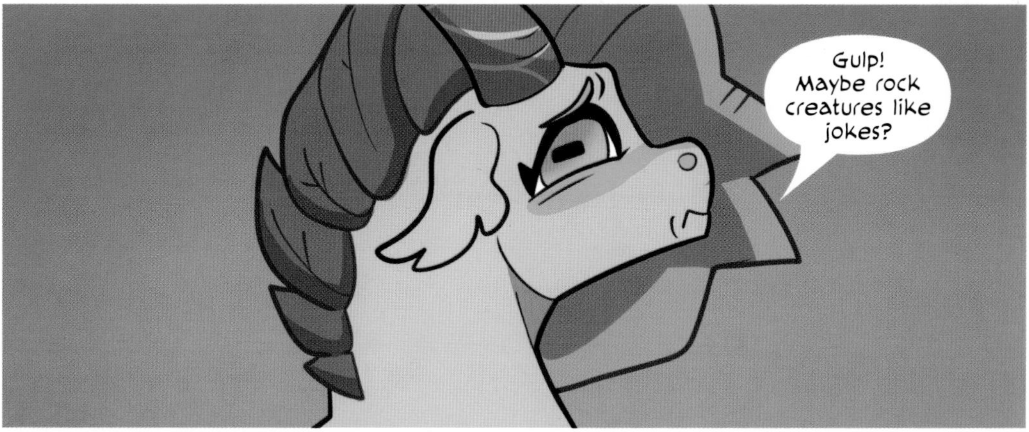
Gulp! Maybe rock creatures like jokes?

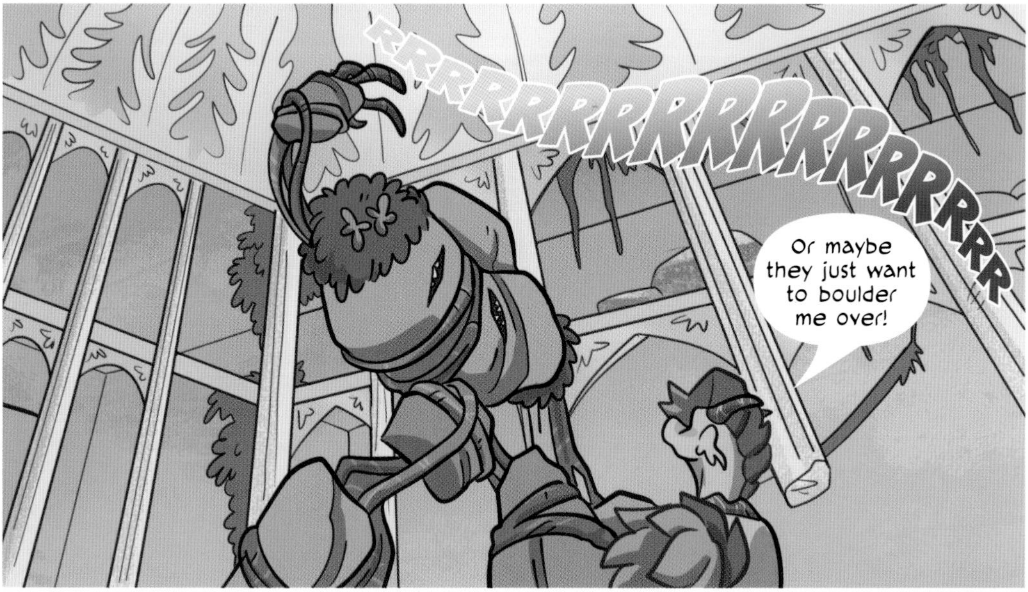
RRRRRRRRRRRRRRRRRRRRRR
Or maybe they just want to boulder me over!

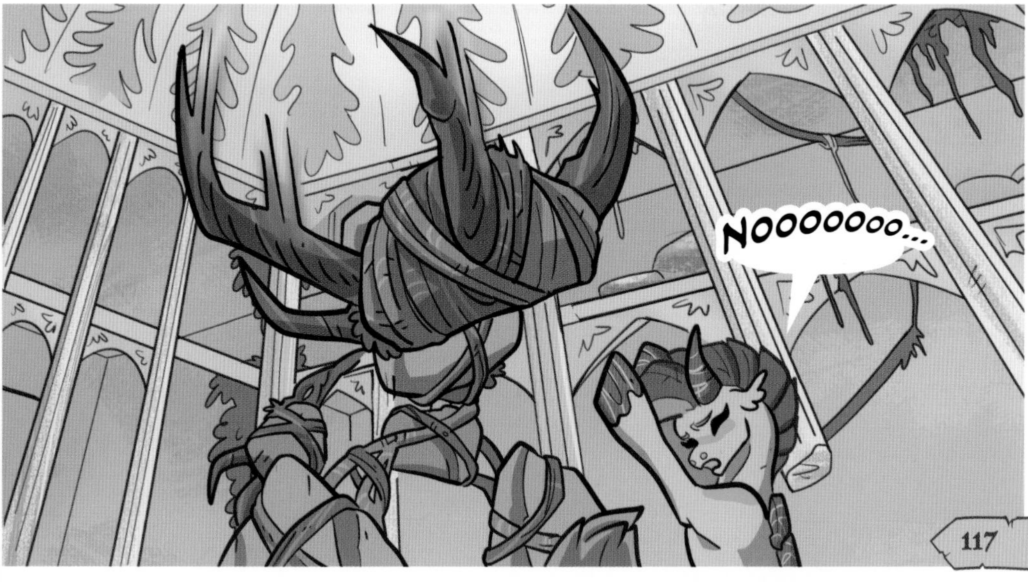
NOOOOOOO...

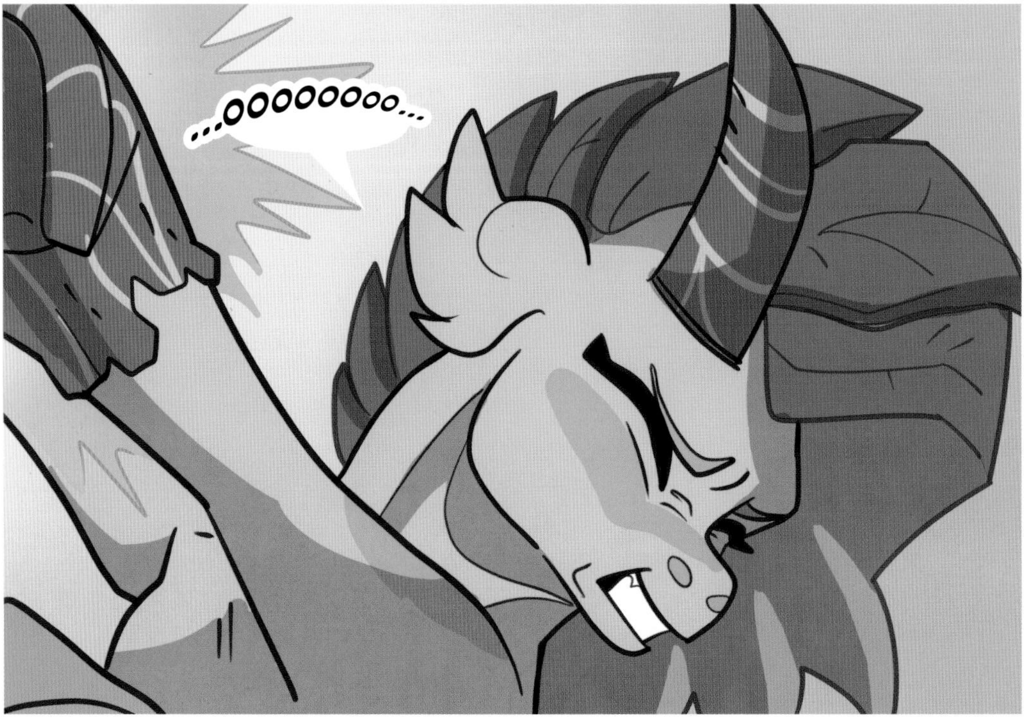
...OOOOOOoo...

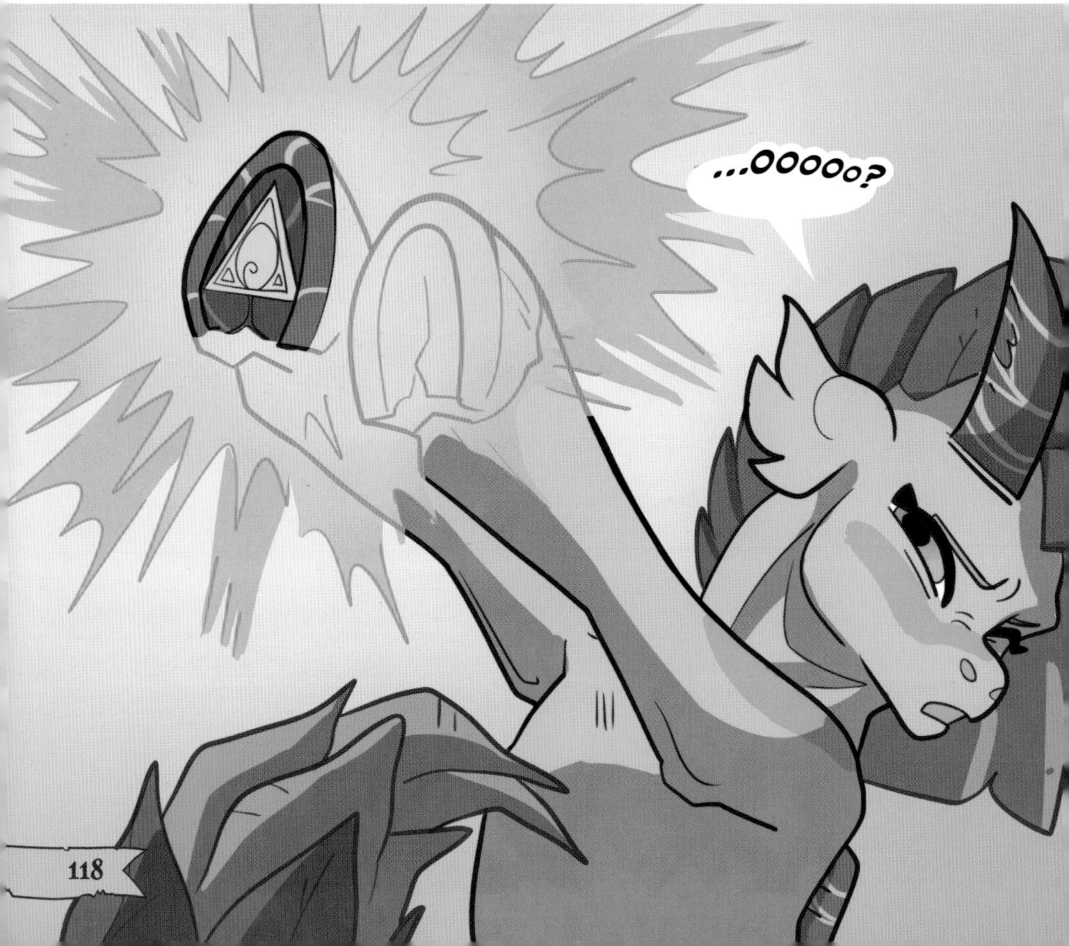
...OOOOo?

Chapter 9

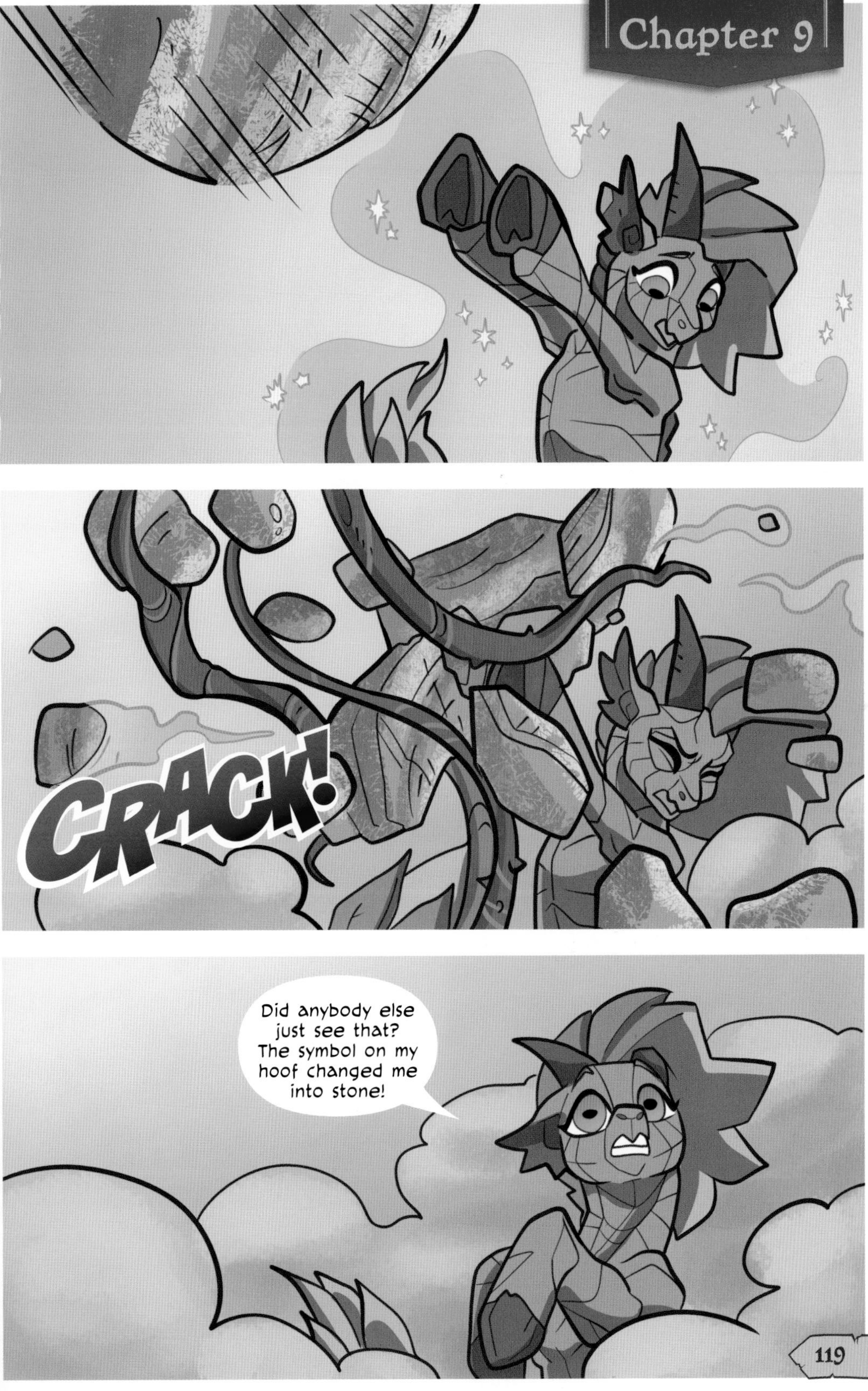
CRACK!
Did anybody else just see that? The symbol on my hoof changed me into stone!

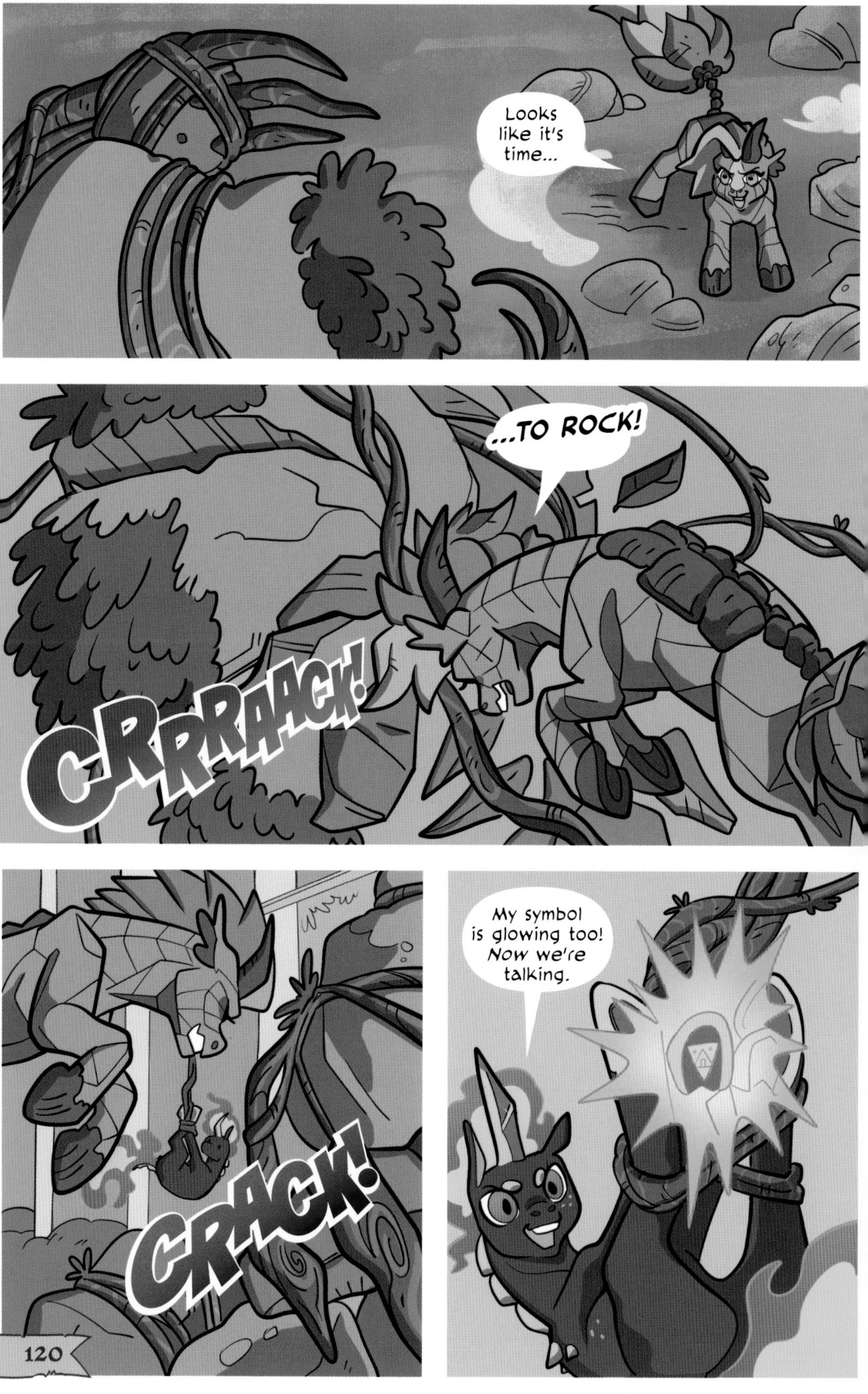
Looks like it's time...
...TO ROCK!
CRRRAACK!
CRACK!
My symbol is glowing too! *Now* we're talking.

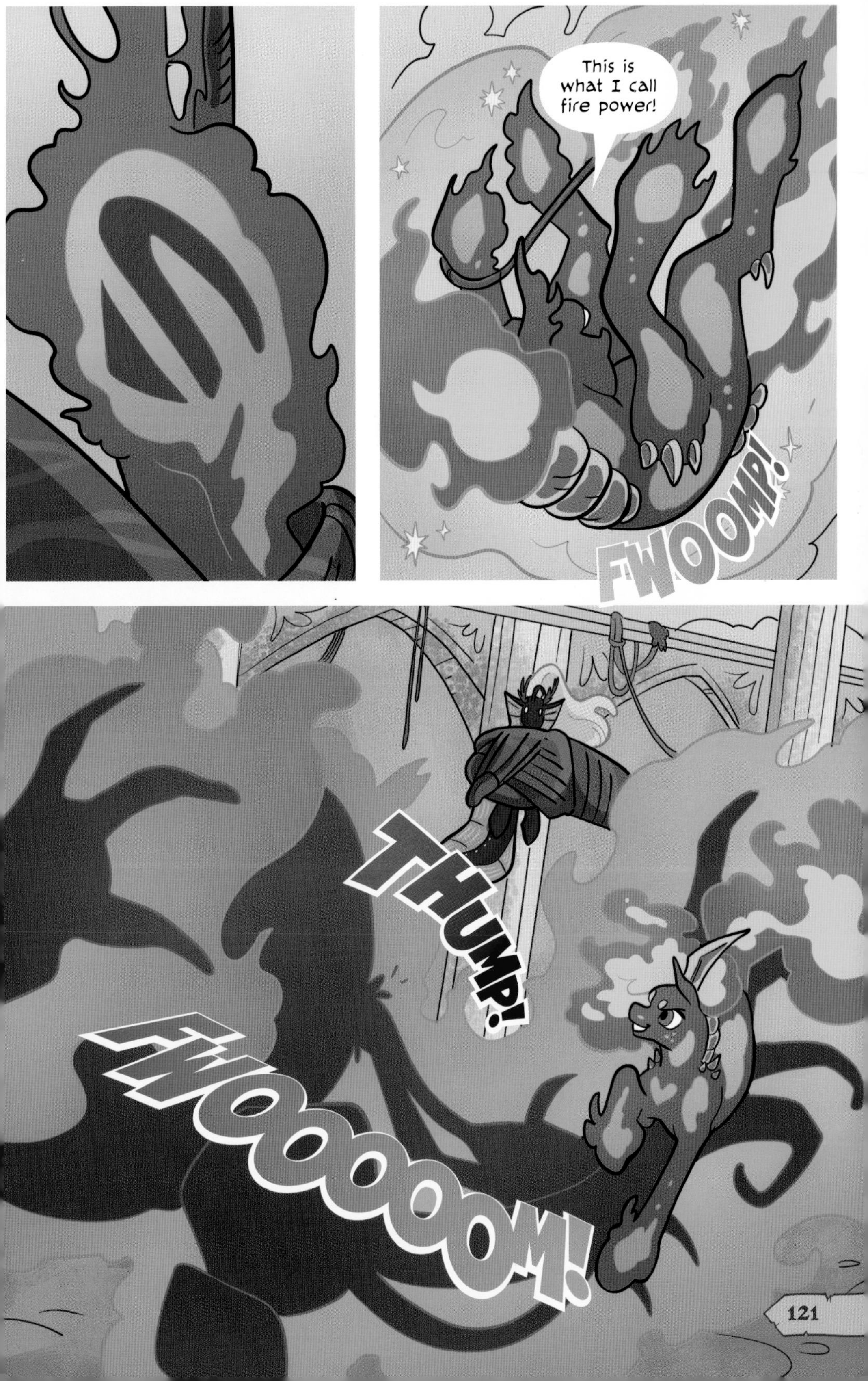

This is what I call fire power!
FWOOMP!
THUMP!
FWOOOOOM!

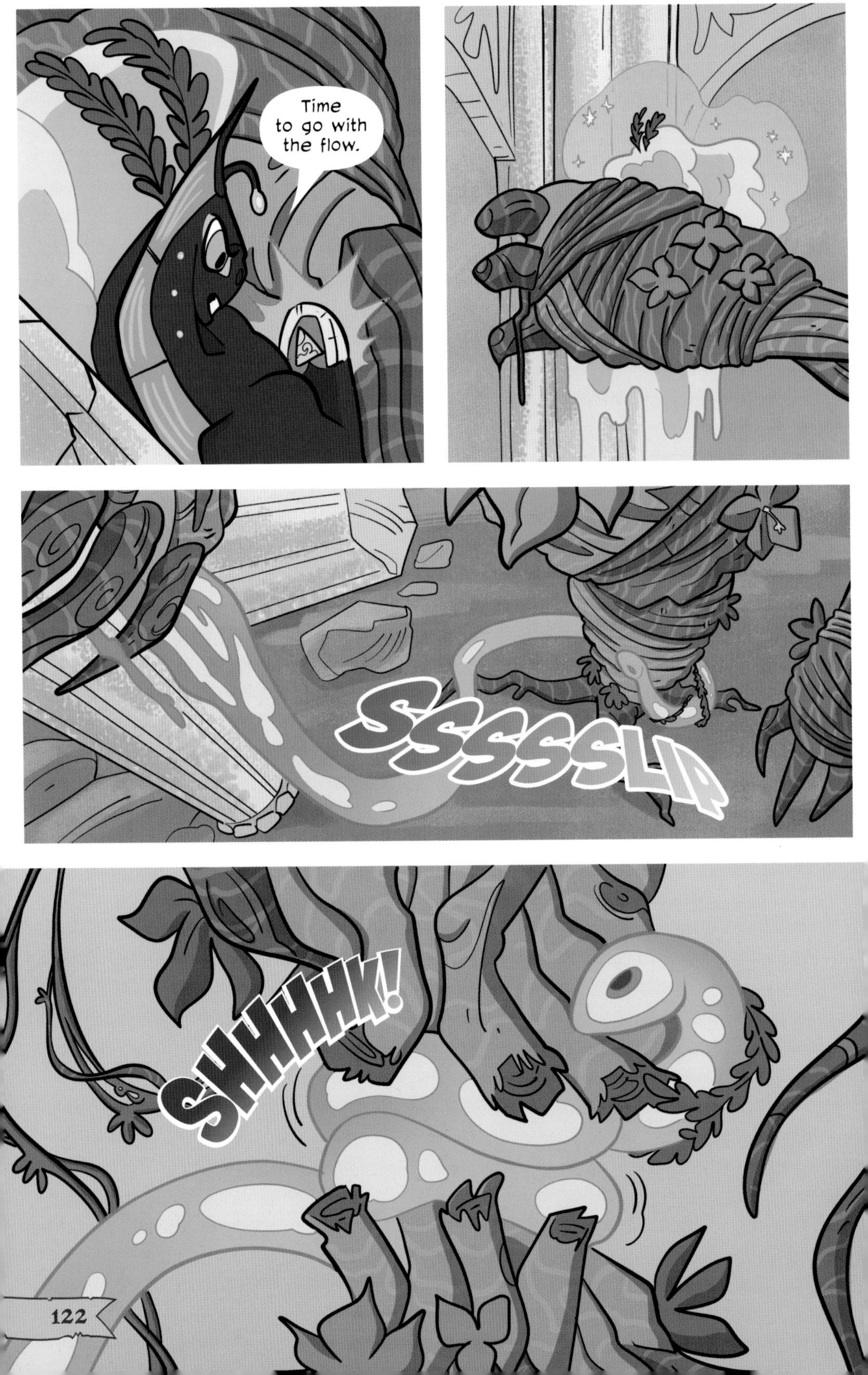
Time to go with the flow.
SSSSSLIP
SHHHHK!

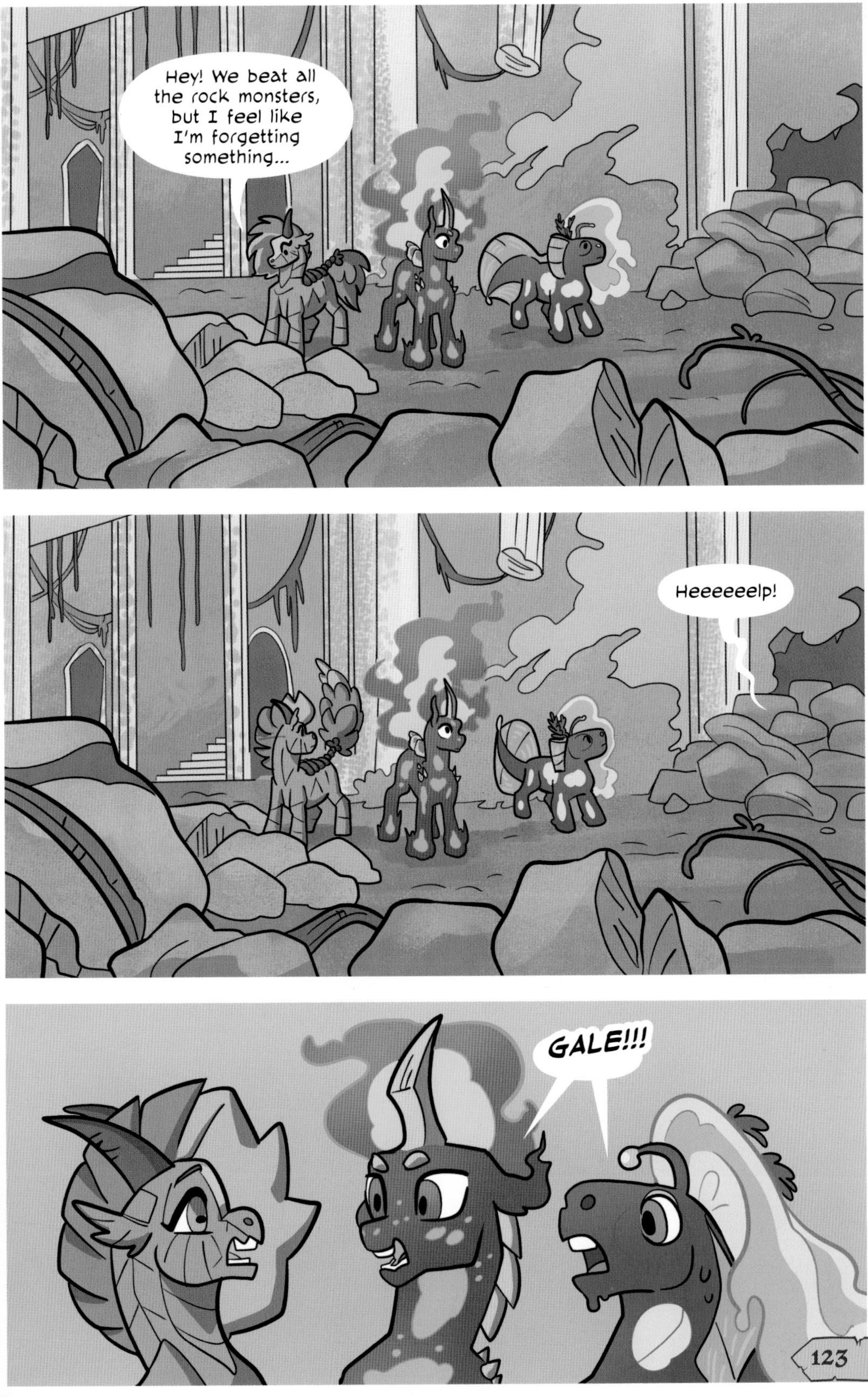
Hey! We beat all the rock monsters, but I feel like I'm forgetting something...
Heeeeeelp!
GALE!!!

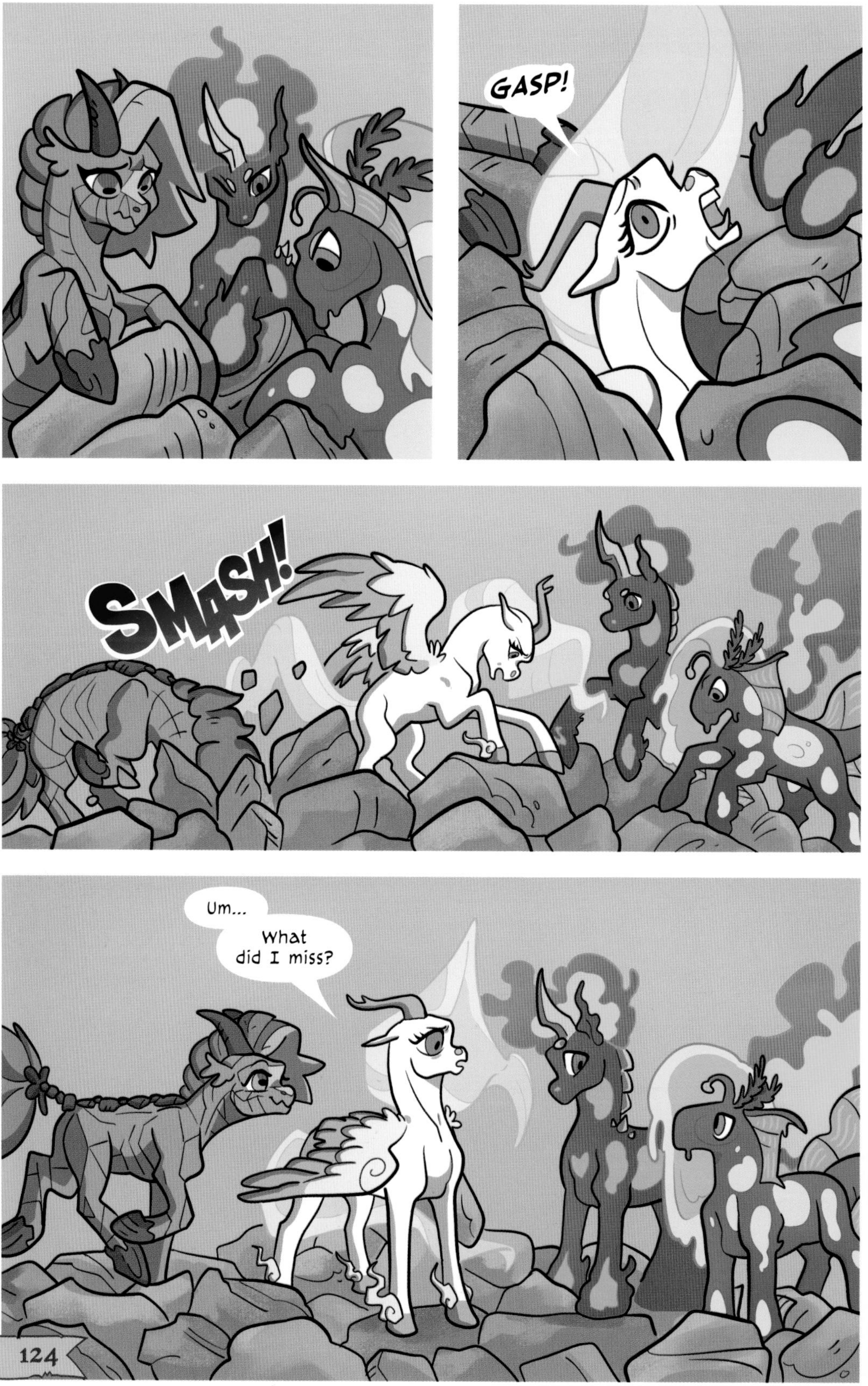
GASP!
SMASH!
Um...
What did I miss?

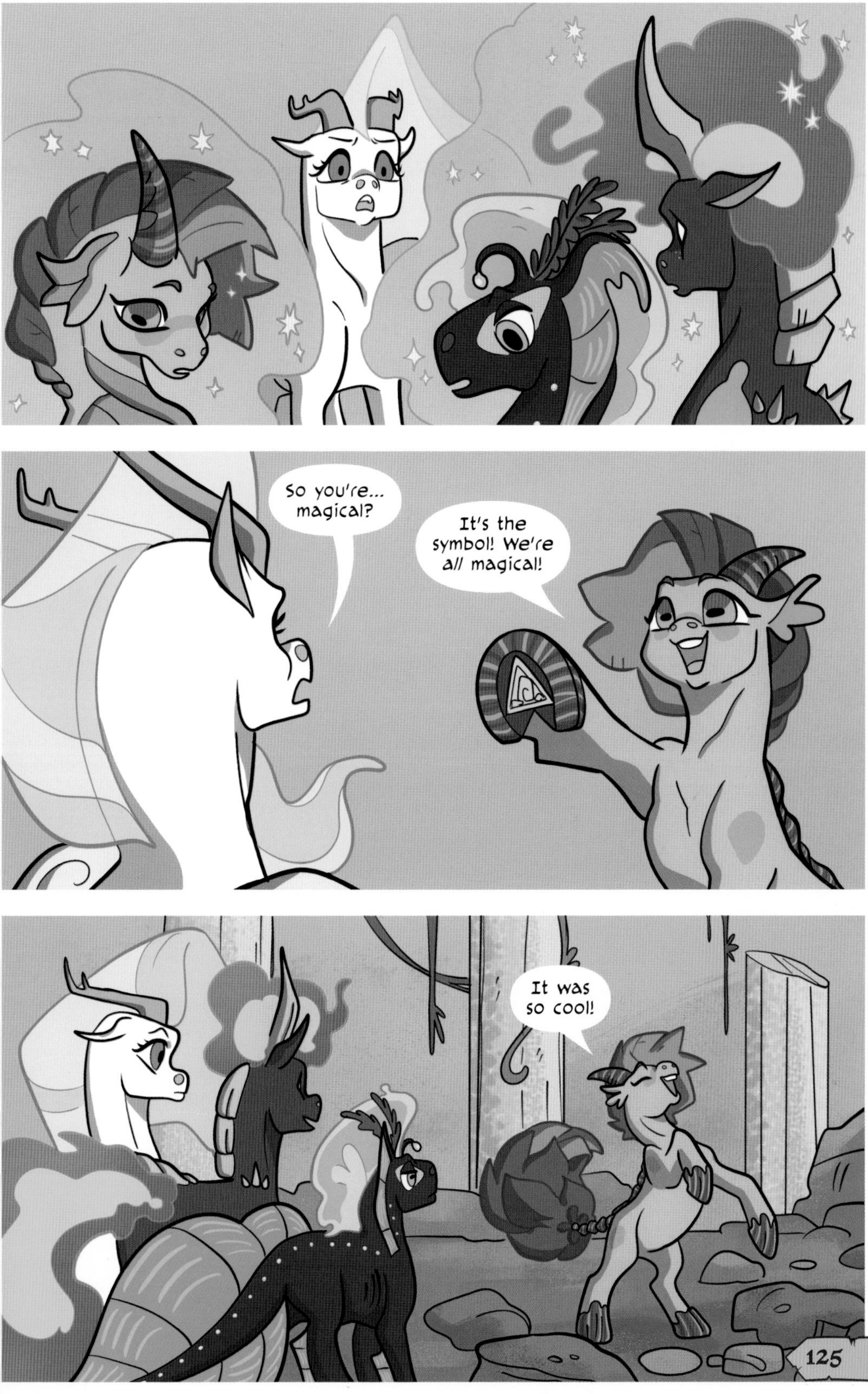
So you're...
magical?
It's the
symbol! We're
all magical!
It was
so cool!

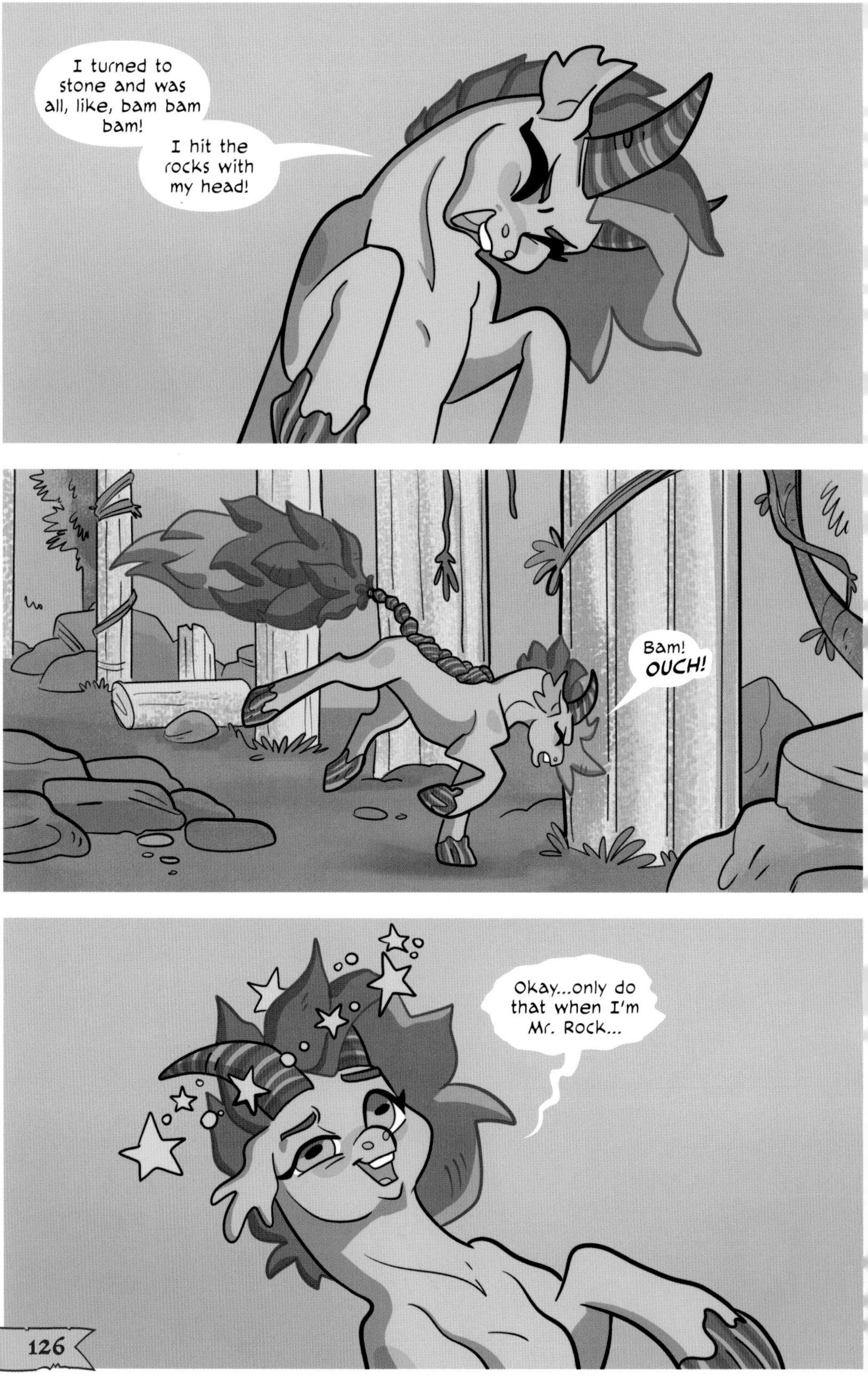
I turned to stone and was all, like, bam bam bam!
I hit the rocks with my head!
Bam! OUCH!
Okay...only do that when I'm Mr. Rock...

I turned into flames! Actual flames!

And Stillwater was a real drip!

I didn't drip. I was a flood!!!

But, Gale—you didn't change?

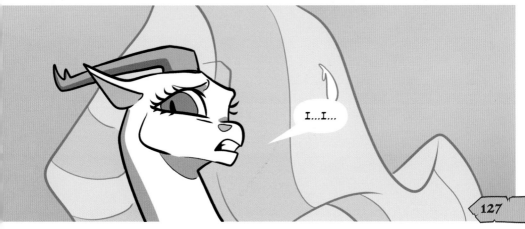

I...I...

127

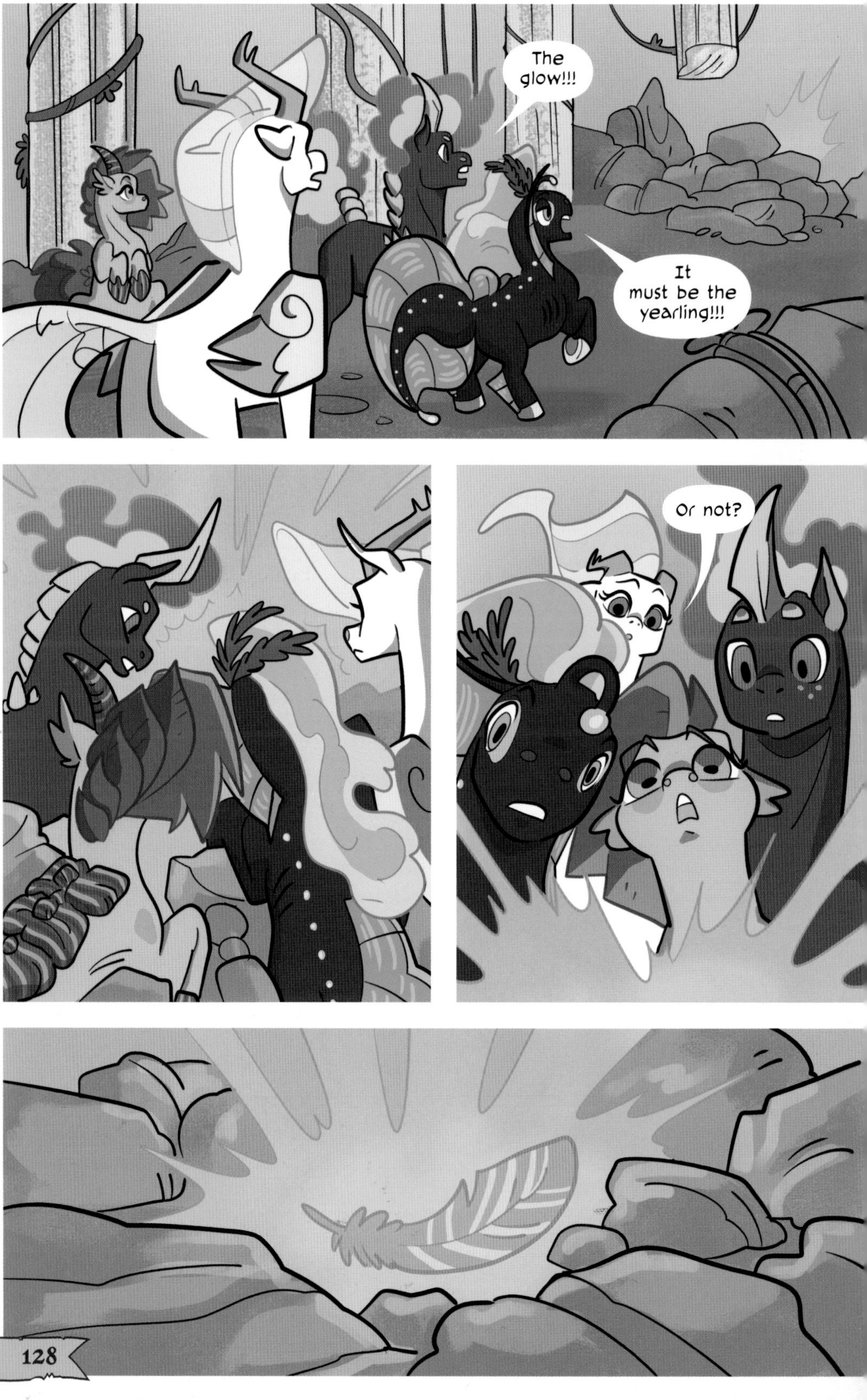
The glow!!!
It must be the yearling!!!
Or not?

Chapter 10

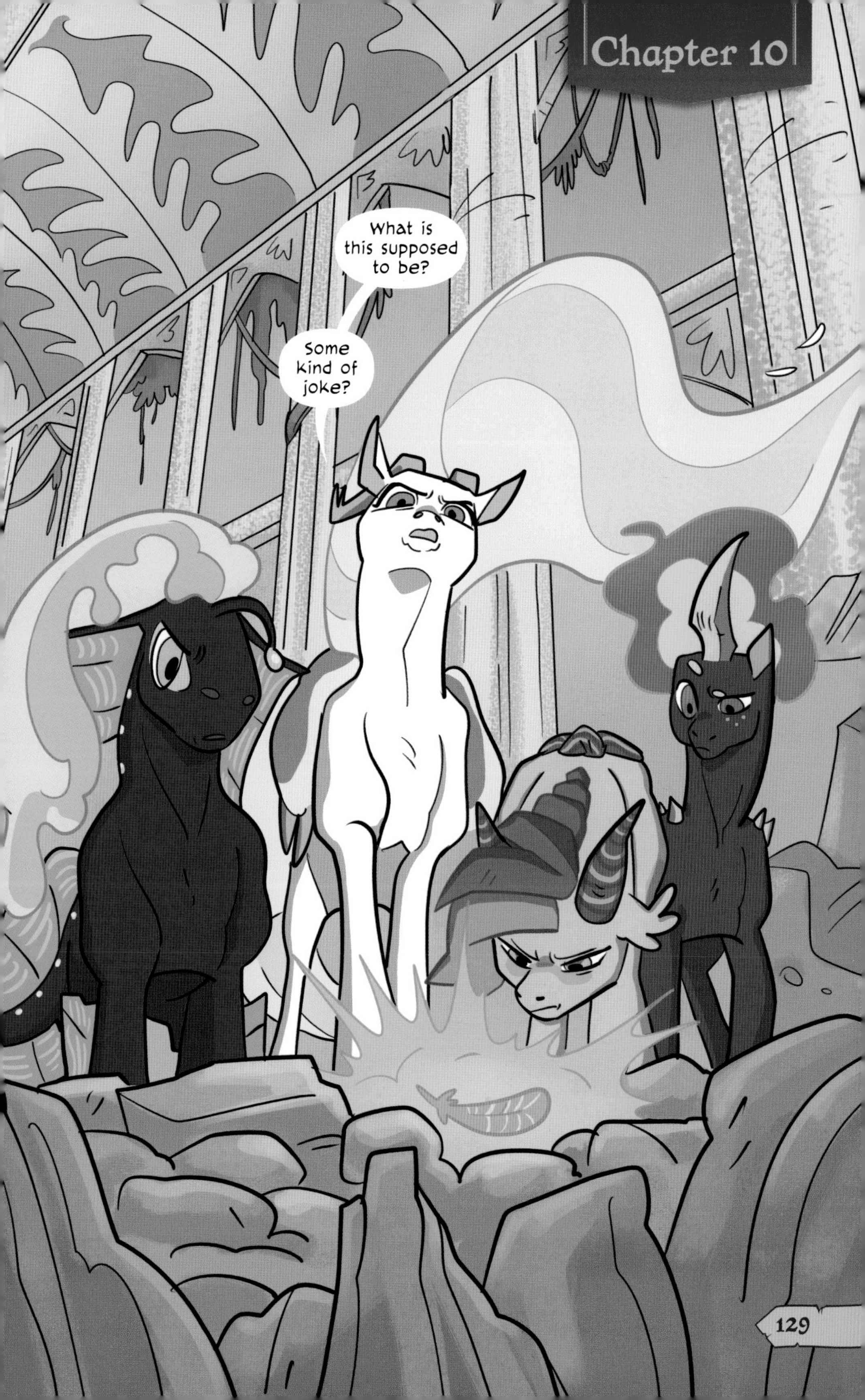

What is this supposed to be?
Some kind of joke?

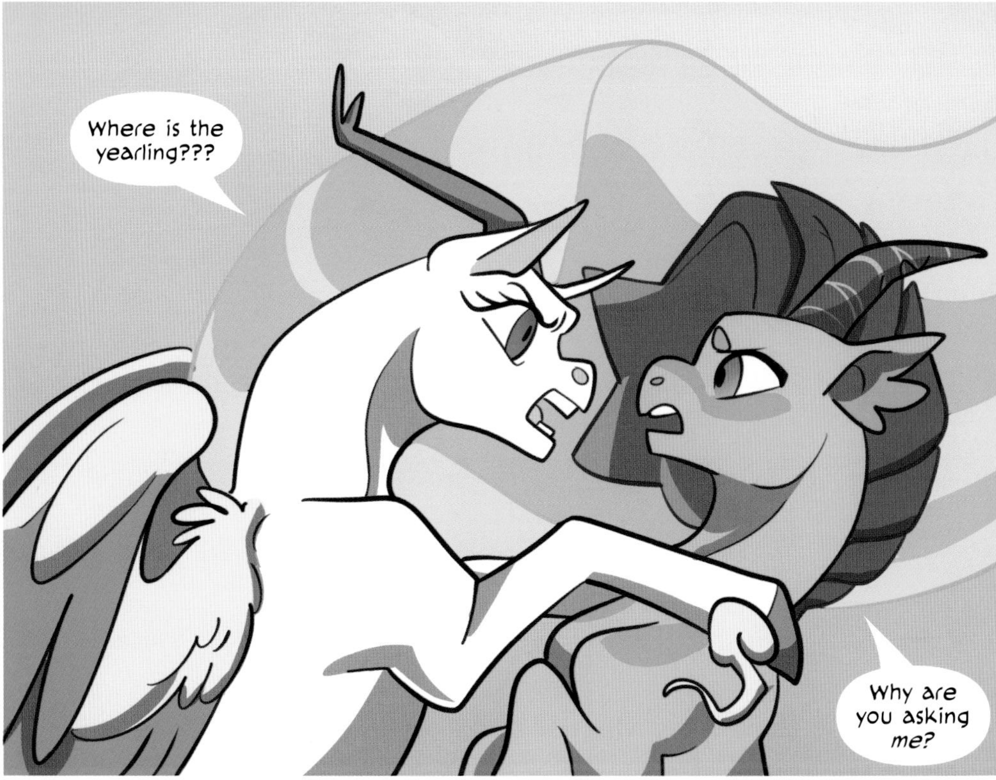
Where is the yearling???
Why are you asking *me?*

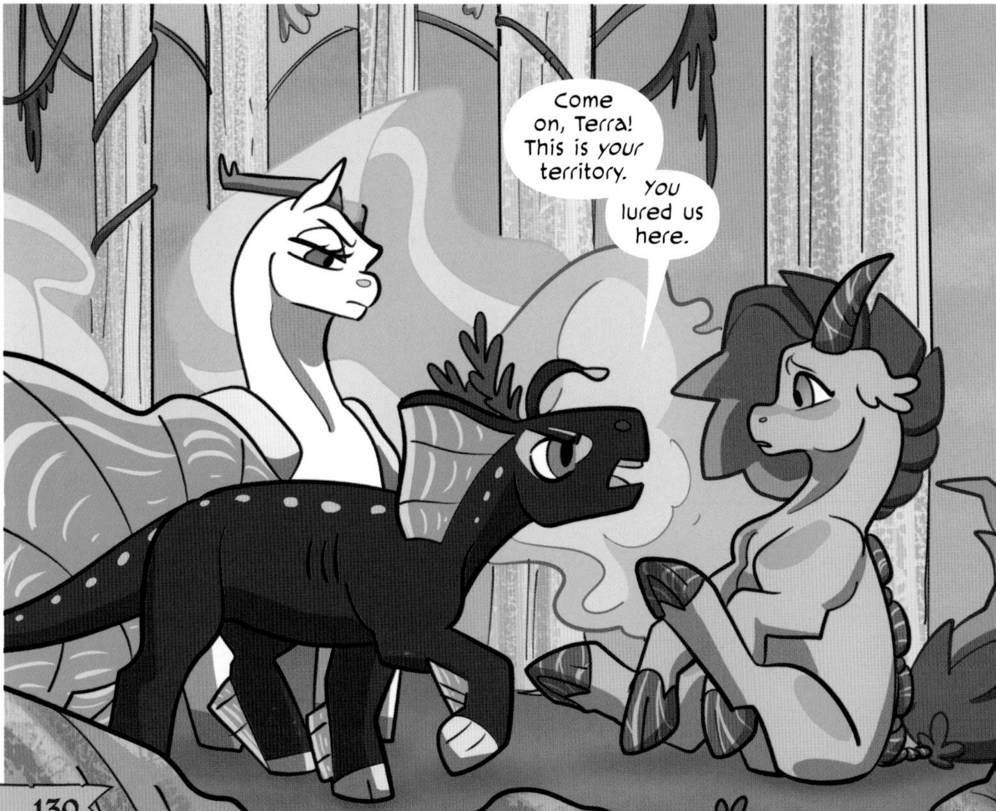
Come on, Terra! This is *your* territory.
You lured us here.

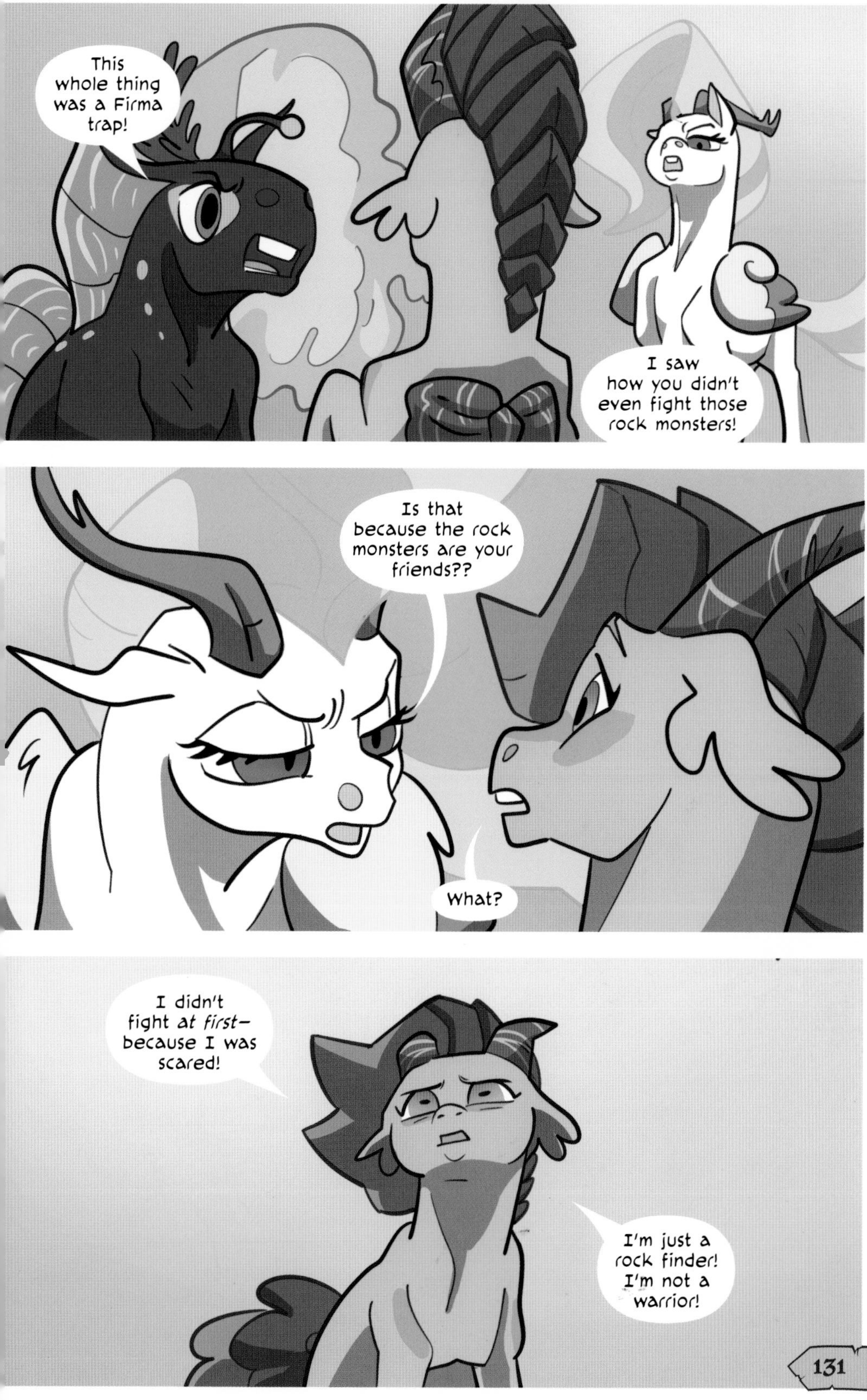
This whole thing was a Firma trap!
I saw how you didn't even fight those rock monsters!
Is that because the rock monsters are your friends??
What?
I didn't fight at *first*—because I was scared!
I'm just a rock finder! I'm not a warrior!

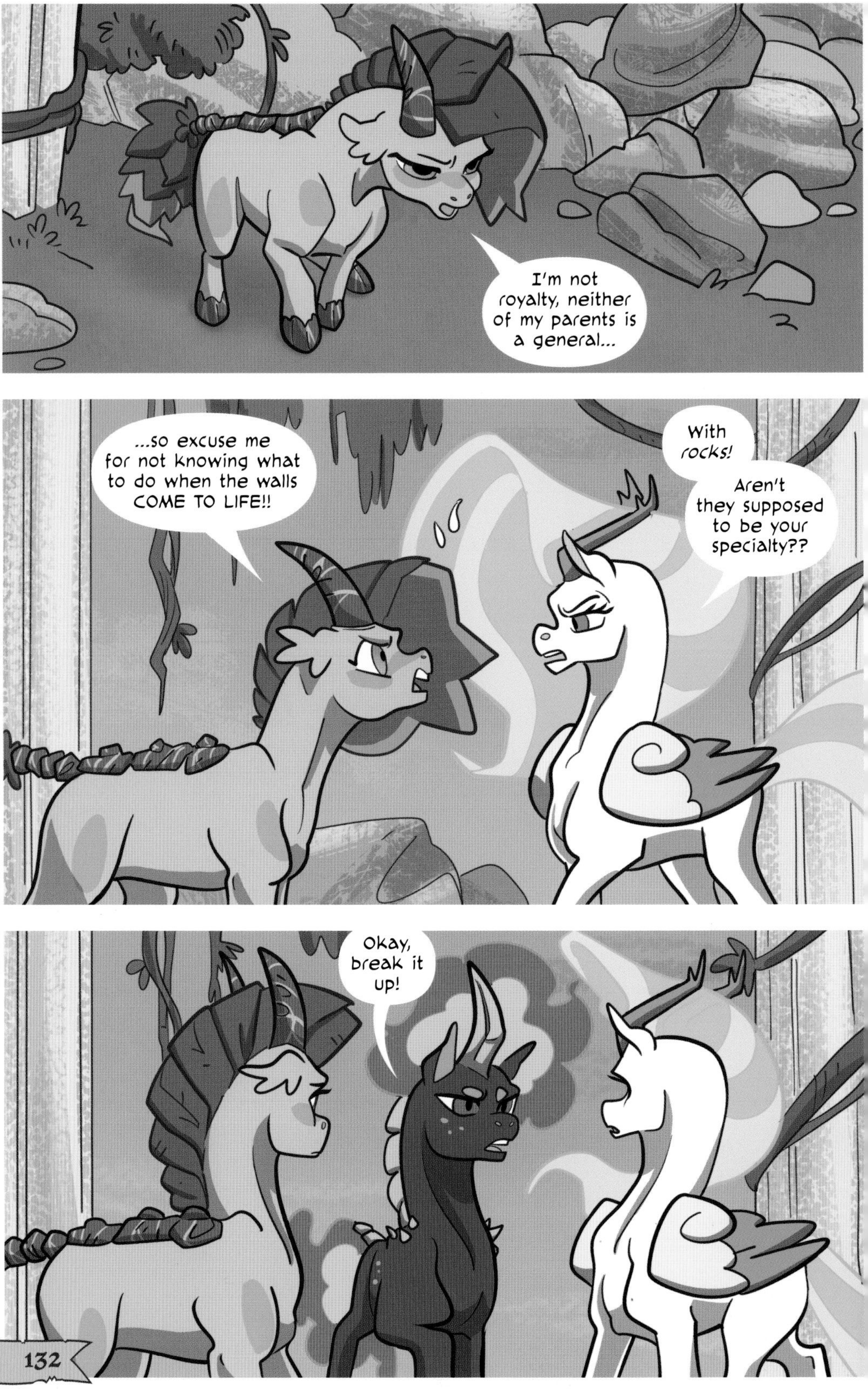
I'm not royalty, neither of my parents is a general...
...so excuse me for not knowing what to do when the walls COME TO LIFE!!
With *rocks!*
Aren't they supposed to be your specialty??
Okay, break it up!

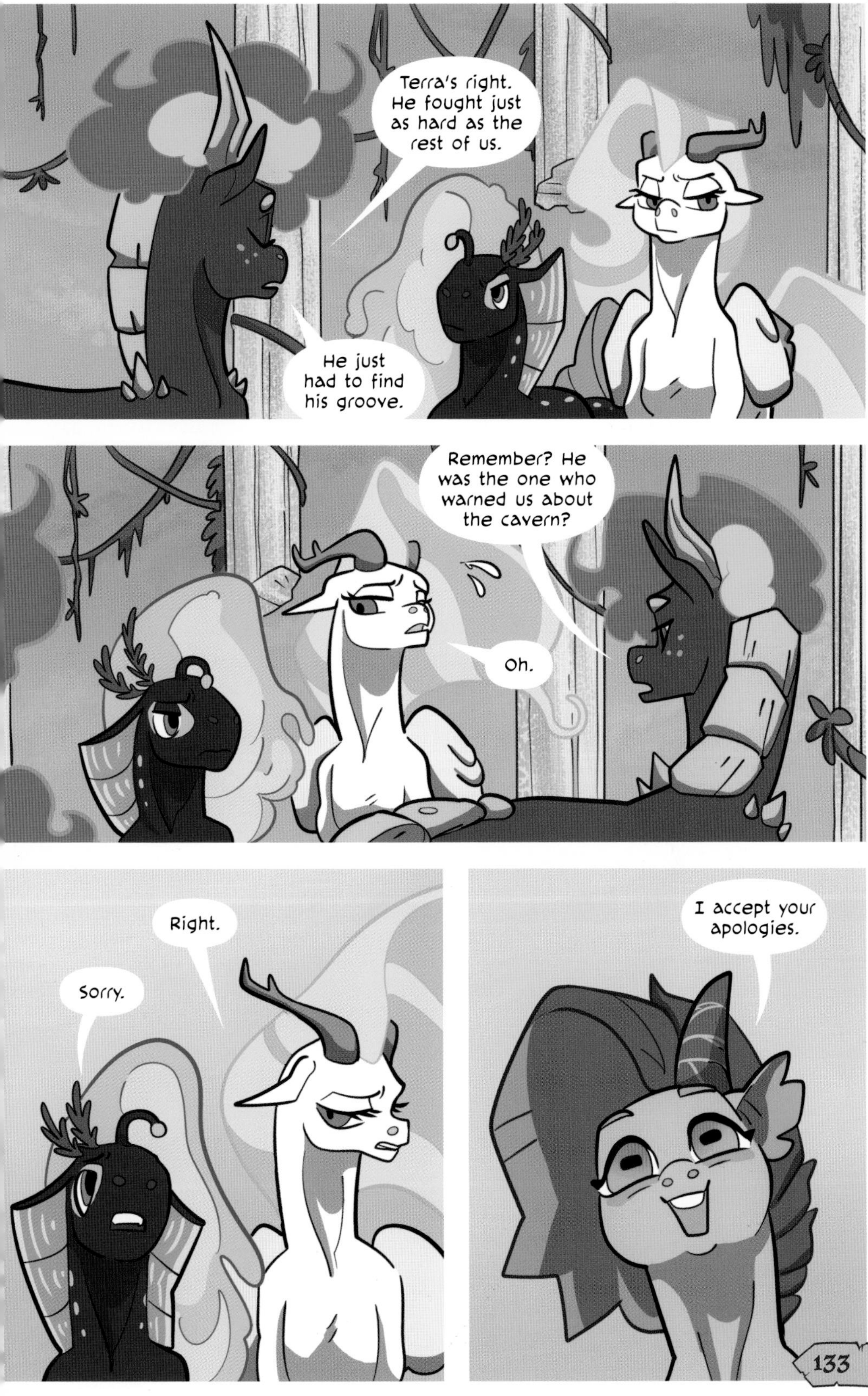
Terra's right. He fought just as hard as the rest of us.
He just had to find his groove.
Remember? He was the one who warned us about the cavern?
Oh.
Sorry.
Right.
I accept your apologies.

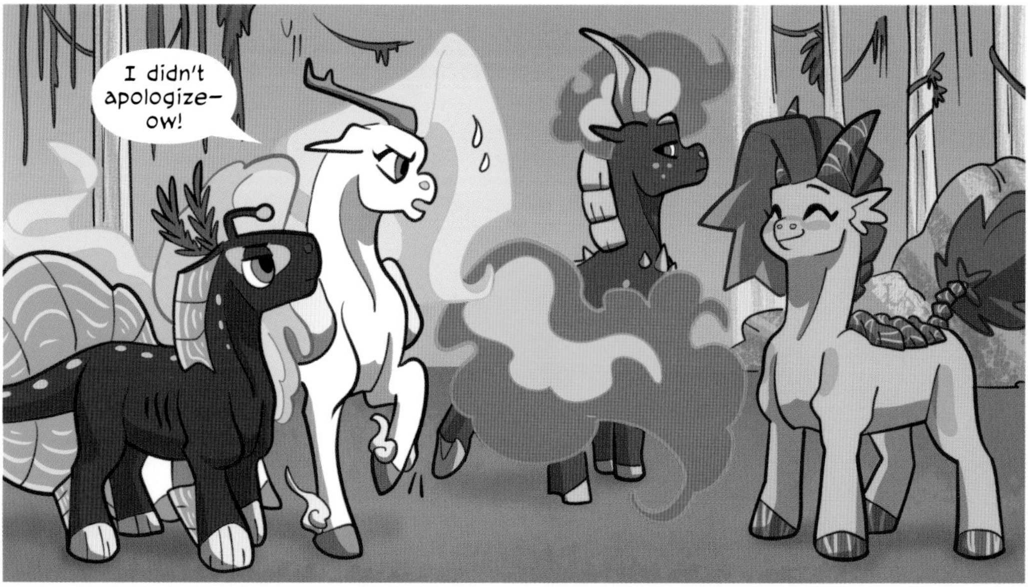
I didn't apologize—ow!

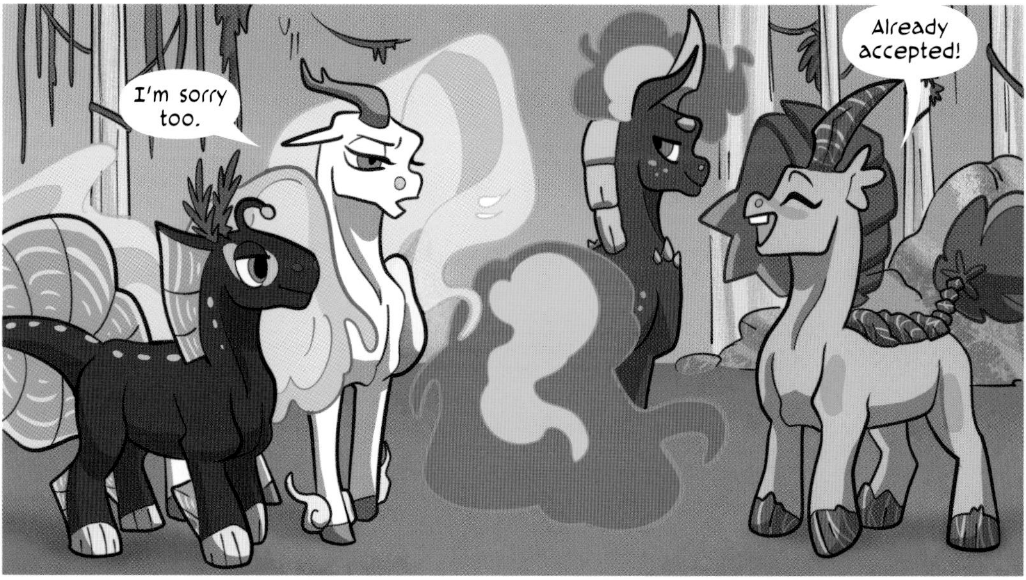
I'm sorry too.
Already accepted!

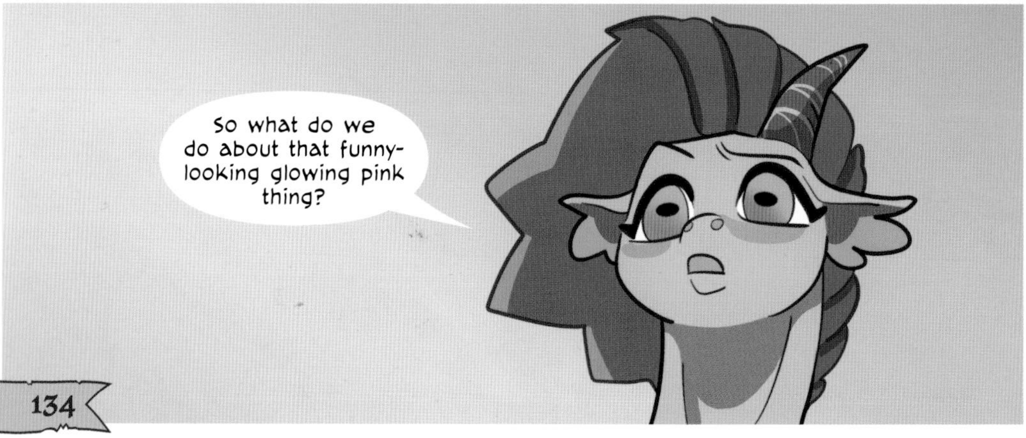
So what do we do about that funny-looking glowing pink thing?

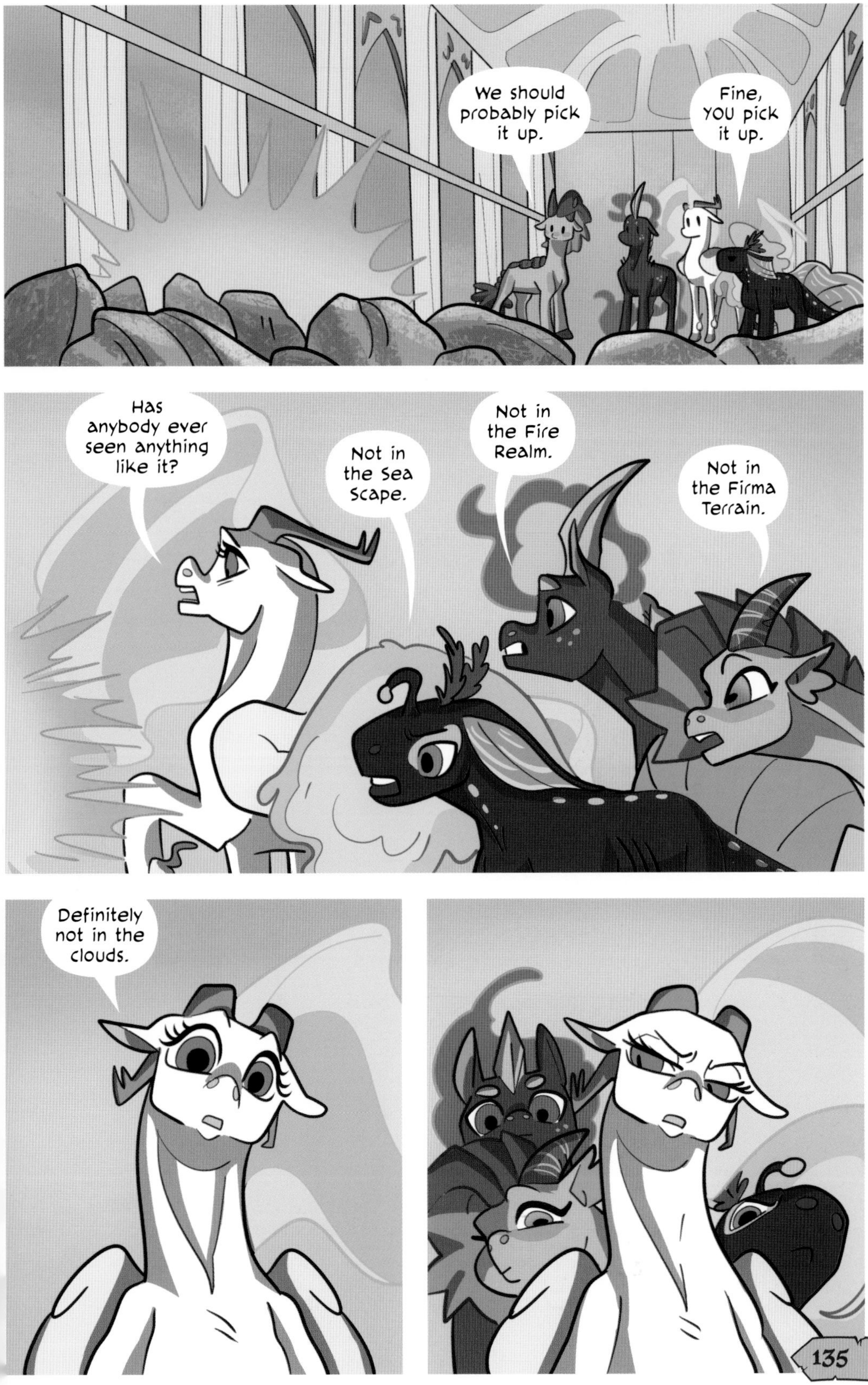

We should probably pick it up.
Fine, YOU pick it up.
Has anybody ever seen anything like it?
Not in the Sea Scape.
Not in the Fire Realm.
Not in the Firma Terrain.
Definitely not in the clouds.

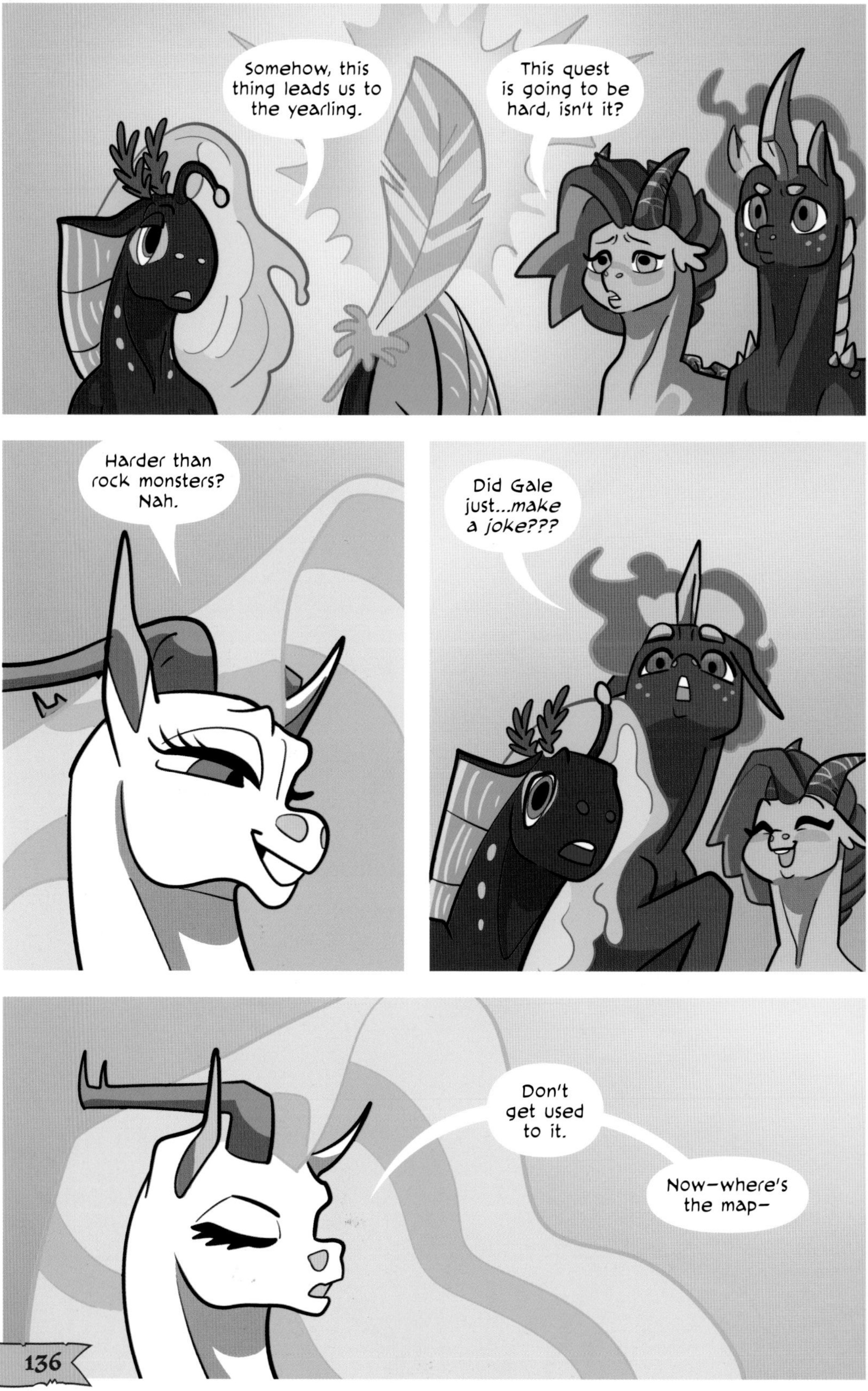

Somehow, this thing leads us to the yearling.
This quest is going to be hard, isn't it?
Harder than rock monsters? Nah.
Did Gale just...*make* *a joke???*
Don't get used to it.
Now—where's the map—

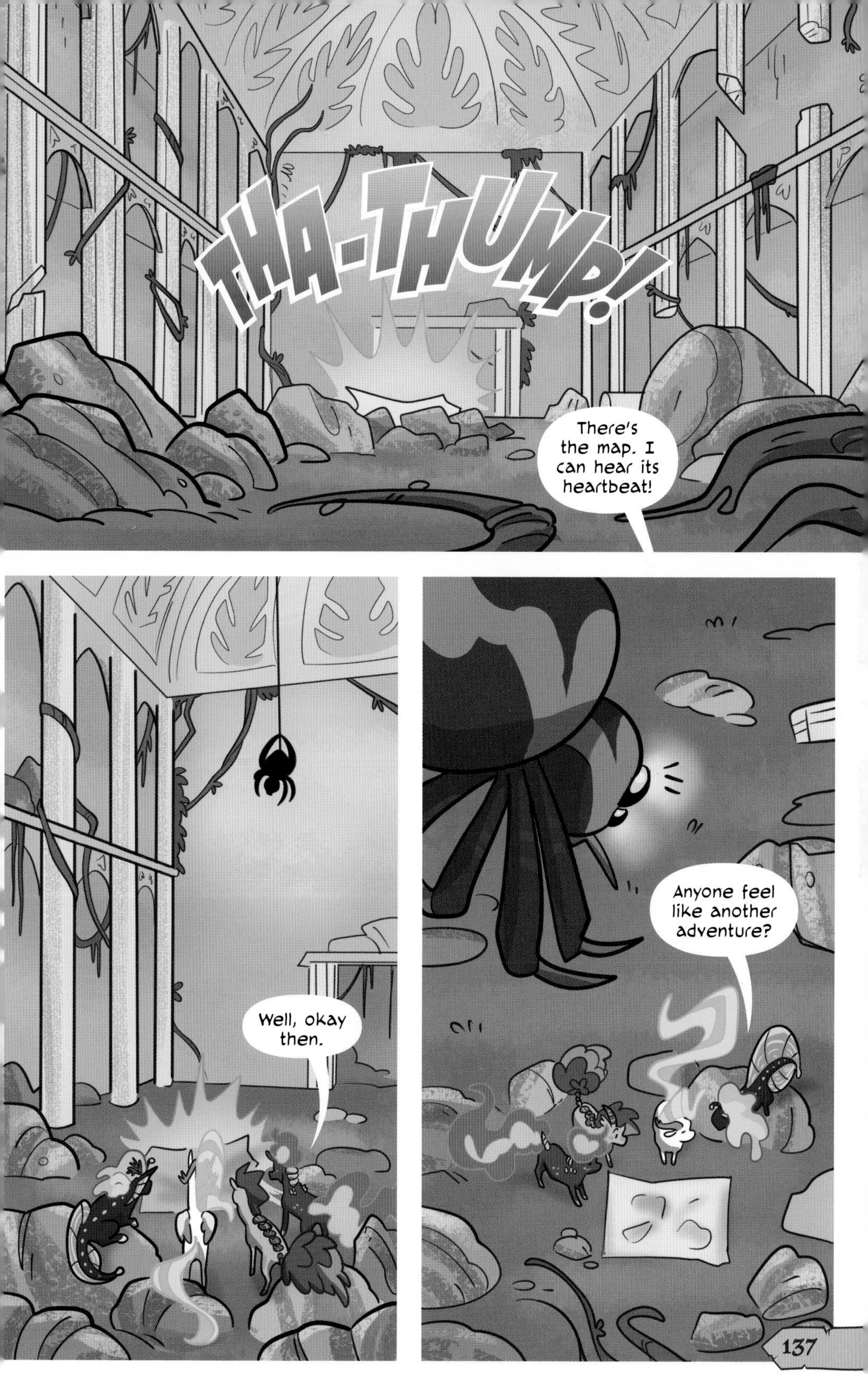
THA-THUMP!
There's the map. I can hear its heartbeat!
Well, okay then.
Anyone feel like another adventure?

Anyone feel like another adventure?

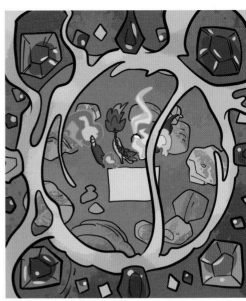

Mmmmmm...

You lived through this round, Guardians...

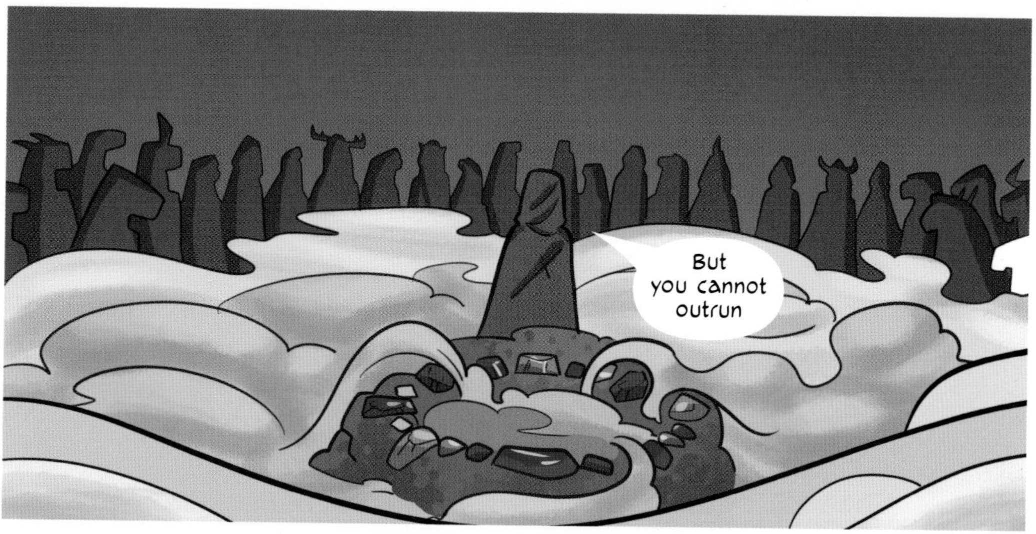
But you cannot outrun

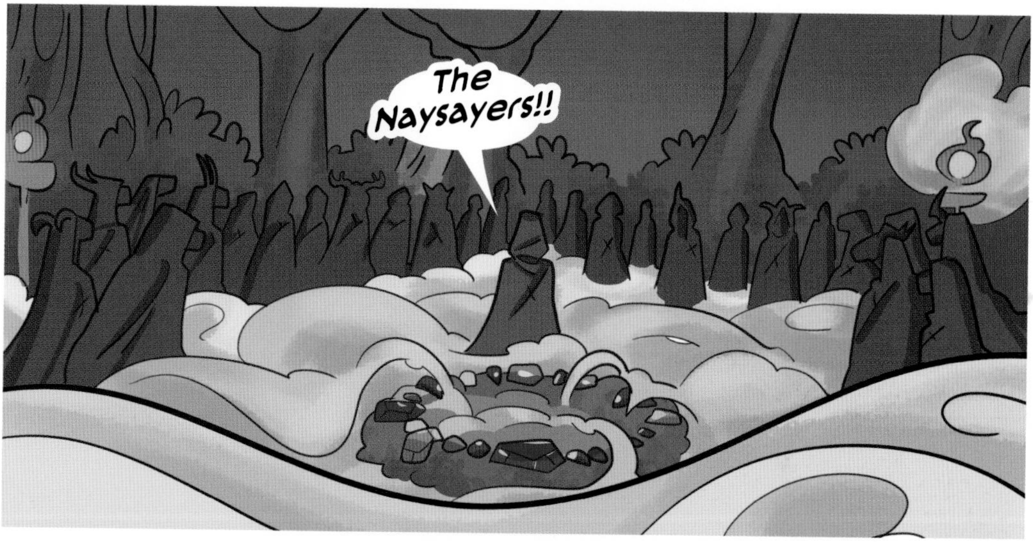
The Naysayers!!

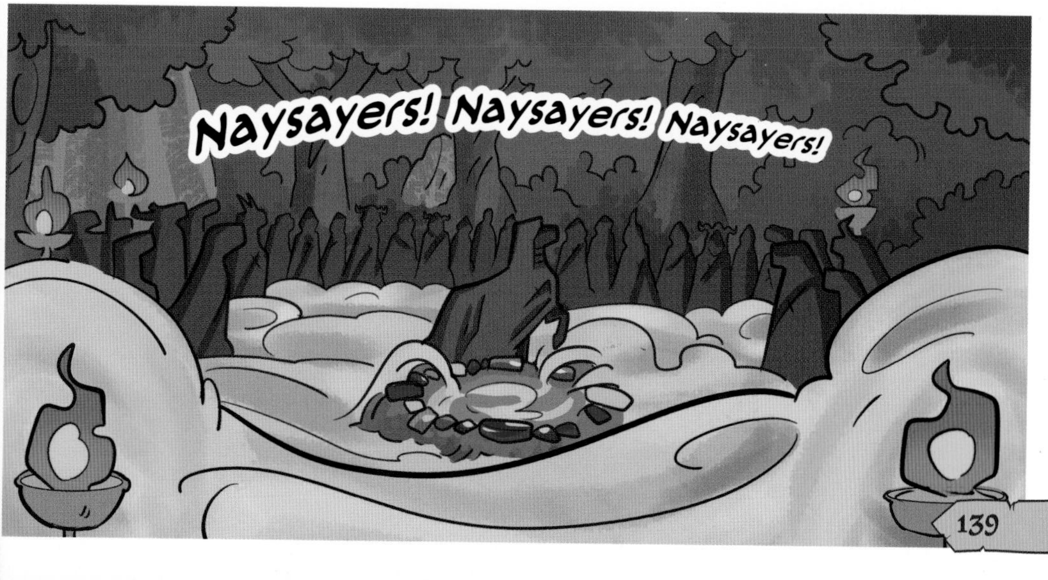
Naysayers! Naysayers! Naysayers!